BILLY BOYLE

This Large Print Book carries the
Seal of Approval of N.A.V.H.

A BILLY BOYLE WORLD WAR II MYSTERY

BILLY BOYLE

JAMES R. BENN

KENNEBEC LARGE PRINT
A part of Gale, Cengage Learning

GALE
CENGAGE Learning

Detroit • New York • San Francisco • New Haven, Conn • Waterville, Maine • London

GALE
CENGAGE Learning

Copyright © 2006 by James R. Benn.
Kennebec Large Print, a part of Gale, Cengage Learning.

ALL RIGHTS RESERVED
Kennebec Large Print Softcover.
The text of this Large Print edition is unabridged.
Other aspects of the book may vary from the original edition.
Set in 16 pt. Plantin.
Printed on permanent paper.

LIBRARY OF CONGRESS CATALOGING-IN-PUBLICATION DATA

Benn, James R.
  Billy Boyle : a Billy Boyle World War II mystery / by James R.
Benn.
    p. cm.
    ISBN-13: 978-1-59722-891-6 (pbk. : alk. paper)
    ISBN-10: 1-59722-891-5 (pbk. : alk. paper)
    1. World War, 1939–1945—Underground
movements—Norway—Fiction. 2.
Sabotage—Norway—History—20th century—Fiction. 3. Large
type books. I. Title.
PS3602.E6644B55 2009
813'.6—dc22   2008042456

Published in 2009 by arrangement with Writer's House LLC.

Printed in the United States of America
1 2 3 4 5 6 7 13 12 11 10 09

For Debbie —
Once a dream,
come true.

A STRAND OF CORPSES

I know a hall whose doors face North
on the Strand of Corpses far from the sun,
poison drips from lights in the roof;
that building is woven of backs of snakes.
There heavy streams must be waded through
by breakers of pledges and murderers.

The Edda: The Deluding of Gylfi
Norse Mythology, 13th Century A.D.

Prologue

I typed the date under my name: Lieutenant William Boyle, August 6, 1942. I pulled the sheets out of the typewriter, separated out the carbon paper, and made two neat stacks. My official report. Everything that had happened during the last few weeks reduced to a neat summary: part confessional, part U.S. Army standard issue after action report. Most of it was even true.

I looked out the window near my desk. August. The only real evidence of that was the calendar on the wall. Outside the sky was gray, people carrying umbrellas and walking with that hurried step you put on when it's chilly and you press your arms to your sides for extra warmth. August in London, inside the U.S. Army headquarters in Grosvenor Square, and it was cold. Lonely, too. Things had changed since I first walked in here back in June. A lot of things.

I reached for a red folder stamped "TOP

SECRET." It was filled with photos, orders, and maps, all marked with notations referred to in my report. One copy went in there. The folder would be taken by a clerk and filed away under lock and key. I doubted anyone would ever read it. The carbon copy would go to my boss, who would read it and then burn it. Top Secret. I looked out the window some more. People came and went. In and out of buildings, hurrying across the small park at the center of the square. There's a war on, after all.

There's a lot that's not in the report. Some of it is unofficial, personal stuff. The things that set everything in motion aren't set down. Events that took place years ago, before America was in the war and while I was wearing a blue uniform instead of khaki.

I can tell you the whole story, secrets and all, right from the beginning. Not the army version, which probably sounds more like a police report than it needs to, but the real McCoy.

But before I start explaining, maybe I should tell you how I ended up here, at U.S. Army HQ in London. I didn't get here by choice, that's for damn sure.

CHAPTER ONE

Over the North Atlantic
June 1942

I wanted to die. No, actually I didn't want to die. Or live. I just didn't care. Dying would have been better than puking my guts out again in a bucket. Which wouldn't have been so bad if the bucket hadn't been inside a freezing Flying Fortress halfway between Iceland and England, trying to ride out a North Atlantic storm. And if there hadn't been a war going on, and I hadn't been headed right for it.

I wanted to reach for the bucket again but the floor dropped out from under me as the Fortress was pounded by powerful, howling storm winds that seemed to scream at the fuselage, clawing at the plane's skin for a way inside. Canvas-covered crates bounced on each other, held down by knotted ropes and the weight of what they carried. I worried about being crushed to death before I ever got to England, a crate of beans or grenades or whatever was important enough to rate air transport ending my military career. The waist gunner openings were closed up. Only a small Perspex window let in what little light there was among the gray clouds at twenty thousand feet. The noise from the storm and the four straining engines pounded in my head like a jackhammer orchestra. I prayed for the plane to steady itself and held on to the hard metal seat for dear life. All I could think about was the fact that, just two days before, I was fat, dumb, and happy, just about to graduate from Officer Candidate School, and ready to enjoy the delights of life as a staff officer at the War Department in Washington, D.C. I was all set. The fix was in. Now I was in a fix.

I never wanted to be in the army. I was happy as a cop on the beat in Boston, just like my dad and my uncles, and seldom even left South Boston, where the Boyle family lived and worked. I had been on the job for three years, and my dad and his brothers and their pals watched out for me. That's how it works. The rich folks on Beacon Hill look out for their own and the Irish in Southie look out for theirs. I guess it's like that all over the world, but I really don't know. Or care. That's the world's problem.

My problem was that I had just made detective three days before Pearl Harbor. It was unusual for a kid in his early twenties to make the grade. The test they gave was pretty hard. While I can usually figure things out sooner or later, I'm no scholar. I would've had a hard time, but a few of the sheets from the test sort of found their way into my locker a couple of days before the exam. I managed to pass. My uncle Dan is on the promotions board, so with a little back-scratching with his buddies over a few pints of Guinness, I was in. That's just the way it works. I'm not saying I'm proud of it, but it doesn't mean I'm not a good cop either. It's not a bad system, actually. The other guys know me and know they can depend on me. I'm not some stranger who got the job just because he's smart enough to answer a bunch of questions on his own. That doesn't mean squat when you need your partner to back you up. Three years walking the beat in Chinatown and around the harbor had taught me a lot, not to mention everything Dad tried to drum into my head. He's a homicide detective, and he always made sure I got assigned to a crime scene when they needed some extra blue-

13

coats for crowd control or knocking on doors. I worked a lot of overtime, saw a lot of dead bodies, and listened to Dad talk me through his routine. Sometimes it was obvious who the killer was, like after a knife fight between drunks. Other times, it wasn't. Watching Dad figure things out was like watching an artist paint a picture. He used to say an investigation was a lot like art, just a blank canvas and a whole lot of different colors in little jars. All the clues were there, just like a painting was already in those little jars of paint. But you had to mix them together and put them on the canvas right, so it all made sense. Well, the only thing I can paint is a house, and sometimes I couldn't see how Dad figured things out, even when he explained it all to me. But he would always go through it with me afterward, hoping some of it would stick.

Anyway, I was pretty disappointed to hear about Pearl Harbor. It was tough for those guys out there, but it also meant the draft board was going to come after me. The Boston PD had more cops than deferments, and we younger guys knew what was coming. I didn't like it much, but it looked like Uncle Sam was going to ship me off to fight the Japs. Everybody was all worked up over the Japs, but it seemed to me that I had enough problems with the Chinese gangs down in Chinatown without taking on the rest of the Orient.

I thought maybe the military police would be a good choice, to stay in the game sort of. Dad nixed that idea right away. He'd hated the MPs he'd run into in France during the First World War and said no son of his would ever earn his keep busting poor enlisted men over a drink or the ladies. OK, that was that.

Uncle Dan didn't want me to go at all. He and Dad went off to war in 1917 with their older brother, Frank. Frank got killed his first day at the front. It broke Grandma's heart and I think Dad and Uncle Dan's, too. I never really knew how hard it had hit them until one night over drinks at Kirby's Bar, right after New Year's, just a month after Pearl Harbor. I could tell they were working up to tell me something. It took a couple of Bushmills Irish whiskeys before they got around to it.

"If somebody comes after the Boyles, then it's personal, and we all back each other up," my dad started. "You know that, Billy. But this war, it's no good for us. The Boyles have finally made it here. No one ever helped us, especially when Da couldn't get work because 'No Irish Need Apply.' We've worked hard to build something for you here, and we're not going to let this war with the Japs and Germans take it away from you. It's not our war. No one attacked Boston or Ireland. So we're going to find a way to keep you safe. We don't want you to get killed, like Frank."

"Especially not fighting for the fucking English, Billy, you remember that," Uncle Dan chimed in. Like any good IRA man, he hated the English. It had galled him to fight on the same side as the English in his war, and he didn't want me to do the same in mine. Unfortunately, their plan didn't go any farther than deciding I shouldn't get killed, which sounded fine to me. We drank some more, and went home. Dad got yelled at. I went to sleep.

In the morning we went to Mass. That always calmed Mom down, and she was nice to Dad as we walked home from church. That's when she got the idea. Her second cousin, one of the Doud clan that had moved to Colorado, was married to a general who worked at the War Plans Division of the War Department in Washington, D.C. Maybe he'd give me some sort of job there. I'd seen him last at a family wedding a few years ago. Since he was an older guy I called him "Uncle." Uncle Ike.

The Boyle family put the wheels into motion. Dad called our congressman, Teddy McCarrick, who owed him for certain favors granted during the election. Teddy was glad to oblige, knowing there was always another election around the corner. Not only did I get an immediate qualification for Officer Candidate School, but he called a week later and told Dad that my uncle had asked Army Personnel to assign me to his staff as soon as I graduated OCS. Well, all right! On my uncle's staff in the nation's capital, where the women outnumbered the men ten to one and I'd be an officer and a gentleman. Not bad for an Irish kid from Boston. A lot better than a grave in France, according to Uncle Dan.

We only forgot one thing. The part of OCS that stood for "School." I did fine in basic training. I'd always played sports and kept in shape. I knew firearms, which is more than I can say about the other guys in boot camp. I figured it was more dangerous around the firing range there than anyplace I'd ever see in this war. But then we went to school. Never liked it, never will. It wasn't the kind of school where you could bullshit your way out of trouble, like I'd done many times back home. They really expected you to learn this stuff: map reading, tactics, command, logistics. It gave me a headache. I kept hoping that I'd find the exam answers slipped under my door, but this wasn't Boston, and the noncoms were all Southern boys. Not an Irish guy among them.

Somehow, I made it. Rock bottom out of my company, but I made it. Before we got our bars my drill instructor told me I was the dumbest Irish Mick he had ever seen, and that was saying something. I thanked him for the compliment and thought, Imagine how surprised he'll be tomorrow when we get our orders, and I go off to the War Plans Division. Ha! I'll show him!

We got our orders all right, and Sarge really was surprised. So was I. I wasn't going to D.C. I was going to London goddamn England, to the headquarters of the U.S. Army European Theater of Operations, General Dwight David Eisenhower commanding. Uncle Ike. In charge of the whole shooting match. Why, I had not a clue. I love my mom, but I had to think that maybe this was not one of her best ideas.

The plane stopped rocking and lurching. The storm had calmed down, and so did my stomach. The sun rose, or we caught up with it, and things started improving. We descended through white clouds, and when I went up to the cockpit I actually enjoyed the view. I was the only passenger, not because I was special, but because a Flying Fortress bomber was not meant to be a passenger plane. I had AAA travel priority, so I had been put on the first flight out of the States headed for England. This was it, or at least for a lowly lieutenant, this was it. I had never flown before — hell, I had never been out of Massachusetts before the Army — and the sight of England from the air was beautiful. So green and lush, small fields marked off by stone walls and clumps of houses at intersections, huddled together like storybook villages. I closed my eyes, mentally apologized to Uncle Dan, and then opened them to admire the greenness unfolding below me as we descended lower and lower.

We landed at a military airfield. I climbed down the metal steps to the runway, stiff from sitting so long on a hard seat. One of the crew threw down my duffel bag and waved so long. I caught it and waved back, wondering what the hell was going to happen now. I walked past the wing of the Fortress and stood on the wet tarmac. Rows of aircraft lined the field. At the end of the runway, off to the side, a twisted black hulk scarred the orderly landscape, its tail fin pointing up to the sky like a cross. A real confidence builder.

A jeep pulled out from a nearby hangar and stopped next to me. It was misting slightly, and the officer driving it had his trench-coat collar turned up and his service-cap visor pulled down. My own trench coat was rumpled from the long trip, and my tie was undone. Scarf. I had to remember they called ties "scarves" in the army, just to confuse honest civilians. I saw the officer, a major, look down at my shoes with a grimace of distaste. I looked down, too. They were flecked with dried vomit.

"You must be Lieutenant William Boyle. Get in."

In my wisest decision since I arrived in England, I kept my mouth shut, and got in.

CHAPTER TWO

The ride into London was damp and chilly, and it wasn't just the weather. It was almost July, but it felt like a cold April day back home, even when the mist let up and rays of sun peeked out between the clouds. Outside the base we drove past fields of thick, wet grass dotted by sheep that ignored the aircraft roaring above them as fighter engines revved and flaps lowered. We put the base behind us, and houses began to appear along the road, then a village, then rows of houses and shops as we reached the edge of London. The mist began again and I turned up the collar of my trench coat, cold hands fumbling with the button at the neck. I shivered. A combination of dampness and lack of sleep sent a chill through my body. The cool moisture felt good on my face.

Major Samuel Harding didn't do much to warm things up in the way of conversation.

He introduced himself without shaking hands, and made it clear he wasn't picking me up in order to be a nice guy, in case I was too dumb to figure that out. Maybe that sergeant from OCS had talked to him.

"Ike asked me to get you settled in. I'll drop you at the Dorchester Hotel. We've got a number of officers billeted there, and it's just a few blocks from headquarters. HQ is at 20 Grosvenor Square. Get cleaned up. I'll expect you at 1100 hours."

"OK."

"The proper response is 'Yes, sir,' Lieutenant."

"Yes, sir."

Having demonstrated the fact that I was a real quick learner, I searched for another way to impress him. Nothing came to mind, so I kept my yap zipped. He returned the favor, a tight-lipped grimace telling me he wasn't happy being chauffeur to Ike's nephew.

The road was narrow and I had to draw in my elbow when vehicles came the other way. It was strange sitting in the passenger's seat as Harding drove on the left-hand side of the road. Every car and truck seemed to come within inches of us, and there was nowhere to pull over. Hedges ran along both sides of the road, and where there were buildings they came right up to the edge. Why the hell did the Brits have to drive on the wrong side? And why these skinny roads? We drove on into London, the road widening a bit but still not enough for two trucks to pass each other with more than inches to spare. Lorries. That's what they'd told us the Brits called trucks. We had been briefed in OCS on language differences and how to make nice with the Brits. Don't flash your money around, GIs are paid more than British officers, stuff like that. Me, I couldn't have cared less. The English had had their time in the sun when they conquered Ireland and ran it like their private preserve, killing and starving out my ancestors. If I hurt a few feelings waving around a sawbuck or two, big deal.

Harding didn't point out the sights on the way to the hotel. Some of those sights were piles of rubble where apartment houses and office buildings used to be. The Blitz hadn't been as bad as it had been the previous year, but the place was still a target. As we passed by a row of white-painted brick houses with a gap like a missing front tooth in a wide grin, I caught sight of a river that I figured was the Thames. A pile of blackened rubble covered the ground between the houses, weeds creeping over the remains of the unlucky home. We turned a corner and had to stop as workers in blue coveralls hauled bricks away from a smoldering pile of debris that had slid out into the street. People going to work walked around the mess, carrying their newspapers, umbrellas, and briefcases as if it were completely normal to walk past bomb-damaged buildings. Shops across the street had OPEN FOR BUSINESS painted on wood planks nailed over shattered windows.

A London cop, his blue uniform a dingy shade of gray from concrete dust that lay thick on his shoulders, stood in the middle of the road and blew his whistle, holding up his hands as an ambulance passed cars on the other side of the blocked street. Traffic was already at a dead stop, but the pedestrians halted immediately, the murmur of movement and morning conversations stopped by the end of the shrill whistle blast. People parted and formed a narrow corridor as three stretchers were carried out of the destroyed building. Two held blanketed, inert forms. The third carried a person covered in soot highlighted by rust-colored dried blood along a leg and a hasty bandage wrapping a head. A thin female arm rose from the stretcher with two fingers raised in the V-for-victory sign as she was gingerly carried into the ambulance. There were murmurs of appreciation from the crowd, and then they drifted back into their morning routine. Another day at the war. The other two stretchers were left on the sidewalk for a journey to a different destination.

"Welcome to London," Harding said as the traffic moved forward.

"Yes, sir." Maybe I wouldn't wave those sawbucks around for a while.

The river was the Thames. We crossed it on a bridge that showed off a scene I had seen on dozens of newsreels as I waited for the main feature to start. Parliament and Big Ben. London, under the gun. I could almost hear Edward R. Murrow saying, "This . . . is London" over the radio in our living room, that pause always giving a sense of weighty suspense as he reported on the Blitz and other war news. Now I was here. It didn't seem real, as if my being here somehow lessened the importance of everything.

The rain had stopped, and the clouds were turning from threatening gray to puffy white. Harding zipped past Big Ben as the clock struck the half hour with that distinctive, authoritative bong that sounded so much louder than it had in the newsreels.

Buildings were much larger on this side of the river, big imposing granite structures mounded with sandbags around their entrances. British soldiers stood guard as well-dressed officers with gleaming leather belts and polished buttons strode past them. We looped around a bit and ended up on a road with a park to its left. HYDE PARK CORNER, a sign said. I had heard of that. Harding pulled into a semicircular driveway in front of the Dorchester Hotel. He stopped. He didn't take his hands off the wheel or look at me. A large lady wearing a hat with a big feather sticking out of it walked by, dragging a tiny dog on a leash. The dog dug in his heels and barked at the jeep, or Harding, or both. The lady kept walking, dragging the dog away, his toenails making a long scratching noise on the sidewalk as he tried to stand his ground.

"Here it is. Remember, 1100 hours."

"Yes, sir."

I got out, grabbed my duffel bag, and he drove away without even complimenting me on my proper military response. Standing on the curb, I could hardly locate the door of the Dorchester. The entire entrance was lined with sandbags, except for a narrow passageway. The front of the hotel was curved, facing the park across the street at an angle. A fountain marked the center of the driveway, and staff cars, after pulling around it, were discharging generals and guys wearing formal coats with vests and striped pants I thought had gone out of style before the last war. I felt out of place and thought maybe lowly Irish lieutenants from Boston were supposed to use the side entrance. I walked through the front door anyway, threading my way between sandbag walls and half carrying, half dragging my duffel bag through the door.

The reception desk was to my left in a small area dwarfed by a long marble hallway that stretched straight ahead. White flowers were everywhere, blending with the color of the marble and highlighted by soft white lights. Footsteps click-clacked all around me, but voices were hushed, as if this were church. Half of me wanted to turn around and find a rooming house with some normal people, someplace a little less fancy and not as heavy on marble and chandeliers. The other half of me couldn't wait to see my room. I snapped out of my daydream of room service and a hot bath and walked over to the counter. A tall, balding guy stood behind it, his fountain pen drifting across paper.

"May I be of some assistance?" He literally looked down his nose at me. I had heard that expression before, but never actually seen it. I could practically count his nose hairs. The way he said it told me assistance was the last thing I could expect.

"Yeah. I need a room. Major Harding told me I was billeted here."

"Your name?" I thought I could hear him shudder as he looked me over. I made a mental note that dried vomit seems to impress folks in England even less than it does in the States.

"Billy Boyle."

"We have a room for a Lieutenant William Boyle?" There was a hint of hope that a more distinguished and cleaner member of the Boyle family would walk through the door behind me.

"Yep, that's me."

"Sign the register, please." I admired him for hiding his disappointment so well. He even smiled when he handed me a key attached to a large disc and directed me to the elevator — the "lift," he called it, which I figured was just what I needed. My room was on the fourteenth floor, but the elevator — lift — went only to the twelfth. There was no thirteenth, but a flight of stairs led to the fourteenth, which was actually the thirteenth floor. Lucky me.

I dragged my duffel bag behind me, thumping up each step. The hallway was narrow; it didn't look much like a fancy hotel to me. I unlocked my door and went in. There was a small bed, a table, and a bureau, and one very small window that jutted out from a slanted ceiling. No bathroom. Then I got it. This was a servant's room. That slanted ceiling was the roof. I had visited our cousin Margaret Boyle with my mom when she came over from Ireland to work as a domestic on Beacon Hill. She'd had an attic room just like this in the mansion where she worked.

Did that snob at the desk sense I was shanty Irish and belonged up here? Or were they just pressed for space with Americans pouring into London? Or had Major Harding made this very thoughtful arrangement for me? Screw it, I decided, a bed's a bed. I unpacked my wrinkled khakis and shined my shoes. I found the bathroom down the hall and washed up. I wanted to sleep, but I was nervous about missing my date with Harding at eleven o'clock. Eleven hundred hours, I reminded myself. It was really a pain in the neck after noontime, but at least in the morning I didn't have to count off on my fingers.

I was feeling good enough to be hungry

and would've killed for a cup of coffee. I think it was still the middle of the night back home, but it was midmorning here and I didn't have a clue where to get some grub. Then I realized I didn't have any English money. Sitting in my little room, putting a final spit shine on my shoes, I felt forlorn. There had always been a relative or friend I could turn to when things got tough back in Boston. Here, I only knew a tight-assed American major and an even more tight-assed English hotel clerk. Oh, yeah, and Uncle Ike.

That cheered me up some, and I headed out to find Grosvenor Square. I asked my pal at the desk, and I guess he saw that I had worked hard at cleaning up, and so I was worth a civil answer.

"Go left out the main door, you'll see South Audley Lane straightaway. Go left again and it's a five-minute walk direct to Grosvenor Square. Are you looking for the American headquarters?"

"Yes, I am."

"It will be directly across the square as you enter it. You can't miss it — sandbags, American sentries, and all that."

"Great. Thanks a lot."

"Thank you for coming."

"Seems like a nice hotel," I said, holding

back half a dozen wisecracks about my closet-sized room.

"No," he said, leaning forward on his elbows and looking me in the eyes. "Thank you for coming to England."

I said something that I hoped didn't sound idiotic and followed his directions. His thanks unsettled me. I didn't want to be here, never was a fan of the British Empire, and the only American I had met so far didn't act like he gave a rat's ass if I was here. I thought about the woman and the V-for-victory sign. Was she still alive? The image of her swam through my mind as I wondered if she had made it. I noticed I had already crossed South Audley without turning left. I tried to forget about her and concentrate on not getting lost.

I saw a sign for Piccadilly and knew that was something a tourist would go see. I was tempted to explore. But duty called and, more important, I thought they'd have coffee at the office. *Coffee at the office.* OK, that sounds almost normal, I thought. It may not be Boston or even the States, but I'm in London walking to the office. How bad can this be?

A few minutes later, standing at my best imitation of attention in front of Major Harding, I began to get an inkling of just how bad it could be. He sat behind his desk, leaning back in a swivel chair, reading a file. My file, I guessed from the expression on his face. He wasn't smiling. He had a row of campaign ribbons and medals on his uniform jacket that made it look like he had been in the army since God was a child. He sported a neatly trimmed mustache, and a brush haircut that almost hid the gray at his temples. He looked pretty trim, like he had been a football player — maybe a quarterback — who worked at not going soft when he hit forty, which is about what I guessed him to be. He wore a West Point ring and no wedding band. Worst of all, he sipped from a china cup of steaming black coffee while he read. I didn't see a service for two.

"Now listen up, Boyle," he finally said, throwing the file on his desk. "Ike wants me to babysit you while you get your feet wet. I've got too much to do already without taking on some relative who pulled strings to get a soft staff job. I don't know what Ike's got in mind for you, but if I had my way you'd be carrying a rifle in an infantry platoon."

"Major, I —"

"I didn't ask for your opinion, Lieutenant!"

"Yes, sir." That phrase sure was coming in handy.

"Do you have any idea at all why you're here?"

Now let's see, I thought. Should I tell him about how my mom and dad and Uncle Dan didn't want me to get killed? Or about the congressman who got me this job? Then the perfect answer came to me.

"No, sir." It was a variation on a theme, but I thought I was beginning to get the hang of it.

"Well, neither do I. However, although I've only worked with General Eisenhower for a few weeks, since he came over here from the States, I respect his judgment. He's made a real difference in a short time. I don't want you screwing things up, Boyle. For some reason Ike thinks you can help him out. Doing what I don't have a clue, but if you step out of line just once. . . ."

"Major." I spoke up quickly to avoid another lecture. "Sir, I don't know what the general wants me for. I don't plan on screwing anything up or getting in your way, but I don't think I'd be much use to anyone in an infantry platoon. I'm a city boy, a police officer." I was beginning to get a little steamed.

"I read your file, Boyle," he said irritably.

33

"I know you're no coward. There's a commendation in here from the mayor of Boston for saving a little girl from a burning house. Why did you bother to risk your life for her, city boy?" Harding leaned back in his chair and seemed to focus on my eyes. It made me feel uncomfortable so I shrugged to show him I wasn't. I wanted him to know he didn't get to me.

"That was little Mary O'Shaughnessey. I saw her every day on my beat. I knew her folks. My dad would have whipped my butt if I hadn't gone in after her. We look out for each other in South Boston," I said rather proudly.

"What if you left here and came upon a burning building?"

"Call in the alarm, what else?"

"Go in and look for another little girl?"

"That's a job for the London cops and firemen, isn't it? Sir?"

"The London cops have quite a lot on their hands right now, Boyle. We're here to help them, not to sit around while they do the heavy lifting."

I'm no scholar, but even a dumb Mick like me knew this was a metaphor. Or a simile, I could never remember which was which. I also knew what the right thing to say was.

"Yes, sir."

A rap on the door saved me from a further lecture on how we have to help our good pals the Brits.

"General Eisenhower is ready to see you now, Major Harding. And the lieutenant." The beautiful voice belonged to a honey-haired young woman in a blue uniform. She spoke like an angel — an English, very upper-class angel.

I stood and introduced myself. "Billy Boyle, Miss . . . ?"

"I know your name, Lieutenant." Her disapproval hit me like a hammer. Harding came to the rescue, which meant her dislike of me must've been pretty apparent.

"This is Second Officer Daphne Seaton, Women's Royal Naval Service, attached to U.S. headquarters. Daphne . . . Second Officer Seaton . . . holds a rank equivalent to yours. She's my administrative assistant."

"Pleased to meet you, Second Officer." She nodded.

"We'll be right there, Daphne. When we're done, please take Lieutenant Boyle to his desk and show him around. He looks like he could use some chow." I almost fell over when I heard Harding say that. He seemed almost human.

"Certainly, Major, I will be glad to." As she turned to leave, she looked at me as if

Harding had asked her to take out the garbage.

I was beginning to get the feeling that the English were pretty good at letting you know that they meant exactly the opposite of what they were saying. I looked at my shoes. No, they were clean and shiny.

"You'll have to excuse Daphne," Harding said as he stood up from his desk. "She's gone through the Blitz from the beginning and lost some friends. It didn't make her and some of the other staff happy to hear Ike's nephew got himself appointed to a soft job here. Especially not with the news that they've just lost Tobruk in North Africa, along with twenty-five thousand prisoners. Now let's go see Ike."

I considered how I could thaw out Daphne while I followed Harding up the stairs. He led me through a suite of offices and knocked on a set of double doors. I stopped thinking about Daphne with some difficulty. I had just time enough to feel nervous about meeting Uncle Ike again. A sergeant opened the doors and gestured us in.

"William, very good to see you!" Though he was a distant relation, Ike grinned widely and extended his hand to shake mine. He looked older, of course, than the last time I saw him. He was smiling but the rest of his face looked serious. His eyes locked on to mine and it seemed like he was trying to see inside my head. It was as if he was looking for something that he wanted, something that I could give him. Only I didn't know what it was. Or if I even had it.

I suddenly didn't know my left from my right. I'd tried to stammer out something while beginning to salute, then finally got my right hand in the right place when I saw he wanted to shake hands. I tried not to sound like the jerk I felt.

"Uncle . . . I mean General . . . ," I managed to say. OK, so maybe I should have tried harder.

Ike laughed, and immediately put me at ease. "Sit down, son. We won't dwell on military protocol today." He sat in a leather chair and motioned for the two of us to seats opposite him, then he lit a cigarette.

"So how are your folks, William? It's been a few years."

"Fine, sir. Mother sends her regards."

Ike inhaled and then looked at Harding. "You know, Major, William was a detective with the Boston Police Department before joining us."

"Yes, sir. I've seen his file."

"There's one thing about family," Ike continued. "A relation, even a distant one, is always bound to you. There's no escaping it. It could be a drunken brother-in-law or a crazy cousin or even a rich uncle. When they show up at the door, they're one of yours."

"We don't get many rich uncles in South Boston, General, but I know what you mean. Family is family."

"Yes, it is." He nodded, paused, and looked straight at me. "William, we're trying to build a family here. An Anglo-American family that will fight together and win this war. A family that will stick together, through thick and thin. To do that, I've got to make sure that everyone is pulling his own weight and putting the family first."

"I'm not sure what you mean, General." I didn't want to sound stupid, but I wasn't too proud to ask a dumb question.

"William, I've got a big job here. I've got to get the British, who have been fighting this war alone and barely holding on, to work with the Americans, who haven't yet been touched by the war, and to take us seriously. I've got to get the Americans to listen and learn from them, instead of coming on like gangbusters. Pretty soon, there will be more Yank soldiers, planes, and ships over here than British. Before that happens, we've got to get everything working smoothly between us. If we don't, it could be our greatest weakness. Disunity."

He stopped and pulled on his cigarette deeply, letting the smoke out with a sigh as if he was himself daunted by the task. He looked at me and smiled that friendly warm grin of his.

"So, I guess you're wondering what that has to do with you."

I nodded.

Harding spoke up. "Frankly, sir, I've been wondering that myself." Uncle Ike lost the smile and looked at him as if he were squinting down the rear sight of a rifle.

"Major, I am not the type of man to grant a post to a family member as an act of nepotism."

Harding looked a little flustered at this rebuke. Since family patronage had been the thing that got me this far in life, I wondered what was wrong with it.

"William brings something special to us, Major. He is a dedicated police detective, decorated for bravery. Sooner or later, I am going to need someone who can handle potentially delicate investigations. Anytime this many people are brought together in an enterprise, with so much bounty in supplies and multiple chains of command, there are bound to be a few rotten apples."

"For the good of the family, they need to be removed, quietly." I surprised myself with this, but I knew exactly what he meant.

"Exactly, William! We need to be sure the top officers running this war are as pure as Caesar's wife. If any of them get into the black market or something worse, the publicity could lead to divisions within our ranks. It would only help the Germans."

"So my job is to hush things up?"

Ike raised his eyebrows and glanced at Harding. "Well, no, William," Ike said, crushing out his cigarette in a glass ashtray mounded with ashes and butts. "Things will have to be handled discreetly, but when the need arises, we will deal with anyone who violates the Articles of War or the laws of Great Britain. No one's going to get away with murder. I just don't want them tried in the Old Bailey for the world to see, that's all."

"How do I fit in, sir?" Harding leaned forward and I could see he was hoping to be let off the hook.

"I hope I won't be utilizing William's talents full-time. He'll need some other work to do to keep himself busy and useful. He can act as your aide." I saw astonishment, followed by resignation, flicker across Harding's face and vanish, buried under that West Point facade that never seemed to relax.

"Thank you, General." With that, I knew Harding could have a second career as a diplomat.

"You're heading off to that briefing with the Norwegians on Monday. Take William along and let him get the feel of things, get to know people. OK?"

Uncle Ike made it seem like a question, as if Harding would be doing him a favor.

"I'm sure he'll be a great help, General."

Ike nodded and the interview was apparently over. As we got up, he took me by the arm and walked me over to the window. Harding closed the door behind him and it was just Uncle Ike and me in the room. From where we stood, we could see all of Grosvenor Square. Some buildings were bomb damaged; the front of one was gone, revealing couches, beds, and tables in the rooms, like a giant dollhouse. He pointed to an intact structure on the opposite corner.

"John Adams, our second president, lived right there when he was ambassador to Great Britain. Just over that way a few blocks is Buckingham Palace and beyond that the Houses of Parliament. There are many ties that bind us to the English, William. We will have to rely on these bonds to get us through this war. They must be strengthened. And protected."

I had remembered Uncle Ike as a guy always ready with a grin. Now he looked like somebody else. Somebody with a grim job ahead of him. Somebody who needed a trusted hand at his side. I trembled a little, realizing that he thought that was me. I wanted to tell him I was the wrong guy, that I was a fake and a cheater. It was the first time in my life I ever felt ashamed of anything, but what could I say? That the Boyles were all talk and no action? His eyes were on me again, and he spoke in a low voice.

"William, I want you to know that I picked you for this job for two reasons. First, you're a trained detective. Second, you're family, and I've always believed in trusting family."

He lit another cigarette and drew on it heavily.

"Can you do this for me, William? And for your country?"

It must have been the lack of sleep. There was something solitary and lonely about Uncle Ike standing there, looking out over the ruined buildings and John Adams's ghost, maybe wondering if he could handle it all. I didn't feel sorry for him. At that moment, I just wanted to help him, more than anything else. If I had been more rested, I would've thought to ask what it was I'd get out of it. But I didn't.

"Sure, Uncle Ike. You can count on me," was what I said.

CHAPTER THREE

As I left Uncle Ike's office I asked a passing
PFC where I could find Second Officer
Daphne Seaton. He pointed toward a hallway and told me to go one flight down. The
stairway emptied into one large room with
about a dozen desks and countless file
cabinets. Maps covered any spare wall
space, and the paint job was a fresh coat of
army green, with some brown trim for flair.
I saw Harding standing next to one of the
desks, talking with Daphne. He looked up,
crooked his thumb in my direction, and
without another word walked away in the
opposite direction. I threaded my way
between desks and a sea of uniforms, American, British, army, navy, all busy moving
lots of paperwork around, the walls echoing
with a constant murmur of low voices and
the shuffling of files. A telephone rang and I
had to dodge an RAF officer as he ran to
grab it. I put on my best smile as I ap-

proached Daphne's desk.

"Do you have time to show me around, Second Officer Seaton?" I asked.

"Please call me Miss Seaton if that's easier for you; saves time all around."

Harding must have said something to her because I actually felt the temperature rise above freezing. I guess he told her that Ike had asked for me, and what he had in mind. I mentally thanked him for the boost and tried to act modest, but it was a new experience for me, especially around a pretty woman.

"Well, Miss Seaton, the first place I'd like to see is the mess hall, and a pot of coffee, maybe some doughnuts." Once a cop. . . .

She finally smiled, and that did me a world of good. I always felt better when I could get someone to smile, especially when they were inclined otherwise. If someone's smiling — a genuine smile, not a leer or the phony grin of a two-bit grifter — then you can be pretty sure they're not going to cause any trouble. And trouble wasn't what I was after.

Daphne led me down to the mess hall, which took up most of the basement. There were long trestle tables, three in a row, and a few small round tables, probably reserved for Uncle Ike and the rest of the brass.

Steam tables fronted the kitchen area, and the smell of cafeteria cooking, the clanging of pots, and the clacking of stacked plates all somehow made me feel at home. It was familiar. First thing I went for was the coffee urn. I grabbed a heavy mug and topped it off with joe that carried a faint whiff of eggshells. We picked a spot on one of the tables that wasn't too crowded and sat across from each other. It was about lunchtime, but the place wasn't exactly packed. Some people were just drinking coffee, or tea if they were Brits, while others ate breakfast or a lunch of sandwiches and some sort of stew. Daphne caught me eyeing the room.

"People pretty much work around the clock here. You can always find somebody looking for breakfast at the oddest times," she said.

"You mean this place doesn't run regular office hours?" I dropped two sugar cubes in the dark coffee and swirled the spoon around, not taking my eyes off her.

"Not anymore we don't, not since General Eisenhower arrived, and thank goodness for that. It used to be a nine-to-five headquarters, with just a skeleton staff on weekends. It was as if the Americans — excuse me, I mean the previous general — didn't take the war very seriously."

"Ike does?" I blew on the coffee, watching her over the rim of the cup. She was animated, excited, explaining how things were to the new kid.

"Yes! Staff here works seven days a week, and long days are the rule rather than the exception. Every section is staffed twenty-four hours a day. General Eisenhower knows this war can't be won on bankers' hours."

"How long have you been here?" I drank the coffee, bitter and sweet.

"I joined the Women's Royal Naval Service — they call us WRENs — in 1940. My father was in the navy, so it seemed a good choice. I started at Portsmouth Naval Base, went through women's officer training, and then went back to Portsmouth to do the same thing I had done before I was made second officer. File papers and make tea. I kept asking for assignments with a bit more purpose. I think all I really did was irritate my superior officers."

"I knew we had a lot in common," I said.

She ignored that opening. "As soon as the first American mission set up in Grosvenor Square, I was posted here. That was five months ago, and there really wasn't much to do before General Eisenhower arrived.

Now, things are different."

"You're making coffee as well as tea?"

That got a bit of a smile. "I've been taken off coffee duty, thank goodness," Daphne said. "I always managed to make it too weak or burn it or something."

"Pretty smart move on your part."

She raised her eyebrows and tapped her fingernails on the table, a bit surprised. "You may be able to make yourself useful, Lieutenant Boyle," Daphne said. "No one else ever suspected."

"You never know," I said, giving her a wink as I got up to get some food. I came back with a full plate of powdered eggs and toast that smelled almost good. We talked more, which means she spoke, I ate like a horse, listened, and learned. She and her sister had both joined up when the war broke out. Daphne chose the Women's Royal Naval Service and her sister, Diana, went into something called the First Aid Nursing Yeomanry, known as the FANYs. I asked her why they had enlisted, and with raised eyebrows, she just said, "One must do one's duty, mustn't one?" I just smiled and stuffed some eggs into my mouth.

Their brother was in North Africa fighting Rommel on the Egyptian frontier. She was worried about him. And she didn't like being called a WREN, but there was nothing she could do about that either. She didn't like lollygagging around the cafeteria with a guy on a long-term coffee break any better, and as soon as I finished my plate we were back on the tour. She gave me the layout of the place and introduced me to people I ought to know and whose names I forgot, one after the other.

Finally she showed me my desk, across the room from her own. It had a pile of books and briefing papers on it that looked like more reading than I did in all of high school. Then she showed her merciful side and told me to go home and sleep. She reminded me that the mess room of the U.S. Army HQ, European Theater of Operations, was the only place I could count on for coffee and "Yank food." I told her that was fine, since we hadn't had tea in Boston since we threw it all in the harbor. She looked blankly at me for a moment and then laughed. It was like sunlight hitting the water.

I thought about that laugh on the walk back to the hotel and forgot to look right instead of left and almost got run over by a London cab. Safely across the street, I decided it felt good to stretch my legs and I wouldn't be able to sleep now anyway, after all that joe. I walked back to the hotel, just so I could trace my steps back to it, then crossed the street into Hyde Park. It was huge, with wide crushed-stone paths leading in all directions. The green spaces between the paths were filled with gardens, shoots of vegetable plants sprouting up everywhere: a giant Victory Garden. I crossed a bridge spanning a long, narrow pond and found myself on a wide pathway called Rotten Row, for some very old historical reason, I hoped. I followed it and found myself back at Hyde Park Corner, which I had seen from the jeep that morning. I wandered some more and ended up at the back of a crowd stacked up outside a tall wrought-iron fence. It was Buckingham Palace itself, and I caught the tail end of the changing of the guard, gray-coated British troops marching back to their barracks and looking very imperial. I followed them for a while through St. James's Park, and ended up back at Big Ben and Parliament. I stood there like a tourist back home gawking at the Old North Church, waiting for the bells to ring. It was the half hour, and I let the sounds wash over me, almost feeling the vibrations in my feet. How could people just walk around me, talking to each other, and not stop and listen? I kicked myself mentally for being such a rube in the city and walked along the Thames until I noticed a side road marked Downing Street. Everyone had heard about Number 10 Downing Street, the home of the British prime minister. I turned the corner and all of a sudden there it was, a couple of bobbies and a Royal Marine standing guard. If I'd moved quick enough, I could've gone up and knocked. Instead, I turned around and went back the way I had been headed. No sense getting Winston all riled up.

Getting my bearings in London made me feel less isolated and alone. I had a hard time realizing that I was simply out for a stroll, passing by places I had heard of all my life, that lately had become even more important as symbols of the fight against fascism. I remembered Edward R. Murrow talking about brave Londoners under the Blitz. Now I was one of them. A temporary Londoner, anyway. I couldn't help getting caught up in all that heroic last-stand stuff, but I wasn't so sure about the brave part.

I thought about what Uncle Dan, with a good dose of Irish Republican reality, would have to say about the British Empire and its capital city, London. I walked on, my feet starting to ache and a gritty tiredness creeping up on my eyelids. It was still light out and too early to hit the hay, so I trudged on, wanting to case the layout of the city streets as much as I could.

I was on Whitehall Street, another famous name symbolizing the British government, a street that Uncle Dan would spit on with joy. Whitehall emptied out into a big square, with a large water fountain in the center and a big, tall column off to the right. Trafalgar Square and the column dedicated to Admiral Nelson. Traffic flowed around the fountain, and young girls, walking arm in arm with guys in uniform from half a dozen countries, craned their necks up and stared. I heard English, French, and other languages I guessed were Polish and Dutch. I heard a Brooklyn accent and a couple of southern drawls, too, but no Boston accents, no one to remind me of home. I put my head down, feeling alone and tired, and turned right, away from the gaiety and this symbol of English world dominance.

I wandered down a crowded wide street jammed with traffic and pedestrians for a while but took a left into a more interesting little side street, deciding to try to loop around and find my way back to the hotel. Wellington Street — geez, did the English name everything after generals and admirals? Anyway, Wellington Street reminded me a little bit of Boston with its shops and narrow, curved turns. Coming from the direction of the river, the smells and the small streets almost made me nostalgic for my waterfront beat in the North End of Boston. I used to patrol the wharves along Commercial Street, and then turn in on Battery Street to check the shops on Hanover, all the way down to Haymarket and city hall. That was my first assignment as a bluecoat outside of South Boston, and it made me feel like a man of the world.

I first worked out of Station 12, at the corner of Fourth and K Street in Southie. I could walk to work, and my beat took me along F Street, right past the five-and-ten and Kresge's, where I used to beg my mom to take me to shop for toys when I was a kid. I'd walk by the big glass windows and practice twirling my baton, like Dad taught me, dreaming of the day I'd be a detective, just like he was. Some days, I didn't feel that much older than the kid who used to press his face against those store windows and dream of buying one of those six-gun cap pistols with belt and holster, just like Tom Mix. But that was the beginning of the Depression, and those six-guns gathered dust, until one day just before Christmas. They were gone, replaced by a display of matching knickers, mittens, and wool cap. I remember thinking that my folks had to have been the ones who bought them, skipping home through dirty slush, counting the mornings left until Christmas.

But there was no gunfight at the OK Corral for me that Christmas. I can still remember my heart breaking when my mom proudly gave me my present, a shoebox wrapped in tissue paper, too small and light to hold a Tom Mix six-shooter. She had knitted me socks, thick wool socks in an argyle pattern, and a set for my brother, same thing but in different colors. His were green and mine were red. Christmas colors. I threw the box down and bit my lip, far too old at ten to cry. Funny thing was, my mom cried. Then I did, too, and finally Danny joined in, just for the hell of it, I guess, since he was too young to know what was going on. Dad sat there, gripping his pipe in his mouth, nearly snapping the stem in his teeth, but not saying anything. Next Christmas, I got a double set of cap pistols, silver with white handles, and the holsters even had those strings so you could tie them down to your legs. Danny got a train set, and I was jealous until I realized he couldn't have it set up all the time, but I could strap on my six-shooters and blast rolls of caps anytime.

It was still the Depression, but something had changed in our house. Dad started bringing presents home, and not just for special occasions either. On a regular weekday, he'd show up with a new coat for one of us, or canned hams, or bottles of whiskey, maybe a toaster. Stuff like that could sit on store shelves for months waiting for somebody with cash left over after paying the rent and the coal bill and the grocery tab to come along and take a fancy to it. But at our house, it was more like the stuff took a fancy to us and just started showing up.

When I finally got a transfer out of Southie, after walking a beat for a couple of years after I graduated from high school, it meant that I could be trusted as a rookie cop, that my desk sergeant, who was my second cousin, thought I could work on my own without a dozen relatives checking up on me every day.

I loved the waterfront, everything from the smell of salt water, oil, and dead fish to city hall, tipping my hat to Mayor Tobin once in a while and then doing the loop again, watching the ships come and go, thinking about where they were bound. How many ships did I watch steam off that ended up docking in the Thames? I never would've thought I'd end up here, too. I made a motion with my hand as if I were twirling my old baton, walking my beat, familiar territory beneath my feet. I wondered about the question Harding had asked me. Would I run into a burning London house to save an unknown English life, or would I stand by, waiting for the bobbies to show up? There was nothing in it for me, but I had a hard time picturing myself on the sidelines. I whistled a jig and went back to pleasanter thoughts, smiling at the memory of carrying fish home on the trolley from the market on Fish Pier. Everyone wanted a patrolman around, and there'd be no end to the cod and mackerel wrapped in newspaper and smelling of brine and ice you'd have pressed on you of a Friday afternoon.

Memories made me feel lonely, so I looked around for a distraction, and saw the Coach & Horses Pub, the front painted in a deep, dark red and a hand-lettered sign in the window that said ALWAYS SOMETHING READY TO EAT and DRAUGHT GUINNESS. Now it felt more like Boston, and this was a memory I didn't mind. I went in.

Inside the pub, dark wood paneling, the color of brown shoe polish, lined the walls. Small lamps every few feet provided the only illumination. Cigarette smoke dulled the air while loud voices and laughter from the rear floated up to lighten the atmosphere. Couples sat at tables in the back and two silent older civilians occupied stools at the bar, pints before them in various stages of consumption. I took an empty seat at the end, and then realized I still didn't have any English money. I would trade dollars for pounds tomorrow, but I wanted a Guinness today.

"What'll it be, Yank?"

"A pint of Guinness, if you'll take American money."

"You've got no pounds nor pence then?"

"I just got here this morning. I haven't had time to exchange my money."

"I don't know. . . ." The barman had an uneasy look, as if he thought I was pulling a fast one.

"Oh come on, Bert," one of the guys at the bar said. "Give the lad a break and take his money. He's come all the way from America just today!"

He smiled and winked at me, his grin showing gaps in his teeth. He wore blue coveralls, like I had seen on the workmen at the bombed-out building earlier that morning. His hands were rough and callused and his gray hair stuck out in wisps above his ears. He had an easy laugh that broke down into a smoker's wheeze that he treated with a pull on his pint.

"A pint of Guinness costs a quarter back in Boston," I said, trying to be helpful.

"A quarter of wot?" Bert's face scrunched up as he tried to figure out what I meant.

"Quarter of a dollar. Twenty-five cents. How about I give you a dollar and that should be more than enough for a pint for me and one each for my friends here?" I nodded in the direction of my bar mates.

"Wot I'll do with a Yank dollar I don't know, but all right. I hope the rest of your lot don't expect the same."

Pretty soon we all ended up shaking hands — Bert, the barman; George and Henry at the bar, both deliverymen for the markets at Covent Garden, which is where I had gotten myself to. I ended up trading that dollar for a five-spot, and hearing stories of the Great War, London during the worst of the Blitz, and where their sons were serving. Bert had a kid in Burma with the army, and was worried since he hadn't gotten a letter in a month. George had two boys, both of whom had signed up with the Royal Navy, one on a destroyer out in the Atlantic and the other a mechanic at Scapa Flow. Henry had a daughter in the WRENs, just like

Daphne, and a boy who had been in France with the BEF but made it out at Dunkirk.

"Lucky we are they're all in one piece still," George said, and Bert made himself busy with the glasses.

"Aye," said Henry quietly, nodding his head as if in prayer. The war was still young.

I told them about Boston and entertained them with stories of all the murders I had solved. If I overstated my contribution, well, it was the Guinness talking. Sometime after dark they led me out to Piccadilly Circus, steered me down Piccadilly, and told me to walk straight until I came to Hyde Park.

"Big bloody green thing, in the daylight anyway, filled with potatoes, it is! Can't miss it," George said. "And good luck, lad."

We all shook hands, and Henry slapped me on the back like an old pal. It was as if I was standing in for all of their kids, and the act of befriending me would spread out all over the world and bring acts of kindness to their children. I thought about Dad, and realized it was the kind of thing he'd do, too.

I walked until I came to Hyde Park Corner again. I thought about everything I had seen today and everything I had been taught all my life about the English. I knew two things for sure: first, that Ireland had to be free and united, and second, that Bert, George, and Henry and the woman on the stretcher with her hand raised in a V sign weren't people I had an argument with.

I was pretty tired now, the flight, the long day, and the Guinness making the slight slope up Hyde Park feel steeper than it should have. I stuck my hands in my pockets and hunched forward, thinking of bed and sleep. The image that came to me was of my room at home and the bed I had slept in every night of my life, until this war came along. The bed I woke up in every Christmas morning, the "socks" Christmas, and the ones after that with toys, jewelry, and sweets for all.

One of those years, Dad converted a small room upstairs into his den. It had been full of boxes and junk, but one day he cleaned it out and the next day a leather sofa and chair showed up. Real leather, with brass nail heads showing. He got himself a used rolltop desk and announced it was a den. I had never heard of a den, except as caves for foxes in stories, and it sounded great to me. But it wasn't for kids. His buddies would come over after work, or to drop off groceries or some special present. Uncle Dan too, and sometimes he'd bring his friends, who were nearly all IRA men. They carried guns, but they weren't all cops. Not gangsters either, but something in between.

Dad carried the key to the room on his watch chain, and the key to his desk, too. No one was allowed in there, except Mom when she cleaned. It smelled of smoke, and she'd empty the ashtrays, open the window, and mop down the woodwork. She always did it after school, and I'd stand outside the door and look in, curious, wondering what the men did in there. I wanted my dad to pull out that key and unlock the door, put his hand on my shoulder, and invite me in. But he never did. Not even when I joined the force.

"Stay away from here," he said. "And don't bother the men."

The men. I was standing there, in my new blue uniform, home from the first day on the job. Two of his pals were clumping up the stairs in their heavy cop shoes, the first guy a sergeant from the Back Bay station, carrying a gym bag.

"How's the rookie doin'?" he said, to my father, not to me.

"Come on in, Basher. The rookie's none of your concern now. Billy, begone with you."

So what? Big deal. Who cares about a bunch of old guys drinking Jameson and smoking cigars anyway? But it was funny.

Dad would spend hours with me at a crime scene, calling me down when I was off duty, to show me how he did things, how he looked for evidence, looked at how a body lay. He had worked Homicide for ten years and had one of the best solve rates in the city. He'd tell me anything about a case. But never in his den.

I realized I'd almost passed the Dorchester. Thinking about home, I almost forgot where I was. It was like I'd slipped back to Boston for a few minutes, and the sidewalk under my feet was leading from the station to my house. I was ready to fall asleep on my feet, and if I did, maybe I'd wake up and see my house, climb the steps, and turn the key in the lock on the front door, inhale the smells of supper, and walk up to my room, past the den and the muffled sounds of talk and harsh laughter.

I spent the next day reading about Norway, drinking coffee, and watching for Daphne to pass by my desk. I was better at the last two, but I did manage to absorb a few things. The Norwegians had gotten beaten pretty bad in 1940 when the Germans invaded. Even though the British, French, and Poles sent troops to help them, they'd all ended up with their tails between their legs. King Haakon escaped to England, where he set up a government in exile. The Norwegians had managed to pull a good one over on the Germans. Just as the Nazis were about to march into Oslo, the Norwegians made a little withdrawal from their treasury, about eight tons of gold. They took it by train, trucks, and even small boats along the coast, until they met up with British warships that carried the king and the gold to England. In the past two years they had used this money to build up an underground network of civilians back home. They called it the Underground Army, but it hadn't done much yet. There was also the Norwegian Brigade here in England, made up of men who had escaped from Norway. They were about three thousand strong and growing, and they were itching to be the spearhead of an invasion to liberate their country. The Norwegians had their own commando units that worked with the British Special Operations Executive. Together with SOE units, they were conducting hit-and-run raids along the Norwegian coast, blowing up fisheries and fish-oil-processing plants. That sounded pointless until I read that fish oil was a key ingredient in making nitroglycerin. War certainly is educational.

I hadn't gotten much farther when I saw

Daphne approaching my desk. I sat up straight and tried to look important, so I could pretend to be too busy to speak to her for a minute. My plan fell apart when I saw that she was with another guy and seemed to be stealing sideways glances at him and whispering as they walked toward me. A quick look told me he was an unlikely guy for me to be jealous of, but that didn't really matter at the moment. My heart was broken.

"Lieutenant Boyle," Daphne said, as if she were introducing two generals, "this is Lieutenant Piotr Augustus Kazimierz. He will be going to Beardsley Hall with you and Major Harding."

I didn't know what a Beardsley Hall was, but I did know my dear Daphne was smiling warmly at this Peter whatever-his-name-was. He was a slight guy, a few inches shorter than me, with thick glasses and a faint smile on his face. His hair was sandy and his eyes a grey-blue. He wore a British uniform with "Poland" stitched on the upper sleeve. He was half the kid you wanted to beat up in school and half Leslie Howard. I could tell which half Daphne saw. But my mother had taught me my manners. I stood.

"Glad to meet you, Lieutenant. . . ."

"Kazimierz. Call me Kaz if it's easier. It is

for most Americans."

"OK, Kaz. I'm Billy. What's Beardsley Hall?"

Daphne held up a hand. "Before you answer, Baron, Lieutenant Boyle has to sign something." She fished through a file folder marked TOP SECRET.

"Baron? Like the Red Baron?"

Kaz looked embarrassed; his pale skin showed a red flush easily. I had almost said I didn't know Polacks had barons, but was saved by Daphne.

"Piotr is a baron of the Augustus clan in Poland, not that I would expect you to know that," Daphne said, as if I were the original colonial clod. "Now sign this."

Polish barons, Norwegian royalty, and top-secret documents. Not my normal day, but I tried to hold my own.

"Sign what?" I asked.

"The Official Secrets Act. It means they can shoot one if one reveals any military secrets. We've all signed it," she added casually, handing me a pen. Almost a little eagerly, I thought. I wrote my name, trying to keep my hand steady and look nonchalant.

"Don't worry, Billy, they haven't shot anyone yet," Kaz offered helpfully. "But I hear there's one chap who drew ten years' hard labor." He spoke the King's English with a slight trace of an accent that was nothing like the heavily accented Polish I was used to hearing in a few Boston neighborhoods. I laughed to show him I knew he was joking. I hoped he was.

"I better be careful. I hate any kind of labor," I said as I handed the pen back to Daphne.

"Do tell," she said, snapping up the form as she turned on her heel and walked away, leaving me with the little Polish guy she'd been flirting with. Kaz smiled, barely able to suppress a laugh at my expense.

"What did I say?" I wondered.

"Daphne works very hard, and expects everyone to do so as well."

"One must do one's duty, right?"

"Well, well, Lieutenant . . . I mean Billy. I think it will be fun to watch you and Daphne work together. A real test of the Allied alliance."

Behind those glasses I could see his eyes twinkle and one eyebrow raise. Most guys would get steamed at a crack about their girl, or at least jealous. Kaz seemed confident, like he knew Daphne could hold her own with me. Maybe even mop the floor with me.

"Have a seat," I said, offering the chair

next to my desk as I sat down. "Don't pay me any mind, Kaz, I just like to ruffle feathers."

"You like to pet birds?" Kaz asked, looking at me like I was nuts.

"No, no, it's just an expression. Meaning that I like to stir things up, rile people up."

"Ah," he said, tapping his finger against his cheek as he looked up at the ceiling, as if committing the phrase to memory. "I am a student of languages, but there is always so much to learn, so many idioms that are not in the textbooks. Ruffling feathers, yes. So, where were we?"

"Beardsley Hall. What and where is it?"

"It is where the Norwegian government in exile holds court, and where we are going tomorrow. North of the city, on the coast. If you will be so kind as to join me for dinner tonight, I will explain everything to you, in more comfortable surroundings. We must enjoy a good meal before we dine with the Norwegians. They are sure to feed us pickled herring and other arctic delicacies. *Okropny.*" He made a face like a kid who was made to eat boiled spinach.

"Lousy?" I guessed.

"Terrible. *Słusznie okropny.*" Kaz had a pleasant smile, the kind that said he found just about everything amusing, including

67

himself. Since I couldn't see the advantage in taking things too seriously myself, I admired this attitude.

"Dinner sounds good, best offer so far today, Kaz. Where?"

"In my rooms at the Dorchester. At seven o'clock." He got up, tossed off a mock salute, and left.

Rooms? Maybe his command of the English language wasn't so great after all. I got his room number and went back to my pile of files. I finished the stack of papers on my desk and very carefully put them back in a filing cabinet and locked it tight, thinking about the Official Secrets Act and wondering if Daphne had been kidding about getting shot. I visited the HQ company clerk and exchanged my dollars for British pounds before calling it a day and heading back to the Dorchester.

I had no idea what the dress code was, but I had only one uniform jacket, so I brushed it and tried to shake out the wrinkles. Kaz had worn the standard-issue British wool battle-dress jacket, but it seemed to have been tailored just for him. For a little guy, he wore a uniform well. I put on a clean khaki shirt and knotted my tie — scarf — neatly. I thought I looked good. At seven I went down the stairs to the tenth floor. I walked down the hall, which was nicely carpeted and well lit. The doors were very far apart. I wonder if Kaz had his own private bathroom.

When I gave his door a sharp rap, I got two big surprises. Daphne opened the door. She wore a smile and the kind of evening gown I had only seen in movies, like the dresses Ginger Rogers wore when she danced with Fred Astaire. And her light brown hair cascaded over her bare shoulders, setting off a necklace that sparkled with more diamonds than I had ever seen, except for the time I caught Tommy Fortunato after that jewelry-store heist.

Three surprises, actually. Daphne and her attire counted as two. Stretching behind her was a wide wood-paneled hallway lit by a crystal chandelier. The triple surprise must have shown on my face. Daphne took my arm in hers and led me in with a smile.

"So glad you could join us, Lieutenant. I take it your clothes haven't arrived yet?"

I almost told her I had all my socks and underwear with me. I almost said, "Yessir," but that only worked with Harding. Was she was needling me or on the level? I had to say something and was stunned to hear myself ask, "Are you needling me or are you on the level?"

She giggled, covering her lips with two delicate fingers, and I got my answer. We finally reached the end of that long hallway. It opened into a wood-paneled sitting room with an even larger chandelier hanging from a domed ceiling. Kaz stood at the window, closing the blackout curtains. I caught a glimpse of Hyde Park across the street, visible in the lengthening evening shadows. My room came with a windowpane the size of my hat that looked out at the next building.

He turned and extended his hand. "Welcome, Billy, to my humble home." He was dressed in a tuxedo that didn't look like a rental. There was a table set for three and champagne on ice.

"Nice place, Kaz. Sure your roommates won't mind us eating without them?" I always thought a wiseass remark was a good substitute for self-confidence.

"Very good, Billy. Roommates. *Współlokatorzy.* I like that." Kaz laughed as he opened the champagne. That pissed me off and at the same time made me like him even more.

"Let us drink to the Dorchester Hotel, an oasis of civility within a world in chaos. Do you know they never closed the kitchens, even during the Blitz?" He poured three tall, narrow glasses, and I decided not to tell him

I preferred Guinness on tap.

We clinked glasses, and this champagne tasted a lot better than anything I ever drank at a Boston wedding. I felt a little nervous, like I'd been invited to a swanky party in Beacon Hill by mistake, and had to figure out how to act with the swells. I looked around, trying to think of something to say.

"OK, Kaz, I gotta admit it. This place is really something. How do you rate this while I'm stuck in the attic?"

"Listen, Lieutenant Boyle," Daphne spoke sharply, "you —"

"Call me Billy, please. It will make me feel so much better when you yell at me."

Daphne smiled a little, and I noticed she was wearing makeup and lipstick. She looked really beautiful all dolled up. The real trick was that she'd also looked beautiful in that WREN uniform with no makeup.

"Very well, Billy. I won't yell at you. But you should know General Eisenhower kicked a colonel out of that room for you. He wanted to have you close by. He also has rooms here. Even for Americans, the Dorchester is exclusive real estate these days."

Kaz refilled our glasses. "For myself, Billy, I must admit that I've always had a weakness for the Dorchester. I stayed here with my parents when it was new in 1932. When I was at Oxford, they would visit once a year and they always stayed here, in this very suite. We spent Christmas 1938 in this room, with my two sisters." His eyes drifted away and focused on something that I couldn't see.

"Where are they now? Still in Poland?"

No response. Kaz just seemed to be in a dream. Daphne reached out to touch his arm. He came back from wherever he was.

"They are dead. All of them."

He set down his champagne at his place and sat. I realized it was the first time I'd met anyone who had actually suffered from the war. Back home it was all newspaper headlines and here it had been file folders, coffee, and drinking buddies so far. I felt bad about asking, but I could tell he had his pain carefully stored in that faraway place. So I asked.

"How?"

"The Nazis decided to eliminate anyone who might resist them. The intelligentsia, officers, government officials. And the aristocracy. We do not have a monarch, but the ancient clans had their leaders, their barons and counts. Or had them." He was quiet for a minute. Daphne and I sat down, and she filled in the rest.

"Piotr was at Oxford, doing graduate work in foreign languages when the war broke out. He volunteered for the Polish Free Corps when they organized here."

"So how did you end up with Eisenhower?"

"The Polish Army was gracious enough to grant me a commission. I have a heart condition that would normally keep me from active service, but I know a number of European languages, a talent that is suddenly in great demand."

"And all this?" I gestured around the room.

"My father had significant land holdings and investments. He was a very shrewd businessman, and knew that sooner or later Poland would be overrun from the east or the west. He was right, except it was from both directions. He kept most of the family fortune in Swiss accounts. I am now the sole beneficiary of his wisdom."

"So you stay here where you have good memories."

"It is all that is left, Billy. In my country, there is even less."

"I hope you've got plenty stashed away. This place must cost a fortune. Hope your money lasts longer than the war." Daphne shot me a glance that said, shut up. Maybe you didn't talk about other people's money in England. Then I saw a sadness in Kaz's eyes as he looked at Daphne.

"That is of little concern. Now, let us talk about Norwegians before the food is brought up." It didn't take a Beantown detective to figure out all that money would probably outlast his heart. I was glad of the change of subject.

Kaz gave me the lowdown on the meetings with the Norwegians. Major Harding was going to Beardsley Hall to give the king and his advisers a top-secret briefing. Kaz was to be his interpreter, although most of the Norwegians spoke English to one degree or another. I was to go as — well, let's just say I was going, too.

The briefing was about Operation Jupiter. When he mentioned that name, Kaz lowered his voice and looked around as if we were standing on a Berlin street corner. Operation Jupiter was the plan for the invasion of Norway. It had been created by the British, but they hadn't had the resources to carry it out until we entered the war. Now it was going to be the Allies' first offensive against the Third Reich. Before winter set in, we were going to invade Norway. British and American forces, along with the Norwegians, were going to take Norway back. This would protect the Murmansk convoys bringing supplies to the Russians, and give the Allies air bases within fighter range of Berlin. It sounded like we were about to win the war.

The Norwegians had been lobbying for Operation Jupiter, and now they were going to be told it was on. We were going to deliver the news jointly with a British delegation headed by a Major Charles Cosgrove. The Norwegians were going to have their government officials there, along with officers from the Norwegian Brigade and commando units. It sounded like we would be heroes.

"Should be a breeze."

"Breeze?" Kaz asked quizzically.

"He means it should be easy," Daphne explained.

"Ah! Yes, I understand, but actually it may be more like heavy winds. *Ciękie wiatry,* my friend."

There was a knock at the door. The food came in, two carts' worth of covered plates and bowls. It smelled great, and we never got back to why it wouldn't be such a breeze.

CHAPTER FOUR

The alarm rang. It was 6:00 a.m. Oh six hundred hours, I thought, as I suddenly remembered I was in the army. What a disappointment. It was dark as a dungeon in my little room, and I had to turn on the bedside lamp to make sure I didn't walk into a wall. It was raining. I could tell by the greasy streaks of water on my tiny dirty window.

Ten minutes later I was dressing and packing for a few days in the country with the Norwegians. I put on a pair of freshly pressed olive drab wool serge pants and a starched khaki shirt with the mohair olive drab field scarf tucked in between the second and third buttons. I bent over to tie my shoes, brown laces on brown oxfords. I was a properly drab soldier, and thought about how dull the olive green and khaki brown were in comparison to police blue. Cops in uniform stood out in a crowd, it said, Here I am, a man in blue. I guess soldiers preferred to fade into the forest instead of standing out. That first day on the job in Boston, my badge had felt solid and weighty as I pinned it on my new blue shirt. It was everything I had ever wanted. Dad had been called out on a homicide during the night, so it was only Mom and little Danny to see me off. Danny had shined my shoes for me, getting more black shoe polish on his hands and nose than on the shoes, but they still sparkled. They both stood at the door and waved, and more than a few neighbors stood on their porches to watch the Boyles send off their second generation to serve with Boston's finest.

Funny thing, it was the First World War that had gotten Dad and Uncle Dan jobs with the department. After the police strike in 1919, none of the strikers got their jobs back. Governor Coolidge saw to that, and it got him into the White House. The city needed new cops fast, and what better source than the veterans, just back from the war, jobless, trained, and in need of dough? Dad and Uncle Dan signed up, along with plenty of their buddies, and that bunch of recruits stuck together, looked out for each other, did favors for each other, protected each other. For more than twenty years.

That's a lot of favors, and now some of those guys were pretty high up in the department. Some were dead, too. Being a cop wasn't all about favors, you know.

Now, it was another world war that was taking me away from the cops. Funny. One generation gets in, another gets pulled out. Like war was a tide that washed over us, leaving some on the high ground and dragging others out to sea.

I stood up, shoes laced tight, and pulled my army-issue Colt .45 caliber automatic pistol out of the duffel bag along with its holster, belt, and spare clips. The damn thing weighed a ton. I was used to my Smith & Wesson .38 Police Special revolver, a piece you could wear snug under your shoulder or in your back belt and not feel like you were lugging around an elephant gun. But that was back in Boston and here I was in London with this cannon. There was a war on, so I didn't see any sense in leaving it behind. I put it in my overnight bag along with a few other things and grabbed my field overcoat, olive drab, of course.

I went down to Kaz's room and knocked. He had promised to have coffee and toast sent up, and I wasn't about to turn down room service on his dime. I shouldn't have been surprised when Daphne opened the door in the midst of buttoning her uniform tunic.

"Come in and help yourself, Billy, we're almost ready."

I made a beeline for the cart with a steaming pot of coffee surrounded by toast and pots of jam. Remembering that I was supposed to be an experienced detective, I turned to her as soon as I had poured a cup and asked, "We?"

"Oh, yes. I'm also Major Harding's driver, didn't you know?"

"A dame? I mean, uh, a lady driver? Why can't Harding drive himself around, or have me do it maybe?" Daphne's eyes were narrowing and she was about to give me what would have been a very unladylike answer when Kaz strolled in from the bedroom, casually knotting his tie.

"Billy," he said with a smile, "I believe that the word 'dame' has quite a different meaning in American English from that which we are used to. You must explain it to me later. And, Daphne, you must forgive our guest for not understanding the special circumstances here in England." He seemed to be enjoying our discomfort, with an expression of detached amusement that he wore as well as his clothes.

"Very well, Piotr. If I must." She took a deep breath, as if she needed stamina to explain the obvious to a blundering idiot.

"Billy, you should know that even General Eisenhower has a woman driver here. It is part of our duties. It wouldn't do for foreigners to be driving around the country on what they would consider the wrong side of the road, and then getting lost. You see, we've taken all the main road signs down, to confuse German paratroopers; they seemed a very real possibility only a year ago. The major does like to drive himself, as he did when he picked you up in the jeep. But today is an official trip in a staff car, and I shall be at the wheel."

To emphasize the point, she picked up a pair of kid-leather driving gloves and idly slapped them against her thigh. Oh, to be a kid again, I almost said out loud. I stuffed toast in my mouth instead.

We picked up Harding at another hotel and headed north out of London. As we pulled away from the curb, Daphne gave me a smile in the rearview mirror.

"Billy," she said, "as soon as we turn up ahead, watch for the street name, it may interest you."

I was game, although I couldn't see why a London street name would be that interesting. We turned and I watched as we drove up a street lined with shops and homes, nice brownstones, except they were all painted white. I craned my neck to see the street sign up ahead.

"Baker Street?" I tried to think what that meant, and I saw Daphne stifling a smile. Next to me in the backseat, Harding shook his head just a bit as he unfolded a newspaper.

"Baker Street! Sherlock Holmes!"

"I thought you might fancy that, being a detective yourself," Daphne said. "There, up ahead on the left, is 221B. Or where it would be, if it were real."

I shifted over toward Harding to get a good look out his window. There it was, a sign above a shop that said 221B BAKER STREET. My mouth hung open. I looked around at the ordinary street and the white-painted buildings, looking clean in the morning rain. Where were the fog, the streetlights, the gray atmosphere? The horses pulling carriages, bringing troubled clients to Watson and Holmes? I had to admit I had been impressed with Big Ben and all, but for a kid who had devoured all the adventures of Sherlock Holmes, this was really something. I was on Baker Street, driving by the rooms of Holmes and Watson! I sort of wished it were all in black and white and gray, like in the movies.

"You a fan of Doyle?" asked Harding.

"Sure," I said, then struggled to keep the gee-whiz quality out of my voice. "Sure, him and a lot of others, too." I didn't want to admit that the only book I had ever read cover to cover was a collection of Sherlock Holmes stories. I turned around and watched Baker Street fade away as we turned the corner and drove around a park, heading out of the city. *Gee whiz, I'm in the land of Sherlock Holmes.*

We left Regent's Park behind us and the buildings started to thin out. Traffic was heavy coming in to the city, but in our lane, out going was light. Daphne was actually a very good driver, and she seemed to know her way around. Without any signposts identifying towns, direction, or roads, it seemed impossible to navigate, but she managed it. Kaz sat up front with her, an open map on his lap, which he occasionally consulted as he pointed out an upcoming turn. He turned in his seat and held up the map for me to see.

"We're going to a little town called Wickham Market, on the Suffolk coast," he said, pointing out the bulge of land that curved out into the North Sea. "About one hundred miles or so from here. Beardsley Hall is an estate on the Suffolk Heath where the Norwegians are headquartered. Ironic, since the hall is built around an old castle fortification, which used to guard that part of the coast against Viking raids. I'm sure some old English bones in the ground protest the current occupants of the hall!"

"Better Norwegian Vikings than Germans," Daphne added.

"Well, yes, if we can be sure of that."

I could see Daphne look in the rearview mirror and cock an eyebrow at Harding, who was silent, reading the *London Times.* He gave her the slightest nod, which she passed on to Kaz. These three seemed to have their own language.

"OK, Kaz, what's going on?" The great American detective at work.

"We have indications that one of the Norwegians may be a spy."

"A traitor?"

"We really don't know," Kaz said, shrugging his shoulders as he turned to half face me. "It could be a traitor, or a German agent planted among the Norwegian troops who made it to England in 1940. It would have been easy for someone with false papers to mix in with retreating British, French, Polish, and Norwegian troops."

"That would have taken some planning. The Norwegian campaign was over pretty quickly."

"Exactly. Which supports the theory that it is a traitor within the Norwegian ranks. All we know from our sources is that such an agent exists. But there are thousands of Norwegians in uniform in England now. The Norwegian Brigade, merchant marine, naval, and RAF units, King Haakon's court . . . a spy could be anywhere. He could be very highly placed or situated where he can do no harm."

"How do you guys know about this?" There was a silence. Harding put down his paper and spoke.

"The British secret service picked up a number of German agents who were positioned in this country before the war. They were mostly sleeper agents, sent here with radios to await word when they were needed. Our man tried to contact one of these agents just when British counterintelligence picked him up. We tried to set up a meeting so we could scoop up the spy, but he evaded us. All we could get from interrogating the sleeper was that there was a spy among the Norwegian forces in England, and his code name. Prodigal Son."

"So we're going to tell the Norwegians

about the invasion scheduled for this fall, with a German agent lurking around somewhere?"

"Looks like you're going to start earning your keep real quick, Boyle," Harding said, returning to his newspaper.

"Don't worry, Billy," Kaz said. "Everybody who is anybody among the Norwegians in England will be there. All we need to do is identify the spy. Before he finds another way to contact Berlin and betray the invasion. No, take the right fork, Daphne." He turned his attention back to the map.

"Are you sure, dear? I swear we go straight here toward Sudbury."

Great. My first assignment is to find a needle in a haystack and these two can't even find the road the haystack's on. I leaned back and shut my eyes, pretending to sleep so no one would ask me how I planned to discover who the spy was.

I pretended pretty good, and woke up a while later when Harding nudged my shoulder. "Cut the snoring, Boyle, we're almost there."

The rain had stopped, but there were still dark clouds rolling in, from the sea, I guessed. We were on the heath, which is British for a damp, cold, treeless swamp.

"What the hell did the Vikings want around here anyway?" I asked. Nobody answered me, and soon my attention was drawn to Beardsley Hall off in the distance, silhouetted against the gray sky. It was massive. Four stories tall, it squatted on green landscaped grounds that stood in stark contrast to the gloomy heath surrounding us. Green ivy-covered granite gray stone nearly up to the top floor. At one end of the building stood a crenellated castle tower. Kaz played tour guide.

"The original foundation and tower were constructed around 900 A. D. Rebuilt in the mid-1400s and expanded during the reign of King George, during your American Revolution. The great hall was built during the Victorian era, with the reconstruction of the tower completed at the turn of the century, at great cost to the Beardsley family. No matter, though, since the patriarch made his fortune investing in African diamond mines. The family line ended when all the sons died in the Great War. The government took over the hall and granted it to the Norwegian government in exile in 1940."

"Will there be a test?"

"Oh yes, indeed!" Kaz laughed. He always seemed to know something I didn't. We turned onto the wide gravel drive and took it to where it made a circle near the main entrance. Daphne slowed the car and the tires crunched the white crushed stone like a prizefighter cracking his knuckles. The long lawn was manicured and green, enclosed by thick hedges trimmed at a uniform height for a hundred yards on either side. I guess having an unemployed army of Norwegians hanging around made for good lawn care. A Norwegian flag, red with a blue-and-white cross, hung limply in the damp air, not even trying to flap a welcome. On either side of the main door sentries stood, armed with Sten submachine guns, grim looks, and polished boots. Only their eyes moved, like cop eyes, on high alert, checking each new person who moved into their domain. As we got out of the car, the double doors of the entrance opened and an officer almost ran out to greet us, followed by two more enlisted men. He wore the same kind of British Army uniform Kaz did, except his shoulder patch read "Norway." He was short and thin, and his movements were quick, almost hurried, his eyes darting among our party until he spotted the brass.

"Welcome, Major Harding." He saluted and then extended his hand. "On behalf of

His Majesty King Haakon, I welcome you to our headquarters. Captain Jens Iversen, at your service. I am in charge of security for the king." His English was precise, clipped, like he was biting off each word as he said it.

"Thank you, Captain," said Harding. "This is Lieutenant Boyle and Lieutenant Kazimierz. My assistant, Second Officer Daphne Seaton."

"Pleased to meet you all," responded Iversen, with a bow to Daphne and the barest trace of an accent twirled around his words, now that his canned speech was over. "My men will show you to your rooms, and then the king requests that you lunch with him at twelve. Baron, the king looks forward to meeting you. Now, you must excuse me. I have to prepare for the exercise tomorrow." With a nod, he scurried off, evidently a very busy man. Or a very nervous one.

"You're famous, Kaz. Kings await you."

"Billy, the aristocracy of Europe is really a very small club. Those of us still free feel the weight of those left behind. It brings us closer together."

"So tell me, what do I call him?"

"Your Majesty will do nicely," Daphne chimed in. "Don't they teach you these things in Boston?"

The enlisted men took Daphne's and the major's bags and led us up innumerable stairs, twists and turns and through corridors, until we reached our rooms on the fourth floor. I stashed my bag and we regrouped a few minutes later in Harding's sitting room. It was a small, pleasant chamber, lace curtains framing the only window, a faint breeze of damp air moving them sluggishly. A couch took up one wall and two upholstered chairs faced it. Doilies and flower vases gave it a grandmotherly air.

"OK, here's the drill," Harding lectured, ticking points off on his fingers. "This lunch is a social affair. We make our manners with the king and his folks and keep the conversation light. The briefing on the invasion is set for tomorrow afternoon. For security reasons we are not mentioning the word invasion until then. Got it?" We got it.

"Boyle, I don't think we made one thing clear about the German agent. The Norwegians don't know about him. And we're not going to tell them."

"Yes, sir." Old reliable.

There was a knock at the door. Daphne opened it and said, "Major Cosgrove! What a pleasant surprise" in such a way that I could tell it was a surprise and not really a pleasant one.

"Pleased to see you, too, Daphne, my dear." An overweight, balding, frowning, and very dignified British major in full dress uniform entered the room. He walked stiffly, using a cane with his right hand. His large form was hidden behind a uniform that even I could tell was well tailored. His leather Sam Browne belt gleamed and his drooping mustache was waxed to perfection, the ends flipping up into little tips.

"Now look here, Harding, you should have informed me you were arriving a day early. Trying to get the king's ear, eh? Who's this young chap?" He spoke this last pointing his cane at me. I didn't know what to expect next but somehow I had the presence of mind to get up and offer him my seat.

"I'm Lieutenant Boyle, sir. Please, sit down."

"Hrrmmph." He sat himself down and looked at me. His way of saying thanks, maybe.

"Major Charles Cosgrove," Harding said to me, "represents the British Army chief of staff. He will be presenting Operation Jupiter with us to the Norwegians tomorrow."

"Bloody awful idea, always has been. Too bad you Yanks talked Winnie into it. Now,

Harding, what brings you here a day early?"

"Perhaps I should ask you how many days you've been here?"

"Just arrived myself, old boy. Some business with the commando chaps. They're putting on a show tomorrow out on the heath with the Norwegian Brigade. Blowing things up, lots of fireworks, impress the locals, that sort of thing. Number Ten Commando, since it includes a Norwegian troop, will assault some positions with First Battalion from the brigade. They'll blow up some old Matilda tanks and chase off the local Home Guard chaps who are playing the Germans. Great fun. Then we'll present this idiotic plan to the king and his men."

"As you can tell, Billy," Kaz offered, "Major Cosgrove thinks Operation Jupiter is doomed to fail."

"Damned right, Baron! I took a Turkish bullet in this leg at Gallipoli during the Great War," Cosgrove said, slapping his right knee. "That was another one of Churchill's grand invasion plans. He mucked that one up and he'll do the same in Norway, and you Americans are encouraging him down that road to disaster!" His voice rose and he punctuated the sentence by rapping the end of his cane on the floor. He sighed and finished in a quiet, resigned voice.

"We are not yet ready to invade any part of the continent." His voice faded off and he tapped his cane on the floor, staring at it while silence hung around him. I didn't know much about Gallipoli except that it was a failed invasion and that Cosgrove was lucky he got out of it with just a slug in the leg. Looked like he knew it, too.

"Well, Charles, that's all been decided above our level," said Harding. " 'Ours not to reason why' — isn't that what the poem says?"

"Quite so, Samuel. Now tell me, what's this young pup doing here?" That was me.

"Ike thinks he can help us with our Norwegian problem. He was a detective back in the States." Harding shrugged to show Cosgrove it wasn't his idea. At least he didn't mention Ike was my uncle.

"He thinks a rosy-cheeked youth fresh from America can succeed where MI-5 have failed! You must be quite the detective, young man."

"I am. As a matter of fact, I've already discovered something."

"And what's that?"

"We're late for lunch."

Cosgrove got up pretty quick for an old guy with a bum leg. It looked like he hadn't missed many lunches lately and didn't want to start now. We all filed out and tried to keep up with him as he propelled himself down the hallway, launching his bulk on each step with his cane. Must have been pretty sturdy wood.

"Don't mind Charles," Daphne half whispered to me. "He's terribly gruff but he doesn't mean to be rude."

"Gruff I can handle. It's the pickled herring I'm worried about."

Daphne giggled and made a face at Kaz, who smiled back. I marveled at their nonchalance. They acted as if we were in a play and were moving on to the next scene. Maybe it was their way of coping with the fact that they were playing with the fates of nations and the probable deaths of thousands. Maybe it was the way of the titled upper classes. What did I know?

Damned little, and as we descended the staircase something about that thought began to bother me. I didn't know why or what, but I felt like I did that time in Chinatown when I knew the guy coming out of the store in front of me was going to pull a gun. Not scared, but stunned at the sudden knowledge of what lay beneath the surface.

CHAPTER FIVE

I had never heard Norwegian before, but I heard it loud and clear down the long hallway heading to the solarium. The sounds flowed out of the double doors and bounced off the paneled walls, doubling in volume as we approached. The words seemed hard and sing-songy at the same time. I had no idea what the voices were saying, but they were saying it at the top of their lungs.

"Don't tell me they're at it again?" Harding asked Cosgrove.

"Have been all morning. Skak is after the king to make up his mind about the senior adviser post. He keeps bringing up the gold." Cosgrove puffed his cheeks and blew out air, in exasperation over the arguing or in exhaustion from hustling to lunch. Or both, but I was concentrating on something else.

Gold. The eight tons of gold I had read about, I supposed. Gold would complicate everything.

Before I could blurt out a question, an enlisted man dressed in a white jacket opened the glass double doors and we entered the solarium. I wondered what rank army waiters held. There were three of them stationed around the room, which was long and narrow, jutting out from the side of the main house, surrounded by high glass windows. If there had been any sun, it would have been plenty hot. The little light that made it through the cloud cover did raise the temperature a bit, just enough to take the damp chill out of the air. A long table was set for a luncheon. Six places on each side and one at the head of the table, that chair just a little bigger than all the others. My first throne.

A heavyset guy who might have been a well-dressed stevedore sat at the table, smoking a cigar and pointedly staring out at the gardens so he wouldn't have to look at the guy across from him. The other fellow, dressed in an old-fashioned frock coat with a starched collar, was visibly trying to keep himself under control, his eyes burning with obvious dislike, even hatred, of the cigar smoker. His hands were clenched and shaking, his face red, and he looked like he was currently on the loser's end of the argument.

As for the third guy — well, I had never seen a king before, but he had it written all over him. Tall and thin, with a thick mustache and a long, aristocratic nose, he looked completely calm, above the fray. He stood ramrod straight, dressed in a naval uniform, and gazed at us with intense interest, as if nothing had passed between the men in the room. It almost made me forget about the gold. Almost.

"Ah, Majors Cosgrove and Harding," King Haakon said in excellent English. "My Anglo and American compatriots. Welcome!"

He stood, smiled warmly, and looked each of us in the eye as Harding introduced us. He had a firm handshake. When he was done, he stepped back just a bit and folded his arms behind his back, as if at parade rest. I could tell there was still some bad blood in the air. Cosgrove jumped in and introduced the two Norwegian civilians.

Vidar Skak, the frock coat, was deputy minister of the Interior. That must have been an important job a couple of years ago, but since the Germans currently held the note on the Interior I thought he might have some time on his hands. At first I thought

96

he was older, but then I noticed it was mostly how he dressed and acted. He looked like pictures of my grandfather on his wedding day, just not as happy. He was bony and pale, like he never spent a day outdoors, and his handshake was indifferent. But there was a determination behind those pursed lips, and I knew immediately he hadn't given up on the argument that still hung in the air.

Knut Birkeland was the king's economic adviser. He was a dark-haired, beefy fellow, barrel-chested, and with a face that had felt the wind. He gripped my hand like a vise and I could feel the hard calluses on his palms. I didn't know how much he knew about economics but I was sure he knew about work. He took Daphne's hand in his big paw and kissed it like a pro. He looked up and caught sight of the latest arrival.

"One of the Three Musketeers! Anders, come here!" He waved the Norwegian officer over to our group and clapped him on the shoulder as they shook hands.

"Major Anders Arnesen, may I present the beautiful Second Officer Daphne Seaton and her Allied escort?"

"Fortryllet," said Arnesen, taking Daphne's hand and kissing it.

"*Enchanté,* in case you are not familiar

with Norwegian," Kaz said.

We laughed and introduced ourselves, and Daphne glowed. What fun. Next maybe we could play charades.

"What makes you a musketeer, Major?" I asked. Anders Arnesen had a confident, easy look about him, the kind of look that well-trained soldiers displayed. Ready for anything — lunch with the king, assault a pillbox, you name it. It made me nervous.

"Three of us escaped from the Germans and ended up with the king when he left Norway. The king's party was small and he was glad to have some soldiers about. He . . . adopted us, I guess you could say. Someone named us the Three Musketeers, but we haven't seen much of each other lately."

King Haakon joined our group and put a fatherly hand on Arnesen's shoulder, much more gently than Birkeland had. For a major, this guy had friends in high places.

"Is Major Arnesen being overly modest again? He and his men were a godsend when we departed Norway. They helped us to load a large amount of our gold reserve aboard ship, in the middle of a German bombing raid, no less! Now one of them is in charge of security here . . . you've met Captain Iversen, yes? And Lieutenant Rolf

Kayser is a decorated commando. The Three Musketeers have done well!"

"And we'll all be together tomorrow. Rolf is participating in the exercise with my battalion," Arnesen said. "He commands Fifth Troop with Number Ten Commando, an all-Norwegian unit."

"You're with the Norwegian Brigade, Major?" Kaz asked.

"Yes. We've been training for two years now, and we're eager to get back into the fight. Do you have any news for us?"

"Unnskyld meg," came a voice from behind us, as an enlisted man in a white server's jacket held a tray of covered plates. "Excuse me," he said again in English. I moved, thankful for the interruption. The eager beaver would have to wait for his news.

"Take your seats please, gentlemen," the king said as he offered his arm to Daphne and led her to the place on his right. I noticed Birkeland and Skak make a beeline for the open seat on his left. Skak was faster. I ended up next to Birkeland and across from Cosgrove, with Kaz on my left. Harding sat across from some Norwegian officers I hadn't met. Waiters served us fish with a yellow sauce, boiled potatoes, and cauliflower. It was quite the white meal. The knives and forks were heavy, real silverware, the kind of stuff you counted after your guests left.

"Ah, Pouilly-Fumé, just my choice for turbot with hollandaise sauce!" Kaz raised his glass to the king. "To your health, Your Highness!" The toast was repeated by all and glasses raised. The wine was all right and the potatoes fine, but I was more interested in a different color.

"So what's all this about gold?" I asked. I noticed several forkfuls of fish suspended in midair, just below pairs of widening eyeballs. Only the king continued eating, royally ignoring my question and me.

"Don't they report the war news in Boston, young man?" Cosgrove snorted at me. "The Norwegians smuggled their entire treasury of gold bullion out of the country in 1940, practically under the noses of the Germans. Hundreds of cases of gold bars and coins. A logistical feat, under any circumstances!"

"So it's all here, in England?" I watched for a reaction from Skak or Birkeland, but Harding cut in.

"No, Lieutenant, the gold was taken to the United States on several different vessels, and deposited in banks to be at the disposal of His Majesty's government." He spoke quickly, as if to close the conversation.

"That's great. I must've missed it in the papers." I turned to Skak and Birkeland with a gee-golly look that came disturbingly easy. "Were you fellows involved with this gold transport?"

Skak looked straight ahead and drummed his fingers on the table. Birkeland spoke very deliberately. "We each were given different duties by the king. I was responsible for transferring the gold from ground transport to fishing boats and British warships, when they were available. We didn't want the gold to be all in one place, in case a ship was sunk or captured."

"How did you manage it — all those fishing boats, I mean?" Daphne asked. I wondered if she was really curious or just trying to steer the conversation in a different direction.

"Many of them were actually mine," Birkeland said, wiping his mouth with a napkin. "I own a small fishing fleet in those waters, and it was relatively easy to coordinate the loading. Most of the boats met up with British destroyers and other vessels. A few came directly to England." He took a drink of wine and set his glass down, adding, "Vidar was responsible for the book-keeping."

He speared a potato and popped it in his mouth. He smiled at Daphne as he chewed, satisfied that the questions were over. Hold your horses, buddy.

"So you got it all to England?" There, that got a reaction. Birkeland's face flushed and Skak looked tense. The king patted his lips with a napkin and stopped eating, which was the biggest reaction I had gotten out of him. It must have been the colonial in me that got a kick out of needling royalty.

"Yes, essentially," Birkeland said. "There were a few gold coins lost when a crate broke in Molde, and a few discrepancies in paperwork when everything got to England. But nothing that affects the balance of our national treasure."

At this, Skak finally turned and spoke. "The leavings of a national treasure may be minor, Lieutenant, but only to nations. To a single person, it is a great fortune."

There was a second of interminable silence. Skak had a good point, but nobody agreed with him. Finally the king spoke.

"Tell me, Lieutenant Boyle. Are there many Norwegians where you come from?"

I said something polite, and then took the obvious hint to drop the questions. I didn't know what the gold had to do with a spy, but sometimes you just had to kick over a few garbage cans to see what was hidden behind them. There would be plenty of time to poke a stick in it later.

Then it came to me. That thing beneath the surface bubbled up and came to the top. It was only a small thing, and it didn't even make sense or have anything to do with the gold. But there it was.

CHAPTER SIX

I was more used to a ham and cheese on rye washed down with a Coke for lunch. I really wanted to take a nap after drinking two glasses of wine and eating that big meal, but it would have been tough the way Harding was yelling at me.

We were in the library, sitting in cozy leather chairs, but I wasn't enjoying it. Not like Kaz was. I could see him lifting one edge of his mouth and suppressing a smile every time Harding looked away. Kaz sat back in a reddish brown leather chair, the brass buttons on his uniform matching the shiny nail heads decorating the leather. His legs were crossed and one arm was lazily draped over the arm of the chair; the other held a cigarette. His eyes darted back and forth between me and Harding, like we were swatting tennis balls at each other.

"I told you, Boyle, that this was supposed to be a nice social conversation. Not an interrogation! We're not here about the missing gold, damn it!"

"Maybe the spy is after the gold," I said, my cop's mind going right to one of the two motives that everything ultimately came down to. Greed. The other was love, or rather love gone bad. I preferred greed. It was more direct, pure in its own way. And usually not as messy. Greedy people just wanted to get away. Ex-lovers wanted revenge, or blood.

"Everyone with half a brain knows the gold is in America, Boyle."

Well, he had me there. I didn't want to go into my theory of investigative techniques, the "poke-everyone-with a-stick" theory. I had come up with that one myself. And if I said, "Yes, sir" one more time to this guy I was going to puke.

"It gives me an excuse to ask questions, Major. We've got to ask questions to find this spy; if he thinks it's about the gold, all the better."

I could see Harding hesitate before he launched into his next lecture. He was actually thinking about what I had said. Ah, the joys of being an Irishman with the gift of the gab. I hadn't even realized it was a good idea until after I had said it.

"OK, Boyle. At least you had a reason.

But keep a lid on it. Lieutenant Kazimierz, make sure he does. You are now officially Lieutenant Boyle's nursemaid. Be certain he doesn't cause an international incident." Harding leaned back in his chair and lit up a cigarette, shaking his head as he blew smoke toward the ceiling.

"It will be my great pleasure, Major. Is he to be allowed to attend this afternoon's meeting?"

"It will be your responsibility if he does," said Harding, still eyeing the ceiling. Kaz cocked an eyebrow at me that seemed to say, I don't care what you do; I'd just like to know one way or the other.

"Don't worry, Kaz. I won't get you into hot water."

"Hot water? Does that mean trouble?"

"Yeah, trouble."

"No hot water, Billy. Lukewarm is all you are allowed for the rest of the day!" Harding rolled his eyes but seemed to accept Kaz's pledge. Kaz smiled at Daphne, pleased with his own little joke. She smiled back as she rose from her chair and walked to the window. She had the patient look of a woman waiting for men to calm down and talk sense.

"Can you at least tell me what's going on this afternoon so I know what not to say?" I asked Harding.

"It's Cosgrove's show," he said, tapping ash into an ashtray balanced on the arm of his chair. "The British have funded and armed this Underground Army the Norwegians have organized. But the Norwegians are hesitant to use it. They want it in place when the country is liberated, some of them say so the Communists won't take over."

"But the British want them to start harassing the Germans now, perhaps take over a northern province," Kaz explained. "They've been after the king to approve some level of uprising, but he's put them off. Today, the British government, in the form of Major Cosgrove, is delivering an ultimatum."

"Time to go, gentlemen," Harding interrupted. "You get the gist, Boyle. Now just keep it zipped. Let's go." He ground his cigarette out, got up, and we followed him like little ducklings.

"Zipped?" Kaz asked in a low voice as we left the room.

"Yeah, like keep a lid on it. Keep it under your hat. Mum's the word."

"Billy," Kaz said, "I think you have a lot to teach me."

We entered a large room with a huge

107

wooden table at one end and maps of Great Britain and Norway taped to blackboards on wheels, like in school. The room was paneled in dark walnut, even the ceiling, and it felt heavy and oppressive, as if the weight of centuries hung over our heads. The king, of course, was at the head of the table. Vidar Skak and Knut Birkeland were on either side, and Major Arnesen and Captain Iversen sat next to them. There was another Norwegian officer, a lieutenant, next to Arnesen. The last musketeer? We took seats opposite Cosgrove. Daphne was in a chair against the wall, a notepad balanced demurely on her knee.

"Now that we are all gathered," King Haakon began, "let us begin. The purpose of this meeting is to hear a request from His Britannic Majesty's government concerning the disposition of Norwegian forces. Major Cosgrove?"

Nice. A request, he calls it. Something easy to say no to.

"Ahem." Cosgrove cleared his throat and shifted in his chair. He stroked his mustache and licked his lips before starting. A nervous tell.

"Your Highness. Thank you for receiving me on this matter. As you know, for the past two years we have worked with your govern-

108

ment to strengthen the Norwegian forces in Great Britain and within Norway. We have built up the Norwegian Brigade, a Norwegian commando unit, RAF squadrons, and extensive naval forces."

"We are eager for these forces to enter the fight against Germany and liberate our homeland," the king intoned. "We are grateful to you for the aid and assistance you have given us, as allies."

"Yes, well. . . ." Cosgrove seemed a little flustered and worked to get his train of thought back. Nice move, king. "We will get to that topic in due course. Today, we must discuss the potential usefulness of the Underground Army. Through our joint efforts, there are now hundreds of small groups of men in nearly every town and village from Oslo to Narvik. The purpose of forming this army was to strike back at the Germans, to fight the occupiers of your nation. However, if the underground is not used, or is kept for some future purpose, that effort will have been for naught."

"Major Cosgrove," Birkeland said, "the Norwegian government and people are grateful. However, we do not propose to order British troops into combat, and do not feel you should order our troops either." Birkeland looked at Cosgrove directly, his voice casual yet firm.

"We do not plan to issue orders to units under your direct control," Cosgrove answered stiffly. "However, it is the policy of His Majesty's government to carry the fight to the enemy with all our power, as soon as possible. To that end, we respectfully request — request, not order — that you bring the Underground Army into action now. If that is not possible, then we will not hesitate to bring the fight against Nazi Germany to Norway via air attacks and increased commando raids along the coast." He sat back in his chair, evidently relieved at having delivered the message. There was no relief anywhere else in the room.

"What exactly do you mean, Major?" Skak asked. "What kind of attacks?"

"We must hinder the enemy's ability to fight," Cosgrove said, gesturing with an open hand, as if astounded that his request was even being questioned. "Whether we do so through actions of the Underground Army or by bomber attacks or commando raids, it must be done! By you or by other Allied forces. It must." With that, the open hand slammed down on the table.

"Are you aware, Major, of what happened after our previous attempts to activate

Underground Army units?" Birkeland asked.

"Civilian losses are regrettable —"

"They are preventable!" Birkeland shouted. "But not if we order the underground to take action. The Germans have promised to continue reprisals against civilians wherever there is an uprising. Every time we blow up a bridge, innocent men, women, and children will be shot!"

"In wartime," Cosgrove lectured, "we cannot be responsible for the atrocities committed by our enemies. We cannot allow them to dictate the terms of battle. Norway is strategically located, and its economy cannot be allowed to work for the benefit of the Nazis."

"So the decision before us," King Haakon stated, "is how to conduct the fight against the Germans. Either use the Underground Army and accept reprisals against civilians or . . . ?"

"Or we will bomb factories and other industrial targets. At night, to minimize civilian casualties. The commando raids we have begun will increase in intensity. We have already hurt the Germans' ability to produce glycerin for explosives through the destruction of fish-oil-processing plants in Nordland."

"Your Highness," Skak broke in, "what will the Norwegian people think when the war is over if we let the British fight our battles for us? We have to use the weapon we have created! The Underground Army is ready to fight. Let them do so."

"No, no," Birkeland protested, shaking his head. "You are too concerned with factories, Skak. What about people? No room in that bookeeper's heart for them?"

Skak pointed a bony finger at Birkeland, his face reddening. "You are the king's economic adviser, you should be concerned about the destruction of our economy, especially if there is an alternative! We will need to govern Norway when the war is over, and that means taxes. No factories, no taxes."

"The people will not accept a government that allowed them to be put up against a wall and shot!" Birkeland started to rise from his seat, thought better of it, and settled his bulk back down.

"What of the British people and all their losses from the bombing?" asked Skak, opening his arms to all of us, seeking an answer. "They have not cried to their king to surrender, that it is too much. Do you expect less of the Norwegian people?"

King Haakon held up his hand for silence.

In the midst of the enraged men in the room, he was quiet, calm, and dignified. He looked at Skak and Birkeland and stared them into submission. He turned to Harding.

"Major Harding, is this the opinion of the American government as well?"

"Your Highness, I only represent General Eisenhower, and we have no opinion in this matter, other than to wish to work with all parties to defeat Germany in this war."

I marveled at Harding's ability to say nothing and make it sound nice. It was definitely a more refined skill than poking folks with a stick.

"I will consult with other members of the government and our military staff. This is a difficult and demanding decision," the king concluded. "The final recommendation shall be made by my senior adviser. I will announce who will be appointed to that post when our meetings this week are concluded."

He stood, folded his hands behind his back, and silently, but very effectively, dismissed us. I watched Skak and Birkeland stand and stare at each other. If there hadn't been a big wooden table between them, they would've been at each other's throats. I'd bet on Birkeland in a hand-to-hand fight.

But I'd bet on Skak in a dirty fight, and this was politics, as dirty as it got.

CHAPTER SEVEN

Beardsley Hall was swarming with Norwegian officials and all sorts of soldiers, sailors, and probably a few doctors and lawyers. Indian chiefs I wasn't so sure about. Events were moving kind of fast, and I wanted to slow down and think things through. I went out a rear entrance, crossed a patio, and walked into the gardens. I knew I was no Einstein, but I did know how to think about things. Slowly. Thoroughly. Quietly.

"Billy! Billy!" Kaz jogged to catch up with me, or at least jogged a few steps. He wasn't the most athletic guy around. He puffed like he had just run a mile, and pushed up the heavy glasses that had slid down his nose. I could tell by the look on his face that quiet was not going to be in the cards.

"Billy, this has been most exhilarating, yes?"

"Did you expect something else?"

"Ah! A question. That is exactly what I

mean. You are full of questions, why is that?"

I thought about that for a minute as we walked along a garden path, framed by red roses on both sides. Red petals carpeted the ground, like velvet drops of blood. I did like asking questions. Asking questions meant that there might be an answer, and that gave me hope. When you ran out of questions, the case was hopeless, and you just plain ran out of everything.

"Questions are a dime a dozen, Kaz. Answers are what interest me. What's so exhilarating for you?"

"You. Your approach to things. Very direct. Even more American than any other American I've met. You are unafraid to go to the heart of the matter, no matter how, how . . . inappropriate it may be. Very un-European. I think it puts people off balance."

"Good way to get a reaction."

"If you can tell the difference between shock and guilt, Billy."

Guilt. I turned down a path in the garden, white roses hanging damp and heavy from thick shoots spiked with sharp thorns. Guilt will out, Dad used to say. Guilt will out, except if you're dealing with a crazy person. Normal people just couldn't keep guilt from showing, and all you had to do was know where to look for it. That was the hard part.

"Guilt has its own special look and sound."

"Sound? What do you mean?"

"A catch in the voice, an uplift in tone. You can hear it all the time if you listen. It doesn't even have to do with crime. It can be emotional."

"How so?" Kaz asked, not quite believing me.

I stopped and looked at him. Well, he asked. "I heard it in your voice the other night. About your parents, and the suite at the Dorchester."

"What? Am I guilty of a crime?" I could hear the defensiveness creep into his voice.

"You're there, and they're not. It was their place, and now it's yours. Any normal person would feel guilty, can't be helped. I'm sorry, Kaz."

Sorry for his parents, sorry for telling him. He was silent for a minute, then turned and started walking again, watching the ground.

"No, no, you are right. Sometimes I feel like an impostor there. But it is all I have left." He shrugged sadly. "I just never thought of it as guilt."

I put my hand on his shoulder, gave a little squeeze, and let it drop.

"People don't usually think about these things, Kaz. They feel them, act on them, but hardly ever think about them. There's no reason to; it's a part of you. A wife will stab her husband one day and honestly think that he said something that made her mad, so she knifed him. Maybe he's been screwing around and it finally got to her, but she never admitted it to herself. She never thought through the little clues that she found, but they were there, eating at her. So one day he complains that the roast is burnt, and she puts the carving knife in his back."

"Are these the things a Boston detective thinks about on a case? Self-deception, guilt, the knife in the back?"

"Cops always look for things that are out of place. Very little things, which sometimes lead to bigger things, like *why* a knife in the back."

"So how do you look for these little things?"

It was like asking how you breathed or woke up in the morning. It was what a cop learned to do first thing, at least in my family. To look, really look, at every little thing.

"What do you look for when you walk into a room?" I asked him.

"A beautiful woman," he smiled. "Books on the shelf, artwork . . . anything else would not be very interesting. Although a bar would attract my attention."

"I like your approach, Kaz; it's better than most. A cop will check the exits, look to see if anyone is carrying a hidden weapon, and sniff out any tension in the air automatically, just like you would scan the bookshelf for a rare book. Without even thinking about it."

Kaz nodded thoughtfully. I could see him taking this in, comparing it with his experience.

"Sometimes you can feel something under the surface, something wrong. You can't be sure what it is. Everything looks normal, but you just get a feeling that something is out of place, that all the little things don't add up."

"What do you do when you feel that?"

An obvious question. It was easy for me to talk about Kaz's family, tell him what was going on inside his head. But it wasn't that easy to even think about the first time I came up against that question, saw just what Dad had always told me about. One night, just after I got home off duty, Basher Mc-Gee came by the house, tipped his hat to Mom, and headed upstairs with Dad to the den. They shut the door, just like always, but their talk was loud, angry, and not contained by the thin plasterboard walls.

Nothing understandable, except that the undercurrent of brewing trouble that Basher always brought with him had boiled over, and neither man was giving an inch.

Then there was silence. The house seemed empty, waiting for the sound of their anger to fill it again. I could hear Mom turn the faucet off in the kitchen as she stood in front of the sink, worried more by the quiet than the yelling. The upstairs door slammed open, bouncing off the wall and almost smacking Basher on the rebound as he crossed the threshold.

"You take it, you're one of us, no better!" he yelled as he clomped down the stairs, tipped his cap again to Mom just as nice as you please, and let himself out the back door. I started to walk upstairs, but Mom put her hand on my arm. I shook it off, and didn't look at her, embarrassed at how Basher had behaved toward Dad in his own house, embarrassed at shaking off the hand of my own mother. I gripped the banister and headed up toward the den.

The door was still open. Dad held a small box in his hand, the lamplight just behind him lighting one side of his face and leaving the other in shadow. The box was wrapped in plain paper, tied by twine tightly knotted. His hand fell to his side, and he tossed the box into the wastebasket next to his desk. I didn't move a muscle. He sat down at his desk, didn't say a thing, just stared at the wall. I tried to move, to walk up to him, to go through that doorway and tell him I'd do anything he needed me to do.

I didn't. I just stood there. He never looked over at me, and finally I walked to my room, shut the door, flopped down on my bed, picked up the latest issue of *True Detective* from my nightstand, and lost myself in the fiction, dreaming of blazing away at bad guys and watching them roll down the stairs.

"Billy? What do you do when guilt shows itself?" Kaz asked, reframing the question as if I hadn't understood it properly.

"Run. Duck. Draw your piece, do something, anything. But don't just stand there."

A stray stone had found its way out of the flower beds and onto the soft grass path. I kicked at it, sending it back where it belonged, with a clump of grass and torn roots for company.

"Billy, you must teach me how to see and understand these things, to help you find the spy."

I could see Kaz was all worked up. He was almost like a kid brother, jumping up and down and begging his older brother to take him wherever he was going. Like Danny always did, and I had hardly ever said no to him.

"Why do you want to know all this? Aren't you already involved in looking for the spy? You know all about everything at HQ."

Kaz took off his glasses, rubbed his eyes, and shook his head. "All I do is read and translate reports and talk to other officers who read and translate other reports. I am sure it is very important work, but it is not getting us any closer to finding this spy. And it is not very exciting," he added a little sheepishly as he put his glasses back on.

"Asking a lot of dumb questions isn't very exciting, Kaz. Ask questions, rile people up, watch things, think about things, then go back and ask more questions. That's it. Not really exciting at all."

"I do find my work not very stimulating, Billy, but it is not really excitement I am seeking. It is . . . revenge. If I could fight, I would, but with my heart, this is as close as I can get. If I can help to uncover a spy, that would be enough. I would feel as if I had done the right thing for the memory of my family."

I didn't get this little guy. He had bad health, good money, a great hotel room and a beautiful girlfriend. If I had that deal, the last thing I'd be doing would be hunting around for a German needle in a Norwegian haystack. But he was probably going to try on his own anyway, so I figured I might as well take him on and make sure he didn't mess things up for me.

"OK, Kaz. You're on. Just watch what I do and keep your eyes open."

"Excellent! What do we do first?"

I looked at him and wondered how much I could trust him. Was he really an eager beaver? Or was he watching me for somebody else? The thought had even occurred to me that I couldn't rule out Kaz as a suspect. How did we know he was really who he said he was? Maybe the Nazis were holding his family hostage? Maybe *he* was the "Prodigal Son?" Maybe I was Sam Spade, but I doubted it. Occupational hazard of being a cop. Everyone's a suspect.

"Go find out where Knut Birkeland is, then come get me. We'll have a chat with him. I'll be out here."

Kaz threw me a mock salute and went off to find Birkeland. I kept walking through the gardens as the sun tried to break through the steel gray clouds. I was thinking about little things and trying to add them up so they made sense. I decided I was a couple of sums short of an equation and stopped to smell the roses, just like they always said you should. I reached out to pull a flower closer to sniff it. It smelled like raspberries and perfume on a beautiful woman's neck. I let go and a thorn caught my fingertip, leaving a slit on my right index finger, and spraying tiny flecks of blood on the blooms beneath it.

About a half hour later Kaz and I were sitting in Knut Birkeland's office on the third floor, where most of the government offices were. There were stacks of papers everywhere. Birkeland looked as disheveled as his room. He pushed aside the open books and folders in front of him, leaned his heavy frame back in his chair, and raised his bushy black eyebrows.

"What can I do for you, Lieutenant?" There was gruff suspicion in his voice.

"I just wanted to apologize, sir. I didn't mean to upset people at lunch by asking about the gold." I put on my meekest voice and enjoyed the look on Kaz's face. He'd obviously hoped I'd pull out some brass knuckles.

"Well, it doesn't bother me, but I don't like it being brought up in front of the king. This is a very delicate time." He stared at me with those dark eyes, and didn't even try to hide the fact that it really did bother him.

"You mean because of the pending appointment of a senior adviser?"

"You ask a lot of questions, young man, especially for someone who just apologized for it."

"I'm sorry, sir. It's just that I was a policeman before the war, and it seems that asking questions is a hard habit to break. I don't even realize I'm doing it." He seemed to accept my humble apology, and relaxed a bit.

"Well, no matter. I have nothing to hide. I didn't take any gold, and I do want the position of senior adviser. If only to keep it from Skak!" He punctuated that statement by pounding his fist on the desk. I could tell he wouldn't mind the next question at all.

"What's wrong with Vidar Skak?"

"He's a coward and a liar! He claims two cases of gold coins went missing while they were in my possession, with no other proof than his own books! He never spent a night standing guard in the snow over that gold or bent his back loading case after case onboard a ship with German planes dropping bombs all around!"

"Why would he blame you for the missing gold? What has he to gain?" asked Kaz, taking on some of the questioning himself.

"Gain? Why the senior adviser job, that's all! Can't you see that? If he discredits me in the king's eyes, then the job is his, and the worse for Norway." Birkeland's eyes slid sideways, as if envisioning a dark future with Vidar Skak whispering in the king's ear.

"Seems to me he just wants to fight back against the Germans." I congratulated myself on avoiding a direct question.

"Neither of you strike me as fools," Birkeland said. "You can see that Skak wants to use the Underground Army to support his own aims. The more glory for him, the better. He can be a hero in Norway after the war, when we lay wreaths on the monuments to the dead."

"There'll be plenty of death to go around before this war is over. Sacrifice can't be avoided." Geez, I sounded like Harding.

"Skak is willing to accept the sacrifices of others. He has lost nothing himself. I've had to watch newsreels of my own fishing boats being destroyed by the commandos, some of them Norwegian! I have a fishing fleet in Nordland, and when the commandos destroy one of those fish oil-processing plants to keep the Germans from producing nitroglycerin, my boats go up in flames. I'm watching my own business, which I've built for twenty years with my bare hands, go up in smoke. But, by God, I'll put the torch to the whole damn thing myself if it will keep the underground from going into battle! We would gain nothing, and the reprisals would be terrible."

The wind went out of him and he sank back into his chair. "Terrible," he repeated quietly. "Let the British destroy our industry if it will hurt the Nazis. But let our people live."

We left soon after that. On the theory that a guy who would rather see his own property destroyed than lose innocent lives would make a lousy candidate for a thief or traitor, I decided it was time to move on to greener pastures. I said as much to Kaz as we walked to our rooms, and to my surprise he responded like a cynical desk sergeant.

"How do we know he really owns a fishing fleet, and that it's being destroyed in commando raids?" Ah, cynicism, the first dawning sign of a rookie cop learning the ropes.

"All right, let's think it through. Skak and the king would know. Hard to believe he could be lying about it."

"Yes, but the key point is his willingness to sacrifice his fortune. We have no confirmation of that."

I thought about that for a minute. It seemed harmless enough, and who knew what the little guy might find out?

"OK Kaz, here's your first assignment. Ask around and see if anybody else knows about it. Ask the Three Musketeers. That Rolf guy is with the commandos; he might know. Just act like you're interested."

"I will be the soul of unoffending curiosity."

"Just remember the cat. He didn't offend anyone either."

I left Kaz to his junior G-man investigation and went up to my room on the top floor. I was tired, the alcohol drifting through my system and weighing down my eyelids, making me think about catching a few z's before the evening festivities. The king had invited our group to some sort of state dinner he was throwing in the main ballroom. It sounded boring, and I knew I needed my beauty sleep so I wouldn't nod off during the third speech.

Evidently, all the big rooms were taken. Mine had a double bed, a bureau, one straight-back chair, and an armoire, with just enough space to walk around the bed if you kept your elbows tucked in. The furniture looked a little worse for wear, the kind of stuff that was too sturdy to throw out but too scruffy to show off. The room did have its own bathroom, and I liked that, a step up from the attic of the Dorchester. Kaz had told me a lot of these old castles and mansions never got around to upgrading the plumbing, but that the Beardsleys were very modern for their day, and each room had hot and cold running water and the usual facilities. I kicked off my shoes, tossed my jacket onto the chair, loosened my tie, and closed my eyes for about a half hour. Catnaps and spy chasing are my specialties.

I woke up two hours later from a dead sleep. It had only been a few days since that flight across the Atlantic, and I guess I wasn't over it yet. I yawned, stretched, and decided I had time for a soak in a nice hot tub before dinner. Maybe it would wake me up and help me decide what to do next. Always thinking of the war effort, that's me. I turned on the hot water and was greeted by clanging and thumps as the pipes summoned up the strength to deliver a lukewarm trickle of water. I was familiar with the sounds of overtaxed plumbing from my parents' house. Everyone probably had the same bright idea I had — take a nice hot bath before dinner. I tried the cold water.

Plenty of that. I soaked my feet in the tub, washed up in the sink, and cursed the plumbing that had robbed me of a plan.

Jolted awake by the cold water, I went downstairs and joined the crowd gathered in the ballroom. Two long tables took up half the room. Chandeliers lit the room and candles burned along the length of the tables, their light reflecting off the gleaming silver. I had thought lunch was fancy, but this was hoity-toity. There was the head table with seats on one side, and another table at a right angle to it with seats along both sides. There were little cards with names to let you know where to sit. I didn't bother looking for mine up at the head table. I was down at the end, surrounded by names I didn't know. Harding and Cosgrove had seats at the head table, along with Daphne and Baron Piotr Augustus Kazimierz. I guess that showed me. I was fingering my place card when Kaz came over. He was wearing a British dress uniform with a gleaming leather belt and a big grin. He handed me a glass of champagne.

"Rank, royalty, and beauty all at one table, Billy. I will be certain to come down here to visit you!"

"I'm sure the other peasants will be honored, Baron." We clinked glasses and drank. The room was filling up with all sorts of uniforms. Mostly British types with "Norway" on the red shoulder flash. A few naval officers and a couple of old Home Guard officers and their wives, from the local village, probably. Harding and I were the only Americans.

Daphne entered, and the room fell silent. In the midst of browns, dark blues, and khakis, she was dressed in a bright green gown that was like a shimmering fountain of color, sparkling off the candlelight in the room. It was tight and low cut, and she wore a matching short jacket that accentuated the whiteness of her bare skin.

"I marvel every time I see her," Kaz whispered reverently as several senior offices elbowed each other on their way to greet her.

"Shouldn't you go rescue the fair damsel from that mob?" She was now being besieged by Norwegians and Englishmen, including a Home Guard captain who was going to be sleeping on the couch tonight by the look on his wife's face.

"No, certainly not! That dress was her doing, and she'll have to put up with it. Let's go talk to Rolf Kayser."

We found Rolf hoisting drinks with his musketeer pals. Rolf was big, muscular, and about six feet tall, square jawed and tanned, probably as much from the wind off the Norwegian coast as the sun. His hair was dark brown and so were his eyes, deep set beneath bushy eyebrows. He stood still, as if he were conserving energy for what lay ahead, watching everyone move around him. Standing next to Jens Iversen, he looked immense, a giant oak tree rooted to the spot. Jens, barely up to Rolf's shoulder, looked like he was using up his energy all at once, shifting back and forth on his heels, turning this way and that, surveying the room, pointing out the top brass as they filtered in. Arnesen stood with one hand in his pocket, a drink in the other, watching both his friends with a calm smile, obviously enjoying their company. They were an unlikely trio, of different sizes and shapes, but thrown together by chance and now good pals with the king, all in top posts. Security chief, commando leader, brigade commander. Kaz introduced me to Rolf and we grabbed some fresh champagne as another white-coated enlisted man came by with a tray.

"*Fortell meg, Løytnant* Boyle," Rolf asked, "is the American Army involved with this ultimatum about the underground? I understand you met with Knut Birkeland this afternoon." News traveled fast. I guess this guy hadn't taken a nap today.

"Not at all. Just chatting with Mr. Birkeland. I was very curious about how he got that gold out of Norway. Quite an accomplishment, for all of you."

"We only helped a little, really," said Anders Arnesen. "Just some heavy lifting aboard the *Glasgow*. There were many Norwegians who did much more, at greater risk."

"Well, Rolf did almost get himself killed," chimed in Jens Iversen, and they all laughed at what seemed to be an inside joke. He waved his hands to get the others to stop laughing.

"When we were loading cases of gold coin on board from a fishing ship, the rope slipped and the cases nearly knocked his brains out. They broke open and Rolf was buried in gold coins, very hilarious!"

"Druknet i gull!" said Arnesen, and they all laughed again. I didn't ask; it was obviously an inside joke.

"Well, it wasn't funny to me at the time," Rolf said with a smile, "especially with *Tysk* bombers coming after us, but it is a good story. I just wish I still had my souvenir."

"What do you mean?" asked Kaz.

"One coin got stuck in the folds of my

uniform somehow. When I changed later that night it rolled out." He looked at us somewhat sheepishly. "I thought it would make a good souvenir. What difference would one gold coin make? Well, after we got to England it began to bother me. Finally, I decided to give it back. I was going to send it to the king on his birthday, hoping that he would appreciate it and not be angry."

"Was he?" I asked.

"It was stolen from my barracks locker before I could give it to him. I told him about it though, and he wasn't too hard on me."

"It probably helped that you told him right after a very successful commando raid," said Jens with a grin, looking up at his friend. Jens spoke in bursts of energy, his eyes always moving, watching everyone in the room. Rolf looked like he could stand in one place all day while Jens danced around him. Anders was right in the middle, of average height and weight, but he carried himself with the self-assured authority of a professional soldier.

After a little more chitchat the group broke up and we headed to our seats. Vidar Skak came in and stopped to talk with Rolf and Major Cosgrove, pointedly turning his back on Birkeland, who was standing nearby. I bet their place cards weren't next to each other.

I sat with the Home Guard officers and wives and spent most of my time listening to complaints about the Americans over-running their village. A newly arrived division had just been based nearby, and to listen to this group they were all girl-crazy cowboys who should never have been let off the base. They were probably right but I said nice things about my countrymen anyway.

The food was bland — more fish and boiled potatoes. Servers brought out plates with the fish already doled out, still piping hot. Bowls of potatoes and turnips appeared, followed by brussels sprouts and cabbage. There was food rationing here and it probably wasn't easy to put on a feed like this, but the local victory gardens must have been overflowing with brussels sprouts.

"Used to love them," said a woman next to me as she passed the bowl, "on Sundays, with a nice roast beef. But every day, it does wear one down."

A basket of bread came from the other direction, but no butter. Even gold couldn't buy butter with U-boats sinking freighters every day in the Atlantic. The speeches were thankfully short, and there were enough toasts to Allied unity to keep my wineglass permanently in motion.

"To the Americans," a Home Guard colonel opposite me said, offering a toast to our group at the end of the table. "May they arrive in sufficient numbers to defeat Jerry, but not so many as to take up all the room in the village pub!"

"Hear, hear," went around the table, and the colonel winked at me, having his bit of fun. He was gray at the temples, and by the lines around his eyes, over fifty.

"Oh dear, Maurice," his wife said, "what terrible manners! Please excuse my husband, Lieutenant, he had to wait fifteen minutes for his pint recently and hasn't been the same since."

"That's all right, ma'am, I understand it must be difficult having so many GIs around. If I remember my history lessons, we had the same problem in Boston a while ago, until the redcoats left."

"Touché," said the colonel. "I deserved that. Don't think we don't appreciate America coming into the war, we do. It's just that, for my generation, having gone through the First World War, and now this, it's all so damned repetitive. And here we are, too old to serve. . . ."

"The Home Guard is service, and important service too," his wife said. "Why, after Dunkirk, you were all that was left to stand up to the Germans if they invaded. And a good account you would have given of yourselves, all of you!"

There was silence around the table, and I watched their faces. Older men, lost in memories of battles past and opportunities lost to prove themselves once again. Maurice patted his wife's hand, and she placed her other hand on top of his and squeezed. There were a lot of jokes about the Home Guard, old men drilling with broomsticks, and all that. Looking at them, I had no doubt that these gray-haired, middle-aged retreads would have gone down fighting if it had come to that. It must be hard keeping their spirits up when the U.S. Army showed up, rich in supplies, arms, cash, and optimism, eliminating the very need for a local guard just by their presence. And not understanding how close things had been for them. I raised my glass.

"To the Home Guard," I said, surprised at the lump I felt in my throat.

"To the Home Guard," came back at me from up and down the table, and I watched the colonel puff out his chest a bit as he raised his glass and basked in the smile his wife gave him, her moist eyes lingering a little as she watched him.

I realized the talk about Americans all around me was uneasy. I was one of the thousands from across the sea, easy with money, informal beyond the bounds of their polite society, a threat and a salvation wrapped up in one. Their young men were spread out across the globe, fighting in North Africa, in the jungles of Burma, sitting in German POW camps, and we were here, well fed and feeling our oats. They scrimped along with food rationing while your typical U.S. Army base probably threw away more than their whole village ate every day. I wondered how we'd react if the tables were turned.

After that toast, the mood lightened a bit. We talked about the last war, in which all of them had fought, and this war, in which their sons were fighting now and, for some, in which their daughters were taking part, too. The colonel and his wife had lost their oldest son on the *Hood,* sunk last year by the *Bismarck.* Their youngest was a pilot in the RAF.

"Fourteen hundred men on the *Hood,* including Michael," said the colonel. "Only three were picked up out of the water."

"At least you sank the *Bismarck,*" I said,

offering what feeble comfort I could.

"I didn't mind hearing that news, not at all," the colonel said, taking his wife's hand.

"What was it, Maurice?" she said. "Over two thousand on the *Bismarck,* and only a hundred survived. The numbers of war are so horrible. We say two ships sank, but that's over three thousand men as well."

The table fell silent.

"They are more than numbers."

"Your Highness!" None of us had noticed the king standing just behind me, making his way down the table to greet his guests. Everyone started to rise.

"No, please, stay seated," King Haakon said, gesturing with his arms, palms down, for everyone to stay in their seats. "I am sorry for your loss, for all the deaths in this war. There are no words worthy of such a loss."

"God bless you, Your Highness," said the colonel's wife. The king walked around the table and stood at her side, reaching down from his height to take her hand.

"No, I ask God to bless you."

I had never thought much about what it took to be a king. Guess I thought it was all giving orders. Shows what I know.

I had another glass of wine and was feeling a little tipsy when the king finished making his rounds and left the room, which I took to mean I could, too. I said my good nights to the Home Guard group and not for the first time wondered what Uncle Dan would say if he saw me now. The party was beginning to break up, and people were starting to file out. I noticed Daphne at the head table, a shock of green surrounded by brown and khaki. Cosgrove arose and intercepted me as I made for the door. For a big guy with a gimpy leg, he could move pretty fast when he wanted to.

"Lieutenant Boyle, I must ask for your assistance. It seems we are a bit short of Home Guard chaps for the exercise tomorrow. We need a few more fellows to fire off some blank rounds at the Norwegians and play the Huns. You've been volunteered!" I looked over at Harding, still sitting at the head table just outside the crush of men around Daphne, and he raised his glass with a smile. Thanks a lot.

"I guess so, Major. What do I do?"

"Be at the main entrance at 0600 hours, and you'll be driven to the exercise area. The baron is going as well, and Mr. Birkeland has offered to lend a hand. They both think it will be great fun!"

Kaz would.

"And wear something more suitable for

140

the field. It's bound to be muddy out there."

He was off, leaving me wondering why all armies seemed to start things before the sun came up, and wishing I had something besides my one dress uniform with me. I walked down the hall and up the stairs to my room, each step increasing the pounding in my skull. Too many damn toasts.

Minutes after I made it to my room there was a knock on the door. An enlisted man stood outside, a pile of clothes and boots weighing him down.

"Mr. Birkeland's compliments, sir. He thought you might prefer to wear these tomorrow." He handed me a brown wool British battle jacket, trousers, and boots. "Let me know if the size isn't right," he said as he went down the hall to knock on the door to Kaz's room. The duds were fine, which was more than I could say for my head.

CHAPTER EIGHT

The bell on the alarm clock sounded like a three-alarmer and my mouth tasted like ashes. I swore I'd punch whoever offered me a glass of wine today right in the mouth. I stripped and knelt in the tub, sticking my head under the faucet and turning on the cold water. The shock drove my headache into submission, if only for a minute, but it was worth it. I dressed in the scratchy wool uniform and clomped downstairs in the heavy boots, ready to play soldier. The uniform stunk of mothballs, and I hoped the open air would clear the smell, which I always associated with my Aunt Bess and the hand-me-down clothes she saved for me, peppered with mothballs for five years in a chest in the attic. I always wished my cousin Owen was a lot less than five years older than me.

Outside, a British army truck was idling, the open bed crammed with eager volunteers, all in the same wool outfit, no rank or unit markings.

"Hurry, Billy!" hollered Kaz, obviously worried I'd miss the fun. Birkeland, beside him, offered me a hand and pulled me up like a fish in a net.

"Come, lad, it's not every day you get to play at making war!" He laughed and clapped me on the back, a hit hard enough to send me tumbling if there had been room to fall. The truck was jammed with other volunteers from among the government workers at Beardsley Hall and whomever else Cosgrove had talked into this charade.

About a mile down the road, the truck turned left off the road and onto a rutted farm lane, bouncing along as the driver gunned it to keep from getting stuck in the mud. He pulled off the path and stopped. We jumped down from the truck and landed with a *squish* on the boggy ground. Delightful. Although it was summer, the dampness crept up into my bones and chilled me from the ground up. I was happy to see a table with big urns of tea, which wasn't too bad with a lot of sugar. We were handed British helmets, which looked like old-fashioned flat helmets from the First World War, and stood in line for our rifles. Kaz was almost jumping up and down with excitement, fixing his helmet at just the right jaunty angle.

A stern British army noncom checked each Enfield rifle before handing it to us, working the bolt and leaving it open, making sure it was unloaded. When we all had rifles he motioned us to gather around him. He picked up a clip of bullets, all blanks, and held it up in one hand, the other grasping a rifle with the bolt open. He spoke loudly, as if there were an exclamation point after every word and we were twenty yards away.

"Now lissen 'ere, sirs. This is the Lee-Enfield Number Four rifle, the finest bolt-action rifle ever there was. In the 'ands of a good marksman it is accurate up to sixteen hundred yards, which don't mean a thing today, as you gentlemen will be shooting blanks at them Norwegian boys. You will each receive three clips of ten blank rounds each."

He showed us how to load the clip and work the safety. Then he handed each of us the ammunition. "Now remember, sirs, even though it'll be only blanks out there, don't shoot 'em off straight at anyone's face. You can still get burned or worse if you're too close. Any questions? Sirs?"

There weren't, and we found the Home Guard troops and followed them into position. A slight rise in the heath led to trenches dug in the wet soil, with tree trunks laid in front of them. Two old retired Matilda tanks sat just out in front, unoccupied and surrounded by sandbags. The commandos were going to blow them up to make a good show before they assaulted our position. In front of us were gently rolling fields of tall grass and beyond that another small rise with a clump of trees. I guessed the Norwegians must be grouped behind there since there were no troops in sight. There were umpires on both sides of the field who would determine when one side or the other could advance or retreat. Since we were playing the bad guys, I guessed they were just window dressing.

Off to the side by the road were benches and chairs for the king and his officers. I could see Harding and Cosgrove standing behind the king. Harding was scanning the fields with his binoculars. Suddenly a referee's loud voice from behind shouted, "Helmets on! The exercise has begun."

We strapped on our helmets and I thought how crazy it was that I was all dressed up as a British soldier, playing a German, firing blanks at Norwegians. We knelt to take up positions with our rifles resting on the logs and pointing toward the woods. The damp ooze soaked through my trousers and I shivered, the warmth of the sweet tea just a memory now. I glanced over at Harding and saw him scan the field again. He passed over us and trained his binoculars on one of the small rises of land — a hillock, I guess it would be called — in front of us. What was he looking at?

Then I saw it. The grass was moving. Here and there I could make out a few crawling shapes, camouflaged with grasses. They must have sneaked forward behind the hillocks and were now crawling out in the relative open, very slowly. Everyone's eyes were trained on the woods, where we expected the opposing force to come from. I tapped Kaz on the shoulder.

"Is that something moving over there?" I pointed. Birkeland, on my left, leaned forward to see for himself. Kaz squinted through his thick glasses.

"Yes! They're here, in front of us!" he yelled as loud as he could and then fired his rifle. It almost knocked him over but he held on, worked the bolt, and tightened his grip for the next shot. He hung on to that one, and kept the rifle at his shoulder as he worked the bolt. All up and down our line the Home Guard began shooting and the noise quickly became deafening. Kaz was grinning up at me and Birkeland was enjoying himself too, playing soldier out here in the fields. It was kinda fun, I thought, in spite of myself. I smiled at Kaz and gave him a thumbs-up, as conversation was impossible with the high-powered crack of rifle fire snapping at our eardrums.

Some of the crawling figures stood up to throw smoke grenades. I could see the rest of the Norwegian force coming out of the woods at a trot, hoping to link up with the commandos who were now returning our fire. The umpires were holding them back — a bit of unexpected victory for us. But through the smoke I could see several of the forward commandos rush up to the Matilda tanks, and then scurry back, diving and rolling to cover. Seconds later, twin explosions wracked the air as smoke and flames blossomed from the tanks. That did it. The umpires signaled all the commandos forward, and gave us the signal to move out or surrender. Kaz was loading his last clip, and I had to tell him it was time to sound retreat. I tapped him on the shoulder and cupped my hand around my mouth to yell as the firing from the commandos drew closer and louder.

"Time to go, Kaz —"

Something exploded in my face and cut

me off, sound and shock stunning me. I dropped to the ground, put my hands to my face, and felt blood dripping between my fingers. I was still breathing, but the thought kept going through my mind that I had been shot. Not possible, I told myself. They're using blanks, aren't they? My face stung like a hundred bee stings. Birkeland and Kaz bent over me as the commandos swarmed over our position, jumping up on the log and vaulting over us, chasing the rest of the retreating Jerries like avenging angels. One of them stood on the log and let loose a burst from his Sten submachine gun, hot shell casings cascading over us. One landed on the back of my neck and added insult to injury.

"Move, you idiot!" I could hear Birkeland yelling.

"Billy, Billy! Are you all right?" I could hear Kaz, too, but couldn't see him. I touched my eyes, hoping to find they were still there. Intact. They were. I wiped away blood and said a little prayer of thanks that I could see.

"What happened?" No one answered, no one seemed to know. I recognized Jens Iversen as he pushed away the men gathering around me. He took my head in his hands and turned it, checking my eyes and neck.

"You've got splinters in your face. Forehead and left side, mostly. It doesn't look too bad, actually, just a lot of bleeding." That sounded bad enough to me. He took a handkerchief and started cleaning away the blood around my eyes.

"Look at this." Birkeland stood by the tree trunk where I had been positioned next to him. There was a ragged bullet hole near the top, and wood splinters were protruding from the gouge it had left.

"A live round," said Jens, stunned. "Someone must've loaded a live round accidentally. Another inch higher and you would have been a dead man." I tended to think that another inch lower and I wouldn't be bleeding like a stuck pig, but hell, I didn't sneeze at being alive.

They half carried me off to a first-aid tent where Jens took over and pulled out several large splinters with a tweezers. "Nothing a first-year medical student can't handle," he said. "I'm glad to have the practice." He poured on some disinfectant that hurt worse than the splinters, then cleaned the remaining blood off my face.

"You're very lucky, you know." Anders stood by the half-open tent flap, eyeing my wounds. "Lucky to still have your eyesight."

"If I was really lucky, Major, this wouldn't have happened at all."

Anders gave a rueful laugh as the tent flap was flung open and Rolf joined the crowd, full of apologies. He stood in front of me, wringing his hands like an abject schoolboy. It was odd, seeing this large, powerful man, his head scraping the top of the tent, almost cringing.

"Jeg er slik trist, gjorde hvordan dette skjer?" Rolf said, looking back and forth between Jens and me.

"We don't know how it happened, Rolf. Slow down and speak English," Jens said as he pulled another splinter out of my forehead.

"Lieutenant Boyle, I don't know how this could've happened! All of our weapons were checked and then loaded with blank rounds. I am *trist* . . . very sorry. I can only think a rifle had a round in the chamber that was unaccountably missed."

"Unaccountably," I agreed. "Don't worry about it. I won't be playing any more war games today."

"We are all sorry," said Jens. "It would have been so ungracious to shoot one of our own Allies!" They all laughed. It hurt when I did. A joke is supposed to relieve the tension, but when I got up to leave and brushed past Anders, he looked grim. I wondered why. I wondered why everyone else had been full of apologies and concerns, and he had sounded like he was issuing a warning. Or a threat. I didn't know anything except my head really hurt, and I wished it was only a hangover.

An hour later I was lying on my bed and Daphne was dabbing my cuts with a warm washcloth, making cooing sounds and telling me everything was going to be all right. That made almost getting a bullet in the forehead worthwhile. Kaz paced back and forth in my small room nerved up from the exercise and the shooting, while Major Harding leaned against the wall and tried to look concerned. What a picture.

"We're due at the conference in a few minutes," he stated, glancing at his watch. "Why don't you stay here and rest up." I tried to get up on one elbow.

"But, Major, I want to. . . ." The room started spinning and my head found the pillow, fast. I spoke looking up at the ceiling. "We need to observe everyone who was at the exercise this morning."

"Why? Are you saying this was no accident?" Harding said in disbelief.

"Think about it . . . sir. Let's say there was one live round loaded accidentally. It could have been fired off into the air or at any one of those Home Guards or Norwegians running around out there. But it wasn't. It ended up a few inches from my head. What are the chances of that?"

"It had to end up somewhere, Boyle," Harding answered. "What makes you think you're so special?"

"Because we're here, looking for a spy." I lowered my voice, feeling like an actor in a bad melodrama. "And I've been asking around about the gold. Either a thief or a traitor or both tried to kill me today."

"And failed," Kaz spoke up, "which means we should not leave Billy alone."

"Hold on," Harding said firmly. "We are about to announce that we are going to invade Norway. I need all of you there. Boyle, keep your .45 handy if you're worried and lock your door. We'll check in on you when it's over. Let's go."

I had Kaz dig out my piece and I put it under the blanket.

"Be careful, Billy." Daphne smiled down at me. "I want you to dance at my wedding." She kissed me on the cheek like a big sister and scooted out of the room after Kaz. Harding looked out the window as if he took the threat to me seriously.

"No way in here except through that door, Boyle. Can you get up and lock it after me?" I swung my legs out of the bed and steadied myself. My head was throbbing but the room wasn't spinning as much as it had. Harding looked at me impatiently.

"I can make it, Major."

"OK. Looks like you've stirred things up, Boyle. Good work. But try not to get yourself killed." He turned and left. Not wanting me to die was the nicest possible thing Harding could've said. It fit right in with my plans. I locked the door and decided to run a tub and bathe away my troubles. With everyone scurrying off to the conference in the main hall I had the water pressure all to myself. Hot water filled the tub and I had a glorious soak. Another hard day at the war. I relaxed and let the steam rise up around me. Was it just this morning that a bullet had slammed into wood inches from my nose? In the safety of the steamy bathroom it all seemed far away. Maybe this army deal was going to work out after all, as long as the bullets didn't get any closer. I wondered what it was going to be like for the poor GIs landing on the cold shores of Norway. They'd have more than one stray bullet to worry about, and there wouldn't be a warm bath afterward. Oh well. Real tough for them, but no reason not to enjoy a good tub.

Hours later a knock on the door woke me from a nap. I threw on a bathrobe and shuffled over, bleary eyed but almost clear headed, my automatic held behind my back.

"Who is it?"

"Room service," answered the singsong voice. Daphne. I opened the door and could smell the soup before I saw it. I settled into bed and let her arrange the tray around me, my .45 on the nightstand. Kaz came in with a bottle of wine, and I didn't even want to sock him. It was all quite cozy.

"Well?" I asked. "How did it go? Were the Norwegians happy?"

"Billy," Kaz smiled as if he were explaining the obvious to a child, "it is impossible to tell if a Norwegian is happy. If we were talking about Poles, there would be dancing in the streets at the news that our homeland was going to be liberated. We would kiss the cheeks of our allies who promised invasion! Instead, the king solemnly stood and shook Cosgrove's and Harding's hands. Moving in its own way, but not very demonstrative."

"Darling, shaking hands is demonstrative for those from the cold northern climes.

Can you imagine Major Cosgrove's expression if the king had kissed him?" Daphne laughed and covered her mouth like a schoolgirl. Kaz looked at her with a smile on his face and an expression that said, Is there any guy luckier than I in the whole world?

Harding knocked and came in, carrying a bottle of Bushmills Irish whiskey in one hand and his briefcase in the other. He raised the bottle in a salute. "Thought we might celebrate. Couldn't have gone better today."

"Well, I might disagree about that, if I were dumb enough to argue with a man carrying Bushmills."

"Sorry, Boyle, I meant the conference. How's the head?"

"I'm feeling fine, sir." It was easy to remember to call Harding "sir" when he was holding my favorite brand. He went up a notch in my estimation as he poured each of us a generous portion. "What happens next?"

Harding took a seat, leaned back, loosened his tie, picked up a glass tumbler, and took a sip. He looked tired, and for the first time I saw him as something more than a hard-nosed paper pusher. Worry showed on his face in the dark circles under his eyes and creases in his forehead. It struck me how close I was to the center of everything, the historic first strike back at the Nazis. I felt like I was . . . important. I tried to sit up a little straighter.

"I just finished a preliminary briefing session with Norwegian Brigade and commando officers in the map room. We went over the basic tactical plan, and we'll finish up in the morning. Then we head back to London and start coordinating with the U.S. and British divisional commands."

"Can you tell me what the plan is?" All of a sudden I thought I was a military genius and I didn't want to be left out.

"I guess so," said Harding cautiously. "Now that we've briefed the Norwegians it should be all right. Remember, this is still TOP SECRET. I just spent the last half hour securing the invasion plans and maps in the map room downstairs. This information can't leave the building, understood?"

We all nodded eagerly, pledging silence, our lives, our firstborns, whatever it took. I was hooked. Just like I was hooked the first time I worked a homicide. I knew then that I was different from everyone else, set apart from the concerns of everyday life that swept everyone else forward, on a river of errands, work, dates, drinking, eating, and sleeping. I was going in a different direction, toward revelation and retribution, and there were damn few of us headed that way. This was like that. I was going to see behind the curtain, see what lay ahead for thousands of people, tens of thousands — Germans, Yanks, Brits, Norwegians, soldiers, sailors, civilians, old men, pretty girls, knee-scraped kids. They all were living their lives, doing what they were told to do, waiting to find out what was going to happen, if they thought about it at all. I wouldn't have to wonder. I'd *know.* Harding had pulled a long folded map of the Norwegian coast out of his briefcase and spread it out over the bed. He tapped it with his pen as he ticked off the main points.

"Primary landings will be just west of Oslo, with the Norwegian Brigade in the first wave along with one U.S. infantry division and a British tank brigade. There'll be a secondary Anglo-American landing at Stavanger in order to capture an airfield. Also various diversionary commando raids up the coast in order to keep the Germans off balance. We're also working on a landing in force in the Nordland province, just north of the Arctic Circle. There's a point near Fauske where Norway narrows to just about forty miles between Sweden and the North

Sea. We'll make a line there to cut off any reinforcements from the Narvik area, secure the airfield at Bodo, and create an area to build up forces to complete the campaign."

"What about air and naval forces?" asked Kaz.

"We actually hope the Germans will commit their navy. With the Royal Navy and the American naval units that are still arriving, we should decimate them if they intervene. The Luftwaffe is another matter. We'll have air cover for the invasion, but if we don't capture those airfields intact and get our fighters in the air over Norway. . . ."

He didn't have to finish, leaving the image of Stukas dive-bombing Allied troops with impunity clear enough in our minds.

"That's why you plan to seal off Nordland?" I asked.

Harding looked out the window, avoiding my eyes as if he didn't want to answer. "There are sound tactical reasons for securing Nordland. One is that it provides a foothold in case the southern campaign goes badly. It also gives us air bases and ample harbors for supply and warships. It's very important, which is why we're committing an American ranger battalion and the 503rd Parachute Regiment, along with British and Norwegian commandos. Once they secure the airfield at Fauske we'll fly in more infantry. Heavier stuff will be landed from the sea at Bodo."

"Major, isn't it dangerous to release all this information with a spy in our midst?" Daphne asked with a quizzical look on her face.

"Yes, it is. We have to be on our guard. He may try something again."

With that cheery thought, Harding filled our glasses and we drank another round. And one more, then Daphne excused herself, and then we lost count.

I fell asleep pretty easily, or passed out, I can't remember which. I woke up in the middle of the night with a dry, parched throat and a throbbing headache. I forced myself out of bed and stumbled to the bathroom. My tried-and-true hangover cure was a big glass of cold water and a couple of aspirin. I managed to shake out the aspirin and turned the faucet on, looking forward to letting the water run long enough to get really good and cold. I was rewarded with less than a dribble. Damn these pipes! The warm water came out full force, though, and I managed to fill a glass before it got too hot and force the aspirin down. I knew that without a tall drink of cold water my head would still be pounding in the morning. So far, the worst thing about being in England was hangovers and the plumbing. And almost getting killed, of course.

CHAPTER NINE

I didn't feel so great a few hours later, standing outside Beardsley Hall as the sun thought about coming up over the horizon. But I was still a lot better off than Knut Birkeland, who stared up at me with lifeless eyes, lying on his back and ruining the geraniums he lay on in the garden below his open window, four stories up.

Jens Iversen paced back and forth behind me, questioning the two sentries who had found the body. He had sent for me as soon as the discovery was reported to him, and right now people were spilling out of the hall like it was a beehive that had been hit with a stick. Harding pushed through the growing crowd just as the first rays of the sun hit the granite side of the building and illuminated the scene without casting light on a thing.

"What the hell is going on, Boyle?" he demanded as he stepped toward the body. I put out my arm to stop him.

"Hold on. Sir. Please don't touch him. We need to move these people back."

Harding pushed my arm away but didn't move any closer or threaten me with a court-martial. "What happened?"

"I don't know yet, Major, but if we let everyone stomp through here we'll never find out. Jens says the sentries woke him at a few minutes past six thirty when they found the body on their rounds. He got me a few minutes later and here we are. All I really know so far is that's Birkeland's room up there." I pointed to the swinging casement window on the top floor. "I've already asked Jens to post a guard outside the door and not let anyone in."

A breeze blew the window back, and it gave out a rusty grinding noise and the old iron hinges protested the sudden movement. The edge of a curtain flapped out of the window as if it were waving a sad goodbye to Knut Birkeland. Harding looked at the crowd, looked at me, and decided I was his best bet.

"OK, Lieutenant, it looks like you've got the situation in hand. You're in charge of the investigation. Let's see what kind of detective you really are." At that moment, Jens came over to us.

"Excuse me, gentlemen. We will remove the body now."

"Not until Lieutenant Boyle completes his investigation of the scene," Harding said, holding his hand up to Jens just as I had to him.

"I am in charge of security here, Major, not the American army." Jens bristled as his men watched him and waited for their orders, but he didn't slap the hand away.

"That's not a very impressive claim to make over the dead body of a senior governmental official," came the voice of Major Cosgrove as he moved closer to us, stabbing the ground with his cane to help make his point. "And since this facility is owned by His Majesty's government, I am certain that you will cooperate with us in this joint investigation. You will agree it is better than calling in the local constabulary."

"We will handle this investigation ourselves," snapped Jens, all the friendliness of yesterday's allies in arms gone.

"Do not force the issue, Captain," said Cosgrove in a low man-to-man tone. "It would not do to rupture relations over a jurisdictional matter, especially one that you cannot win. This is Crown property, provided for your use. It is not Norwegian territory."

Cosgrove had laid his cards on the table as neatly as if he were showing off a royal flush, which wasn't far from the mark. Allies or not, the Norwegians were foreigners, dependent upon their hosts, even with all that gold safe in America. Gold. A dead man. Jens' quick attempt to preempt any investigation. Was he just trying to do his job or did he have another motive?

"As guests in your country, we can do nothing but cooperate," answered Jens with a sneer, and turned away on his heel, spouting rapid Norwegian to the sentries. Touchy. I saw Kaz coming out the door and told him to head straight up to Birkeland's room and make sure the guard was there and let no one inside. Now there was nothing left to do but investigate. I glanced at Harding, who had shooed the gathering crowd away and was standing back, arms folded, watching me.

I stood there, trying to remember what my dad and uncles did at a crime scene. They'd always called me in for crowd control when a homicide came up on the board, to show me the ropes. Now I wished I had paid more attention. This is why they did it, so when I made it to the big leagues I'd know what to do. So I'd make the Boyle family proud. It felt like Dad was standing behind me, just shaking his head a little, wondering why he'd wasted all that time teaching me. I had to stop myself from turning to look for him.

Instead, I got down on my hands and knees close to the body, after checking to be sure there were no footprints or drag marks in the dirt around him. Just like Dad used to do. I looked at the flowers just in front of his feet. They weren't crushed or disturbed. He hadn't been standing and then been knocked down. This fella had come straight down, for sure.

I felt his jaw and neck for the first signs of rigor mortis. Nothing there, which is where rigor first sets in about four hours after death. His head was turned to the right, and the skin close to the ground was darker in color, where the blood had begun to settle. I pressed my finger firmly against the darkened cheek, and watched the skin whiten under the beard stubble and then return to the same crimson color. As the coroner would say, no evidence of fixed lividity. Around six hours after death, the blood settling in the body becomes clotted, and won't blanch at a touch. That's what fixed lividity means. I looked into the dark eyes below the bushy, thick eyebrows and saw they were flattened, as fluid drained out and the eyeball collapsed. That happened thirty minutes after death. I stood up triumphantly.

"He died no less than thirty minutes ago and no more than three hours ago, probably closer to an hour ago."

"Boyle, it's almost been thirty minutes since the sentries found him. That doesn't tell us much." Harding was unimpressed. I frowned and crouched down again, looking at Birkeland. I remembered seeing my father in this pose so many times. He would squat and stare for a long time, then suddenly get up and start barking orders. I was squatting and staring just fine, but I had not a clue what to do next. A clue. I really needed a clue. Dad, what was it you looked for? What did you see?

I looked Birkeland up and down. I tried not to assume anything, to take in everything that was in front of me, just as it was. He was fully dressed, in a dark blue suit with a matching vest. I picked up one hand and looked for anything he might be holding. The hand was empty. Clean fingernails too, no sign of a struggle there. I opened the other hand, which felt soft even with those calluses, and found the same thing. I could feel the coolness creeping into his skin. I patted down his pockets, looking for the Norwegian gold shipment. Even in the dimly lit room, it gleamed, shining brightly like the devil's left eye. I almost ran the few steps to the desk, with Harding, Jens, and Kaz following me. I nearly fell over when I read the note beneath the coin.

I know this is a great disappointment. I have always tried to serve Norway and my king as best I could. This final step is unfortunately necessary given the current situation.

The gold coin was carefully placed just below these lines. The paper was small, of a high quality, and there was a stack more of it at the side of the desk. A closed fountain pen was carefully positioned at the top of the blotter. I turned to Jens.

"Is this Birkeland's handwriting?" He stepped closer and reached for the note.

"Don't touch it," I said, "please."

Jens halted his movement, nodded his head, stood, and studied the note for a few seconds.

"Yes, absolutely. I see his handwriting nearly every day. This is it."

I walked around the room and looked on top of the bureau, the nightstand, felt in the pockets of the coat hanging on the coatrack

a note. There was nothing. No billfold, matches, handkerchief, or anything. I guess he'd dressed for a very short trip.

I signaled for Harding to help me roll him over. I took the shoulders and Harding pushed at the hips. Birkeland was a big guy, and it took both of us. No surprises there, just evidence that the body had come from a height and wasn't dragged and dumped here. A visible indentation in the garden soil showed where his torso had hit. We rolled him back. His neck hung at an unnatural angle. I was pretty sure it was broken. Nothing jumped out at me, nothing to say there was anything here to be seen but Knut Birkeland, unable to defy gravity.

"So?" Harding said as he looked up to the window on the fourth floor. "Suicide?"

"Looks like it, doesn't it?"

"You don't think so?"

"I really don't know. I just wonder why a guy who was on a mission to stop Vidar Skak from becoming senior adviser would jump out a window."

Harding was silent for a moment. I could tell what he was thinking but couldn't say out loud. Could this be the work of our neighborhood Nazi spy?

"There's a doctor from the Norwegian Brigade heading over here. He'll act as medical examiner and conduct an autopsy as soon as he gets here. You done with the body?"

I was. Harding ordered a couple of guards to take the body away, and we headed upstairs. Kaz was standing at the door to Birkeland's room, arguing with Jens Iversen.

"No, Captain, you must not enter . . . Billy!"

The sight of the little guy standing up to the obviously frustrated head of security almost made me forget my hangover.

"Billy, I've let no one in!"

"Good job, Kaz."

"Now that you are here, Lieutenant," Jens said, stressing my lesser rank, "perhaps we can enter?"

"Listen, Captain, I don't mean to get in your way, but I've got a job to do. It's nothing personal, I just used to be a cop, so I drew this assignment. OK?"

"All right. Are you ready to go in?" He seemed agreeable, but I wondered why he was in such a hurry to get into Birkeland's room.

"Not yet. First, tell me, is the room locked?"

"Yes."

"Do you have the key?"

"I have a key, Lieutenant, a spare from

the housekeeper. What exactly do you mea[n] by that question?"

"Nothing, I didn't mean to imply an[y]thing. Just want to know what to look f[or.] Let's open the door, but I go inside first."

"As you request," Jens said with hea[vy] sarcasm, stressing the last word. He u[n]locked the door and stepped aside. I w[ent] in. I took two steps and stopped and ca[re]fully looked around. The room was la[rge] and spacious. Besides the bed, which [was] unmade and looked slept in, there w[as a] desk and chair by the open window. [The] lace curtains blew in as a light breeze s[wept] through the room. There were no signs [of a] struggle. I looked into the bathroom, w[hich] was done in marble and much more ele[gant] than mine. Not that it mattered, but [I] think about how nice it would be to so[ak in] a tub in such a fancy bathroom. I fe[lt the] towels hanging on the rack. They [were] damp. The bathroom had that stea[my] damp smell that you get after a bath[. Evi]dently Birkeland had wanted to me[et his] maker squeaky clean. I walked bac[k into] the bedroom and signaled the oth[ers to] come in.

Then I saw it. On the desk, on to[p of a] piece of writing paper, sat a single gol[d coin.] A Hungarian gold piece, just like th[e

near the door. I thought about Knut Birkeland sitting at that desk, writing that note. I thought about him down below, dressed for a date with the daisies. Something was wrong. I scanned the room again.

"What are you looking for, Billy?" asked Kaz.

"Tell me what's missing from this room."

Kaz looked around, shrugged. "Nothing obvious."

I walked over to the bureau, where some coins sat in a ceramic ashtray, a penknife on top of the pile. His billfold was next to the ashtray.

"What else belongs right here?" I asked. "If this were your room, what would be lying next to coins and a pocketknife?"

I saw the lightbulb go on.

"The key! The key to this room, of course."

"Yes, good! It wasn't in any of his pockets, and the door was locked when we got here, so it has to be in this room." We began a thorough search. We looked in the obvious places again, then everywhere else. Lifted the mattress, moved the desk. Nothing.

"What's so important about the key?" Harding looked irritated at what he obviously thought was a waste of time.

"Sir, if the door was locked, and Birkeland didn't have the key on him, then it must be outside the room. Which is really important. It means someone else took it out, after Birkeland was dead, and locked the door from the outside."

"After they threw Knut Birkeland out the window," Kaz added.

"He catches on fast," I said to Harding, jerking my thumb in Kaz's direction.

"There's just one problem with your theory," Jens interrupted.

"What?" Harding growled. His temper wasn't improving any.

"Look at this room." Jens gestured with open arms at the order around us. "What do you think a room would look like if someone tried to throw Knut out this window? He was a very large man. It would not have been easy."

"Maybe he was killed first," Kaz suggested halfheartedly.

"Once again, it would not be easy to kill such a man without a struggle." Jens looked smug. I looked down at my shoes. Kaz gave it another shot.

"Maybe he was poisoned? Last night at dinner?"

"What, a delayed-action poison?" Jens laughed. "He obviously got up this morning early, as was his habit, bathed, dressed, wrote that note, and committed suicide. Skak must've been right about the stolen gold. . . ."

His voice trailed off as he looked at the gold coin. "I wonder where the rest of it is?"

"Why would anyone bother taking a bath and getting dressed if they were going to kill themselves anyway?" Harding asked. I could tell he hadn't been around dead bodies a lot, or at least not after the fact.

"Actually, sir, suicides are pretty careful about their appearance, in their own way. I found a guy once who had shot himself in the heart. He took his shirt off before he did it. I guess it made sense to him, although he still left a bloody mess."

"So the bath and good suit make sense to you?"

"I'd say it's consistent with suicide, but the missing key bothers me."

"What about the suicide note?" Jens asked. "Isn't that clear proof that he took his own life?"

"It seems so, Jens, I have to admit. But, still, where is the key, and who has it?" He seemed to have an answer for everything, except that.

Harding did, though.

"Well, find the damn key, Boyle! It's probably just been an hour or so since Birkeland went out that window. No one's been allowed off the premises, so get cracking!" He turned to Jens.

"Captain Iversen, we should find the king and report to him now."

"Very well. Would you like some of my men to assist in the search? It is a very large building." Harding glanced at me and I gave a slight shake of the head.

"No, thank you, Captain. Lieutenant Boyle will take care of it." He shot me a look as they left the room. I knew he understood we didn't want any possible suspects in on the search, and that right now anyone with the slightest Norwegian accent was a suspect.

I sent Kaz to fetch Daphne. We'd make better time in the search if we split up, and I figured a rookie like him could use an extra pair of eyes. First, I went outside and searched the flower bed again, in case the key had been in Birkeland's pocket and bounced out. No dice. I didn't think it would be there anyway. He had nothing else on him, so why should he put a key in his pocket?

I found the housekeeper and got the spare keys. There was a metal ring of keys for each floor, each one marked with a room number on a small metal tag. I sounded like sleigh bells a-jingling as I trotted up the stairs. Reindeer came from Norway, didn't they? For the first time I wondered if I'd be going to Norway after the invasion, or maybe as part of it. It then quickly occurred to me that I had just about had my fill of Norwegians, and that they couldn't take back their country soon enough for me.

CHAPTER TEN

By lunchtime I had rummaged through more Norwegian underwear drawers than I ever thought I'd see in my life, which, if I had really thought about such things, would have been zero. I had learned a few choice Norwegian curses based on comments made by the occupants of rooms as I searched them. I didn't know if they were referring to me, or my mother, but they weren't happy with either of us.

Vidar Skak was unexpectedly cordial. He was on his way out, but he offered to let me search him for the key. I realized that word of our search was spreading faster than we could possible conduct it, and that if someone had the key he or she would have to be a complete idiot to be found with it. I patted him down anyway. He must've been in a good mood with his rival for senior adviser dead, because he smiled when he left, and probably would've whistled if he were a whistling sort of guy.

His room was about the same size as Birkeland's, but at the other end of the building, maybe so they wouldn't have to bump in to each other in the hall. His bathroom was even larger, but no marble finishes. His fixtures were pretty new, probably installed by the government. He had a fireplace, and I poked around the ashes for anything incriminating, getting nothing but soot for my troubles. I went through the motions in the rest of his room, feeling that the search was increasingly useless. Searching a room can actually be interesting, if there's only one room or even just one house to search. But a repetitive search of a whole bunch of small rooms is very, very boring. What is personal and sacrosanct individually, like family pictures, old photos, and letters, becomes mind-numbingly more and more like the debris of everyday life, devalued a little bit every time you see it again with only the faces changed. I longed to find the room of a monk, someone who had renounced the world and all connections with it. No such luck. Even Vidar Skak kept a picture of his mother or grandmother on the mantel. I hoped to God it wasn't his wife.

I walked out of his room and shut the

door. The hallway was silent, everyone busy in their offices or at lunch. I put the key in the lock and turned it, withdrew it, and started to walk away. Something stopped me. I went back to his door, unlocked it, and then locked it again. For the first time, maybe because of the quiet or because I had lost focus on the search, I noticed something. The key, turning in the lock, made a loud or at least noticeable metallic *click clack* sound. What would that sound like in the early morning hours, when you were close to waking up? Could someone in an adjacent room have heard that sound just before dawn?

I headed to the stairway to see how far Kaz and Daphne had gotten up on the fourth floor. I wanted to test my theory out in Birkeland's room. I heard rapid footsteps, heels racing on the wooden floor, and Daphne's high voice calling out "Billy? Billy, we found it!" I hotfooted it to the stairwell and caught her before she made it all the way down.

"Where?" I asked as I took her arm and turned her around.

"Anders Arnesen. In his room," she answered breathlessly, "and I found it!"

Major Arnesen. Hmm. I had a strange feeling about him yesterday. He seemed relatively indifferent after I almost took a shot to the head. Had he been the shooter? Was he the killer? What was he thinking about when he left the key in his room?

Kaz was standing in the open doorway. "Billy, we haven't touched or moved anything. Come, see."

This room was more like mine, a small guest room, suitable for temporary visits but not outfitted for living space. His bathroom was even smaller than mine, which made me happy.

"It was so easy, wasn't it, darling?" Daphne gushed as she squeezed Kaz's arm. "It was terribly gauche going through these people's personal possessions, don't you think? But there it was. We didn't even have to look hard!"

She was thrilled with her find and would probably be walking on air for the rest of the day. Kaz silently walked to the corner of the bed and picked up the mattress. There, lying about ten inches from the edge, was a key.

"Daphne found it just like that. I checked the spare key to this room against it; it's not the same."

I pulled the housekeeper's spare for Birkeland's room out of my pocket and laid it next to the key. It was a perfect match. Well,

well, well.

"Daphne, will you please find Major Arnesen. He should be in his office or the map room. Tell him we need his assistance up here. Don't let on that we found anything. Then find Captain Harding and tell him we'll meet him in the mess hall. I need some chow."

"Shall I tell him what we found?"

"No. Don't tell anyone anything, OK? Can you pull it off with Arnesen?"

"Darling, at dinner last night I pretended I was interested in the business of fish-processing and canning. I can handle a little white lie with the major." She winked at me and scurried off.

"What is your plan, Billy?"

"Poke him with a stick, Kaz, and see how high he jumps."

"I think I will like this part. What do you want me to do?"

"Sit right here." I motioned to the edge of the bed where the key was hidden. "I'll ask him a few questions, and we'll watch his reaction to where you're sitting. Then we'll spring it on him." Kaz grinned like a sly fox in a henhouse and I leaned up against the wall near the window, trying to look casual. I wasn't sure the presence of the key in his room meant he was the one who put it there, but it didn't mean he wasn't either. I thought about how that really meant I didn't know a damned thing. A minute later, Anders Arnesen walked in.

"Major." I greeted him with a smile. "Come on in!"

"It is a little strange to be welcomed into one's own room, Lieutenant. However, I understand the necessity. How are you, Baron?" He nodded at Kaz politely.

"Very well, Major. Searching is quite a tiring business, though. I am glad Billy has given us a respite." I watched Anders closely. He gave no hint that he was doing anything except engaging in polite chatter.

"Have you found anything yet? I hear you are looking for a missing key."

He stood with his hands in his pockets, looking extraordinarily nonchalant. He didn't look like he was in mourning for Knut Birkeland, but, he wasn't acting like a guilty or nervous suspect either. I watched for the telltale glance at his hiding place, but, aside from his exchange with Kaz, his eyes never darted anywhere. He looked at me idly, waiting for a response. Already this wasn't going the way I thought it would.

"Word travels fast. Did you know Knut Birkeland well?"

"Actually not very well at all. After our

escape from Norway, I saw him only a few times here at Beardsley Hall. I have been busy training the Norwegian Brigade at our base. New volunteers are coming in from Norway constantly."

"How do they get here?" asked Kaz.

"Every commando raid along the coast returns with a large number of volunteers. When we land near a town the word spreads and young men pack up and return with us. Sometimes a fishing craft will slip through the German coastal patrols and make the journey to Scotland."

"What did you think of Birkeland's position on using the Underground Army?"

"I have just requested permission from the king to go to Norway and assess the effectiveness of the underground. I believe it would be a waste of resources to organize and arm this force and not use it. However, if they are not capable of a sustained uprising, it would be criminal to order them into action."

"Makes sense. What did the king say?"

"His initial reaction was that he wanted me to stay here and get the brigade ready for the invasion, but he promised to think about it. Lieutenant —"

"Major, unless you want to stand on ceremony, please call me Billy. When people say 'lieutenant' I can only think about my supervisor back at the Boston Police Department." I wanted to put him at ease, figuring that he'd assume a friendly approach meant he wasn't a suspect.

"We are very lucky to have a trained policeman here. Quite a coincidence . . . Billy." He smiled and lifted a questioning eyebrow at me. Wow, this guy was confident. He was either innocent or very experienced at interrogations. Or both, which was also possible. An attack is a good defense when you're being questioned. The interrogator needs to know not to respond, not to give up the rhythm of the questioning by answering the attack. I knew that. Kaz didn't.

"What do you mean by that?" Kaz demanded angrily, jumping up from his seat on the bed and standing in front of Arnesen, arms akimbo, defending my honor.

"Baron, you must admit it is quite odd. First, our American friend Billy is almost shot yesterday, and then Birkeland is found dead this morning. Beardsley Hall has not seen so much commotion since the days of the Vikings. Before your party arrived, things were very quiet here. One has to wonder at your real reason for coming." Again, the smile. So disarming. He'd make a great interrogation partner. Kaz was fuming, so I put my hand on his shoulder and tried to calm things down. He sat back down on the bed, his eyes shooting daggers at Arnesen.

"Major, there's nothing I'd like better than to leave you all here and get back to London — or Boston, for that matter. I just came along for the ride and now I'm stuck with this assignment, just like you're stuck here with the Brigade instead of taking off for home. So give us a hand, will you?" He studied me for a minute. I could practically see the wheels turning, and I wished I knew what he was really thinking.

"OK, to use an American expression. How can I help you, Billy?"

"We have a little experiment to perform. Your room is two doors down from Birkeland's, right?"

"Yes."

"You and Kaz stay here with your door shut. I'm going down the hall. Tell me what you hear." I left the room and went to Birkeland's door. I unlocked it, trying to be as quiet as I could. The key turned in the lock and the mechanism rotated with a clear metallic *clack*. I opened the door, closed it carefully, and locked it. *Clack*. It was a distinct sound, not really loud, but probably more audible in the quiet of night. I walked past Anders's door, stopped, then walked back and knocked. Kaz let me in.

"Major, please tell me what you heard, in detail."

Arnesen closed his eyes and held up one finger. "First, your footsteps down the hall." Another finger came up. "Then the faint sound of the key turning the lock, twice. I assume you unlocked and then locked Birkeland's door. Then, and probably only because I was listening for it, the sound of your footsteps going by my door." He ended with a fourth finger up and opened his eyes. I looked at Kaz, who nodded his agreement.

"So this experiment, it was to show that others on this floor could hear the door being locked?" Arnesen asked.

"Yes. Did you hear anything like that last night?"

"Billy, my American friend, you have discovered what every man on this floor discovered when the female staff moved in!" Arnesen started to laugh, adding, "Congratulations!" Now I was really off my rhythm.

"What are you talking about?"

"Of course these old locks make a terrible noise at night, when everything is quiet. They echo in the hallway off the wooden walls and floor. I was here six months ago just after they brought in female clerical and housekeeping staff. The king's staff had grown so large Jens decided they needed additional help. Late-night visitations were forbidden, but that first night it sounded like a symphony of locks as men left their rooms to meet their newfound girlfriends. As Skak and Birkeland were at opposite ends of the building, and were early risers, no one ever tried to bring the girls up here."

"But what's so funny?"

"There was a crackdown on the nocturnal visits, and several officers were disciplined when they were caught in the act. They learned to leave their doors unlocked at night, and slip out quietly. You could walk down this hallway at night and probably every other door would be unlocked and the room empty. So even if Birkeland or Skak were awake, they wouldn't hear any coming or goings. Excellent, Lieutenants!" He gave each of us a mock bow. "You have uncovered a dastardly plot to steal the virtue of young English women!" By now he was almost howling with laughter. That did it. I was mad. At my own stupidity mostly, but it was never fun to take things out on myself. So I went for Arnesen. I flipped up the edge of the mattress.

"Do you think this is funny?" I picked up

the key and held it in front of his face. My dad had taught me to hold off confronting a suspect with a piece of evidence long enough for the guy to think he'd gotten away with it. Let him feel relief at having put one over on you, he used to say. That way he'll have even farther to fall when he finds out he's wrong.

I watched Arnesen. Not just his eyes, but the muscles in his face. I wanted to see his fear when he realized I had found his hiding place. The shock of being found out, the little twitch that gives off the aroma of guilt. He had been riding high, laughing at us, and I was going to enjoy watching him reveal himself.

There was none of that. Genuine amazement, round-eyed surprise showed on his face. He was still half laughing as the fact that Knut Birkeland's key was in his room dawned on him.

"What's that doing here? Who put that there?"

Now I've seen plenty of guys who have been through questioning try to fake it. Everyone tries too hard, tries to show you how honest and innocent they are. The trouble is, as soon as you start thinking about it, it's harder and harder to sound convincing. Because the really convincing thing is when you aren't prepared, because you are innocent. You sound just like Arnesen did.

"Were you off on a nocturnal adventure last night, Major?"

"No. I have not had time to get to know any of the women here."

"So how could anyone but you have put this key here?"

"First, Lieutenant, you are holding the answer to that in your hand. There are spare keys kept by the housekeeper. Anyone could walk through the kitchen area and pick them up, as you did." I had to admit he was right. I had to find the housekeeper myself to tell her I was taking them.

"And secondly, why would I be so stupid as to keep the key to Birkeland's room? I could always get in later with the spare, if that's what I wanted. And if I needed to get rid of it, I could have easily found another open room as I've explained, and hidden it there."

Anders stopped, the cold logic of his words hanging in the air between us. It made no sense, he was right. What did make sense was that someone else had done just what he suggested he could have done himself. He rubbed his chin with his hand, thinking it through. It looked like the same thought occurred to him at about the same time.

"So someone did kill Birkeland and then hid the key in my room. . . ."

I could see he was considering the possibilities. I was trying to stay one step ahead of him and find out if he knew anything he wasn't telling us. Kaz beat me to the punch.

"Maybe you were next on the list, Major," said Kaz, "and when you weren't here, perhaps the person thought framing you would be the next best thing."

I had to admire Kaz for that one. It was the first thing we threw at Anders that shook him. His eyes widened fractionally and he hesitated just a second before agreeing it was possible. He nodded his head but turned away, not meeting our eyes. Or not letting us see his. Once he collected himself, he turned around, as if his thoughts had just wandered. I decided to leave on a high note.

"That must be it," I agreed. "Better watch your back, Anders."

"I will, Billy. It seems there are enemies on all fronts."

CHAPTER ELEVEN

Kaz double stepped to keep up with me as I strode down the hallways of Beardsley Hall, fists slammed into my pockets and a black cloud over my head. I didn't feel like chatting and Kaz mercifully got the point, remaining unusually silent.

I was fuming at looking like a rookie in front of Kaz and Anders. I hadn't placed much stock in that key being proof of Anders's guilt, so I didn't mind that it hadn't worked out. We took a shot and missed, no big deal. I hated being shown up about the locks, though. I was certain that within the hour my big "discovery" of the loud locks would be making the rounds, getting a big laugh about the American detective and his powers of deduction, or was it seduction? Ha ha. It reminded me of what my kid brother, Danny, said after his first few months at college. He took a class in sociology and said a sociologist was someone who would do a year's worth of research to find out where all the whorehouses in town were, when all you had to do was slip any cabbie a sawbuck.

I had no idea what a sociologist did for a day's pay, but I felt about as low as that dumb guy doing all that research. The worst thing — well not actually, but it sure felt that way at the moment — that could happen to a cop in an investigation was to look stupid or be the butt of a joke. It's hard to put the fear of God in someone who's laughing at you. You're more than likely to beat the guy like a drum, which may feel satisfying at the moment, but doesn't get you anywhere. And it wasn't an option here in merrie olde England anyway.

We went down the last flight of stairs to the basement, following a sign for the mess hall. This place wasn't for state dinners, and the king probably never set foot inside. It was basically a cafeteria for the military and civilian staff working in Beardsley Hall. Linoleum floors, shiny aluminum fixtures in the kitchen, ladies with hairnets and paper hats, warming trays along the line, and a mixture of yeasty odors all signaled that the British version of institutional food was in ready supply. Small round tables with wooden chairs pulled up to them were scattered throughout the room. At the far end, Daphne was sitting with Harding. She smiled and waved. He didn't. I gave it a try and came up with tight-lipped grimace.

My spirits rose just a bit when the aroma of coffee drifted out of the kitchen. Was it possible? A break from tea, here in the heart of England? Yes! There were two large urns, industrial-size jobs, one for tea and the other containing the blessed black brew. I poured hot, steaming black coffee into a tall, thick mug with the seal of the Norwegian navy on it. I dumped in some sugar, grabbed a couple of hot hard-crusted rolls from a basket, and scooped strawberry preserves onto my plate. I was a happy man again, and thanked my lucky stars that I was a simple soul at heart, satisfied with such little things that could take my mind off being the laughingstock of Beardsley Hall. Armed with java and jam, I made my way to the table and sat next to Daphne. Not a hard choice.

"Go ahead, Boyle, eat your chow. You probably haven't had anything yet today." Harding confused me when he was nice, which fortunately didn't happen often enough to be a real problem. I ate, gulped, went and got a refill on the coffee, and sat down, ready to report.

"So, what have we got?" Harding demanded. There, that was more like it. That dependable tone of voice always let me know right where I stood.

"We've got the key. Daphne found it in Arnesen's room. Most likely it was planted there. A lot of the fellows here leave their rooms unlocked at night so they can slip out quietly and visit the ladies. We interrogated Arnesen but it just didn't add up."

"Loud locks give the men away to senior staff?" Geez, did everybody know this dodge except me?

"Of course, sir." I smiled my best man-of-the-world smile, which was also my David Niven impression.

"So run me through a likely chain of events, as best you can."

I looked around, wanting to be sure no one had sat down at the table behind me. No worry there, the only other people in the place were halfway across the room, talking and glancing over at us, probably laughing at me.

"OK. The suicide version goes like this. Knut Birkeland knows that he is about to be exposed for the theft of gold from the Norwegian treasury. He's about to lose everything: position, honor, the friendship of the king. He decides to end it all. He gets up early, writes a note, and places a gold coin on it to make his point. He takes a bath and dresses in his best suit, wanting to go out in style. He opens the window and jumps. Breaks his neck."

"And you say that's not out of the ordinary for a suicide? The bath and best-suit routine?" Harding sounded skeptical, and Daphne and Kaz looked up at me like I was a professor at How-to-Kill-Yourself U.

"Look, I'm not an expert on suicides. But from what I've seen, yeah, it works. Maybe he decided to sleep on it, woke up, and found everything still bleak."

I tried to visualize what had gone on in that room and in Birkeland's mind. I closed my eyes, gripped the coffee mug, and tried to see things as they might have happened.

"Maybe he hadn't decided when he first got up. He took a bath, dressed, and maybe thought about it some more. He reached the same conclusion: dishonor, failure. He decided to go through with it. He wrote that note. Placed the coin on it, an admission of guilt, and a nice paperweight, too. Then opened the window and jumped."

I opened my eyes.

"Sounds plausible," Daphne said, looking at each of us for our reaction.

"Except for the key," I sighed. "If he committed suicide, we have to explain how his room ended up locked and the key got into Major Arnesen's room."

"You've eliminated Arnesen as a suspect?" Harding asked.

"No, we haven't eliminated anyone, but Arnesen seemed genuinely surprised when we showed him the key. He pointed out, with some logic, how easy it would have been for him to hide it elsewhere. And how stupid it would have been for him to hide it in his own room."

Harding rubbed his chin and frowned. "OK, tell me how a murder would have gone."

"That one's a little harder, sir." I took a deep breath and tried to place myself in that room, watching the events unfold. Standing there, up against the wall, real quiet, observing.

"It's early morning, and Birkeland was already up and bathed. We know he was an early riser. Probably he's already dressed. Someone knocks on the door and Birkeland unlocks it, lets them in. Maybe they talk a while. Somehow the killer gets Birkeland to write that note, then kills him, quick, probably by breaking his neck. No signs of a struggle, so we have to assume it was done rapidly and efficiently. He opens the window and tosses out the body. Then he probably put the coin on the note, although I don't know if he or Birkeland originally had it. Could've been either one of them. He unlocks the door and goes out into the hallway. He locks the door behind him, not wanting anyone to get into the room too soon because he needs to get away before the body and the note are found. He's standing in the hallway, trying to figure out what to do with the key. He quietly tries a few doors until he finds one unlocked. Figuring he can kill two birds with one stone, he hides the key in Arnesen's room so suspicion will be cast on someone else."

"Wouldn't that mean that Major Arnesen can't be a suspect?" asked Kaz.

"If that theory held up, it would, except for the fact that Arnesen says he was in his room all night, so his door should've been locked. But before we even think about that, tell me how anyone could force Birkeland to write a suicide note and then kill him? He was a big fellow, and not exactly meek. Why would he go along with it? It doesn't make any sense." I shrugged.

"A commando could kill quickly and quietly," Harding offered.

"Rolf?" asked Daphne. "I think he's the only commando who stayed at Beardsley

Hall after the exercise."

"Unfortunately, that theory doesn't fit either," Harding said, negating his own idea. "Rolf met with the king before five o'clock this morning to go grouse hunting. According to Boyle, the murder, or death, occurred shortly after that. Rigor mortis and blood settling gave a pretty good estimate of the time of death. It occurred when Rolf and the king were out hunting, and the king provides a pretty good alibi."

My head hurt. Nothing added up. Birkeland couldn't have committed suicide in a locked room with no key in it, and there was no way I could see for anyone to force him to write a fictitious note and then kill him with no fuss or muss. Even if someone like Rolf had pulled a quick one and snapped Birkeland's neck, how did he or she get him to write that note? Neither option made any sense. Maybe it was time to tell these guys that I never actually headed up a murder investigation before. Crowd control for my dad didn't really qualify me. Maybe it was time to tell them I was basically a fraud. I decided to go at that one sideways.

"Major, are you going to call in the military police to conduct a real . . . an official investigation? They've got all kinds of resources that we could use."

"No way, Boyle. This is exactly the kind of affair Ike wanted you on board for. If we bring a truckload of MPs in here, word would get out in no time. It would be embarrassing for the Norwegians and hurt the war effort, especially with the invasion coming up. You've got to track this thing down yourself. Lieutenant Kazimierz and Second Officer Seaton will assist you. If I can help, let me know what you need. Otherwise, it's up to you. Plus, it will be an excellent cover for taking care of that other concern. I know you can handle it."

I wanted to tell him he had the wrong guy. I wanted to tell him I was just a Boston Mick and I was like a fish out of water here in England. I doubted I could find out how Birkeland died, and I sure was no spy catcher. He needed to know that maybe our congressman oversold me a little bit to get me a job with Uncle Ike. Probably a lot. Yeah, I had been promoted to detective just before the war started, but I never even got to work a single case. Sure, I had worked a few here and there with my dad, but never as the detective in charge. Now, I was between that old rock and a hard place. If I told the truth about myself, Harding would send me to a rifle company and I'd find myself landing on a cold, stony shore in Norway in no time flat. If I didn't, I'd probably screw up this investigation and never find the murderer, much less the spy. I was feeling pretty bad.

Maybe I should come clean and get it over with. Admit that what I did, what my family did, was wrong. Face the music. Easier said than done, if you want my opinion. It wasn't just me who had pulled this off, it was my whole family. What was I supposed to do, turn state's evidence on them with Uncle Ike? I thought about Dad throwing that package in the garbage. At some point, when you were in over your head, what became important wasn't whatever you'd gone after in the first place, but something more indefinable. You couldn't call it honor, not at this stage, not after you had gotten yourself in this deep. Avoidance of shame, that was more like it.

"Billy, darling, we'll help you," Daphne said, reading the struggle on my face, but not understanding how far back it went. "Look at everything we've found out so far! We can do it together."

She reached out and put her hand on my arm while Kaz solemnly nodded his agreement. Well, maybe I was being too hasty. Why agonize over it? Why disappoint

Daphne and Kaz? So what if the murderer got away? It had happened before and would happen again. Uncle Ike might not be too happy if I didn't take care of this little problem, but he'd be a lot madder if he found out . . . found out the truth about me. It didn't sound real pretty when you just came out and said it, did it? I shivered a little inside and tried to forget it.

"Sure we will, Daphne. We can do it. Major, we'll ask a few more questions and then the three of us will regroup and decide what to do next."

Harding nodded, as if he really believed I knew what I was doing. He seemed to have changed his opinion about me. It was as if he trusted me to get the job done.

"Very well, Lieutenant," he said in a formal tone, sealing the deal on my assignment. "I'm going to meet with the king. He was very upset at hearing the news. He needed some time to compose himself. He and Birkeland had evidently been close friends for some time."

"How did Rolf take it?" asked Kaz as Harding got up to leave.

"Surprised, but he seemed to take it in stride. He's seen plenty of death and destruction in this war already. One more body wouldn't shake him."

"Did he come back with you?"

"Yes, but he's gone by now. He had to get back to his unit. The Norwegian commandos have been moved to a new base at Southwold, up the coast, along with our Ranger and paratroop units."

I'm not the most experienced detective around, but I knew that didn't sound right. When you didn't have one suspect, everyone was a suspect, and you didn't let anyone waltz out the front door. I drank some more coffee, but it was cold.

"We should have questioned him first, sir."

"Why? He obviously wasn't involved if he left with the king to go hunting before Birkeland died."

"It's hard to explain, sir, but I need to talk to everyone. Rolf may know something he doesn't even know is important."

"I'll pretend I understand that, Boyle. Don't worry. They've got a big fence around the Southwold base. If you want him, you can find him there. Keep me posted."

Harding strode out of the mess hall, confidently leaving his staff to solve a murder while he went off to hold King Haakon's hands. It must be nice to be in command. Oh yeah, I was, too. In command of a little Polish baron and his beautiful English broad. If the guys at the precinct could only see me now. I was beginning to think I had gotten stuck with the short end of my own stick. How could I find the murderer if I couldn't even keep track of the suspects? The suicide theory was beginning to look better by the hour. I tried to sound confident for my rookies.

"OK, here's the deal. We've obviously missed something important, and we have no idea what it is. So we've got to split up and ask a lot of questions. Daphne, you've got the hardest job of all, one Kaz and I couldn't even attempt." I could see her eyes widen at the prospect. She was a real trouper.

"Tell me what to do, Billy."

"Chat up the young ladies and make some friends. We need to know if any of them had visitors from the fourth floor last night."

"You mean ask them about. . . ."

"Yes, dear," Kaz said with a smile. "Ask them about that."

"Well, it's usually not done, but I'll try my best."

"Really?" I asked. "Don't girls talk about . . . that?"

"If we did, we wouldn't let you men in on it, would we?" With a sly smile, she got up and stood in line for a cup of tea along with a gaggle of giggling WRENs who had just entered the cafeteria. On the job in a flash.

"Do you understand women, Billy?" Kaz asked, his eyes still fixed on Daphne.

"I understand they make me crazy, Kaz. Other than that, not a damn thing. What about you?"

"She is a constant, wondrous mystery." He refocused on me. "Now, what do I do?"

"You talk to the housekeeper. Find out if any of the household staff saw someone walking around early, from five o'clock on. They must have been up and about. Maybe we'll get lucky and one of them will have seen something."

"What will you do?"

"I think I need to talk to Vidar Skak some more," I said.

"Why Skak?"

"So far, he's got the most to gain from Birkeland's death. Nothing else makes sense, but that always does. My dad always says when you're stuck, go back to the guy who benefits the most."

We left the mess hall and I headed to Skak's office, praying that Dad's advice would provide the solution to this mess. I didn't have any other cards to play. If this didn't work I was going to need a whole new deck.

Chapter Twelve

Vidar Skak didn't have the casual open-door policy of Knut Birkeland. In his office on the third floor I was confronted by a severe gray-haired Norwegian woman, seated at a desk way too small for her big-boned figure, in an anteroom way too small even for the desk. She spilled out over it, big droopy arms lying on papers as if she was holding them down. Her arms moved as I entered, hands poised to push her body up from the desk, ready to leap in front of Skak's closed door if I tried anything. A piece of paper stuck to the underside of one forearm, which she shook until the paper fluttered down, freed from the thin veneer of dampness that had bonded it to her. I backed up, not wanting to get in the way of those elbows and arms.

I gave my name and asked to speak to her boss. She told me to wait as she moved away from the desk, which took no more than two steps in that little room, keeping her eyes on me at all times. She guarded Skak's office like it was Fort Knox. I still didn't know exactly how the gold fit in, or even if it really did, but it was never far from my mind.

Brunhilda, or whatever her name was, knocked on the door, waited a beat, then went in, half closing the door behind her. Maybe Skak took naps and didn't like the help walking in on him. She spoke to him in hushed tones and then, grudgingly, opened the door and nodded me in. I tried to make myself small as I went past her sideways.

Vidar Skak rose but didn't come out from behind his desk. The cherrywood gleamed, every carved corner shining. There were three folders on the desktop, lined up perfectly. Nothing else, not even a pen. Glass double doors behind him opened onto a small balcony. The wall on my right was covered in bookshelves; a quick glance showed that most of the titles were in Norwegian. They looked like law books and bound government reports. Had Skak brought all those books with him? While Knut Birkeland was breaking his back carrying his country's national treasure, was Skak transporting cases of books? The other wall was covered with photos, all arranged neatly, above a leather sofa. Skak with the king, Skak shaking hands with Winston Churchill, Skak seated at another desk, in another office, probably in Oslo. No trace of family photos, no other picture of that woman on his mantel.

This was Skak's true surroundings, not his sterile room upstairs. Here, at the center of his power, was the place he called home. No one else would see his bedroom, so it served no purpose other than as a place to sleep and get ready for another day of politics. And this was a good day for Skak, a day of elimination and gain. But was it as simple as good fortune for him and bad luck for Birkeland? Or had Skak made his own luck?

He looked severe, his forehead wrinkled with all the important thoughts going on behind it. He raised his lips in the semblance of a smile, the phony politician's grin that looks the same in Boston or Oslo. I wondered if they bothered with that anymore in Berlin. Watching Skak trying to smile was like looking at a crack in a mirror; I thought the effort might break his face. He put his hands behind his back and rocked back and forth on his heels, like he was full of energy and life. It made me think of Knut Birkeland, still and cold on the damp ground.

"What can I do for you, Lieutenant Boyle?" He gestured for me to be seated as he adjusted his frock coat so he didn't sit on the tails. His high starched collar dug into his neck and he twisted his head just a fraction, adjusting the angle he looked at me from to suit the collar. I had seen pictures of men dressed like that, I just didn't know they still did.

"Nice office. Will you get a new one when you're the senior adviser?"

"Don't be impertinent, young man!" The smile vanished.

"My apologies, sir. I just assumed you'd get the job now with Mr. Birkeland out of the way." He looked at me through angry, narrowed eyes, assessing my value, my ability to help or hinder his advancement.

"Is rudeness a technique of American policemen?"

"Do Norwegian police solve crimes through politeness?" He eased back in his chair and I thought I saw a half grin, half sneer try to creep up one corner of his mouth. It was entirely natural, a real emotion playing out over his face. Gone in a flash, it gave the hint of a highly intelligent man who enjoyed this sort of game.

"Perhaps not," he admitted. "But why did

207

you refer to crimes? Did not Birkeland jump from his own window?"

"Perhaps not," I shot back. "Do you think Birkeland was the kind of man to kill himself?"

"I am not qualified to judge such things. I have never known anyone who has taken his own life. It seems abhorrent to me, but perhaps he had his reasons." Skak leaned back, quietly satisfied at leaving the thought of Birkeland's reasons dangling in the air, bait for me to rise to. I wasn't ready to walk into that one yet.

"Well, if you don't know if he would have killed himself, do you know anyone who wanted him dead?"

"Lieutenant, we have many disagreements here," Skak pontificated, looking over my shoulder at the photographs on the wall. "Some of those disagreements are about matters of state policy, and some are about military strategy. Most involve the lives of many people. Naturally, these disagreements can become quite heated, and even personal. But to wish someone dead — no, I cannot conceive of that." He sounded smug, as if he had rehearsed these words until they sounded just perfect. Time to poke this guy.

"Don't you wish many people dead, sir?"

"What do you mean?"

"The Underground Army. Won't many of them die if the king authorizes the uprising?"

"You know that's not the same thing, Lieutenant."

"No, you won't have to get your own hands dirty. It's not the same thing at all."

"Lieutenant Boyle, this discussion is pointless. If there is something specific I can do for you, please let me know. Otherwise, I am very busy."

"Mr. Skak, I think you don't quite understand. This questioning is not voluntary on your part. I'm under orders to investigate the suspicious death of an Allied government official. You are as much a suspect as anyone. More so, perhaps." The smugness and the smile vanished. He looked like he suddenly realized that it might not be smooth sailing for the future senior adviser. I had no idea if my authority, if I really had any at all, extended to the Norwegians. All I had was Harding's orders and some backup from Cosgrove. It looked like Skak bought the bluff, though.

"A suspect? More so? Whatever do you mean?"

"The most basic rule of a murder investigation. The one who has the most to gain is automatically a suspect. Birkeland was your competition for senior adviser. He's gone and now you're it. Simple."

"That is idiotic! You don't even know if he was murdered or killed himself!"

"I know that things aren't what they seem. And that I will find out what really happened, and why." I went silent and stared at Skak. Sometimes a confident bluff and determined silence can work on a guy. As I stared at him, I started counting how many pairs of clean socks I had left. It wasn't many, but it didn't take Skak long to start talking either. He didn't strike me as a man comfortable with his own silence. Maybe he didn't have any clean socks to count.

"I have been told you are looking for a key. What does all this have to do with your search for that key?"

"Good question, Mr. Skak. There was no key inside Mr. Birkeland's room, which was locked. That means that someone was in his room and locked it from the outside when he or she left."

"The murderer."

"Maybe. Or maybe Birkeland did kill himself and someone entered the room after the fact, for some other reason then left and locked it. Did you visit him in his room last night?"

"We were not in the habit of visiting each other in our personal living quarters. We were not . . . friends, I regret to say."

"You don't look like you regret it at all, Mr. Skak."

"Oh, but I do, I do, young man. If he were alive, I could expose Knut Birkeland for the thief he was. I could have ended his influence with the king and won the post of senior adviser for myself. But now that he is dead, by whatever means, I will certainly be appointed by default, and we will never know what he did with the gold he took." It was a good answer, and there was a rage in his voice that seemed real to me.

"When did this problem with the gold start?"

"Aboard the *Glasgow,* after we left Molde. You heard about the crate of coins that broke open. I had been keeping a tally of the crates during our journey. I kept track of every small shipment that Birkeland sent off. It was a good idea, I must admit, to use the fishing fleet. It protected the entire shipment from capture by the Germans, but it also allowed it to slowly leave our control."

"Did you lose much of the gold?"

"No, the Norwegian people rallied around us through every step of the journey. Everyone helped and no one informed the Germans. But when the last of the shipment, about two hundred crates, distributed to Birkeland's fleet of fishing vessels in Nordland was unloaded, we ended up two crates short."

"Only two? How could that have been Birkeland's fault?"

"Lieutenant, first you must understand that each crate weighed sixty-five pounds. That makes one hundred and thirty pounds of gold, a fortune for anyone. Each ship's count was right, which means the two crates were diverted in the off-loading. Which was supervised by Knut Birkeland."

"Means and opportunity, but no motive," I said.

"Pardon me?"

"Police first look to see if a suspect had the means, the motive and the opportunity to commit a crime. Birkeland had two out of three, but what would his motive have been?"

"Money. A great deal of it."

"Would you have stolen it?"

Skak paused for a second to actually consider the question. "I would like to say no, but then again, I have never had the means and the opportunity, as you say, presented to me. Who can say what they would really do? Would you commit such a crime?"

"Good question," I admitted. I thought back to the last big bust I had been involved with before I left the cops. We had got the jump on the Riley brothers as they were about to fence a shipment of stolen watches: ladies' watches, fourteen-karat gold plated, a gross of them. While we were unloading the boxes into the evidence locker, one of the guys dropped one and it busted open. I had given my mom a fourteen-karat gold plated watch for Christmas that year. I never really thought of it as stealing. Hell, it had already been stolen, and we got it back! So, yeah, I took my share when it wouldn't hurt anyone, so who was I to judge Birkeland, up in Nordland on a little fishing boat, watching all the gold in the world pass him by? I looked Skak straight in the eye and answered him.

"No. Once a police officer, always a police officer. I wouldn't steal."

"Exactly. Your training prohibits you from doing so. My family is quite wealthy, and I have few needs, since I have dedicated my life to government service."

"In other words, you prefer power to money."

"Lieutenant, you are rude and overly

blunt. But not incorrect. Wealth by itself is nothing more than an amusement for those who are born to it. Knut Birkeland, however, was born to a poor fisherman, and built up his fishing fleet and his political fortunes by hard work alone. To such a man, great wealth is an aspiration, and a temptation."

"I have to agree with you, Mr. Skak, about money. But it also applies to power. Once you've had a taste of it, you can never have enough. The motive you're describing for Birkeland's theft of the gold is the same one I could apply to you. You wouldn't have been able to stand the humiliation and loss of power if Birkeland had been appointed senior adviser. It's a perfect motive for murder."

Skak gulped. He didn't like the picture I was painting. I could see him mentally calculating the chances that just a hint of guilt would keep the king from appointing him, even if I had no proof. Then he brightened.

"Let me grant you that, in your mind at least, that is a sufficient motive for murder. What about your own rules? Where are my means and opportunity? How could I have overpowered and killed Knut Birkeland?"

"I'm not sure," I admitted.

Skak's face lit up as he warmed to the task of destroying my theory.

"Another thing, Lieutenant. Why do you suppose I was the only one with a great deal to gain from Birkeland's death? Why don't you look into who will inherit or take over his business interests? He could have a relative or partner in England who would have much to gain by his death."

It was a very good point. It was also a long shot, but one worth taking, as well as one I hadn't thought of. I decided not to thank him for the swell idea.

"Where were you between five thirty and six o'clock this morning?"

"I am a man of very precise habits, Lieutenant. I awake each morning at five thirty. I dress and take a morning walk at six o'clock, rain or shine. I find it clears my head for the day's work and keeps me fit. I breakfast at six thirty and am at work by seven. This morning, Major Cosgrove joined me on my walk. He wanted to talk about the Underground Army and my plans for it."

I made a mental note to talk to Cosgrove. He hadn't mentioned that he'd been up and around, and I hadn't figured him for the early-exercise much less the walking type.

"Did you see anything unusual in the

house or on the grounds?"

"No, just the usual house staff about. Except for Captain Iversen, now that you mention it."

"Was it unusual for him to be around?"

"I don't usually see him that early. As I came down the staircase from the fourth floor, I saw him walking down the third-floor corridor very quietly. His back was to me, so he didn't see me there. He opened his door, which was unlocked, and closed it behind him, very slowly without a noise. I thought it a bit odd at the time, and only remembered when you asked me. Why would he go out and leave his room unlocked and act so furtively?"

I was glad to hear that someone else besides me hadn't caught on to the unlocked door dodge, until I realized it put me in the same company as this lifeless bureaucrat. I'd have to ask Jens about his excursion, and why he hadn't mentioned it. That made three guys already up and around the building when Birkeland was killed: Skak, Cosgrove, and Iversen. And maybe Anders, since he couldn't account for how someone got into his room to leave Birkeland's key, although that could have been done anytime up until it was found.

"Well, Mr. Skak, maybe he just didn't

want to wake up his neighbors. Anything else?"

"No. Major Cosgrove and I met at the front entrance and walked briskly for half an hour. When we returned I went straight to my room, where I have my breakfast delivered." The thought of Cosgrove walking briskly for thirty minutes was pretty funny, and it made me wonder why he was so interested in Skak's plans.

"Lieutenant Boyle, will you be reporting on your investigation to the king?" I could see the worry in his eyes.

"I doubt it, sir. I report to Major Harding, who reports directly to General Eisenhower. He will probably inform Major Cosgrove as a courtesy, but what they do with my report is their business."

"And when do you think you will complete your investigation?"

"When I understand exactly what happened and why."

"Well, good luck then, Lieutenant." I could see that Skak's faith in me didn't lead him to foresee a speedy conclusion to this case. His face visibly relaxed and his smile looked almost natural. He must've figured that word of his potential involvement wouldn't get back to the king until he was safely enthroned as senior adviser.

I left and smiled at Brunhilda on my way out, trying to work the Irish charm. Nothing. I'd have had more of a chance with cod on ice at Quincy Market than with her.

I walked downstairs to the second floor, where Jens had his office amid a cluster of other officers and lower-level functionaries. No ample secretaries pulling guard duty in sight. I found him at his desk and on the phone, jotting down notes and nodding his head. Someone on the other end was doing a lot of talking. I stepped back a bit and looked around as I waited.

Down here on the second floor accommodations were a bit more spartan. Jens's office was actually a rectangle, three walls and an open front. There were four others like it along one wall, and a nest of desks, map tables, and file cabinets filled the rest of the room. Norwegian soldiers in brown British battle dress, WRENs in their blue uniforms, and some civilian women buzzed about. I watched them talking, tracing movements on a wall map with their fingers, dancing over the North Sea from Scotland to Norway as if they were planning a Sunday drive, eyes alive with anticipation. There was a sense of purpose in everything they did, every little thing filled with great importance, even filing papers and typing forms.

File cabinets were closed with determined thuds like mortar rounds going off, and the rapid chatter of typewriter keys sounded like machine guns strafing the paper into submission. There was excitement in the air, the unspoken fervor of anticipated action. The invasion was *on.* It had been two years since some of these people had seen their homeland, and now they were on their way back. This wasn't just a government job; it was a cause, something they all believed in and would fight for. Die for.

Leaning against the wall, with Jens jabbering on the phone and the murmurs of activity all around me, I felt a stab of loneliness. Or maybe just a kind of difference that separated me from these eager beavers. They were all doing their bit for the cause, and here I was, an outsider, searching their rooms, questioning their leaders, and generally getting in the way. I sure didn't want to go along with them, but I did feel left out, as if I were watching a parade pass me by. But that was the price I paid, the trade-off for making my living by uncovering what people wanted to stay hidden. Separateness. Everybody had their secrets, and no one liked having them aired in public. I didn't either, which was why I was trying so hard not to make a fool of myself in this investigation.

The beehive continued to buzz as I stuck my hands in my pockets, whistled a low tune, and wondered how many of the people in this room would still be alive by the end of the war. I had never been so patriotic that I was willing to charge blindly into the jaws of death. As a matter of fact, I thought anyone who was needed his head examined. The brass was going to think up plenty of ways to get us all killed, while keeping themselves safe and cozy, sipping good brandy in comfortable quarters. I saw no reason to help them get me killed. I planned to do my best to get Mom's oldest boy home again, safe and sound. I shook my head, like a drunk trying to get ahold of himself. I needed to watch out for this Norwegian liberation fever. It might be catching.

"Yes, Lieutenant Boyle?"

I was so lost in thought that I hadn't noticed Jens hang up his phone. He was looking at me as if I were a door-to-door salesman. I stopped whistling. I could tell he was still steamed at having his claim to jurisdiction overruled by Major Harding and by my role in charge of the investigation. I didn't blame him a bit. No cop would want an investigation taken away from him, and the head of security here wouldn't feel any different. Didn't mean I was going to cut him any slack.

"Captain Iversen," I began in my best imitation of military formality, "I need to ask you a few questions." I watched him carefully. There was no surprise on his face at being approached as a witness or perhaps a suspect. Instead of indignation, I saw resignation.

"Please, sit down." He gestured at the chair facing his desk. I pulled it closer to his desk, sat down, and leaned forward so we could speak quietly. Jens moved aside a map, then thought about it and folded it up so I couldn't see it. He was the head of security, after all.

"Captain, first let me say that I didn't ask for this assignment. I don't like interfering with your work here, but I have to follow up every lead that comes my way."

"Lieutenant, I don't like finding the dead body of one of my officials and then having the responsibility for the investigation taken away from me. This should be a Norwegian matter. But as a soldier I understand the need to follow orders, so ask your questions."

He was hanging on to his dignity. Not only

had the death of Knut Birkeland happened on his watch, but his authority had been undercut by Harding, and now here I was to question him. Part of me felt bad for him. Most of me liked it. It meant he was off balance, worried about his status and what it was I knew. It was all a good start for an interrogation. I leaned in even closer.

"Jens," I said in a soft and friendly voice, "why didn't you tell me where you were this morning?"

His eyes widened and he gave out a nervous little laugh. "What do you mean? I was with you."

"No, Jens, before we found the body. Before he went out the window."

He leaned back in his chair and exhaled deeply. He kept quiet, which was the smartest thing anyone being questioned can do. Unfortunately for him, my dad had taught me well how to deal with a quiet suspect. Be quiet right back at them. Let them fill the silence. We sat there, looking at each other. He twitched a bit, and his eyes darted around the room behind me. I stared at him, thinking confident thoughts. When he started tapping a pencil on the desktop I knew it wouldn't be much longer.

"Billy, what do you want more than anything else?"

That was easy; so easy that it came out with a sigh.

"To go home," I said.

Jens laughed again, not nervously but the kind of laugh that hides a real pain or shares one. "Yes, to go home. Imagine that you haven't been home for years instead of weeks, and that the Nazis occupy your home. Now think about how badly you'd want to get back." I had the fleeting thought that some parts of Boston at night would be tough even on the Nazis, but I knew what he meant.

"I'd want to get back real bad, to even the score. Just like you do now."

"Yes, I do, now that everything has changed. Within a few months we will be in Norway, taking it back from the Germans. We've been dreaming about this since 1940."

"You're telling me all this because . . . ?"

"Because as much as I want to be part of this invasion, as important as it is to me, I won't answer your questions. No matter what the consequence."

"Jens, I already know that shortly before six o'clock you were seen returning to your room. You had left your door unlocked and went in very quietly. Then you told me the sentries woke you about six thirty after they found Birkeland's body. I know you were out of your room in the early morning hours and that you lied about the time you were up. Why not just fill in the blanks?"

"No."

"Were you in Birkeland's room that morning?"

"Not until I entered with you."

"Were you in anyone else's room that morning?" I could see him think about that question. Evidently he didn't mind answering questions that skirted the issue of why he was out of his room. I was beginning to get an idea.

"No, I can tell you that much."

"Did you see anyone else?" He shook his head.

"Does that mean you didn't see anyone or won't tell me?"

"Billy, I am not withholding any information that would bear on Knut Birkeland's death. I know you are somewhat single-minded, but not everything that happens here has to do with his death. Some things are personal . . . private."

"Until I know that something doesn't matter, it does."

"That does indeed make you single minded, or childlike, as if the whole world revolves around you and your needs. It doesn't, Billy. The world goes on, with or without us or even Knut Birkeland. The invasion will go on, regardless of what you find out."

Not exactly, I thought to myself. Maybe the invasion, yes. It will go on. But this is my world — the investigation, the intrusion, the hanging on until it's solved or I run out of air speed and ideas. Until then, this is my universe and I'm the center of it, and I like it just like that.

"Are you telling me to back off?" I asked.

Jens shrugged, as if it didn't really matter.

"You cannot even be sure Birkeland was murdered. It may have been a suicide. You have to admit it is somewhat ironic that one death receives so much attention in the midst of a war with thousands of deaths. Here we are working on plans for the invasion and the Underground uprising. Who knows how many on both sides will die?"

"So what's just one death when we can look forward to so many more?"

"I mean . . . there is so much to look forward to, so much to do. And we will need every man to help. Why not just leave things to the Almighty? Perhaps if Birkeland really was murdered, God will punish the killer. As you say, there will be death enough very soon."

"I'm only a cop, or whatever I am now in this job. I make it a practice to leave God's punishment up to him, as soon as I send a bad guy his way. You need to understand something, Jens. I'm going to find out what happened. In order to do that, I need to know everything that went on this morning, whether you like it or not. Even if it hurts somebody. Even if it hurts her."

Jens jumped like he'd been poked with a sharp stick. Wow, had I been right.

"Who?"

"Her. The woman you're protecting. The woman who was in your room last night. The woman who you probably escorted back to her quarters, being such a gentleman. Am I right, or were you off killing Knut Birkeland instead?"

Jens just about collapsed into a chair. His hands covered his face as he tried to mask his emotions. *"Gudshjelp meg,"* he said in a whisper. "God help me." He rubbed his eyes as if he were very tired.

"I did not kill Knut Birkeland, Billy. If you can figure out everything else, you should know that much."

"What about her? Who is she?" Well, he was the one who called me single-minded.

"It's more . . . complicated than you might

226

think. If it would help you, I would tell you, but there is nothing she could know. And it would cause . . . great pain."

"Tell me one thing, Jens. Did you take her all the way back to her room?"

"No, I didn't want us to be seen together. I took her down to the first floor, and then she went on from there."

"Then I need to talk to her. She may have seen something after she left you, something she's not even aware of."

"No. I will not put her through this."

"It sounds like this goes beyond your normal slap and tickle, Jens."

"What does that mean?"

"How do you say 'romp in the hayloft' in Norwegian?"

A limp smile lifted his lips. "I think I understand. As I said, it is complicated. Much more complicated than that."

"You love her, and she's married?"

"That would be simple. I have fallen in love with her, but. . . ."

His voice trailed off, and his eyes wandered to some distant place. Suddenly I realized that he was right. It probably was very complicated. So complicated that it made him miserable and might lead him to give up his dream of fighting his way back home.

"But what, Jens?"

"Her husband is missing in action. He is a ghost that haunts her. Now leave me alone."

CHAPTER THIRTEEN

I left him alone as soon as I realized I wasn't going to get another word out of him. I walked down to the main entrance, went outside between the twin grim sentries, and gazed along the road we had driven down just two days ago, unaware of the undercurrents in Beardsley Hall that were stirring, as someone was getting ready to kill Knut Birkeland. I took a deep breath and let it out, hoping the fresh air would clear my mind and let me see a pattern emerging. Nothing. Nothing but the smell of flowers, damp greenery, and the faint pungent smell of gun oil hanging in the still air. The sentries' Sten guns gleamed, the dark metal glistening with the perfume of death. I stepped off the smooth steps and onto the crushed stone driveway, liking the feel and sound of it underfoot.

I wondered about Jens and his female friend with the missing husband. That would throw a monkey wrench into his plans. It was one thing for a woman to have an affair right under her husband's nose, at least then he had some chance of finding out. But missing in action? Maybe dead, maybe not? Maybe never to be seen again, maybe about to walk through the door tomorrow? That's competition.

He was intent on protecting her, whoever she was, and I was lucky to have gotten anything out of him before he clammed up. Now I needed to talk to Major Cosgrove, to ask about his early morning stroll with Skak. He hadn't been straight with me, but then again, who had? Every time I turned around I found somebody where they shouldn't have been. I wasn't any closer to finding a spy, the missing gold, or even figuring out if there really had been a murder. Suicide still didn't make any sense to me, not for a guy like Knut Birkeland. He might have killed somebody if he got mad enough, but I couldn't see him taking his own life. It was too introspective an act for a fellow like him.

But even with every Tom, Dick, and Lars wandering around Beardsley Hall before dawn, I couldn't place anyone in Birkeland's room, much less figure out how they could've killed him. I was tired and I was getting a headache. I was fed up with

Norwegians and their holy crusade and healthy early morning walks. Maybe Jens had it right. Let God sort things out. I thought about saying a little prayer for help, but it had been so long since I had been to confession that I figured it would only piss God off. Maybe I should go to Mass this Sunday. I could write Mom and tell her about it, which would definitely make her day. But though it seemed like a good idea now, I knew come early Sunday morning, I might feel differently. I thought about food and drink and Daphne, not in that order. And sleep. Sleep would be good, too. But Cosgrove was bugging me. Why hadn't he told me he was out with Skak at six o'clock in the morning? He might have seen someone or something, like blood on Vidar Skak's hands. OK, that was a little overboard, but it would have made things a lot easier. I knew it would bother me all night if I didn't deal with it now, so like a good little investigator I went back inside to find the major.

Cosgrove and Harding had set up shop in the map room. It was a long room on the first floor, looking out over the gardens, a row of high windows illuminating the room with the gray light that filtered through the thick clouds. It was summer, but damp and cloudy seemed to be what passed for summer weather here. There were large map tables set up on trestles under the windows, and a long conference table along the opposite wall. File cabinets and map cases filled the middle of the room, and Harding and Cosgrove were standing in front of one of the map cases, its wooden front panel open. I was about to make a crack about English weather when I saw the look on their faces. Something was wrong.

"Boyle!" Harding snapped. "Shut that door and get in here."

I turned and closed the heavy oak door behind me. I walked over to the map case. Harding was peering inside while Cosgrove examined the lock on the open door. They looked like a couple of fancy dress cops on burglary detail.

"Someone steal the Beardsley family silver?"

"Nothing has been stolen, Lieutenant," Cosgrove said. "But someone has been in this map case. All the Operation Jupiter maps are stored in here." I looked at the case, but nothing appeared to be disturbed.

"How do you know someone got into the case, sir?" I asked Harding.

"Look in here, Boyle. See these compartments?" The inside of the cabinet was subdivided into sixteen small compartments, four rows of four, each large enough for a rolled map and accompanying documents. Ten of them, starting at the top left, were full.

"These ten maps represent the overall strategic plan for Operation Jupiter. Naval, air and ground forces, plus special operations. They include unit strength, dates, everything. And they've been moved. Each map is numbered, one through ten, the first in the upper left-hand corner, then the rest in order."

"They're out of order?" I asked.

"No. They're exactly in order." Harding allowed himself a sly smile as he looked up at me. "I reversed maps six and seven when I put them away. I figured if anyone unauthorized got in here, they would think it was their mistake and put them back in the right order."

"This confirms it, young man," Cosgrove said. "The spy is here among us."

"Why would a spy need to break in to see these? Aren't you briefing the Norwegians on all this?"

"Need to know, Lieutenant, it's all about need to know," Harding answered. "No one here needs to know all the details. We briefed the king and his top aides on the big picture, without much detail. Then we worked our way through the ranks, by branch of service. The navy people got their briefing, but nothing about parachute drops or Underground activity, for instance. Each group got a detailed briefing, but only on their part of the plan. Whoever broke in here got detailed information about everything."

"Look here, Harding," said Cosgrove as he pointed to the lock. There were faint scratches on the inside of the keyhole.

"Yep," I said, sticking my nose between them, "the lock's been jimmied. Think he took pictures with a miniature camera or some sorta spy gadget?"

"I doubt it," Harding said. "It would be too incriminating. It wouldn't be hard to memorize the key elements. Or write them down later. The advantage we have is that he doesn't know we're on to him."

"It occurs to me, gentleman," Cosgrove said as he retreated to a comfortable chair and settled his bulk, "that this may have happened while poor Birkeland was meeting his maker."

Cosgrove puffed out his cheeks, as if the act of sitting had taken all his energy. I looked at Harding, who nodded his head thoughtfully as he gazed into the case. Then I looked at the lock. It was a simple job, nothing an apprentice second-story man couldn't pop open on the first try.

"You're right," he said. "I checked these last night and they were fine. The room was empty all night until 0800 hours. Then people have been in here all day and there wouldn't have been any opportunity to break into the case. We had a briefing scheduled for this afternoon, and this was the first time I've opened the case today."

"It could have happened during the night, or perhaps it is connected with the Birkeland business," huffed Cosgrove. "If it was murder, that is. Have you found anything today, Lieutenant?"

My mind was reeling with possibilities, but I tried to focus on what I had originally come in for. I looked at each of them and thought about how much I could say. Or should say, if I cared about my military career. Not caring much had its benefits, I decided.

"I learned that I need to ask you a few questions, sir," I said to Cosgrove. "Do you mind?"

"What is this, Boyle?" Harding demanded. His eyes narrowed in irritation. Cosgrove appeared amused.

"I need to talk to everyone who was up and around early this morning. Major Cosgrove never told me that he met Vidar Skak for a half-hour walk at six o'clock this morning. I wonder why, sir."

Cosgrove just laughed and pounded his hand on the arm of the chair. "Very amusing, young man! Very amusing indeed. We have a dead government minister, invasion plans have been read by a spy, and you want to know what *I* was doing this morning! Shall we ring up the prime minister and ask him for his whereabouts while you're at it?"

Cosgrove stroked his mustache and continued to chuckle as he looked at Harding with a raised eyebrow that said: See what an idiot this boy is.

Harding sighed and shook his head. "Boyle, not everything that goes on here is your business. Some things are beyond your reach, and Major Cosgrove is absolutely beyond suspicion. Got it?"

"Yeah, I get it," I said, my voice going up a bit, even though I tried to keep it under control. "You guys want me to investigate a death and find a spy, but not if it bothers you and your little plots. Well, it don't work that way!"

"Lieutenant," Cosgrove said, "I don't know if I am more offended by your tone, your atrocious grammar, or the fact that you've referred to me as one of 'you guys.'

I've been accused of many things, but never that!"

He kept his look of amusement, but his eyes drilled me. Harding was steamed. I was nowhere. I wondered if the whole war was going to be like this. I tried to speak calmly.

"Look, sirs, in order to find anything out, I need to ask a lot of questions. Most of them lead nowhere. Once in a while, they lead to something that doesn't add up. Something out of place. Maybe just a little innocent lie, or something left unsaid. That's the kind of thing I look for. I can't work on solving a crime when some of the main players are out of bounds. It doesn't mean that I think Major Cosgrove did it, but maybe something Skak said this morning will help. Or maybe you saw something, something that means nothing to you but could be an important missing piece to me."

"Young man," Cosgrove said as he leaned forward earnestly, "I understand and sympathize, actually. But there are certain reasons of security that apply. Need to know and all that. You'll simply have to make do."

"Boyle," Harding added, "we need you on the job, but we can't tell you everything. There are plenty of generals who don't know half of what you know already. We have to draw the line here. Do whatever you need to do to find out what happened, but you must trust us on this. Besides, what could the major tell you that would help you find out if Birkeland was murdered or killed himself?"

I sat down, feeling defeated. They were actually making sense. This was war, not the cops. There were different rules here. Cosgrove sat back in his chair, smiling at his own logic. Harding stood next to him, arms folded, watching me, waiting to see if I'd fall in line or cause more problems.

"Well, I don't know which is my big problem right now. I hate not knowing, having a blank spot in my investigation. But I guess I understand what you're saying."

I felt like I was surrendering to some superior logic that had proved me wrong but might let a murderer get away. My head was pounding, and I rubbed my temples to ease the pain building up inside.

"Boyle, you're bleeding," Harding said, pulling my hand away from my head. "You must have opened up one of the cuts from the wood splinters."

Harding held my hand in front of my face so I could see. My fingers were stained sticky red and I felt a stream trickle down the side of my face like a tear. I pulled out my handkerchief and tried to stop it before it hit my collar. It seemed so long ago that Kaz, Knut Birkeland, and I were standing out there playing soldier. Blood on my face, blood on the roses — where would it show up next? I felt dull and stupid, a child in the company of adults, needing a bandage. Something wasn't adding up. I felt an idea trying to claw its way up from the back of my mind. I looked at the blood on the handkerchief. Where would it show up next?

"Wait a minute!" I said. I held up my hand as if to stop any other thoughts, to clear my mind. I knew the answer had to do with that bullet. Where would it show up next? I tried to visualize that morning. Kaz had been on my right, and Birkeland on my left. There had been smoke and confusion. I closed my eyes and watched it all happen, trying to slow things down. The commandos sneaking up on us . . . explosions . . . burning tanks . . . shots . . .

"Knut Birkeland *was* murdered," I said. "On the second try."

"What? How could you know that for certain?" Cosgrove's mouth gaped open, as if he had just heard a monkey guess his birthday.

"The bullet that almost got me was not a stray or a mistake in loading. It was an assassination attempt, intended for Knut

Birkeland."

"But the bullet struck just inches from your head," Cosgrove sputtered.

"Which also put it inches from Birkeland," Harding said slowly, one step behind me, as the thought took hold and he started to see how it might have worked. Everything fell into place.

"Yes, sir. Whoever fired was low and to the left. I just happened to be there. Maybe it was his rifle or maybe he got jostled. It was a good idea, though. All he had to do was slip one live round in the chamber before the exercise. When he loaded the clip of blanks, it would have been waiting there, ready to go on the first shot. With all that firing, no one would notice that the shooter didn't work his bolt, since he already had the live round loaded. He could just aim and fire."

"You might be right, Boyle," Harding said. Cosgrove nodded, as if he was reluctant to agree, but couldn't find anything to criticize. He wasn't amused anymore.

"I know I am. There's no reason at all to try and kill me, I've got nothing to do with this Norwegian business. But we know someone wanted Birkeland dead, so it fits perfectly."

"Could it be the spy, I wonder?" asked

Harding.

"Not unless the Germans prefer bomb-ings and commando raids to an uprising," said Cosgrove. "Can't see the spy making that decision in favor of Skak and acting on it. Doesn't make sense."

"None at all," I agreed. "I think that we've got a murderer and a spy, and if we're lucky, finding one will help us find the other. Their paths had to have crossed at some point. Maybe one of them even knows about the other."

Cosgrove and Harding exchanged glances, and then looked away from me, back at the map case. I got up and headed toward the door. Then I remembered something I needed Cosgrove to do. I stopped and turned around. I drew myself up into what I hoped looked like parade rest and tried to look and sound military. I thought it might improve my chances.

"Major Cosgrove, sir, I do have a request for some information. I don't believe it would conflict with security concerns."

"Very well, Lieutenant," Cosgrove said, pleased to grant a small favor. "What do you need?"

"I'd like a list of all British and Norwegian female staff posted here who are married to military personnel listed as missing in action, or who we know are POWs."

"Should be a simple matter. I will have it looked in to," Cosgrove said dismissively. "Now what are these other questions you have for me?"

"Oh, that's on a need-to-know basis, Major. When I need to know, I'll ask you." On my way out it occurred to me that if I hadn't been one myself, I would have had to conclude all officers were bastards.

I tracked down Daphne and Kaz and found them in Daphne's room, sitting on a couch with a tea service in front of them. Kaz had his feet up and his eyes closed, his head resting on Daphne's shoulder. Thinking, I'm sure. Teatime had come and gone, and I was tired, frustrated, hungry, and jealous that it wasn't me napping on the couch next to Daphne. I wanted a change of scenery and a drink. Or two.

"Daphne, is there a pub around here?"

"Yes, in the village, but we need permission to take the car —"

"Permission granted," chimed in Kaz, his eyes still closed.

Daphne nudged his shoulder. "Dear, you can't decide that. Either Major Harding or the ETOUSA transport officer —"

"Daphne, let's not get all official. I just met with the major and he told me to utilize all available resources for this investigation. That must include the staff car. Now let's get out of here."

It was a short drive to the village of Marston Bridge, one of the many rural farm hamlets surrounding the town of Wickham Market, which we had passed through on our drive in. Marston Bridge was a small cluster of houses and shops surrounding, naturally enough, a bridge. We drove over the arched stonework span and Daphne pulled the staff car off the road, next to a timber-framed white-plaster building with a thatched roof. The once whitewashed masonry looked like it hadn't seen a brush and bucket for a century or so. A worn sign hung over the door with a picture of a big red deer, although the lettering below it told me this was the Red Stag Inn. Our staff car looked out of place next to the collection of bicycles that leaned against an old oak tree in front of the inn. It looked quiet, cozy, and comfortable, like a neighborhood bar back in Southie, the kind of place where folks were naturally suspicious of strangers and foreigners. It didn't look a thing like it, but it made me think of Kirby's Bar, a local joint on the corner of D Street and Broadway. Guys coming home from work on the streetcar would get off there, have a beer or two with their buddies, talk about baseball or politics, then go home for supper. I can't remember a time I saw anybody in there I didn't know well enough to say hello to on the street, except maybe those crazy cousins of Packy Ryan's from Back Bay. I thought about those guys and wondered what our reception in this neighborhood bar would be.

As soon as Kaz opened the door for Daphne, I could hear the low murmur of voices and laughter. We entered and stood in the darkened foyer as I blinked my eyes to get used to the change. As soon as I could see clearly, the voices died down; a few oblivious souls in the back cut off in mid-sentence as they noticed the silence. Heads turned. I guess a beautiful WREN, a little Pole, and a Yank didn't walk in here every day. We took off our hats and stepped in, pairs of eyes following us in frank assessment.

It was a low-ceilinged room, with dark oak timbers spaced out every couple of yards. To our left was a small front room, a bench along the walls and small tables scattered about, just big enough for pints and ash-trays. The bar filled the rest of the room — rough, wood stained, dark with spilled ale and nicotine. It was all men on the left, at the bar or sitting on the bench, watching a dart game in progress. About half a dozen larger tables were arranged on the right side of the room, and small groups of men and women were seated at those, some eating and others drinking. Daphne headed for the only empty table, being at least from the same country as the locals.

"Good evening," she said to the barkeep, nodding her head in respect. He was a stout older guy, who stood behind the bar like a drill sergeant surveying new recruits. He had a pipe clenched between his teeth and nodded back, a clipped "Evenin' " delivered in response. Muted whispers filled the air, our presence seeming to push the liveliness out of the room. Figuring a village pub in England couldn't be that different from Kirby's, I put on my best friendly grin and walked up to the bar, doing a quick calculation of the pound notes in my wallet and the number of people in the pub. Lucky for me I had researched the cost of drinking in England at the Coach & Horses.

"Good evening," I offered with a smile. "Would it be out of place to buy pints all around?"

"A Yank are yer? First one we've seen here. About time, too!"

Now all eyes were on me, Americans and

free pints being in short supply. He turned and called into the kitchen just behind the bar. "Mildred, come out here. We've got a rich Yank visiting us offering to buy pints all around!" Mildred emerged from the kitchen, carrying two plates of fish and chips in each hand. She delivered them to a table and turned, wiping her hands on a dishrag she had slung over her shoulder.

"Well start pulling pints then, why don't you, like the young gentleman asked for? You don't want the first Yank you meet up with to think you don't appreciate his business, right?"

I could see Mildred was the brains of the operation. The barkeep chuckled to himself as he grabbed glasses off a shelf and started pulling pints. The locals gathered around and I was greeted with "Well done, Yank" and "Thank ye" as well as smiles and slaps on the back. We were all pals in minutes.

"You'll have to excuse my man, Lieutenant," Mildred said as she took me by the arm. "He's been waiting for you Americans to show up and drink yourselves silly in his pub for months now. Plumb struck him dumb when the first one to show up buys drinks all around. Now sit down with your friends and let me know what you'd like. Don't need ration cards for the fish and chips, seein' as we're so near the coast and can get all the fish we want, long as the men don't go too far off shore and catch a U-boat instead, hee hee! Chips aren't a problem either, since we got plenty potatoes planted out back."

"Fish and chips will be great, Mildred. It looks delicious."

"Oh, well, thank you." Mildred blushed at the compliment, and then turned back to her husband, raising her voice to command level. "Now, Robert, you pull the next three pints for our visitors here. No need for them that's bought 'em to wait 'til last!"

Robert obeyed, and with an anticipatory smile set up the three pint glasses on the bar in front of me, the thick foam perched on top. I could see he was envisioning me as the first wave in an invasion of Yanks, all thirsty and gripping pound sterling notes in their hands. I decided it was best to let him believe what he wanted. Kaz came over and took two pints back to the table. I sipped mine. It was ale, dark amber colored. Then I took a gulp. It was good, real good, sharp on the tongue and easy going down.

"Is this a local ale, Robert?"

"Aye, Wickham's Ale, they make it in the brewery over in Wickham Market."

"What do the Norwegians like to drink?"

"Them folk up at Beardsley Hall? Don't see too many of 'em here. They tend to stick to themselves. Got their own food and drink up there, I guess. Once in a while, some of them come down here for a meal, but they have to cycle in. They don't come in a grand car like you did. Do all American lieutenants have their own car and driver?"

"No, Robert," I chuckled. "These are my friends. We're at Beardsley Hall for a few days and we wanted a bit of a change of fare. What about the British civilians working at the hall? Do the ladies come here often?"

Robert glanced at the table, and took in the fact that Kaz and Daphne were together. He gave me a knowing look and leaned over the bar as he handed out pints. "Sorry, Yank, but all the girls who work there go to Wickham Market for their fun. They have a bus what brings 'em in and carries 'em back. There's restaurants, pubs, and a movie house. Not like little Marston Bridge at all! Look around you, and you'll see all the entertainment that's to be had for miles. A few farmers and old folk throwing darts, that's about it. You'll have to look elsewhere for a pretty lass."

"Thanks for the tip." I raised my glass to Robert and left him happily pulling pints as

I walked over to our table.

"You look quite at home in an English pub, Billy," Kaz said as he lifted his glass in salute.

"Yes," said Daphne, "you've made friends for life already. That was very nice of you."

"Yeah, I'm a swell guy. I was really hoping for some inside dope on the Beardsley Hall staff from the local gossips, but they don't seem to mix very much."

"What is dope, inside?" asked Kaz, turning to Daphne. "Do you know, Daphne?"

"Yes, I saw a film with James Cagney and he used that expression. Information, right, Billy?" Daphne asked me.

"Yeah. Same thing as the skinny. The low down. The truth. Why do you want to know all this stuff?"

"I want to learn to speak American," said Kaz with a straight face. "I know the king's English, but someday we want to go to New York City. I want to fit right in and understand all the slang."

"We love American gangster movies," Daphne added, "but sometimes they're terribly hard to understand. We'll count on you for the low down skinny." She said the last words dramatically, proud of the new phrase.

"It's the skinny or the low down, but not

both. So, tell me, what's the low down on what you two found out today?"

"Not much, I'm afraid," said Kaz. "Or at least not much of any help. The household staff are mostly Norwegians or of Norwegian ancestry, drawn from those already living in England before the war. They're a tight-lipped group, very protective of the king and their cause. They all know about the late-night carryings-on, but won't name names. I did find out that a number of people were out and about in the early morning. The king — and Rolf of course — went hunting together at four thirty. Skak and Cosgrove were out around six o'clock, taking a walk. Did you know that?"

I nodded.

"Skak was up early, about five thirty, which was his usual routine. Several people also saw Jens going back to his room from somewhere about the same time," Kaz continued. "One maid said she saw someone turn a corner up the stairs, perhaps either Jens or Anders, she couldn't tell. No one else claimed to have seen Anders out until after the body was found. Of course there were staff on duty all night in the radio room, guards outside patrolling the grounds, that sort of thing. But no one else in that wing of the hall, as far as I can tell."

"That's it?" I asked.

Kaz nodded, gave an apologetic smile, and drank his ale.

"I didn't do much better," said Daphne. "The girls didn't exactly bare their souls to me. They don't think much of the strict rules here, and they've probably all broken a few of them. No one would admit to leaving their rooms at night or having guests, but there was enough giggling to tell me some of them are expert at it."

"Any of them see anything in the morning?"

"No. They were adamant that they sleep as late as humanly possible. Probably true, they're fairly young. They were all sad about Knut Birkeland. They thought he was a kind man."

"What do they think of Vidar Skak?" I asked.

"Not much. He's the source of most of the rules they hate. Jens Iversen seems to be the buffer between Skak and the staff. They like Jens, but think he's a little odd. Needs to relax, one of them said. Then another girl said he looked more relaxed lately, and they all giggled again. I couldn't get anything else out of them."

"Jens has a lover," I said. "Someone he's protecting. I know he was escorting her

251

back to her room, but he won't say who she is."

"Gallant sort," said Kaz.

"She's married," I explained. "Her husband is missing. That's all I know."

"He feels guilty?" Daphne asked.

I thought about that. There was guilt, and then there was a deeper layer, when you felt guilty that you didn't feel guilty about something bad you did. The remnant of conscience, I remember Dad telling me. It was a few days after the argument with Basher, when he threw away that package. I came home from the evening shift to find him sitting out on the front stoop, smoking. He had started sitting on the stoop instead of up in his study for some reason, which was nice. It meant we could relax and talk. It was a fall evening and I unbuttoned my coat as we sat there, watching the cars drive slowly by and the front-porch lights wink out, one by one. Dad started to tell me about an interrogation he had run, and how he had to get at that remnant of conscience, to get a guy to show his remorse at his lack of remorse. To crack him open, he said, and start leading him down the road to confession. I remember all that he said, but what always stuck in my mind was just how nice it was sitting out there, shooting the breeze with my old man, and wondering what had led him out of his study and down to the front steps.

But that was then, and now I had to answer Daphne. Jens didn't strike me as the strictly guilty type, but he did have a certain sadness to him, as if he had disappointed himself. Remorse could fester into guilt, especially when there was a woman involved. And a war.

"He or she or both. All I know is that she might have seen something. Jens says it's complicated, and I can't disagree. I asked Cosgrove to find out who on the staff might have a MIA or POW husband."

"Maybe that's why the girls wouldn't tell me anything about her," Daphne said. "They must feel sorry for her. If they disapproved, they would've offered her up on a plate of gossip."

It made sense. Complicated, like Jens said.

"Did you find out what Cosgrove and Skak were doing on their walk?" Kaz asked.

"Skak takes a walk every morning at six. A man of precise habits, he says. Cosgrove, whom I don't see as the walking type, supposedly asked to go along to talk about Skak's plans for the underground. When I asked Cosgrove about it, he politely told me that it was a matter of security and to butt out."

"So we found out nothing today," Daphne said sadly.

"Something else happened." I gestured for them to lean in closer and whispered to them about the maps. Their eyes widened in surprise. It felt good to impart something new, even if it didn't help to figure out who the spy or the killer was.

"Who do you think —," Kaz asked before I cut him off.

"We shouldn't talk anymore about it here," I whispered. "But there's something else. It hit me today that the live round fired during the exercise wasn't aimed at me. It was a near miss, aimed at Birkeland."

"That means it was a planned murder," Kaz said thoughtfully. "The killer missed Birkeland at the exercise, so he got him in his room."

"In both cases, he went to great lengths to cover his tracks. If that bullet had hit Birkeland, there wouldn't have been any suspicion at all. It would've been just a tragic accident," I said. "But once you see both events as connected, then it's obvious it was premeditated murder."

"Murder? Or assassination?" Daphne asked in a low voice. "Are the maps and his death connected?"

"Connected, maybe, but I can't really see the same person at work on both. What's the advantage to the Germans of killing Birkeland? He was an important member of government, but what effect would his death have on the war?"

"None, really," shrugged Kaz.

"That's awfully callous, darling," responded Daphne.

"Yes, it is. But detectives must be objective and dispassionate, yes, Billy?"

"That's a good place to start, Kaz. But it usually gets complicated, much more complicated than you ever bargained for."

I thought about Jens again, and how he had described his relationship with the mystery woman. Complicated, but how complicated? Just how deep had he gotten himself? Were we sure the spy was a man? I drained my glass and went to the bar. This was thirsty work. Robert pulled another pint for me and I returned to my seat.

"Daphne," I asked as I sat down, "what do you know about Major Cosgrove?"

"He seems very well connected to intelligence circles. We think he works for MI-5, British military intelligence. But he claims to be just a liaison from the British General Staff, which fits in with his role here, so maybe our imaginations are overactive. Why? You don't suspect him of anything, do you?"

"Before we got here, did either of you ever tell him anything about me?" Kaz and Daphne looked at each other, maybe thinking I had drunk my limit. They each shrugged.

"No," Kaz answered. "We hadn't seen Major Cosgrove since a week before you got here. Why?"

I leaned in and whispered again. This was getting to be a habit.

"When we first got here, and Cosgrove walked in on us, he said two things about me. First, in Harding's room, he said he doubted a lieutenant fresh from the States could find a spy when MI-5 had failed."

"So?" Daphne asked.

"So how did he know I was fresh from the States? I could've been here for months."

"Well," said Kaz, "most Americans are here fresh from the States. It could have just been an informed guess."

"Could have," I agreed. "But I doubt he could have guessed I was from Boston."

"What do you mean?" Kaz asked.

"Later, at lunch, when I said I hadn't heard about the gold being smuggled out of Norway, he got snotty and asked if they didn't report the war news in Boston. It didn't strike me until later, but then I asked myself — how did he know those two things — that I was new here and from Boston?"

"You do have a distinctive accent, Billy," Kaz said, thinking it through. "You tend to drop your r's at the end of a word. It's noticeable, but then I'm a student of language. Is that a purely Boston accent?"

"Yeah, I guess so. But would an Englishman know what a Boston accent sounded like? Not a Beacon Hill accent, but a real Irish South Boston delivery?"

"No," said Daphne. "You do sound terribly American, but I wouldn't know a New York accent from a Boston one unless you pointed out the difference. I doubt Major Cosgrove would either. He's not very fond of Americans, you know, thinks them brash and arrogant. He'd think it beneath him to discern any difference."

"What do you think," I asked her, "about Americans?"

"You are brash and arrogant, or at least more so than we English. We could use more brashness and you a bit less. But, back to Cosgrove. What do you think it means, if he knows more about you than he lets on?"

"I think it means he can't be trusted."

"Here you are, my dears!" Mildred's

singsong voice interrupted us as she laid down three steaming plates of fish and chips. "You tuck into that now!"

I inhaled the delicious aroma of the fried fish. I glanced up at Daphne and Kaz, who were looking at each other in stunned silence, taking in what it might mean not to be able to trust a representative of the General Staff, if that was what he really was. Kaz's glasses steamed up, and I thought, Right, that's just how I feel. Can't see a damned thing and no clue as to what the hell is going on.

"Not trust him? What does that mean?" asked Daphne, as she absorbed the implications. "Why would the major hide the fact that he knows something about you? There must be a reasonable explanation."

"Yes, what purpose would it serve?" Kaz asked as he wiped his glasses.

"Excellent questions. I mean to pursue them tomorrow, among other things. Right now I intend to demolish this plate of food."

I tried to sound confident and upbeat. In charge. Three pints later I almost believed it myself.

CHAPTER FOURTEEN

"No, Boyle, you cannot question the king!"

I was sitting across from Major Harding, who was at his desk in the map room. He was sitting upright in his chair, not a wrinkle showing on his uniform, his clear brown eyes drilling me dead center. I was trying not to slouch, my uniform jacket smelled faintly of ale and smoke, and last time I looked in the mirror my eyes were more red than their usual blue. I was trying to ignore the jackhammer going off in my head and concentrate on being told off. I vaguely remembered buying some more pints the night before, someone, maybe me, singing; and Daphne driving us home. Wait, make that an angry Daphne driving us back, and it was me and Kaz singing.

By the number of pound notes left in my wallet, we must've had a really good night. I know Robert, the innkeeper, did. Harding wasn't too happy about us having taken the car without permission, but he was more interested in learning how the investigation was going. He must've been in a fairly good mood, though, since there was coffee for two. On the other hand, it was six thirty in the morning, or rather 0630 hours, as the orderly who knocked on my door a while ago had informed me. But that was pure Harding. He must've been up early playing another round of switch the maps.

After the first cup of joe had cleared the fur off my tongue, I told Harding I needed to speak to the king. Rolf had gone up to the base at Southwold, and I needed to know if he and the king had run across anything suspicious. They were the first ones up and about the house, I explained to Harding, as if that was enough reason to question royalty.

"King Haakon is off limits to you, soldier, and that's an order. Understand?"

"What I understand is that I've got one hand tied behind my back. I've got nothing new to report because you won't let me do what I need to do."

"You've got nothing because you're sitting on your ass around here whining to me. Get out of here and question Rolf if you want. Do something useful, but keep out of my way. And away from the king."

"That settles that. Sir." I reached for the silver coffee pot and poured myself another cup. No reason to try another frontal assault. I added a sugar cube and thought maybe I should ease off a bit. After all, here I was, pouring coffee from a silver service and stirring in real sugar, not that saccharin stuff they were using since sugar got rationed. Why rock the boat? I could end up living in a tent somewhere, standing in line for chow slopped into a tin mess kit.

"I didn't expect you to give up so easily, Boyle, but I'm glad you're wising up to how we do things around here. You may end up being useful after all."

Damn! I had just about talked myself into going along. It would've been fine because I was ready to believe it was my own idea. Now I had to respond, even though it was to a know-it-all superior officer spouting off at me. I always hated being told what I had to do. Probably why I never did well in school. Looked like I wasn't going to do any better in the army. I took a gulp and let the hot, sweet black coffee kick in.

"Yeah, I'm beginning to get the picture. But there's one thing I don't quite understand, Major."

Harding set down his coffee cup with a little clink as the cup hit the saucer. A delicate sound, and it made me think of coffee cooked in the field, served in a tin cup in the rain. No clink, just the pitter-patter of rain on your helmet, rain in your coffee, water squishing in your boots. Harding looked pleased, like his slowest pupil had finally come around. I set my cup down, the coffee swishing around and spilling over the edge, hot on my fingers and overflowing the saucer. A real mess.

"What's that, Lieutenant?"

"What are you and Major Cosgrove setting me up for?"

There it was. The slightest blink registered and his pupils widened. In just a second everything was back to normal. Hard-ass Harding with the frozen face.

"We've been over this, Boyle. Just because we can't tell you everything —"

"That's not what I'm talking about, Major, and you know it. Or is Cosgrove running this little game all by himself?"

Harding half stood and slammed his right hand, palm down, on the desk. His coffee cup rattled and now he had coffee spilling into his saucer.

"Listen, you insubordinate son of a bitch —"

"No, you just listen, Major, sir!" We were both up on our feet now, spilt coffee forgotten. "When we first got here, Cosgrove and I were perfect strangers. So how did he know right away that I was just in from the States and that I came from Boston?"

"I don't know, Boyle, and what the hell would that mean anyway?"

"It means that Cosgrove knew about me, and then pretended not to. He lied. Why would he do that? More important, why would a lowly American lieutenant be involved with the schemes of cloak-and-dagger officers like you and Cosgrove?"

"What schemes? Maybe Cosgrove saw your file somewhere. He's very well informed."

"Why would MI-5 have my file?"

"Major Cosgrove works for the British General Staff, as special liaison to various governments in exile, not MI-5."

"Or at least that's the party line for those without need to know."

"Have it your way, Boyle: you're the center of a conspiracy by the British secret service, the proof of which is that Major Cosgrove knows you're from Boston."

Harding sat down again, gave out a little sharp laugh, and reached for a pack of Luckies. Lucky Strike Green, "Lucky Strike Green has gone to war." Just like me. Shake one out whenever you need it, use it up, grind it under your heel. Harding tapped the pack against two fingers and drew a cigarette out. He looked at me while he snapped his Zippo open and flicked the wheel, a tiny spark hitting the flint and producing a fine blue flame. He blew out a stream of smoke and spat out a stray bit of tobacco, shutting the Zippo with a metallic click and playing with it, turning it over in his right hand as he smoked. He shook his head and laughed again, but he didn't fool me. I had seen his tell, that little blink.

"Joke about it all you want, sir. I know something's not right here."

"Damn right, Boyle! One dead government official, one active spy, and your investigation is a bust. When are you going to uncover the truth about what's going on here?"

"Let me share a little professional secret with you, Major." I sat on the corner of his desk and leaned forward. "It's something my dad taught me about investigations. He's a cop too, better than I'll ever be. Last year I was banging my head against a wall, trying to find out the truth about a killing. Know what he told me?"

"What?" Harding sounded interested, and maybe a little worried.

"Never go after the truth; that's a waste of

time. Chase the lie, and let it lead you to the truth. And I know where the lie is here." I pushed off from his desk and stood at attention. "Permission to leave, sir?"

"Sure, Boyle," Harding said, shrugging as if all this made no difference at all. He stopped playing with the Zippo, set it down, and pointed at me with two fingers holding his cigarette. "But first, tell me, did you ever find that killer?"

"Yeah. The guy's wife shot him in the chest, then blamed it on a burglar."

"What'd you do, send her to the chair?" He smiled as if the thought amused him. I heard a door open behind me, and the sound of footsteps stopping, like when you walk into a room in the middle of an argument and realize you should have knocked. Two more footsteps backward, the door shut, and we were alone again.

"No, I didn't send her anywhere. Far as I know, she's still back home, looking after her two kids."

"So you didn't have enough evidence to arrest her?"

"I had plenty."

Harding stubbed out his cigarette, another little soldier gone. Don't worry, plenty more where that one came from. Lucky Strike Green has gone to war. Now he was irritated. This little story wasn't working out the way he thought it would.

"Damn it, Boyle, spit it out! Why didn't you take her in?"

"The bastard was screwing his own ten-year-old daughter. The wife caught him. First time the kids were out of the house she plugged him good. Two shots in the chest and he was toes up. She and her kids had been through enough, as far as I could figure it, and the guy would've got worse in prison anyway. Not a happy ending, but the best one I could come up with under the circumstances. I found the piece in the icebox, not exactly the hiding place of a master criminal. I dumped it in the Charles River and wrote it up as a burglary gone bad, the story she gave us."

Harding drummed his fingers on the desk, then picked up the Zippo again. He stopped and looked me straight in the eye. "What was the lie?"

"The burglary story. They didn't have a damn thing worth stealing."

Harding slammed the Zippo down, turned away from me, got up, and walked over to the window and looked out over the heath.

"Have Daphne drive you up to South-wold. Talk to Rolf Kayser. And be careful, Boyle."

I left, confused by his change in attitude. He sounded like he suddenly gave a damn. I mentally shrugged, chalking it up to the inscrutable ways of senior officers. I went off to find Daphne and Kaz, to begin to chase down a different lie. Time I took my own advice.

"Pack your bags, kids, we're blowing this joint."

I found Daphne and Kaz working their way through breakfast in the mess. I grabbed a cup of coffee and sat down with them. They both looked at me quizzically.

"I understand that we are leaving, Billy, but what are we blowing up?" Kaz asked, as if he were totally ready to set off explosives at my request.

"No, wait, we heard Humphrey Bogart say that in a film!" Daphne said excitedly, turning to Kaz and grasping his hand. "Remember, dear? This house is a joint, and we're leaving quickly, blowing out!" Her brown eyes gleamed with excitement at deciphering American slang. I was glad she liked it, since my supply of ten-dollar words was pretty short.

"Close enough, Daphne, and pretty good for an English gal. Harding gave his OK for you to drive me up to the base at Southwold. I'm going to question Rolf about what he might've seen that morning. The king, apparently, is off limits."

"You didn't ask Harding if you could interrogate King Haakon?" asked Kaz.

"Yep, and I've got the imprint of his boot on my backside to prove it. So, the next step is to talk to our friend Rolf and see what further confusion he can add to this investigation."

"I'll draft some orders for Majors Harding and Cosgrove to sign," Daphne said, warming to the idea of an excursion. "We'll need clearance just to get through the gate. It won't hurt to have English and American officers co-signing."

"Good idea. Add something about authorizing us to draw supplies while we're there. I only packed for a couple of days up here. I'm wearing out my Class A's and my only two shirts."

"What am I to do, Billy?"

"I need you to check out something for me, Kaz. We need a way to get you back to London to investigate Birkeland's business records. I want you to go through his bank accounts in England and look for any large deposits or withdrawals. Go to Lloyd's of London and see if he has insurance on his business and on himself. If so, who's the beneficiary? Go to SOE headquarters and find confirmation of damage done to his fishing business by the commando raids. Was that for real or just a sob story? Find out everything you can about his business and anyone who stands to benefit now that he's dead."

"The Special Operations Executive, not to mention Lloyd's or the banks, is not likely to let me walk in and go through its records," Kaz pointed out.

"I'll add a directive to the orders," Daphne spoke up, clearly taking charge of the planning, "giving permission to Lieutenant the Baron Piotr Augustus Kazimierz to review such records. I'll list it as a direct order from Major Cosgrove of the Imperial General Staff. The combination of continental aristocracy and the British General Staff should open doors for you, darling. That and your charm, of course."

She smiled at Kaz, eagerness and intelligence showing on her face. Daphne was enjoying this assignment as much as Kaz. He wanted to do something important for the war effort, understandable after what the Nazis had done to his family and his country. Daphne had a natural ability to solve problems, and it was being put to better use here than filing security forms back at headquarters. I could tell she knew it, too. She was blossoming with the added responsibilities, happy to be using her talents.

"Between my title and your brains and beauty, we can do anything!" Kaz kissed her, and Daphne blushed, looking around in mock horror at this un-English display of emotion. I sighed to myself, wishing I had a couple of my more-experienced buddies from the force helping me instead of these two lovebirds. Still, I could do worse. And they were great company.

"OK. Calm down, you two. Let's put our brains to work on how to get Kaz back to London quickly. Is there a train station around here?"

"No," answered Daphne, "not close by. But I do have an idea." She raised her eyebrow at Kaz. It took him a second, but he quickly brightened up.

"Oh, yes! Excellent idea, dear. Especially if I get to drive the Imp!"

Imp?

"OK, your turn to explain the lingo to me," I said. Before he could even ask, Daphne answered Kaz's unspoken question.

"Lingo means patois, dear," she said helpfully as she turned to me. "The Imp, Billy, is not some sort of rascal, but a 1934 Riley

Imp sports car. A red two-seater, and a complete delight to drive!"

"Where is this sports car, and how do we get gas for it?"

"It's at my parents' house, outside of Bury St. Edmonds, which is east of Cambridge. We can drive there today, pick up the Imp, and then Piotr can take the staff car to London."

"That's unfair," Kaz protested. "Billy, as the officer in charge of this investigation, deserves to be delivered to Southwold in an official staff car. Billy, you must insist!" I just smiled and held up my hands in surrender, not wanting to get between them.

"Darling," Daphne said soothingly, "I'm just thinking about the petrol. It's a shorter drive to Southwold, and Father probably doesn't have much to spare. Besides, the Imp is so much more fun to drive in the country."

"Billy, see how she mistreats me," Kaz appealed to me.

"Don't look at me for help. I'm trying to figure out if she'll let me drive!"

"Father gave me the Imp for my eighteenth birthday. I drive, Lieutenant!"

I didn't dare argue.

About an hour later Kaz and I were packed

and waiting for Daphne by the front entrance. We were in the main hallway, sitting on a hard wooden bench, our bags on the floor beside us. Kaz had one leg draped over the other, the cut of his trousers making him look casually elegant, like Ronald Colman in a tux. I looked at my pants. Baggy, wrinkled. My wool socks were itchy, and my feet hurt in their standard-issue size nine cordovan service shoes. Kaz's black shoes sparkled like he had just gotten a spit shine, and his socks didn't look like army issue. He looked at home in this grand house, as if he owned the place. I felt like the house dick at the Copley Plaza Hotel, the kind of guy whose job it was to hang around and try to fit in, but who knew he never would. I glanced at my watch after fifteen minutes. Kaz was whistling softly to himself.

"This, Kaz," I said, "is called cooling our heels. Get it?"

"Ah, yes. Since we are waiting, our feet are not moving and staying warm. Yes?"

"I guess so. The expression is used whenever you're waiting for someone, but especially women."

"Some things are worth cool heels, yes, Billy?"

"Yes, Kaz, especially in your case. Daphne is a beautiful woman."

"Beauty is not as hard to find as intelligence and a certain charming independence. Daphne combines all those attributes. Sometimes I can't believe how lucky I am."

"How did you two meet?"

Kaz smiled slyly. "Do you really mean what does such a beautiful woman see in a little Polish man with a heart condition, even if he has 'Baron' in front of his name?"

"No, I was just curious, really," I protested quickly, maybe too quickly. "But since you put it that way, tell me. How did you end up with Daphne?"

"You won't believe me, Billy."

"Try me. We've got time to kill."

"Murdering time. I must file that one away, Billy. I like it, especially in light of our investigation. A race against time to find a killer and perhaps a spy, and here we are killing time. Ironic, yes?"

"Sure, Kaz. Now, back to Daphne."

"Yes. It was one night at the Dorchester. I was dining alone and two couples were seated at the next table. Daphne and her younger sister, Diana. They were escorted by two young Royal Navy officers. They all looked elegant and quite dashing."

Kaz stopped, a smile on his lips as he remembered. Then a look of embarrassment swept over his face and he reddened slightly.

"This sounds melodramatic, but our eyes met. I was frankly staring at her, and when she looked up at me, I didn't look away. We just stared at each other, as if we were long-lost lovers who could not remember what the other looked like. It was actually quite uncomfortable, but I couldn't look away. I think her sister noticed, but the young men didn't. They were too busy trying to impress the girls. Then the air-raid warning sounded. Everyone got up to go into the shelter, but I stayed at my table."

"Why?" I asked.

Kaz stared down at the floor, his elbows resting on his knees. He took a minute before answering. A minute is a long time to wait when a guy has his eyeballs locked on to the linoleum.

"At the time, I had recently received word that my parents were dead. And I was recovering from an episode with my heart; I had been in hospital. There just didn't seem to be much point in . . . life. I was commissioned in the Polish army, but they wouldn't assign me any duties at all because of my condition."

"You didn't care if you lived or died."

"No, I didn't. It was quite inconsequential. Until that night, anyway."

"What happened next?" I asked.

"The most extraordinary thing. I heard Daphne tell her companions that she wasn't going to the shelter with them, that she was going to drink champagne with the Polish officer. Me. I was stunned. They got into an awful row over it, but you've seen how determined she can be."

"Uh huh. I assume she stayed?"

"Yes. I introduced myself as her sister dragged off the two officers. We sat by the light of a single candle, talked, and drank an excellent Cristal. I forget the vintage, but I remember her eyes sparkling in the candle-light. The bombing was mostly down by the docks, but a few strays dug up potatoes in Hyde Park across the way. I told her every-thing — about Poland, my family, my heart, my desires and fears . . . things I had never spoken out loud before. I tell you, Billy, it was as if an angel had floated down from heaven and sat beside me. When she touched my arm, it was as if all my burdens were lifted from me."

I didn't know what to say. My most ro-mantic experiences usually took place after three or four Guinnesses wore down the resistance of whatever girl would go out with me. This was the real thing, the kind of moment I'd only heard about in the movies. I didn't even know it actually happened. It made me feel strange, like an inexperienced high-school kid at his first dance. I struggled to find something to say to Kaz equal to the importance and depth of what he'd just told me. I came up with nothing.

"What did Daphne say?" popped out. "I mean it's kinda forward. . . ."

"She told me that she couldn't let the moment slip away and always wonder what would've happened if she had not spoken to me. And that if I thought that was improper, to tell her immediately, so she wouldn't waste her time with a bloody fool." He smiled fondly. "Pure Daphne. I told her I had always dreamed of a woman with her strength of character, and now that she was at my table, I wouldn't dare let her leave. That was right when one of those stray bombs dropped in Hyde Park. We both jumped in our seats and laughed. It was excellent punctuation! We talked for hours, and didn't even notice when the bombing stopped."

"Did her date come back?"

"No, but her sister did. Diana had sent the naval officers to another club on their own. She said they were rather boring, and that she couldn't wait for the bombing to end so she could come back and see what all the fuss was about. She's a remarkable young woman in her own right. Since that night, I always go down to the shelter when a raid comes over."

"So how did you guys both end up working for Ike?"

"Daphne was already assigned to the first American mission here, before General Eisenhower arrived. I was having no luck getting an assignment with the Polish Free Corps, so Daphne had her father contact the Foreign Office about securing the services of someone fluent in a number of European languages for the rapidly expanding American army headquarters staff. Suddenly I had an assignment, working for Major Harding, doing interpretation as needed, mostly of intelligence documents and memos to other governments in exile. And being with Daphne every day. It worked out rather well, don't you think?"

Before I could even think about the fact that with a bad ticker, in exile, with all his family dead and gone, Kaz was content and happy while I was miserable here, we both heard the click-clack of Daphne's heels coming down the hall.

"Ah! Daphne, and her heels are hot, right, Billy?"

"Don't you know it, buddy." I resisted the

impulse to say it wasn't just her heels. Kaz's story must've softened me up a little bit.

"As usual, my dears," Daphne said, standing in front of us, "you men lie about while I do the real work." She flashed a sheaf of official papers at us.

"Daphne, are these orders all for us?" I asked in astonishment at the multitude of sheets in her grasp.

"Of course they are. In triplicate, of course, a full set for each of us." She handed Kaz and me our copies. There was a cover sheet describing the issuing office — U.S. Army Command, European Theater of Operations — the effective duration of the orders, which was thirty days in this case, as well as the priority designation AAA.

The second sheet went into detail about the orders, numbered one through four. The first granted Daphne and me permission to enter the Southwold base. The second directed the base commander to make Lieutenant Rolf Kayser available to assist us, which was a nice way of saying we needed to question him. The third order directed the base commander to allow me to draw supplies from the quartermaster as needed. The fourth order was the longest, detailing Kaz's duties in London at the request of the Imperial General Staff, as ordered by Major Charles Cosgrove.

The orders spilled over onto a third page, with a final directive to all Allied personnel to assist us, named individually, in pursuit of our specific orders. Below that item were the scrawled signatures of Majors Harding and Cosgrove, as the authorizing parties. Pretty impressive.

"Looks like these could get us into Buckingham Palace," I said. "Nice work, Daphne. Let's hit the road."

Kaz took Daphne's bag and grabbed his own. As I headed out the door I heard him ask Daphne, "Explain to me, why must we hit the road? Has it been unruly?"

As I turned around to explain what I meant, I caught Kaz winking at Daphne and stifling a laugh.

"Oh, it's time to make fun of the Yank and the funny way he talks, is it?"

"What do you mean, Billy?" Kaz said, almost dissolving into laughter, "we'd love to assault the roadway with you!"

OK, I thought, as I dug down into my memory of gang talk from South Boston, you asked for it. "Look, I may be tooting the wrong wringer, but if we don't take a powder quick and tighten the screws on this jasper, it'll be a trip for biscuits."

I winked back at them and went out to

the car, hoping indeed that this wouldn't be a trip for biscuits: a trip somewhere with no clear purpose and no results.

CHAPTER FIFTEEN

"Billy, wake up, we are almost there!"

I had been stretched out in the backseat sawing logs when I awoke to Kaz hollering up front. I sat upright and rubbed my eyes. We were in the country, driving down a tree-lined lane with green fields and low rolling hills on either side. The sun was out for a change, lighting up the sky to a deep blue and reflecting off clumps of white puffy clouds moving swiftly above the landscape. It was a beautiful day.

"Here we are," said Daphne as she turned the staff car onto a gravel driveway. Ahead, a fair-sized stone cottage sat on the left side of the road. A line of white fence came from behind the cottage and ran down the length of the driveway beyond.

"Nice place, Daphne," I said.

Kaz turned and smiled at the look on my face.

"Yes, it is, but that's the gatekeeper's

house. Closed up for the duration right now."

"Daphne, are you a princess or something?" I asked as we passed two horses on the other side of the fence running or galloping or doing whatever horses do out in the country.

"No, silly," she answered. "You won't find any royalty here. Father has his knighthood, but that's not hereditary."

"Your father's a knight?" Images of a man in armor riding one of these horses floated through my mind. The Black Knight galloping across the pages of a picture book Danny loved to look at with me.

"Sir Richard Seaton," Kaz explained, "was knighted for his lifelong service to king and country. He was a captain in the Royal Navy in the Great War, now retired."

"If your father's a knight, what does that make your mother?" I asked.

"Mother died when we were quite young. Father raised all of us here, taught us how to ride and shoot, and tell right from wrong. It's been too long since we've all been together, Diana, Thomas, and I. I do miss them terribly." Daphne trailed off into silence and I decided to follow her example rather than ask another stupid question. The gravel crunched beneath our tires as I watched Daphne in the rearview mirror, her eyes staring at the road and maybe beyond, to images of children at play, when the world had been a far safer place.

We slowed to cross a stone bridge arched over a small stream and through the trees I could see a house up ahead. "Seaton Manor," Kaz announced, as if he had produced it from thin air. The house was long, whitewashed brick, two stories high, with a slate roof and tall chimneys at either end. Around the left side a low gated wall encompassed a courtyard with a stone barn at the opposite end. The white fence ended at the barn, and there were more horses gathered there, standing with their necks craned out over the fence, staring at us as we pulled up to park.

It was a warm day and I left my uniform jacket in the car. As I got out, I checked my reflection in the window and tightened up my tie, made sure it was tucked into my shirt properly, and adjusted my fore and aft cap at the jauntiest angle possible, just teetering on the edge of falling off. I knew I was no Beau Brummell, but with Daphne's father being a knight and a captain and all, I figured a little extra effort was required.

"Daphne!" A high-pitched scream came from the barn, followed by a figure running out with arms widespread. "Daphne!" she repeated as she flew through the gate, long blonde hair falling down past her shoulders as a tweed cap hit the ground.

"Diana! Oh my goodness!" The two sisters embraced, laughing and clinging to each other.

"I didn't know you'd be here —"

"— just for a couple of days . . . how long?"

"— pick up the Imp. . . ."

"You look wonderful!"

"How've you been?"

". . . the same. Father?"

"Fine. Working terribly hard. . . ."

It went on like that for what seemed a long time. Bits of sentences, phrases and expressions, laughter and arms intertwined, the shorthand of close siblings. My kid brother and I could catch up with each other after a month with a few mumbled exchanges and a punch to the shoulder. It was like that with Daphne and her sister, just more genteel, English, and feminine. It made me homesick.

"Oh, Piotr," Diana exclaimed, finally noticing us leaning up against the car. "It's so good to see you!" She grasped Kaz's hands and kissed him with genuine affection.

"Diana," Daphne said, taking her sister by the arm and turning her toward me, "This is Lieutenant William Boyle. Billy — my dear, sweet, quite impetuous younger sister, Diana."

I held out my hand and looked into her eyes. They were deep blue, and a shock of her bright blonde hair draped itself down one side of her face. She was wearing blue coveralls with the sleeves rolled up and rubber Wellingtons, probably for working in the barn. There were beads of sweat on her forehead. Horse manure and straw were stuck to her boots, and the general odor was of, well, a barnyard.

She took my hand and I felt her soft, warm skin, as well as the strength in her handshake, almost like a man's. I could see a faint ripple of muscle in her forearm and I held on to her right hand as she wiped her forehead with the other.

"Please forgive me, Lieutenant, I've been shoveling a mountain of horse shit for the last hour."

"Diana! What did I tell you about foul language?" an angry, stern voice said from behind the gate.

"Father!" Daphne said as she ran over to him. His sternness dissolved as she kissed him. "Is Diana still cursing like a trooper?"

285

"Yes, she is. A terrible affliction in an otherwise wonderful daughter. Now, tell me, what are you doing . . . ah, Baron, so good to see you!" Sir Richard walked over to Kaz and extended his left arm. His right sleeve was empty, pinned up at the shoulder. He had a full head of white hair and a short white beard, very neatly trimmed. He was tan and looked in good shape for a one-armed retired naval officer. He was wearing the same outfit as Diana and had also obviously been at work, one-handed.

"Sir Richard," Kaz said, with a slight bow as he shook his hand, acting every inch the aristocrat. "Allow me to present my associate, Lieutenant William Boyle." For a second I didn't know what to do, whether to bow or which hand to shake with. Then I noticed I was still holding Diana's hand. I could feel myself redden as I let go. She smiled and Daphne laughed. Sir Richard's forehead wrinkled up as his eyes darted between Diana and me. I tried to gather what few wits I had.

"Very glad to meet you, sir," I said as I gripped his offered left hand somewhat clumsily. "Most folks just call me Billy."

"You see, Father," Diana said, obviously picking up the thread of a previous argument. "See how informal Americans are, offering their first name right off. Billy probably feels more at home having someone curse around him, don't you, Billy?"

"Well, we don't shovel much horse . . . manure in South Boston, Miss Seaton, and not every American is as friendly as I am."

Diana's smile vanished, her attempt to rally me to her side having failed. She tossed her hair back and turned toward the barn.

"I just need to finish up a few things. Daphne, dear, come chat with me while I clean up. Father, will you show our guests inside?" Without waiting for a response, Diana and Daphne went off, arm in arm, whispering to each other, ignoring the three of us.

"Well, gentlemen, I am glad to welcome you to Seaton Manor," Sir Richard began, "but would you mind telling me the reason for this unexpected visit?"

"Daphne wants to take the Riley Imp out," said Kaz. "I need to get to London and Daphne has to drive Billy up to Southwold. It is a matter of some urgency —"

"The Imp hasn't been driven in months," Sir Richard cut in, "what with rationing and the petrol shortage. I put her up on blocks and drained the crankcase. She's under a tarp in the barn, waiting for better times."

"These are hardly better times, sir," I said,

"but it would really help us out to have the use of another vehicle."

"I take it this is a military matter?" Sir Richard asked Kaz, cocking an eyebrow in my direction.

"It is indeed, Sir Richard. Perhaps we should explain —"

"Explanations can wait," Sir Richard said, the authority of a former captain easily asserting itself. "We need to get to work on the Imp. Follow me."

Within minutes Sir Richard had us in coveralls and was pulling the tarpaulin off the Imp. It was a bright red two-seater sports car, slung low to the ground and as sleek as a Spitfire.

"It's a beautiful car," I said.

Sir Richard smiled. "Yes, she is. Ships and fast cars, they have their own certain beauty, don't you think? Now man that jack, will you?"

We worked for an hour or so, mounting the tires and adding engine oil. Sir Richard brought in a can of gasoline and we poured it into the fuel tank as he ran a clean rag over the hood where we had left some fingerprints.

"Well, shall we start her up? Baron?" Sir Richard handed him the keys. Kaz slid into the driver's seat as Sir Richard walked to the barn door to swing it open. The Imp started up smartly and Kaz shifted into first gear, rolling forward toward the door, the engine rumbling with a low, sustained growl.

"Switch off, Baron!" Sir Richard held up his hand, as heavy raindrops started to splat across the dusty courtyard. Kaz cut the engine and we watched as thick, gray clouds blew across and obliterated the blue sky.

"Looks like a storm blowing in from the northeast, probably a North Sea front. Could be nasty. Just leave the Imp there for now. I must see to the horses. . . ."

His eyes scanned the fenced fields beyond the barn as we heard the growing sound of hoofbeats coming toward us. Daphne came into view, dressed in one of the blue coveralls that seemed to be the uniform of the day at Seaton Manor, astride a brown horse — chestnut, I think they called that color at the racetrack. She was leading about a dozen horses, or ponies maybe, by their size, to the safety of the barn. We walked over to the fence and watched them draw near, satisfaction showing on Sir Richard's face. I saw Diana riding a jet black horse at the rear of the little herd, when suddenly a thin slash of bright light seemed to hurl itself into the trees to our right, followed by a loud crack of thunder that split the sky above us. I jumped. The horses began to swirl in an agitated mass. One of them reared up on his hind legs and let loose a terrifying sound, all teeth and wide fearful eyes. He took off from the herd crazily and ran back the way they'd come, tail flicking wildly in the electric air. Diana turned her horse on a dime, pulling down on the bridle with her right hand, leaning in the direction she wanted to go, kicking her heels into him at the same time. The horse responded as if he knew exactly what she wanted. Diana galloped past us after the stray, her long blonde hair flowing behind her, as another bolt of lightning arced through the sky. She turned her head for a split second and smiled at me, so fast that I wasn't sure it had happened. I climbed the fence and watched her vanish over a rise, her horse's hooves sending clumps of dirt and grass flying as if a machine gun was chewing up the ground behind them. My heart was pounding. It was the most beautiful thing I had ever seen. Everything about the moment — Diana, the black horse, her hair, the lightning — was burning itself into my mind. I stepped down from the fence and saw Sir Richard fixing his gaze on me as the rain began to beat down harder. Kaz was shaking his head wearily.

"The girls will finish up with the horses. They're quite capable. Let's get ourselves indoors and cleaned up," Sir Richard said. He turned and walked toward the house, Kaz talking long strides to keep up with him. I followed, since it sounded more like an order than a suggestion, but I did it with my head turned toward the field, where that black horse still ran with a vision on its back.

By the time we got inside it was a real downpour. We shed our boots and coveralls in the kitchen, while the cook brewed up a pot of tea. She was a stout, white-haired matron with ruddy cheeks. She stood with arms akimbo and held a wooden spoon in one hand like a field marshal's baton. Her eyes narrowed sternly as she watched us doff our wet and dirty garments, as she had warned us not to venture any farther into her kitchen before they were hung properly on the hooks near the doorway.

"It's right nice to have both girls back home, isn't it, Captain?" she said to Sir Richard as she eyed our progress.

"Indeed it is, Mrs. Rutledge. Do you think you could accommodate three more for dinner tonight?" he answered.

"Sir," I interrupted, "we need to be on our way —"

"Young man!" Mrs. Rutledge thundered,

"you will not drive in here for the afternoon with Miss Daphne and then drive out before eating at least a proper meal, you hear me?" She shook the wooden spoon at me and I was instantly reminded of my drill instructor.

"And specially not in a rainstorm like this, not in that little red automobile, you aren't. Right, Captain?" She looked to Sir Richard, daring him to contradict her.

"I believe Mrs. Rutledge is correct, gentlemen," he said diplomatically. "You could leave in daylight but you'd both soon be driving in darkness, and rain, if this keeps up. With the black out restrictions that could be dangerous. You'll stay here tonight and get an early start in the morning. Right, Mrs. Rutledge?"

"Right, Captain, quite right indeed."

"Kaz, she's incredible!" I half whispered as we walked down the wide hallway to our rooms.

"You looked like lightning had struck you when she rode by," he said.

"That's what it felt like. I've never met anyone like her before."

"Don't get carried away, my friend," Kaz said. "We're only here for one night, and remember, Diana is in the First Aid Nursing Yeomanry. She could be assigned any-where, anytime."

"I don't care. I have to see her." I felt like nothing else in the world mattered. I didn't know what FANYs did or where they went, and I didn't care.

"As I said, don't get carried away. She may not be as interested as you are, Billy. And you have to deal with Sir Richard."

"First, she smiled at me. That's all I have to go on, but it's enough for me. Second, why would I worry about him? He seems to think you and Daphne are an OK item. What's wrong with me?"

"Well, first, I didn't jump up onto a fence to stare at his daughter's behind bouncing on a horse the first time I met him. . . . That's your room, I believe." Kaz leaned on his doorknob and pointed to the room op-posite.

"Thanks, buddy."

"Billy, seriously, some advice. Sir Richard is very rare among upper-class Englishmen. He does not seem to have a built-in bias against all foreigners. There are many men in his position who would not want a Pole to court their daughter, even if he is a baron. They would also not look kindly upon a young American of Irish extraction. But do not depend on his liberalism. He is very protective of his daughters. Especially Diana, who seems to have no fear."

"No fear of what?"

"Fast horses, cars, whatever attracts her fancy. Perhaps you are now in that category."

"One can only hope."

I was in my room, dressing after a hot bath. My uniform had been brushed and pressed while I soaked. So far, except for stray bullets and dead bodies, life in fancy English houses wasn't too bad. There was a knock at the door, and a servant told me that dinner would be served in an hour, and that the captain had asked if I would be so kind as to have sherry with him in the library, first. Again I could tell this was no suggestion, and said I'd be right there. I walked downstairs, hoping to bump into Diana on the way. No luck. I found the library, and Sir Richard walked in a minute later. He was dressed in a dinner jacket, and I tried to picture everything in black and white, like in the movies, which was the only place I had ever seen anyone in a tux, outside of a wedding or the mayor at the policeman's ball, and dollars to doughnuts those had been rentals.

"Lieutenant Boyle, I'm pleased you could

join me," he said as he poured out two glasses of sherry from a decanter. No first names between us, I guess. He replaced the stopper on the decanter and it settled in with that nice glassy clunk that said real crystal.

"Glad to, Sir Richard . . . or do you prefer Captain?"

He handed me a glass and gestured toward a chair. We sat. Books lined the wall in front of us, some of them really old, their faded leather bindings thick on the shelves. Others were new, with bright-colored covers showing off among the fading tones of the older books. I wondered if he had read them all. And if he had any Sherlock Holmes.

" 'Captain' suits me better," he said. "I feel as if I've at least earned that title. The knighthood, well, that's so much politics. As a military man, perhaps you understand."

"My military experience as an officer is really measured in weeks, but I think I do. My father and uncle were in the last world war. They lost their older brother in France."

"The shared experience of death. It tends to stay with you." He shook his head sadly, and I wondered what else we were going to talk about. I figured more small talk was in order.

"What sort of ship were you on, Captain? I'm afraid I don't know much about the Royal Navy."

"A cruiser. She went down in the Battle of Jutland. The captain is supposed to go down with his ship, but all I could manage to send down was one arm."

He smiled to himself at what was now probably a well-worn joke.

"It must've been tough."

"Losing the arm? No, that was easy, compared to losing my ship. And my men. Very difficult to come to grips with. You probably have yet to meet the enemy in combat, Lieutenant?"

"No, I haven't."

"Once you do, you will need to keep all your wits about you. You must be totally focused on the job at hand."

I nodded. I waited. I couldn't disagree with him, but I also didn't know what he was getting at.

"You work with Daphne and Baron Kazimierz at the U.S. headquarters?"

"Yes."

"She seems to be quite happy these days. With the baron, with her post there."

"Yes. They seem quite devoted to each other." Thunder boomed, a distant, low sound. Rain pelted the windows as the winds blew it sideways against the house. I wondered what in hell we were talking about.

"It is ironic that people in wartime find each other who never would have met otherwise. For some it can be very good, having a relationship forged during time of war. For others, it can be . . . dangerous. It may entail a loss of focus."

"You mean, like thinking of loved ones back home when you're dodging bullets?"

He took a drink, keeping his eyes leveled on me over the rim of the glass. He set the glass down, still gazing at me. "Yes, that sort of thing. It's why the commandos don't want men with families. On a dangerous job, one shouldn't be thinking about anything but the objective."

"Well, at HQ the most danger we ever face is a paper cut." I couldn't very well brag about almost getting shot by accident to a guy with one arm at the bottom of the North Sea.

"Every job has its rigors. More sherry?"

I drank a second glass of the stuff and we talked some more. About Eisenhower, U-boats, London, lots of idle chitchat. Maybe this was how the swells entertained a guest. Tiny glasses of liquor my grandmother might drink and lots of small talk. It went on until a butler, in a swallow-tailed coat even fancier than the captain's, announced that dinner was served.

I followed the captain out of the library and down the hall, thick carpeting deadening the sounds of our footsteps. We passed portraits of two men in naval uniforms from the last century. I wasn't introduced.

We turned a corner and came to the main staircase at the front, the formal entrance to the house. Diana was waiting at the bottom. She looked a lot different than she had earlier. The absence of horse manure on her shoes was nice. She wore her FANY uniform, a light gray outfit that wasn't designed for fashion, but she looked like a movie star in it anyway. Her hair was brushed and gleaming, falling over her shoulders like sunlight.

"Billy, there you are," she said. "I thought you might have gotten lost."

"The captain invited me to the library for sherry," I said, trying to sound cheery about it.

"Oh, how nice of you, Father," Diana said, falling in beside me and taking my arm.

The captain bowed his head. "No trouble at all, my dear."

Daphne and Kaz were already in the dining room. I walked with Diana to the table to pull out her chair, but the captain had other plans. He seated his daughters to his left and right, and put me next to Daphne. There were only five of us at the table, but somehow I ended up as far away from Diana as possible. Out of footsie range, anyway.

The dining room was wood paneled, a dark cherry color. It was lit entirely by candlelight, candlesticks on the table, sideboard, and flickering in wall sconces. It produced a mellow, golden light, reflecting off the polished wood and giving the room a sense of age and dignity. A brisk fire in a huge fireplace behind the captain kept the damp chill from the rain outside from creeping in. Firewood snapped and sparked as wine — claret according to our host — was poured. He raised his glass in a toast.

"To our American allies. Lieutenant Boyle, I hope you are the first of many more to come."

"They're on their way, sir. You can depend on that."

We clinked glasses, and there were smiles all around.

"We are depending upon it," Captain Seaton said. "After fighting alone for two years, 1941 was a godsend to us. First, Hitler attacked Russia in June, taking the pressure off England, and then America came into the war in December. Made us breathe a little easier over here, I can assure you."

"When will the Americans get into the fight?" asked Diana. "It's been over six months since Pearl Harbor was attacked, and we're just beginning to see you Yanks over here."

"Diana!" barked the captain. "Don't be rude!"

"That's OK," I said, trying to avoid an embarrassing moment. "Miss Seaton may not understand how difficult it is to mount a military campaign." I took another swig of wine, warming to my subject. I was on Eisenhower's staff, after all.

"You see, there's the matter of strategy, logistics, target selection —"

"Billy," Daphne interrupted, "I think you can spare us the lecture. Diana actually has more experience with military campaigns than any of us, excepting Father."

"Diana was with a FANY detachment that served as switchboard operators with the British Expeditionary Force in France," Kaz said, jumping to my rescue. "In 1940."

"Well, Belgium at first anyway, Baron." Diana cocked an eyebrow at me while she took a drink. She had a look that said she was about to enjoy humiliating me. "We were in Brussels, at BEF headquarters with Lord Gort. Supposedly safe behind the lines, working the switchboard and freeing up men for the fighting units. Although nobody told the Germans."

"Especially Rommel." The captain said this gazing between my eyes. I could tell I was getting a message.

"Yes," Diana went on. "Rommel and his Ghost Division, they called it. Kept showing up in our rear areas. Quite a nuisance. We abandoned headquarters, fell back. Bombed, strafed, and otherwise inconvenienced for most of the month of May. We were among the first to be transported out of Dunkirk, with the wounded."

"Are you a nurse?" I asked.

"No, although I did learn a few things about caring for the wounded. They call us the First Aid Nursing Yeomanry, but one doesn't need to be a nurse. It's rather a catchall organization, providing support in various ways. Working switchboards, clerking, that sort of thing."

"Well, I'm glad you got out OK." This was greeted with silence.

Finally the captain spoke. "The destroyer Diana was on was sunk by Stukas. The wounded were packed like sardines on deck.

Most of them didn't survive a night in the water."

More silence. Kaz dropped a knife and the dull thud of silver hitting the table filled the room. I looked at Diana, trying to visualize her bobbing in a life jacket in the cold channel water, dead and dying men all around her. She gave her father a look that said, Please, don't say anymore. She started to speak, stopped, and then seemed to rally. A smile crept back onto her face. She speared an asparagus and looked at me.

"So, Lieutenant, you were telling us about the difficulties of military campaigns?"

I could feel my face redden. I was glad to see she wasn't so upset she stopped needling me. I raised my glass.

"To our English allies. They still have a thing or two to teach us colonials."

I drained my glass. Daphne smiled approvingly, in a silent message of goodwill.

There was more wine, and several courses of good country food. The captain explained that the farm provided for most of their own needs, so rationing didn't hurt them too badly. It was a working horse farm, and even with mechanization, there was still a big demand by the army for horses. He was evidently doing OK. After the servants cleared away the last of the dishes, the brandy and cigars came out. I had never been a big smoker, but I thought I ought to give it a try, since they were on the house. I put the cigar in my mouth before I noticed there was no hole at the end to draw the smoke through. I took it out quickly when I saw Kaz snip the end off his with a little cutter that had come with the box. For the second time that night I felt my face redden. I sincerely hoped they hadn't noticed. Then I saw Daphne dabbing her mouth with a napkin, hiding a grin none too well.

I gave her a glare as Kaz handed me the clippers. At least Diana wasn't laughing.

The captain was puffing on his cigar already, getting it going. Finally he exhaled. "Daphne tells me you're a criminal detective, Lieutenant," he said.

"Yes sir, Boston Police Department, now U.S. Army." Criminal detective sounded a little fancier than cop, but I kinda liked it so I let it go.

"Apparently, you are conducting some kind of investigation? Anything you can tell us about?" I looked at Kaz and then Daphne. I wasn't too sure about who should know what at this point.

"Father is actually very well informed about a number of military matters, Billy," Daphne said. "He's a frequent visitor at

303

Chequers."

The blank expression on my face must've said it all.

"Chequers is the prime minister's country residence," Kaz explained.

"Oh."

"That would be Winston Churchill, dear," added Daphne helpfully. I ignored her as she tried to stifle another bout of laughter.

"Father is too modest to explain," Diana said, "but during the thirties, when Winston was trying to warn the government about the Nazi threat, he was only a member of Parliament, without much of a following or resources. A small group of influential men, some on active duty and some retired, advised him. Father was one of those. Still is, actually, when Winnie wants to sound out ideas and that sort of thing."

"Winnie?"

"Oh yes," Daphne added. "He's quite a dear. He used to tell us stories of his adventures in Africa when we were children."

"Suffice it to say, Lieutenant, I know all about Operation Jupiter. I helped Winston work out the naval logistics when it was an entirely British operation. I can only assume that's why you've been consulting with the Norwegians at Beardsley Hall. As for Diana, she already has a top-secret security clearance. MI-5 cleared her before she went over with the BEF."

Kaz gave a little shrug and nodded his head toward me. I guess we weren't in a nest of German sympathizers.

"Do you know Knut Birkeland, sir?"

"I've met him in London. He advised the Royal Navy on coastal defenses and likely landing spots. Owns a fishing fleet over there, I believe, knows the coastline like the back of his hand, if I remember correctly. Decent chap."

"Yes, he was. He's dead."

"It was supposed to look like suicide, Father," Daphne broke in eagerly. "But Billy thinks it was murder! We're helping him investigate. It's all very exciting."

"How was he killed?" Diana asked.

"Defenestrated," Kaz said. "Pushed, thrown, or jumped out a fourth-floor window. Which one depends on whether or not you believe the suicide note."

I went over the note, the gold coin, the accusations by Vidar Skak, and those who we had identified as being up and about during the early morning hours: Skak, Captain Jens Iversen, Major Anders Arnesen, Lieutenant Rolf Kayser, an unidentified female in the company of Iversen, and of course, the king.

"So," the captain said slowly, thinking out loud, "if it wasn't suicide, it was probably one of those individuals? Certainly you can't suspect the king?"

"A cop . . . a criminal detective should never assume someone is incapable of murder. But leaving his royal status aside for the moment, King Haakon is one of the least likely suspects. Rolf Kayser is the other. They were out very early, hunting. The timing doesn't work, based on the condition of the body."

"Rigor mortis, that sort of thing?" the captain asked.

"Yes. Lividity, too." I described the condition of the body as I found it.

"But you sound certain that the suicide note was actually written by Mr. Birkeland?" Diana asked, puzzled.

"Yes, it is in his handwriting."

"His handwriting, no signs of a struggle inside a locked room," Diana said as she ticked off these points on her fingers. "How can you say it wasn't suicide?"

"He wasn't the type. We found the room key in Arnesen's room later that morning. How did it get there? Someone may have planted it, or maybe Arnesen thought no one would search every room for the key, but I doubt it."

"So who does that leave as a prime suspect?" Diana asked.

"Skak had a motive. He and Birkeland were rivals for the position of the king's senior adviser."

"Yes," the captain said, "I seem to remember a difference of opinion about the role of the underground in Norway. Birkeland was dead set against it, right?"

"Absolutely. Skak was just as adamant that they be used in an uprising. Birkeland favored commando raids, even though that meant his fishing fleet was a prime target."

"Ah, nitroglycerin!" the captain said. "The commandos have been destroying fishing boats and processing plants."

"Correct," said Kaz. "I am going to London to try to find out if anyone stood to gain financially by halting those raids. Someone in England, that is."

"So, Skak has a political motive, and you're looking for someone who might have had a financial motive," Diana said. "What about this mystery woman?"

"I have no idea," I admitted. "Until we find her, anyway. Daphne and I are going up to the Southwold base to talk to Rolf Kayser. He left the hall soon after Birkeland's death and we haven't had a chance to question him. I'm hoping he and the king saw something, or somebody, that morning that will give us a lead."

"It sounds like you've gotten nowhere," said Diana, her blonde eyebrow arched and her eyes aimed at me, drilling me right through the heart.

"That's not fair!" Daphne protested.

"Unfortunately, it is," I admitted. "At this point in an investigation, the only thing to do is to go over everything again, carefully. They always make a mistake somewhere, it's just a matter of patience."

"But are you a patient man, Lieutenant Boyle?" asked Diana.

I tried to think of something suave to say, something that Franchot Tone or maybe Cary Grant would have come up with. The captain cut that short, as if he read too much into Diana's question.

"I suggest we turn in. It will be an early start for you all in the morning. Mrs. Rutledge will have a breakfast ready at six o'clock."

He stubbed out his cigar, grinding it in a glass ashtray with his left hand as he watched us get up and leave. I thought I could feel his eyes on my back.

CHAPTER SIXTEEN

I was in bed, leafing through a two-year old magazine about horses and thinking of Diana on horseback, galloping past me like the answer to a dream I'd never had, when there was a knock at the door. Before the last rapid rap of knuckles faded my heart was pounding hard in my chest.

"Hang on!" I stumbled out of bed, throwing on a robe over my skivvies and praying it wasn't Kaz. I opened the door. It wasn't.

"May I come in?" Diana asked in a whisper, as she worriedly looked up and down the hallway.

"Sure. . . ."

Before I could say anything else she slipped in and closed the door, carefully and quietly, holding her left hand flat against the panel as she moved the doorknob with her right, turning it slowly only when the door was shut tight. She was wearing a light blue dressing gown, her golden hair was loose, and there were tears in her eyes. She turned and leaned back against the door, not moving except for her nervous hands.

"Want to sit down?" I moved to a small couch under the window, feeling like I was coaxing a frightened deer.

"I don't know what I want . . . I feel like a fool, really . . . if Father finds out . . . I should go. . . ."

She turned and put her hand back on the door, but she didn't open it. Her head fell forward and rested against it, next to her hand. Her back heaved and she began to cry silently, teardrops raining down. I gently took her by the arm, just touching her elbow, led her to the sofa, and sat her down next to me. Her sobbing lessened and she sheepishly pulled a lace handkerchief from her dressing-gown pocket. She dabbed at her nose and eyes, giving me a little smile and not much else to go on.

"Diana, tell me what's wrong. How can I help?"

"I can't, Billy. I can't tell anyone. That's why I'm here."

"I don't understand —"

"Listen, Billy." She perked up a bit as she gathered her wits about her and swung her legs up onto the sofa, tucking the ends of her dressing gown underneath them. She

310

looked off for a second, her fingers fluttering in front of her eyes, as if she wanted to pull something away, something invisible between us.

"It's not that anything is exactly wrong. Everything is happening as it should, just as expected. I'm worried . . . scared, actually."

"About what?"

She put a hand up to her face to hide her eyes. It was as if she was battling a secret that wanted to come out, and the fight was costing her. Finally, she looked me straight in the eye, as her words flowed out at me.

"Billy, if there were all the time in the world, if you were here on holiday and all I had to do was train Father's horses, things would be different. I would be very coy and flirt a little bit. After a few weeks, I would admit to you that the first time I saw you I thought you were handsome, attractive, and intriguing. I would then let you kiss me, once. But there isn't time, not much time at all."

She searched my eyes, looking for me to understand something she couldn't explain. She overwhelmed me — her voice, her face, the blue of her gown reflected in her blue eyes. Everything overloaded my mind until I couldn't think of anything except a wisecrack.

"Yeah, I hear there's a war on. You haven't said what you're scared about."

"What I'm trying to tell you is that even though we've just met, I feel comfortable with you, as if we've known each other before. And that I need a friend right now, someone to talk with. And, I have to admit, I like talking to you, even if I do make fun of you a bit."

"Yeah, a bit. But what about Daphne? Can't you talk to her? You two seem pretty close. My brother, Danny, and I are like that, though I'd never admit I was scared of anything to him."

Diana avoided my eyes and looked out the window at the darkness beyond. I didn't mean to turn her down, but I just didn't understand what she was after.

"I can't burden her, or Father. I don't want them to worry."

Then I understood. Even a thick-headed Irishman like me could understand now, and when I did, the bottom seemed to fall out of everything.

"Oh, I get it. Since we're attracted to each other, you can burden me with your troubles, without actually telling me what they are, of course. But then, because we're not really close yet, it won't bother you to leave me to worry about you."

"Why, Billy, you must really be a detective! So, you're attracted to me, too?"

It was my turn to look away. I had never felt this shy with a girl before. I was trying to be mad at her but it just wouldn't stick. She knew it, too.

"Yeah, I guess so." I wanted to tell her about how I felt when I first saw her, but all I could manage was a mumble.

"Well, there's some truth in what you say. I wanted to talk to somebody — I wanted someone to talk to me — who wouldn't lecture me, and with whom I could cry if I wanted. But being with you, I don't feel like crying as much as I did before. Unless that makes you uncomfortable, and you want me to leave?"

She started to get up, and I was pretty sure she was kidding, but I didn't want to take any chances.

"No, stay as long as you want. I was tired of reading horse magazines anyway."

She granted me a smile and adjusted herself on the couch, making herself more comfortable.

"Diana, tell me what the problem is; maybe I can help. Maybe General Eisenhower can —"

She leaned forward and put her hand on the back of my neck and pulled me toward her. She pressed her lips against mine and kissed me like we were hungry lovers who had been apart too long. Just as suddenly as it began, it was over, and she pushed me away.

"There, that was our first kiss. I told you I would let you kiss me once. Now don't ask me again about my problems!"

I was looking at her lips, still feeling the warmth of them pressed up against mine. I didn't know what was going to happen next, but I knew I didn't want to miss it.

"OK, OK! Instead, tell me what that little visit with your father in the library was all about. I couldn't figure out what he wanted."

"I think he was keeping me from you. From being alone with you."

"Why? I'm a nice enough guy."

"Father can be quite headstrong, but never mind him. I can be headstrong, too."

Now she looked angry. I could tell she was trying to forget something as she spoke with a forced gaiety. "Tell me all about yourself. Tell me about your life in Boston. Do you go to parties much? Do you know any gangsters?"

"I'll tell you I liked that first kiss. . . ." I leaned in for another and was rewarded by a firm push against my chest that was almost a punch. Her strength surprised me and then I remembered how firm her handshake had been.

"I told you I'd let you kiss me *once.* Once was it — for tonight, anyway. You don't take me for a loose girl, do you?"

I was about to mention that she had kissed me and not vice versa, but I rubbed the sore spot on my chest instead and thought better of it.

"Not at all. Can't blame a guy for trying. You don't hit like a girl."

"So I've been told. Now, tell me all about Boston."

I talked to her about my family, my kid brother, Dad, and Uncle Dan, and all their cop pals. I told her about being a cop — the real thing, not bragging about being a criminal detective or anything. I told her about the Boston neighborhoods, Southie, Back Bay, Chinatown, and the docks. I explained how I got here, Uncle Ike and everything. I didn't even try to make myself sound like a big deal. It was so easy to talk with her that I never felt a need to lie or even dress things up.

We started out sitting with our legs up on the sofa. Soon we were stretched out with our legs intertwined. By the time Diana finished telling me about her life growing up at Seaton Manor, we were cuddled up together pretty good, my arm around her, her soft hair smelling like a warm summer day.

"It was a good place to grow up, but I missed having a mother. All my friends had mothers, and I couldn't even remember what mine looked like. Father was wonderful, but there was always a missing piece, some part of me that felt like it could never grow up. I still wonder about her, what she was like, really, not what Father remembers or tells us."

"I think I know," I said.

"How could you?" Resentment crept into her voice, as if I had trespassed.

"You and Daphne. You're both wonderful, special in your own way. Some of that comes from your father — how you were brought up, sure — but there has to be quite a bit of your mother in both of you. Look to the best of yourself."

Diana was quiet for a minute, staring into space, thinking.

"Yes, I never thought about it that way. Does the best of you come from your father, Billy?"

"I think so. My best efforts, anyway. I don't know if I can ever live up to him."

"That's the same mistake Thomas always

makes. He thinks he needs to equal Father in everything. But that goes after it backward, don't you see?"

"No, I don't."

"If you want to play that silly game of competition between father and son, think about what your father was doing when he was your age, not what he's accomplished since then. What was your father doing when he was as old as you are?"

"Shipping out from the States in the last war," I said, seeing where she was going.

"Was he an officer?"

"No. He ended up a sergeant."

"See?"

I did. We laughed a bit, and I tried not to think about Dad's time in the trenches, and how all the gold braid in the army wouldn't make up for living through that. We talked some more about Seaton Manor, horses mostly.

"Then the war came," she sighed, a sigh burdened with all the sadness the room could hold. Memories of childhood at the manor with Daphne and their brother, Thomas; growing up with horses and the peaceful English countryside all around them; replaced with bombing raids, defeat, and death.

"Thomas was the first to leave, when his

Territorial Army unit was called up. The Essex Brigade."

"He's in North Africa now?"

"Yes, did Daphne tell you? Thank God he wasn't at Tobruk. Twenty-five thousand boys captured, can you believe it?" Neither of us could. I tried to imagine what twenty-five thousand men marching into prison camps looked like, and failed.

"Did you and Daphne join at the same time?"

"No, you must know it's always up to the oldest to break new ground. Daphne was quite smart about it, too, joining the WRENs. It appealed to Father, with his naval background, even though he was against it at first. When I joined, there was hardly a squabble."

"Why didn't you join the WRENs, too?"

She shrugged, dismissing the idea of following in the footsteps of her older sister. I knew the look.

"I wanted to do something on my own, to go to a place Daphne and Father never had been. I heard that FANY units were being trained as telephonists to serve at headquarters in the field. It seemed terribly romantic at the time, to free a man to fight and be at the front at the same time."

"In my limited experience, HQ is never at

the front."

"Well, closer than anywhere in England, and closer than we ever thought it would be."

"Blitzkrieg," I said, sounding out the word the world had never even heard of just a few short years ago.

"Yes. I was with Lord Gort's headquarters, as I said. We were in Belgium. It was May, and I remember there were flowers blooming everywhere. Warm days and sunshine greeted us. We had our communications all set up; everything was working perfectly. The Germans hadn't attacked yet. They were to our front, the Belgians on our left, and the French to our right."

"And then?"

"Then the Germans were everywhere. They hit us from the front and cut right through the French lines south of us. Panzers and Stukas, that's all anyone talked about. We had to fall back, and at first it seemed just like a setback, that we'd take up new positions and stop them. But nothing stopped them. Telephone lines were all cut, we pulled out, and found ourselves on a road full of refugees. The Stukas came, making that awful screaming sound, almost worse than the bombs."

She was wringing her hands, staring off

into space, listening for the sound of dive-bombers. I had heard them, too. In newsreels. The Stuka dive-bomber had sirens built into their wings, so when they dove on a target it made a god-awful screaming noise. Maybe I had seen her in one of those newsreels, a haunted face in a truckload of FANYs, while I waited for the first reel of Charlie Chaplin in *The Great Dictator.*

"Pull back, pull back, that's all we ever heard. The Germans started out in front of us, and then we couldn't withdraw fast enough to keep them out of our rear areas. Headquarters actually was in the front lines, since we were nearly surrounded." She laughed bitterly.

"But you got out OK? From Dunkirk?" I wanted this story to end well, but I knew there was something else, something that had happened to her there.

"Yes, I got out. On a destroyer. We had been pressed into service as nurses, since we all had some basic first-aid training. There were a lot of wounded. Quite a lot. We took doors from houses when we ran out of stretchers."

Diana wasn't talking to me anymore. Her voice was low as her eyes stared straight ahead and saw the ghosts of Dunkirk, long lines of men standing in the sand awaiting deliverance or death. Her cheeks were streaked with tears as she told of the wounded men being loaded onto the destroyer, and tending to them on decks slippery with blood.

"It was terrible, not while I was actually doing something, but as soon as I stopped moving for a minute, it would just all be too much. When we left the pier it was crowded with men, some yelling and screaming, but most silently waiting their turn. I thought I had seen the worst of it at that moment, sailing away aboard that destroyer, watching those faces on the shore disappear as we headed into the Channel."

She shook her head, wiping tears from her eyes as she did so. I took her hand in mine, gently, to let her know I'd wait. I could hear the alarm clock on the nightstand ticking. Her hand slipped from mine as she spoke again.

"We heard aircraft, high above us, and we thought they were ours, since they didn't attack. But they must have been German fighters, flying cover. Some of them dove down and strafed the smaller boats. I was standing at the rail on the stern deck, checking my life vest, when I heard them. Stukas." She spat out the word, and pressed her hands to her ears.

"Everything was so loud," she said, her eyes squeezed shut and her head bowed, as if she were taking cover. "The Stukas and those sirens, the guns on the destroyer firing up at them, some of the men screaming, everything happening while the ship was zigzagging at top speed. We had to hang on to the men on stretchers so they wouldn't slide off the deck. There were men everywhere — below decks, on every surface above deck. Everyone wanted to get out. Isn't that funny? They were the lucky ones!"

"You don't have to —"

"The first group missed us. I could see their bombs as they let them go. Each one would dive, drop its bomb, and then zoom up, as if it was suddenly lighter than air. It was almost beautiful. I followed each bomb down, and each one missed, either to the side or behind us. We were drenched by the splashes, but it seemed we were charmed. Five planes, five misses."

Diana looked up, as if those bombs were still falling above her. I wasn't even there.

"But then five more came, right after those. The gunners were still firing at the last of them when the second wave came. The first bomb hit just forward of the bow, but it must have damaged the ship. We were all thrown forward, and it started to slow.

The second hit square on the forward deck. There was a huge explosion, and I was thrown backward by the force of it. Black smoke was everywhere. I couldn't see a thing. I could feel the heat, though, coming up from the bow. We were practically dead in the water, just our forward motion keeping us going. Then the ship started to list."

"You went into the water?"

She looked at me as panic crept into her eyes. Her voice was shrill and I had to put my finger to my lips to get her to lower it, so her old man wouldn't wake up and lower the boom.

"You know, even if there had been enough life vests, we couldn't have put them on some of them wounded. They couldn't have endured it. But there weren't enough, not nearly."

"No, there must've been hundreds of wounded. How could there have been enough?"

"Yes, yes, there couldn't have been," she said loudly, as if trying to convince herself. I put my finger to my lips again and listened for footsteps in the hallway.

"It wasn't our fault," she said in a lower voice. "But I didn't know what to do!"

I almost wished for Sir Richard to break down the door.

"There was nowhere to move them. The fire was coming toward us, and the ship was keeling over. I tried dragging one stretcher out of the fire, but we all slid toward the rail when the ship went over —"

"Oh no," I couldn't stop myself from saying. "Oh, no."

"I wanted the ship to sink faster, to put out the fires, but it was so slow. So slow. The men on stretchers couldn't move. Smoke rolled over them, enveloping them. Then they all went into the water, toppling over one another. It was so cold. I managed to swim away from the ship before she sank. But the wounded . . . they couldn't."

"You did your best," I whispered. "You did everything you could; it wasn't your fault."

She leaned forward and thrust her face against my chest, sobbing from someplace deep inside, choking on her tears as she tried to suppress them. She needed a deep, angry screaming, crying jag, but all she could do was smother her tears on my chest. It lasted a long time, until she was whimpering, worn out by her agony. Then she was quiet. I looked at her, trying to imagine her slipping off that deck into the channel waters, the dead and dying all around her.

I held her. Finally, her breathing became

regular. She had fallen asleep, like a baby. I lay awake, like any guy would whose arm was dead because a beautiful woman was lying on it. Very uncomfortable, glad, and confused. I struggled up off the sofa, picking her up, and carried her to the bed. She was half asleep when I pulled the covers over her. I headed back to the couch, ever the gentleman. Besides, I didn't want another rap in the chest.

"Billy?"

"Yes?"

"Come hold me. Please."

Her tears came again, softer this time. I held her until she fell asleep again and wondered at the way my life had changed in a day.

"I've got to leave, Billy."

Her whisper, the warmth of her breath in my ear, woke me. My arm was still around her and the first rays of dawn were filtering through the curtains. I smiled, inside and out.

"Father will be up soon. I must get changed and feed the horses," she said as she untangled herself from the sheets and me and got up.

"Can I help you?"

"You already have. Thank you, Billy.

Thank you for listening."

I shrugged. "Not a problem."

"Well, I do appreciate it. Especially since you were a gentleman. I'm sorry if it was frustrating." She smiled and I blushed, as I thought of her waking up snuggled next to me, with me in that . . . condition.

"I'll take care of the horses," Diana said, laughing, "and you take a cold shower. I'll see you at breakfast." She blew me a kiss, opened the door, and slipped out quietly.

I was a little embarrassed, but I figured, what the hell. It didn't seem to bother Diana, so I wouldn't let it bother me. I got up and stumbled sleepily into the bathroom, thinking about cold showers — they weren't big on showers in England — she must've heard that expression in an American movie. I glanced at the tub in the bathroom and thought about how English guys must have to soak in a cold tub. Ha! That'd sure cure 'em.

I stopped in my tracks. Wait a minute. A cold shower . . . a cold tub . . . I reached down and turned on the faucet. Cold water poured from the tap. In a minute it was even colder, coming up from deep underground. Why does a love-crazed guy take a cold shower? What does cold water do? Lessen the flow of blood? Slow things down? Yeah.

Bingo. That was it. It answered everything. Well, everything except the maps, and a little thing called motive. And who. So maybe not everything, but now I knew how and when. The rest would come soon enough. Ideas were buzzing through my head as I washed, packed my kit, and thought about how smart the killer had been, and how maybe that was a clue. I was knotting my field scarf when there was a knock at the door. I sprinted over, hoping it was Diana. I opened the door and saw the captain. He must've read my face.

"Sorry to disappoint you, Lieutenant. May I come in?"

"Sure . . . of course." I moved back into the room. He shut the door behind him. Not the best sign.

"I'll come straight to the point, Lieutenant. I don't wish to be rude, and I'm sure you're a decent young man. . . ." He sort of trailed off, looking around the room as if he had forgotten something, then back at me. He didn't sound like a strict father who knew his daughter had spent the night with me.

"What do you mean, captain?"

"I mean that you should stay away from Diana." The words came out in a rush, and he took a deep breath. I couldn't figure out why he was saying this. I struggled to find words to make some sense out of it.

"But . . . what about Daphne and Kaz?"

"It has nothing to do with them. Neither of them will be dealing with the enemy."

"Captain, I don't know if I'll ever be anything but a staff officer —"

"That does not matter to me," he said, "if I may be blunt. There is nothing else to say. I'm sure you are a fine officer. Daphne speaks well of you in any case. But I stand by what I say. Diana is very. . . ."

"Impetuous?" I remembered how Daphne had introduced her.

"Impetuous, yes," he nodded, "and quick to form opinions, sometimes to her own detriment. I know her quite well, and I can tell she sees something in you. I understand she was plying Daphne with questions about you, which is unusual. She thinks most young men are pompous fools, and is not shy about telling them. For you, she shows off her horsemanship. Quite a compliment, actually."

He stood as if he were still on the bridge commanding his crew. "For now, do not attempt to see my daughter again." There was sadness in his eyes that didn't match the sternness of his words. "Breakfast is ready. We will not speak of this again, Lieutenant." He turned and left.

I finished dressing, stunned by his ultimatum and what it meant. Of course I wanted to see Diana again, as soon as I could get some leave. Why was he against me? I went down to breakfast, and he greeted me like an old chum. More small talk, mostly the weather this time. It was going to be a nice day.

After breakfast, we all stood around outside with our bags stacked near the driveway, saying some awkward good-byes. Diana and Daphne hugged like there was no tomorrow, until Daphne pulled away and ran to the barn to get the Imp. Kaz put his bag in the staff car and left the captain, Diana, and me alone. Great.

"Good luck, Lieutenant," said Sir Richard formally as he extended his hand. I didn't have any problem taking it in my left hand and shaking it this time. I wanted to show him I didn't give up easily.

"Thank you, sir. Thanks for your hospitality. Diana, perhaps you'll teach me how to ride someday?"

She smiled and was about to speak when her father broke in. "Diana will be back on active service very soon. She'll not have time for riding lessons, and neither should you, young man, if General Eisenhower is keeping you sufficiently occupied!"

"Father!"

At that moment, Kaz started up the staff car and backed up as Daphne drove up in the Imp.

"I'll see you in a few days, darling!" she yelled as he waved and drove off. The captain took advantage of the interruption and busied himself with stowing our bags. As he did, Diana gave my hand a gentle, surreptitious squeeze. Before I could say a thing, she let go, kissed Daphne on the cheek, and ran toward the barn. I saw her run the back of her hand across her eyes as she went.

The captain and Daphne fussed over each other for a bit. I had already said thank you, and since even that hadn't turned out well, I decided to sit in the passenger's seat and keep quiet. Eventually we drove off down the long driveway, away from the captain, who waved, alone.

"What's the matter with your old man?" I asked Daphne. "Does he hate all Americans or just me?" She didn't answer. I looked over at her. She had a grim look on her face, and tears streaked across her cheeks, blown by the wind.

"Why the hell is everyone crying?"

Again, silence. It wasn't until we pulled

out onto the main road that she spoke.

"I'm not supposed to say anything. I'm not really even supposed to know."

"Know what?" This family sure had its secrets.

"Diana volunteered for the Special Operations Executive. She just finished her training. That's why she was home. She's going off on a mission."

"SOE? She's a spy?" I couldn't believe what I was hearing. "When is she leaving?"

"Next Sunday at the latest. Maybe sooner."

"Where?" Silence again.

"Across the channel. Exactly where doesn't really matter, does it?"

Neither of us spoke for a long time.

Now I understood why she had been so desperate to talk with a stranger rather than lie awake in her room, alone with her thoughts and fears.

CHAPTER SEVENTEEN

Daphne drove single-mindedly, focusing on the road and putting the Riley Imp through its paces. There was no chatting. She took corners like a pro and wasn't afraid to open up on a long, straight stretch of road. If I hadn't known she was thinking about Diana and worrying, I would have believed she was enjoying herself. I watched her gloved hands flex, fingers opening, then gripping the leather-bound steering wheel, over and over again. The desperation inside her had to come out somewhere.

We drove through farmland and small villages, mostly green wooded land and cultivated fields separated by hedges and stone walls. The land dipped down to the sea the closer we came to the base at Southwold. I was looking at the scenery but seeing Diana. I had never met anybody like her, and no woman had ever made me feel this way, like all the air had gone out of a room when she left it. It seemed that everything else had been just going through the motions before I met her, as if my life had been empty without my realizing it. I felt strange, like I had left some part of me behind.

Damn! Why did she have to get all gung ho and volunteer to be an SOE agent? Would I ever see her again? At least the captain made sense to me now. He knew Diana was about to leave on a mission and didn't want her mooning over some Yank. He was trying to help her keep focused. Focused on staying alive. He didn't know how badly she needed a shoulder to cry on, how desperate she'd been for distraction from her spiraling fear — and shame. All that "one must do one's duty" stuff had worn too thin after what she'd been through. I hoped I was more to her than just a handy shoulder. I kinda thought I was, but then how would I ever find out with her off sneaking around behind enemy lines? Not too much I could do about that right now.

Daphne downshifted as she took a sharp turn, then punched the accelerator hard enough to snap my neck back. At least she had a machine to take out her frustrations on.

I thought about cold water and its effect

on the human body. How did that fit together with maps, spies, suspects, and suspicious British majors? It was all still a jumble, but a few things were beginning to stand out. Unfortunately, other things still lurked — vague images that failed to clarify into answers, or even connections. I looked at my watch.

"Almost there, Billy." Daphne gave me a weak smile and then downshifted again, passing a farmer on his cart, causing the Imp to growl in low gear as we sped by the country perfume of manure ready to be spread.

"How're you doing? You OK?"

"Better, yes, thank you. Nothing like a morning drive in the Imp to cheer one up!" she said with a false bravado that was almost convincing. "Look there, Billy, that must be the way to the base."

Up ahead a column of U.S. Army deuce-and-a-half trucks was turning off the main road. We followed slowly, and as the distraction of fast driving faded, I could see the traces of worry working away at her face, bringing the corners of her mouth down.

"I'm sure she'll be all right," I said, trying to reassure both of us. "Diana seems like a tough cookie."

"That must mean she knows how to take

care of herself, which she does indeed. It's the emotional price she has to pay that worries me. She made it back from France in one piece, but it wasn't easy for her afterward. She saw so many terrible things."

"Why do you think she volunteered? And please don't give me any of that 'doing one's duty' stuff. Why her?"

Daphne took a deep breath and exhaled. "I asked her exactly that. She said she owed it to those men who died when the destroyer sank. She wouldn't say any more."

"Think she feels guilty that she lived through it?"

"How would joining SOE help?"

I shrugged, as if it were too much for me to figure out. But I knew. I knew Diana was going to tempt death again. To see if she deserved to live. To see if those men slipping beneath the cold Channel waves would finally stop calling out to her.

We crested a small hill and saw the Southwold base ahead and to our left. The column of trucks was entering the gate. A fence extended in both directions, ending on the left at a river and on the right continuing into a stand of trees. I could smell the saltwater–laden air blowing in fresh off the North Sea. We slowed as we approached the gate and Daphne pulled out her orders, ready for inspection. She stopped next to the white-painted gatehouse, manned by one American and one British soldier. The American, a corporal with "Ranger" stitched on his shoulder patch, approached the car.

"Ma'am, sir. Can I help you?"

"We have orders to enter the base," Daphne said, offering up a set of official documents, "and we'd like to see the base commander."

The corporal glanced at the orders and handed them back to Daphne.

"You can try to see him, but he's pretty busy. Better try the exec, Captain Gilmore." He lifted the gate blocking the roadway. "Go straight and take your second left. Headquarters building is right there. Big sign on it."

He smiled and waved us through. I turned around as we drove past. Neither sentry watched us as we went down the road.

"Pretty sloppy security," I said. "He didn't even check our IDs. We could be heading anywhere on this base."

"Now that you mention it, Billy, isn't it usually military police who guard base entrances?"

"Yeah, you're right. Those weren't MPs. Those clowns would let anyone in here." Daphne took the second left and parked in front of a Quonset hut with HQ painted in red letters above the door. Pine trees rose up in back of the building, shading it from the weak warmth the June sun gave. The Imp attracted a few stares, and Daphne attracted quite a few looks herself when she stepped out. Nobody paid me much attention.

"Can I help you, miss?" A GI walked up to Daphne, his hands in his pockets and a grin on his face. There was a parachute patch on his fore and aft cap, and he wore paratroop boots shined to a mirror finish.

She smiled for a second. "That's 'Second Officer' to you, Private. Accent on *officer.*"

Two of his buddies had hung back and were now laughing as his face reddened. He turned away from Daphne and nearly collided with me.

"Excuse me, sss-sir," he stammered as he tried to pull off a salute and back up at the same time.

"Take it easy, soldier," I said, returning the salute. "Just tell us where we can find the CO or Captain Gilmore."

"The CO's out on maneuvers, but Captain Gilmore's here. He's down by the trucks. Our battalion is getting our winter gear today and he's in charge. We're headed there. Would you like to follow us, Lieutenant? And the Second Officer, of course." He offered a tentative grin toward Daphne.

"Sure, boys. Lead the way."

We walked past a long row of Quonset huts, each bordered by a neat row of whitewashed rocks. In back of that row was another row, then another. Thick green grass, still wet from last night's rain, gave off a damp, earthy smell.

"You boys ever get out of here?" I asked.

"Yessir. They give us passes most weekends. We go into Southwold or sometimes up to Halesworth. There's pubs, movies, that sorta thing."

"You're all paratroopers, I see. The girls must like that. What's your unit?"

"Third Battalion, 503rd Parachute Regiment," our new friend said proudly. "But there's a lot of us, plus the rangers and commandos. There's fewer girls than GIs around here. Makes it kinda tough."

"Lots of competition, huh?"

"Yeah, I mean yes, sir. Especially with the Brit commandos. They think they have first dibs on the local girls. But they're out with the rangers on maneuvers today, so I thought I might have a chance. . . ."

"With the Second Officer," said Daphne wryly.

"Yes, ma'am. Sorry."

"Don't worry about it at all. It was most gallant of you to guide us," she said, giving him a forgiving smile. "Are the Norwegian commandos on maneuver also?"

"Probably. They're part of Number Five Troop, and I think all the commando units are out with the rangers. They're doing an exercise, attacking the airfield at Lowestoft."

Just what the brass had planned for them in Norway, where the plan was to take an airfield in Nordland. At the end of the row of Quonset huts was a large parking area. Two rows of five trucks each had their tailgates down and lines of paratroopers were passing along each, laughing and joking as men handed down heavy coats and other winter gear.

"We've got to get in line, sir. That's Captain Gilmore over there, guy with the clipboard."

"Thanks." We walked along the queue of men, some already burdened by parkas, heavy pants, fur hats, and mittens. It was cool for June, but the guys looked hot just carrying all that stuff.

"Captain Gilmore?" I asked as Daphne and I both saluted.

"Yes, what is it, Lieutenant?" He seemed busy, and didn't even bother looking at Daphne, which meant very busy in my book. He had his knee up on a crate, balancing his clipboard on it and jotting down numbers as fast as he could.

"Sir, we have orders granting access to your base in order to speak to Lieutenant Rolf Kayser, of the SAS commandos, Number Five Troop."

"I don't give a good goddamn. . . ." He finally noticed Daphne. "Excuse me. I mean I don't care what your orders say. All commando troops are out on maneuvers today."

"Up at Lowestoft," I offered.

"Right. They should be back this evening, when you can talk to Lieutenant Kayser all you want. Until then, I would appreciate it if you would just stay out of the way. I've got a lot to do." He turned and walked to the next row of trucks, checking his clipboard. I kept up with him, although that had sounded like a dismissal.

"I see that, sir. But what's the rush? Winter's not due for months."

"Then you must be the only guy they didn't let in on the secret. Hey, Doc!"

"Yes, captain?"

A British officer walked over in response to Gilmore's summons. He wore the commando shoulder flash along with the insignia of the Medical Corps. He was a little older than the American officer, with a tanned and lined face that looked like a sailor's or a mountaineer's. It was a hard face, but the blue eyes were soft and expressive. A doctor and a commando. Quite a combo.

"Doc, could you take these two off my hands? Give them lunch, a tour of the base, whatever. They're waiting for one of the Norwegian guys to get back." He walked off, still writing on his clipboard and counting off paratroopers, not even waiting for a response. The doctor eyed him as he walked away.

"Executive officer is not a job I'd wish on my worst enemy. Nothing but paperwork and details, no glory. You have to excuse Captain Gilmore; he's just up to his eyeballs in it." He turned toward Daphne and smiled. "I am Captain Stuart Carlyle. Pleased to meet you."

I took that to mean he didn't care two figs about meeting me, so I horned back in the conversation. "This is Second Officer Daphne Seaton. I'm Lieutenant Billy Boyle. We're attached to U.S. Army headquarters." Daphne handed him a copy of our orders, which he scanned and gave back, with the casual disdain for headquarters types that was quite natural among field officers and hardly even offensive.

"How come you're not out with the commando troops, sir?" I asked.

"I have some training accident patients that needed looking after. A few broken bones, that sort of thing," he said, moving away from the trucks and the noise of the paratroopers. "First let's have some lunch, then I'll show you around."

"I didn't know the commandos had their own medical staff," said Daphne as we followed him.

"We usually avail ourselves of the regular Army Medical Corps," Carlyle said, "but there are times when a doctor is needed on a mission. Such as when we are in the field in hostile territory for a period of time."

"So you're a trained commando?" I asked.

"Absolutely. Had to go through the same basic courses these younger chaps did. Although it helped that I'm an experienced mountain climber. Probably why they wanted me along."

"What do you mean?" I asked. Before he could answer, we all had to step to the side of the road as two more trucks rumbled by, probably loaded down with scarves and mittens. We walked on quickly, waving the dust away from our faces.

"Since you two are on Ike's staff, I'm surprised you don't know. Norway. Lots of mountains there," Carlyle said, looking back at us as we worked at keeping up with him.

"Oh, sure. The invasion. You guys are headed to Nordland, right?"

"Now that bit's top secret. It seems the General Staff figured they couldn't keep Norway a secret, what with the cold-weather gear and training we've been doing. The troops on this base know we're on for Norway, but they don't know exactly where or when. I've been told three different landing spots myself. So keep a tight lip, Lieutenant."

"Sorry, sir."

Sufficiently chastened, I shut up for a bit and let the captain chat with Daphne. I thought about that pathetic attempt at security. With practically anyone able to get on base and hundreds of GIs descending on the local villages and drinking themselves silly, word about the upcoming invasion of Norway was bound to spread. These guys would probably be talking about their new winter gear after their second pint. Our German spy wouldn't even need to get on base to hear about it, he could just sit at a bar and drink. I looked up at the sky and imagined the Luftwaffe sending bombers across the North Sea and blasting this place and these elite troops into oblivion, just on the basis of what their secret agents would hear in Southwold pubs this weekend.

I felt a pang of fear for Diana, and hoped to hell that the SOE had better security than whoever was running this operation. Then Carlyle mentioned lunch and we followed him into the officers' mess. Nothing fancy, just a long, narrow rectangle of a building, so new that piles of sawdust still showed on the ground outside, little sprinkles of dirty yellow in straight lines where boards had been cut. Inside, the usual smell of coffee, grease, and cigarettes hit my nostrils and reminded me of break time on the beat in Boston, of unbuttoning my blue coat and sipping a cup of good diner coffee, my biggest decision whether to have apple or cherry pie. On the house, of course.

It didn't smell like a diner, though; it was too new for that. The smell of sawdust hung in the air inside, too, almost palpable above the cooking odors. The wood was rough cut and unpainted, the windows not yet framed in, as if they had thrown this place together in a couple of days, and didn't care if it lasted more than a couple of months.

I was still worried about Diana and confused about most everything, but that never had an effect on my appetite. The kitchen had hot green pea soup and ham-and-cheese sandwiches stacked up a foot high. Daphne cut her sandwich up into sections and ate them in delicate little bites. It was cute. I ate mine holding it in one hand and slurping up soup with a spoon in the other. Daphne sort of rolled her eyes so I put the sandwich down and finished my soup, trying not to make any loud noises. If I was going to hang around the Seaton sisters, I would have to brush up on my manners.

"So, Captain, do you know Lieutenant Rolf Kayser?" I asked, once I had polished off the soup.

"Quite well, in fact. Kayser is one of our finest junior officers. He's a born leader, very rugged, and his men are totally loyal to him. He looks after them better than any lieutenant I know. But tell me, why is U.S. Army headquarters staff interested in a Norwegian serving with the British commandos?"

"He may be a witness to a matter we are investigating for General Eisenhower. I can't say more than that. Got to keep a tight lip on it, sir." Carlyle didn't seem to notice I was giving his own line back to him, but Daphne did. She jumped in to avoid any unpleasantness.

"Captain," she said, "what does Rolf do, exactly, that makes his men so loyal?"

"Well, I suppose it has something to do with all of them being Norwegian. In exile together, fighting to free their country: I think that forges a bond between them that we English can't fully understand. Thank God. But Kayser also makes a point never to leave a man behind, not even the dead. He's had me put his entire troop through medical orderly training, so they can stabilize a wounded man in the field and try to get him back alive."

"That must make a big difference," I offered.

"It does, for a seriously wounded man. Treating him quickly for blood loss and shock can keep him alive until he can get regular medical treatment. Any member of Kayser's troop could act as a competent medical orderly. He's learned quite a lot of battleground medicine himself by watching me and asking questions. He's not in any trouble, is he?"

"We need to talk with him, before he goes off on another mission. Have you been with him in the field?"

"Yes, several times."

"On missions to the Norwegian coast, to destroy fishing vessels and processing plants?"

"That would be classified information,

Lieutenant."

"Sure. I wonder what it must be like to have to destroy your own country's livelihood. It must be tough."

"War is hell, Lieutenant. Isn't that what one of your generals said?"

"Yes," I answered. "General Sherman during the Civil War, commenting on the burning of Confederate cities. He was from Ohio. I always wondered if he would've sung a different tune if it had been Columbus going up in flames."

"Interesting viewpoint, Lieutenant. You sound like a cynic."

"No, just a cop, but maybe that's the same thing. We tend to see the underside of society most days. Kind of makes you view things differently."

"Not unlike our commando chaps. They live with death and killing every day. It seems to make the question of property destruction somewhat inconsequential. You were with the police before the war?"

"Boston Police Department. Now I'm just a lowly staffer picking up loose ends for Ike. Are you familiar with Knut Birkeland and his fishing fleet in Norway?"

"One doesn't have to go on a raid to know that name. He left behind a rather large fishing fleet in northern waters when he came to England with the king."

"Would it be safe to assume that his ships would be among those destroyed in commando raids?" I could see Carlyle giving that one some thought.

"Yes. One could safely assume that if such raids were carried out, Mr. Birkeland's boats would be amongst those destroyed. If only by the law of averages. He probably owns a third of the fleet in those waters."

Daphne and I exchanged glances. At least now we knew that Birkeland was telling the truth. He indeed had supported a policy that was ruining him financially.

"Did Rolf ever mention a gold coin to you?" I asked.

"Do you mean his lucky coin?"

"Maybe."

"Well, lots of the boys have their superstitions and lucky charms. Rolf was beside himself over a month or so ago when his gold coin went missing. He claims it must have been stolen. He said it was his souvenir from when he helped Birkeland get the Norwegian gold out of the country."

"Had you ever seen it?"

"No, he didn't mention it until it went missing. He wasn't supposed to have it in the first place, so that's understandable. Is he in trouble?"

"No, he fessed up to King Haakon. All was forgiven."

"Good. We'd best be going if I'm going to give you a tour of the base. There are a few interesting things to see. We'll need to finish by 1600 hours. I have to make my rounds."

We left the officers' mess and got into Captain Carlyle's jeep. He drove us around the base, showing us barracks for American paratroopers, rangers, and the British and Norwegian commandos. Same basic spindly wood-frame construction, with metal Quonset huts scattered between them, looking even more temporary and uninviting. Next to those were an exercise field and an obstacle course. I didn't like them much in basic training and wasn't impressed with them here either. He drove along the beach, pointing out a dock with several landing craft and small boats tied up to it. There was also an airstrip with cargo planes and a couple of those small Lysander single-engine jobs that the Brits used to land agents at night. As we drove on, I tried not to think of one of those leaving Diana in some French hay field.

We got out of the jeep at the weapons range. There were firing pits for rifle practice, with both American and British machine guns set up in front of a long shed.

Carlyle showed us a number of German machine guns that had been captured on previous raids. There was even a Norwegian Madsen M/22.

"Everyone goes through the heavy weapons course here," Carlyle told us. "We might need to use captured weapons if things get dicey over there. Care to fire a few rounds, Lieutenant?" Carlyle tapped a German MG-34.

"No thanks, captain. I don't plan to get that close to either end of one of those things."

"Well then, come in here. We have a few subtle tricks that may be more to your liking, the kind of thing I'm sure you haven't seen before."

He opened a door to the shed. Inside there were long benches, boxes marked PLASTIC EXPLOSIVE, disassembled guns, and all sorts of tools and metal devices. It was like an insane Santa's workshop.

"What is all this?" asked Daphne, looking around incredulously.

"The SOE special-devices chaps work in here," Carlyle answered. "They're wizards at coming up with all sorts of nasty tricks for the Jerries."

I walked over to a crate filled with what looked like oversized jacks, the kind kids play with when they bounce a rubber ball and try to pick up a bunch. Except these had three-inch sharp-tipped steel prongs.

"Those are caltrops," said Carlyle. "Any way you throw them, they end up with a sharp point sticking up. We scatter them in the road to inhibit pursuit. They'll pierce any tire."

"I'll bet," I said as I tested the tip with my finger, almost drawing blood. "Isn't it dangerous having plastic explosive lying around, especially so close to a firing range?"

"Absolutely not, Lieutenant," Carlyle said as he led us over to a workbench stacked with blocks of the stuff in different forms. "Plastic explosive is completely malleable and harmless without a detonator. Why, you could even eat the stuff if you had to get rid of it."

"Yum." Daphne laughed.

"Here," he said, handing me a block about six inches by four by two. "This is a clam. With a detonator attached, it would be deadly. Without it, you could jump up and down on it with no effect."

"What's it used for?" I asked, handing it back without bothering to test his claim.

"A single clam could bend a piece of railway line, break an axle on a large vehicle, that sort of thing. These larger pieces are limpets, waterproofed and magnetized, to be placed against a ship's hull. Three or four of these could sink a good-sized ship."

"Ahhh! A rat!" Daphne, startled, grabbed my arm. She pointed at another bench at the end of the room.

"Not to worry, my dear," Carlyle said calmly. That's just one of the chaps' latest ideas. The explosive rat!" He walked proudly over to it and lifted it up by the tail.

"An authentic black rat, quite dead, its body cavity hollowed out and stuffed with plastic explosive. Fitted with a time-delay fuse, it can be safely left about under a building or just about anywhere. The idea is that no one wants to bother with a big black rat, so there would be ample time for an agent to get away."

"I suppose that this thing operates on the same principle, or is this item not too sanitary?" I asked, pointing at a pile of well, shit on the bench as Daphne wrinkled her nose.

"Exactly. The explosive turd, believe it or not. Not the real thing, but filled with plastic explosive and set up with a pressure switch. It's made to look like horse or cow droppings."

"So an officer orders some poor slob of a

private to clean it up, and boom?" I asked, somewhat dubious about the military value of this thing.

"Well, that's the general idea. One hopes the officer is nearby, or it's under a vehicle."

"Do you bring all this with you on raids, captain?" Daphne asked.

"These items are more for single agents, or the underground. We do use the clams and limpets, as well as this little device, which the SOE agents also like."

He picked up a short round tube with one end flattened. There was a small switch at the flat end. He handed it carefully to Daphne.

"This is a pressure switch. The tube is filled with plastic explosive. You jam the flat end under a tire, which depresses the switch and activates it. When the vehicle pulls away off the tube, the switch pops up and the tire bomb instantly explodes."

"Should do a good job of discouraging pursuit," I offered.

"Exactly. We once placed them at night under the tires of a row of trucks outside a German barracks. Then we went on to hit our target, about two miles away. A few minutes after we began, there was a lovely row of explosions off in the distance as the fuel tanks went up!"

"Delightful," said Daphne, gingerly putting the tube back down on the bench.

"Oh yes, quite," the captain said with unabashed enthusiasm.

I could see Carlyle enjoyed all these devices. I couldn't begrudge the commandos anything that might give them an edge, but there seemed to be a glint in his eye that said he was in it for the thrills as much as for God and country. Maybe that was natural for someone who climbed mountains for fun. Me, I didn't even like walking up Beacon Hill.

CHAPTER EIGHTEEN

Captain Carlyle had to get back to his patients. He offered to drive us to the headquarters office to wait for Rolf, but we decided to walk. It was a nice day, and we could take the roadway along the beach. I wanted to talk, and I didn't want to talk about murder suspects and spies with a company clerk listening to us.

A cool breeze blew in from the ocean, or the North Sea it was, I guess. There were puffy white clouds high in the sky, and the sun came in and out as they passed over, sunlight drenching us for a minute until the next cloud rolled by. A couple of Lockheed A-28 Hudsons with RAF markings flew overhead and straight out to sea, their engines snarling as they took off, the sound fading as Daphne watched them disappear toward the horizon.

"Probably hunting U-boats, or watching for surface raiders sneaking out from Wilhelmshaven along the Norwegian coast," she said.

"Like the *Bismarck*?" I asked.

"Yes. It's hard to believe how worried we were about one single German ship. Everything seemed to be hanging by a thread in those days."

"There's still plenty to worry about."

"Worrying about Diana is not quite the same thing as worrying about the Nazis marching into Buckingham Palace. That's something Americans safe across the Atlantic may not understand."

"Safe across the Atlantic is just where I'd like to be right now. But I'd settle for Diana safe on this side of the channel."

"Until this war is won, Billy, none of us will have the luxury of such choices. I wonder if even then we can ever relax again, knowing what evil the world is capable of."

"Daphne, you don't need a war to learn about evil. Spend a few days with a cop in any city and you'll get a fair taste of it."

"But it never touched us before. Now it's reached out and grabbed all of us. My brother, my sister . . . I don't want to lose them, too. Losing Mother was awful enough. I can't imagine. . . ." She started to cry and dabbed at her eyes with a handkerchief.

I didn't know how I could tell her everything was going to be OK, so I didn't.

"I'm sorry, Billy. Let's talk about something else, all right?"

"OK." I smiled and gave her hand a squeeze.

"So tell me, Billy, why did you ask Captain Carlyle about Rolf's gold coin?"

"Just to see if Rolf's story holds up, about someone stealing his little souvenir."

"You didn't believe him?"

"I just wanted some verification. Maybe that was the coin that showed up in Knut Birkeland's room. Maybe it wasn't."

"But if Carlyle never saw the coin, and only heard about it after Rolf said it was stolen, then maybe it wasn't stolen at all."

"Daphne," I smiled, "you have the makings of a good cop. Suspicious of everyone. What do you think happened to it?"

"Maybe Rolf gave it to somebody. Maybe he gave it to Knut Birkeland? Perhaps they were in on the theft together."

"If there really was a theft. We don't know that either."

"How do you keep all this straight, Billy? My head's spinning."

"Pretty much my permanent condition."

"But the real question is why would Rolf lie about the coin? I can't think of a single reason, can you? He seems a decent sort. He certainly cares for his men, insisting on all that medical training."

That reminded me of something.

"When I got those splinters in my face, back at Beardsley Hall, Jens Iversen patched me up. He said something about its being something any first-year medical student could do."

"Yes, I think he mentioned that he had been in medical school when the war started. Second year, I think."

"So two people involved in this had some medical knowledge. Rolf Kayser, through his medical orderly training, and Jens Iversen, after two years of medical school."

"Yes, I guess so. What does that mean?"

"Probably nothing."

I did think it might mean something, but it was too soon to tell. I needed a few more connections to pop up before I was sure.

"With all these suspicions, Billy, there's just one fact for certain: that we found Knut Birkeland's key in Anders's room. Of course, that doesn't mean Anders put it there."

"You're learning fast, Daphne. But it also means something else."

"What?"

"That if someone other than Anders put

it there, it was when Anders was out of the room, which he says he wasn't."

"Hmmm. Or it was put there by someone who was in the room with Anders, when he wasn't looking."

"Which still means he's lying."

"Everything seems to go around in a circle! This is so frustrating!"

"Hang in there, kid. Sooner or later we'll come across something that will put everything in perspective. Then it will all make sense."

Daphne shook her head in frustration and disbelief that we'd ever figure anything out. We walked in silence up the road to the headquarters building. HQ was the last of three wood-frame structures, each up on cement blocks. The windows were open and somebody had the radio on. "GI Jive" was playing on Armed Forces Radio, and the words floated out as we climbed the four steps to the door. We opened the door, and there was Major Anders Arnesen, feet up on a desk, a cigarette between his lips, his fingers keeping time to the tune.

"There you are, Billy! I've been looking all over for you. You know, American music is simply fantastic. Jazz, swing, I love it all."

"That's great, Anders. I like it, too. What are you doing here?"

"I can't say in here," Anders said, looking around at the clerks at work at the other desks. "But I can tell you more at dinner. Rolf is back from maneuvers and will meet us in that beautiful little café they call the mess after he cleans up." He stood.

"Miss Seaton, I trust you will join us?"

"Certainly, Major," Daphne said. "You seem to be in a cheerful mood. It must be good news."

"I think so. Now, I must make some arrangements. We will meet in the officers' mess in one hour." He started toward the door.

"Oh, I almost forgot, Billy." He reached into his uniform jacket pocket and pulled out a sealed envelope. "Major Cosgrove asked me to give you this."

"What is it?"

"I'm just the messenger, Billy. See you both in an hour."

He left, whistling the tune to "GI Jive" and snapping his fingers like he didn't have a care in the world. Daphne and I walked over to a bench set against the wall, under a curtainless window. I opened the envelope and took out the papers so we could both read what was inside. Cosgrove had come through on his promise to look in to any women working at Beardsley Hall whose husbands were POWs or missing in action. There was only one. Victoria Brey, subaltern with the Auxiliary Territorial Service. Twenty-six years old and her husband served in the RAF, bomber command. He had been listed as missing in action when his bomber went down over the Dutch coast earlier that year. Several parachutes had been seen, but he hadn't shown up on any POW lists. He could be dead, or he could be in hiding. He probably was long gone, washed out to sea and now forgotten except for a grieving and guilty wife. I thumbed through the sheaf of documents.

"Damn!"

"What is it, Billy?"

"She's been transferred out of Beardsley Hall. Here's a copy of her travel orders. Dated two days ago, giving her five days' leave."

"Where has she been transferred to?" asked Daphne.

"To the Norwegian Brigade base in Scotland."

"Why would she be transferred out of Beardsley Hall?"

"Maybe to protect her. Or maybe she's becoming an embarrassment. As head of security, wouldn't Jens Iversen have something to say about transfers?"

"Everything," Daphne answered as she took the papers to look at them. "He'd be the one to authorize any request or initiate the orders. Look here, Billy, she lives in Greenchurch. That's only two hours north of here."

"She still has three days' leave. I hope that she's spending it at home. We'll talk to Rolf tonight, then head to Greenchurch in the morning. Between the two of them, maybe we'll learn something new."

"Good. Otherwise, this is just a tour of the East Anglia countryside."

"Thanks for reminding me. Let's do something useful while we wait for Rolf and square away our quarters for the night."

I asked one of the company clerks where the HQ company first sergeant was.

"Top is in Captain Gilmore's office, through there," he said, indicating the rear hallway with his thumb, which I guess doubled as a salute.

"Top?" Daphne asked.

"Top kick," I said, "is what we call the first sergeant in a company. Top enlisted man in the company, and usually ready to kick GIs in the ass to motivate them."

"Let's hope he can motivate someone out of their quarters so I have a place to sleep. I haven't seen any female staff here at all."

I stopped at Gilmore's door and knocked. The steady sound of slamming typewriter keys echoed off the bare wood walls.

"Top?"

"Whaddya need?"

His back was to us and he was hunched over a small table that held a typewriter and a stack of forms. Smoke drifted up from a cigarette stuck in his mouth. It bobbed up and down as he spoke, scattering ash over the keys.

"Quarters for some visiting officers."

"We're not due for any brass. . . ." He turned, probably figuring it was some private bothering him for no good reason. He saw me, and frowned in irritation. Lieutenants were just a burden to any sergeant worth his salt. Second Louies didn't have the rank to get anything worthwhile done, and took up a noncoms valuable time. Then he saw Daphne, and stood. I guess lady junior officers were a different story.

"First Sergeant Frank Slater, ma'am. I didn't know we had a female on base."

"That's all right, Top," Daphne said, obviously enjoying the new slang. "As long as you can find me a room for the night. I'm Second Officer Daphne Seaton, Women's Royal Naval Service. This is Lieutenant —"

"We have very nice visitors' quarters, and no one there at the moment. It's all yours, ma'am."

She smiled at him, and I saw a face that could freeze enlisted men in their tracks soften like ice cream in August. He crushed his cigarette, grabbed his cap, and brushed by me to offer Daphne his arm.

"May I show you the way?"

"Yes, you may, Sergeant Slater. I assume you have someplace for Lieutenant Boyle?"

"Who?"

Daphne tilted her head toward me.

"Oh, sure. Do you have luggage?"

"Yes, in a little red car right out front."

As they walked down the hall, Slater yelled to one of the GI clerks. "Hanson, get the lady's luggage and bring it over to the VIP quarters. Then show this lieutenant to a spare room in the officers' quarters."

Again, the thumb hooked over the shoulder. Must be a local custom.

After stashing my gear, I visited the quartermaster, showed him my very authoritative orders, and persuaded him to part with some shirts, socks, and skivvies. He didn't like issuing supplies to someone not in his table of organization, but that was tough. Orders from ETO HQ countersigned by a representative of the Imperial General

Staff were hard to ignore. I washed up, put on a clean shirt, and felt like a million bucks heading over to the officers' mess.

The feeling didn't last long. Rolf was already there, sitting alone at a table for four. He waved me over. An orderly brought us a couple of beers.

"*Hei,* Billy. Welcome to Southwold. You should like the food; it's an American mess. I must admit I'm becoming spoiled by it." He lifted a bottle of Rheingold, almost covering it in his big hand, and took a long drink, draining half of it. He put the bottle down and looked me in the eye.

"What can I do for you?"

"Tell me about the morning of Knut Birkeland's murder. What did you see at Beardsley Hall? Anything unusual?"

He shrugged. "No. It was early. It was dark. I went to the king's rooms at exactly four thirty. . . ."

"What time did you get up?"

"I had set my alarm for four fifteen. I got up, dressed, and left my room. I didn't see anyone. It was quiet. The king's valet had provided a thermos of coffee and some bread and cheese sandwiches. We walked out front to the car and drove away. It was entirely unremarkable."

I went over it all again, probing for any

little thing he may have seen, anything out of the ordinary. I got nothing, except that it was dark and quiet. Not exactly revelations about a country house on the heath at four thirty in the morning.

Daphne and Anders walked in and came over to the table. Rolf stood and made a little fancy continental bow to Daphne. I half stood, then slumped back into my chair.

"Rolf, how good to see you again," Daphne said.

"And you," said Rolf. "Please sit and cheer up Billy. I have been unable to help him at all and he seems quite depressed."

"Still no closer to finding the killer, Billy?" asked Anders as they seated themselves.

"Doesn't seem so."

"Are you sure there was a killer? I thought Birkeland left a suicide note," said Rolf. "Has something else happened?" There was a moment of uneasy silence.

"Rolf," said Anders, "you had to leave, so you probably don't know that the key to Birkeland's locked room was found. In my room."

"Well, Billy, you seem to have your man!" Rolf lifted his glass in a mock toast to Anders, who raised his hands in surrender. They both laughed and Daphne joined in. It looked like it was going to be a real fun evening. We all ordered another drink, and then my curiosity got the better of me.

"So, Anders, tell us. What's your big news?"

"What are you up to, *min venn?*" asked Rolf. Anders looked around and leaned in to whisper to us.

"Let me just say that the king has agreed to my plan." Anders leaned back and smiled. He had wanted to return to Norway and make contact with the Underground Army to evaluate its effectiveness. This plan had represented a middle ground in the argument between Vidar Skak and Knut Birkeland, and it looked like the king was playing it safe.

"Is Vidar angry?" asked Rolf.

"Yes, of course, but he's pretending to be very friendly. I'm his next best hope if he can't convince the king. I'm to make an initial report in thirty days."

"So you're going soon?" I asked.

"I fly from here to Scotland in the morning." He didn't say anything else, but he didn't have to. Scotland was the jumping-off point for commando raids and agent drops to Norway. They went in by fishing boat, submarine, or sometimes airplane. So another suspect was getting out of Dodge before I was done with the investigation. I knew there was a war on, but I still didn't like it one bit.

"Congratulations. You deserve such an important mission," said Rolf. "But I'm surprised the king let you go. He seemed intent on keeping you with the brigade."

"I think he finally decided a report from a trusted source was the most logical way to decide about the underground," Anders answered. "But I shouldn't say any more. I'd trust one of the musketeers with my life and I'm sure General Eisenhower's staff is above suspicion, but my orders are top secret. Please do not repeat anything I've said."

"Or didn't say," I added.

"Yes, that also."

"So," Rolf said, "to change the subject, where is the baron? The three of you seemed to be a team." He raised his eyebrow at me, as if asking if I had ditched Kaz to get Daphne alone. Or maybe he just had a twitch. Whatever it was, Daphne must've caught it, too, because she spoke up quickly, defending me against the insinuation.

"Oh, Kaz is in London, doing some research. He's looking into who else might benefit from Mr. Birkeland's death."

"Good idea," Rolf said. "Like who would inherit his business, that sort of thing?"

"Yes," Daphne answered, "and —"

I jumped in. "It's just a long shot. He probably won't have any business left to inherit if the raids keep up."

"We're ordered to destroy the fishing plants, *forbann det!* How do you think it feels for Norwegians to ruin their own fishing industry?"

"Whoa, Rolf, hold on," I said. "I never blamed anyone. It's Allied policy, that's all. Don't get all hot under the collar."

"It's bad enough that we have to do it, Billy, but it adds insult to injury that you are investigating the motives of patriotic Norwegians."

"First, it may turn out that Birkeland wasn't killed by a Norwegian. Second, if he was, the killer wouldn't be very patriotic, if he killed the king's trusted adviser."

Rolf seemed to calm down. He looked at us a little guiltily. "I understand. I apologize," he said. "I know you are only doing your duty."

"As are we all," Anders said very seriously. He raised his glass. "To duty, wherever it takes us." We clinked glasses and drank. Dinner came. It was good American food. Roast beef, mashed potatoes, and succotash. But my appetite wasn't what it should have been. The roast beef sat in a twisted ball in my stomach as I pushed the rest of my food around the plate and looked at Daphne, trying not to be mad at her. It was kind of sweet that she had spoken up for me and real dumb to have let the cat out of the bag.

We talked about the war news for a while. There was a lot of it. We had just sunk some Jap carriers off an island named Midway in the Pacific somewhere. Churchill was in the States for talks with Roosevelt. The Afrika Korps was driving deeper into Libya. Daphne was fairly sure her brother, Thomas, was with the Eighth Army in Egypt but wasn't certain, and it worried her. That meant her two siblings were in danger. I wondered how she felt, safe here in England. Did she, like Diana, want to tempt fate, too?

After dinner I walked Daphne back to her quarters. She looped her arm around mine and I had a hard time staying mad at her. Since meeting Diana I was beginning to think of Daphne as a kid sister and that made things a lot easier.

"Are we off to Greenchurch tomorrow, Billy?"

"Not we. I am, but I want you to drive back to Beardsley Hall and talk to Harding or Cosgrove. Get them to intervene and have Anders's orders cancelled. I don't want him leaving the country until we get this thing sorted out."

"Do you think he's the killer?"

"I don't know yet. But now he knows we're looking into Birkeland's business, and if there's any connection it'd be a breeze for him to vanish into the countryside once he gets to Norway. Until he's in the clear, I want him here."

"Oh, Billy! I didn't realize —"

"Don't worry about it. See if you can get in touch with Kaz, too, and find out what he's got. I'll commandeer some transport here and join you at Beardsley Hall after I drop in at Greenchurch."

"All right. I'm so sorry, Billy. I feel as if I failed you."

"You didn't. You've done great so far. You just have a few things to learn. You don't become an ace detective overnight, you know!"

"Billy, you're a dear!" She kissed me on the cheek. "I'll see you back at the hall." She pranced up the stairs to the door of the VIP quarters and waved good night. I waved back and walked off, thinking about what a swell kid she was. It's funny how silly a crush on somebody can seem after you've met the real thing. I stuffed my hands in my pockets and slowly walked over to the officers' quarters, the setting sun behind me lighting up the sky over the gray sea ahead. I kicked a stone, tried not to think about Diana and the night before, and wondered where she'd be tomorrow.

CHAPTER NINETEEN

"I don't give a rat's ass about your orders, Lieutenant," said Captain Gilmore.

The bad mood fit him like a glove. Yesterday I had thought it was just due to the confusion of handing out all that winter gear. Today I found him sitting at his clean desk, drinking coffee, chewing on a cigar, and looking for someone to scowl at. The pile of reports that Sergeant Slater had been working on the day before were all neatly stacked up in his out basket, signed and ready to go up the line. He should've been happy, but that probably didn't come easy for him.

"But they're from ETO Headquarters, sir. . . ."

"All I get from HQ are headaches, sonny. If they want to send someone who outranks me up here, I'll salute and give them anything they want. But I'm not giving a vehicle to some Louie who drove in here in a sports car, I'll tell you that."

"But sir —"

"Enough!"

It came out as a growl, wrapped around a wet stogie. I was wondering what to do next when Slater appeared out of nowhere and walked over to the captain's desk. He pointedly ignored me again and spoke directly to Gilmore.

"Begging your pardon, captain, but this might be a good opportunity to fix that little problem we were talking about."

Gilmore looked at Slater like he was another fly the captain was going to swat. Then I could almost see the lightbulb go off over his head as he dropped the scowl and nodded his head in agreement.

"Yes, very good, Top. Show the lieutenant to the Brit motor pool while I make the call."

Since they were talking about me as if I weren't there, I didn't see any percentage in asking what was going on. My chances had improved since Slater came into the room, so I picked up my kit and followed him out of the exec's office. Gilmore was almost cackling with glee as he dialed the phone. At least it made him happy.

"Thanks, Top, I think. What's this all about?"

"Well, we got two motor pools here, one Brit and one U.S., so we can take care of both types of transport. The motor-pool guys have taken to tinkering with a few vehicles and having races. The latest thing is motorcycles. You ever ride?"

"Sure. My cousin is a motorcycle cop in Boston, where I used to work. I've ridden his Harley."

"That's what we got here. We being the Yanks. The Brits have a BMW — a sweet thing from before the war, I have to admit. We have a race scheduled for tomorrow. Thing is, our guy crashed the Harley yesterday and they can't get the spare parts to fix it until after the weekend."

"And you forfeit the race if you don't show?"

"That's the rule."

"Fair bit of money bet on this one?"

For the first time, he actually looked at me, giving me a practiced once-over to decide if I was a by-the-book or a let-things-slide kind of lieutenant.

"Now, Lieutenant, you know that would be against army regulations."

The faintest smile passed over his blunt face, then he quickly looked away — no need to waste words on a very junior lieutenant.

"In other words, a bundle."

"I don't intend on losing my next paycheck on a no-show. I was waiting for the captain to think of this, but it didn't look like he was going to, so I jumped in."

The top kick opened the door and held it for me as we stepped outside. The air smelled damp and clean, a fresh sea breeze drying the dew from the grass as the sun struggled to come out from behind a low cloud layer. Not the worst day for a motorcycle ride.

"Whatever would the army do without sergeants?"

"I ask myself that question every morning, Lieutenant."

He led the way to the British motor pool. All the walkways were laid out with those whitewashed rocks that seemed to crop up at every army base I'd ever seen. I wondered what they did in Alaska or Greenland.

"Am I going to ruin your racing plans if I don't bring the BMW back?"

"Oh, you'll bring it back. It's British army property, and a couple of hundred commandos, all trained to kill silently, will be looking for you if you don't. Lieutenant," he added, as if it was an afterthought.

He led me into a wide garage, not much more than corrugated sheet metal nailed on to a wooden frame. The floor was hard-packed dirt, and the smell of oil and damp soil was oddly pleasing. Several British army vehicles were in various stages of disassembly and repair, and we walked past those to the darkened rear of the building. In a corner next to a workbench neatly stacked with gleaming tools, on a drop cloth and under a hanging light, was a BMW motorcycle, painted British army brown, polished to a high gloss and clean as a whistle. Three men, also in British army brown but not all that clean, stood with their arms folded in front of us.

"Now what's all this about taking our motorcycle? Just because yours —"

"Hold on, Malcolm," Slater said. "You know ours is still being worked on. This officer needs transportation and the BMW is the only vehicle not signed out."

"Neither of us ever signs out these machines!"

I knew I had entered some special part of the military world, where noncoms ruled and officers were just an irritation, an insistent itch that demanded once in a while to be scratched. They gave me a glance, read me like a field manual, and decided I wasn't going to give them any trouble, except for taking their bike. They ignored me, rightfully understanding this was a matter between guys with stripes, not bars.

"It's just for a day or so. We'll have the race when he gets back, no problem," Slater said.

"Aye, if I'm dumb enough to believe you. Very convenient to come up with this story just after that corporal of yours runs your Harley-Davidson into a ditch," Malcolm said. The others laughed, and he joined them, enjoying the position he was in.

"Malcolm, take a look at these orders of his. Signed not only by Ike's office, but by some guy from your own Imperial Staff!"

Slater held the orders in front of Malcolm, who wiped his hand on a greasy rag and took them by the edges. He looked at each page and then over at me, then back again, as if he couldn't believe they were for the guy he was gazing at. He shook his head in disgust and handed them back to Slater.

"All right, but you'll have to sign a few forms, Lieutenant."

"Thanks, Malcolm," Slater said as he turned to leave, "and good luck, Lieutenant. Make sure you bring her back in one piece."

That earned me even blacker glares from the Brit mechanics, so I dug into my kit and came up with three packs of Lucky Strikes.

I handed them out along with my apologies and promises to return the motorcycle in a couple of days. I must've sounded convincing, because although I didn't really give a hoot about their motorcycle race, and they didn't care a bit about what I needed, pretty soon we were all smoking and trading war stories about bikes and cars. After chewing the fat for a while, they left me with one mechanic, a Scottish corporal, who was giving the BMW a final check over.

Corporal Roddy Ross was of indeterminate age, the skin of his hands and even his face covered in a sheen of grease and oil. He was rail thin, but his forearms were muscular, and he had a certain grace as he moved around the machine, tightening connections and wiping her down with a cloth as he went. He had a Lucky stuck in the corner of his mouth and smoked as he talked, blowing out smoke with each phrase and squinting his right eye against the blue smoke curling up from the tip of the cigarette.

"Now, laddie, are ye shur ye kin find yer way? Greenchurch is but one of a dozen wee small villages yonder." He pointed with his thumb toward the northeast as he rested his other hand protectively on the handlebar of the BMW. I had to concentrate on listening to him to understand his thick Scottish brogue.

"I've studied the map, Corporal, and copied down my route. If I get lost, I can always stop and ask for directions." This brought a chuckle.

"Oh, yeah, as if the English wouldn't mistake a Yank for a Jerry and blow yer young head off with a shotgun! That far inland, there's been hardly a single Yank yet."

I could tell from his tone that Corporal Ross was certain that any Scotsman could tell the difference between a Yank and a German, but that he wasn't about to vouch for anyone south of Hadrian's Wall.

"Well, Corporal, what do you suggest? Maps are in short supply."

"You know that all the road signs have been taken down hereabouts. But I should be able to draw up me own sort of directions. Fer a man who knows his pubs, it should be easy."

With that, he set down his rag and pulled out a stub of a pencil from his overalls pocket and a small pad from the workbench. He licked the end of the pencil, wrote studiously for a minute, ripped off a sheet, and handed it to me.

Pittsfield — straight at the Red Hart
St. Paul — left at the King George Inn
Midbury — straight at the Blue Swan

"Corporal, you're a genius. It must've taken a lot of research to come up with this!"

"Well, ye know what the English say about the Scots: we know the value of a shilling. I wanted to find the best value for a pint and I had to go far and wide in search of it. Now this road at Midbury should take ye right into Greenchurch, though it's a long stretch. Ask there at the Miller's Stone for where ye need to go. And take good care of this machine!"

"I will, Corporal, if you let go of it."

He took his hand off the handlebar, smiled weakly, and stepped back to give me some room. I stowed my pack and got on. We shook hands. He opened a wide side door with a narrow wood-plank ramp. I adjusted my goggles and kick-started the engine. It came to life immediately and purred like a kitten. I sat for a minute, getting the feel of the machine while I let the quiet rumbling vibrate through my body. I nodded to Ross, who got his hand halfway up to his forehead, executing an absent salute as he kept his eye on the bike. I took the BMW slowly down the ramp, did a turn, waved, and rode off. Out of respect for the corporal and his work I didn't open her right up, but rode at a sedate pace up to the main gate. On the way out, Rolf Kayser pulled in front of me in a jeep. He gave a friendly salute, went through the gate, and drove south. I passed the gate and went north on the main road, giving the bike full throttle, hoping the sound would carry back to the motor pool, where I knew Corporal Ross would still be standing just as I had left him, straining his ears to follow the nuance of each gearshift.

The BMW responded like a champ. The throaty rumble of the engine echoed off the hills rising up on each side of the road, and I felt like a schoolkid playing hooky. For the first time in days I was alone, off on my own for a little side trip to the quaint village of Greenchurch, where I doubted I'd find anything new. Even if Subaltern Victoria Brey had seen somebody that morning as she made her way back to her room, did it make that person the murderer? Half a dozen people were up and about, in their own private little worlds, when Knut Birkeland took his dive. Would one more really make a difference? Yeah, maybe it would.

I opened up the BMW on a straightaway to see what it could do. The acceleration pulled me back in the seat and I hunched over, made myself smaller and watched the road unwind in front of me. I eased up on the throttle as the road narrowed where it passed along a hillside, white stone markers on either side. A grassy slope went up on my right, down on my left. I could see muddy paths where cows made their way among the fields and could smell them, too, the odor of green grass and manure flowing over me as I opened her up on another straightaway.

I hoped this trip would make a difference, almost prayed for it. Right now, if someone asked my opinion based on pure logic, I'd have to say Knut Birkeland really had killed himself, if only because that answered the most questions. If I had to answer from my gut, though, I'd bet my next paycheck that he'd been murdered. I had a working theory of how, but it didn't lead me anywhere. Why and who were still mysteries. If only Birkeland had been poisoned. Then I would've clapped the irons on Vidar Skak. He was just the kind of snake who would use poison. Unfortunately, he wasn't the kind of snake to wrestle Knut Birkeland out the window. Cosgrove still bothered me, too. There was something off about him, but I had no idea what. Yet. My thoughts drifted into all the possibilities, all the suspects, and all the reasons why.

It came around a curve I hadn't realized was there — a big, dusty gray vehicle with the driver laying on his horn. The bike wobbled and started to skid and I almost lost control as I tried to recover from my surprise. I caught myself and banked into a curve, just as a truck — or a lorry or whatever the hell they called it over here — came around the bend. I slowed down and pulled over to the side of the road, waiting for my heart to slow too. I decided to stop thinking about the case and keep my mind on riding on the wrong side of the road or else they were going to be scraping me up off it. I started up again, slow, and just rode.

Fields and woods thick with oak trees flowed by as I got used to the BMW and let it go at its own pace, not gunning it but not holding back either. Everything else fell away until there was just the motorcycle, the road, and me. Once you got down to basics, things were simpler. The low cloud cover had given way to light fluffy clouds and blue sky, and I could feel the sun on my back. I passed the Red Hart and kept going straight, feeling my worries melt away with the miles. I wondered why I hadn't gotten one of the thousands of office jobs in this war. Everywhere I went, I saw guys pushing paper, stamping paper, filing paper, carrying files of paper. That was supposed to be me. Those guys worked a full day, five or six days a week, but they didn't have to worry about murderers and spies, and coming up with answers for Ike. I knew guys in the combat outfits would have it rough, but, hell, I had already been shot at, and as of right now, not a single GI had even fired a rifle at the Nazis!

I was getting myself all riled up and almost missed the next pub. I calmed down, and took a left at the King George Inn as I wondered if it was the same King George we had given the heave-ho to at Bunker Hill. It was almost midday by the time I had nearly reached the very small village of Greenchurch. I saw a large round stone, like the wheel from a windmill, propped up in front of a low whitewashed building. The Miller's Stone. I turned around in front of a church — it wasn't green — and pulled the BMW up in front of the pub. There were a few bicycles leaning against the wall. Not a single car. Real quiet little town. Houses with window boxes overflowing with flowers lined the street. Across from the pub was a small white building, its plain front broken by two doors, one marked POST OFFICE.

The other led to a small store. A dog sleeping in the sun on the stone step leading up to the store entrance raised his head, gave me the once-over, then laid his head back down, unimpressed.

I figured that since I had to ask directions to Victoria Brey's house, and since I was also hungry and thirsty, it would be the most efficient use of my time to visit the pub. That actually made it my patriotic duty. I dusted myself off and went inside.

It was a small village pub, low ceilinged and dark. There were just a couple of tables, a bench along one wall, and the bar itself on the right side of the room with a few stools along it. I sat down and nodded to two old gents who were nursing pints that looked like they'd been pulled when the place opened. Neither said hello, but one of them pointed his pipe at me.

"Now what kind of uniform is that?"

"You mean my United States Army officer's uniform?"

"So you're a Yank, are you? About time. I haven't seen one since 1918!"

They both thought this was real funny. I turned my attention to the barkeep, or publican, I think they called him here.

"A pint, and what do you have for food?"

"A ploughman's lunch is all today."

"OK, but hold the onion. I've got to see a lady this afternoon."

I smiled, he didn't. I decided he really wasn't such a bad sort when he brought out bread still warm from the oven, a slab of cheese, and a homemade pickle in place of the onion. Along with the ale it was a meal fit for a king.

After he brought the food he ignored me, which I guess was better than lecturing me on the late arrival of the U.S. Army. After I had inhaled about half the meal, I slowed down and half turned in my seat, speaking to both the publican and his customers.

"Do any of you fellows know where Victoria Brey lives?"

At the sound of her name, the old fellas looked at each other and just shook their heads. Not at me, but just at the mention of her name. "Sad, so sad," one of them said. The barkeep walked over, drying a glass in his hand.

"Why do you want to know?" The expression on his face said he'd be glad to bean me with the heavy glass if he didn't like the answer.

"Just some routine army business. About her transfer, just some paperwork to finish," I lied.

"She's in the ATS, not the bloody American army."

"Yeah, but we're all on the same side. Right?"

"I don't know you, mate. I don't know if you're trouble or not, but I do know Victoria's had her share. More than her share."

"I've known her since she was a babe," the old guy said. "So sad."

"I just need to talk with her a bit, that's all. I know she's had it tough, with her husband missing in action."

"Have a care with her. She's still not well. And she's well liked 'round here, so don't cause her any problems." The barkeep walked back to the bar, carrying the well-dried glass. He had made his decision, but I could tell he didn't like it much. Or me.

"Take the first right up by the church. Then take the left fork. Her place is on the left, a small stone cottage." The barkeep put the glass on the bar, loud enough to punctuate the sentence. I didn't say anything about the implied threat. I could take a hint. I finished up, paid, and left. No one said good-bye.

I found her place easy enough and her, too, for that matter. She was sitting on a worn wooden bench in a small garden in front of her cottage. It looked like a house to me, but I figured it was one of those

English things. I pulled the BMW into the drive and switched it off. The driveway was packed dirt with weeds sprouting out of it, wildflowers forcing their way through the hard surface. She looked over at me as calmly as if Americans on motorcycles showed up every day. I took off my goggles and Parsons field jacket, and attempted to make myself presentable. I brushed the dust off my pants, put on my fore and aft cap at just the right angle, and walked into the garden. She sat still, gazing at the flowers.

"Nice garden, Mrs. Brey." She nodded, ever so slightly, and looked up at me with moist eyes. She was twisting a handkerchief in her hands, limp and damp from her tears.

"Yes, isn't it? They'll probably all die now. . . ."

"Now that you're being transferred?"

"No. Now that Richard's . . . gone. He always tended them. Said a home needed flowers blooming around it first thing in the spring. He always looked forward to spring-time."

Her head swiveled back to look at the flowers. She dabbed at her eyes with the handkerchief she held crumpled in one hand. I could have jumped on a broomstick and flown away for all she cared. She was someplace else. There wasn't another chair and I had to make eye contact, so I knelt down in front of her.

"Mrs. Brey?" Her eyes wavered and finally found me.

"Yes? Who are you?" That was progress.

"Lieutenant Billy Boyle, ma'am. I'm investigating the death of Knut Birkeland at Beardsley Hall."

She laughed. The laughter seemed to break the spell for her and she focused on me as she smiled.

"That's terribly funny."

"What is?" I asked.

"One old man dies and they send a lieutenant. Thousands die in the air, at sea, all over the world, and then who do they send? No one." She laughed some more. At first, I thought she was crazy, and then I thought it over. It really didn't add up, did it?

"I'm sorry, Lieutenant Boyle. I'm not usually so distracted. I haven't been back here since Richard . . . disappeared. The memories were . . . I'm afraid I've been rude."

She wiped her eyes and tried to smile again. There wasn't a lot of happiness to work with, so it wasn't a big smile. She was pretty in a plain English country-girl sort of way, and even that frail grin lit up her face. Her hair was dark brown and pulled back, showing off a long and graceful neck. Her skin was flushed from the heat and a tiny bead of sweat worked its way down her throat and vanished beneath her pale green sundress, open at the neck and cinched tight at her waist. The curves of her hips and breasts were noticeable under the light material.

"Come inside, and tell me why you've traveled all this way."

She stood and walked toward the house, glancing over her shoulder at me. She caught me looking, and smiled. It was quite a change, as if she had awakened from a trance. She offered to make tea, but it was too hot a day for me. She poured lemonade, and we went into her front parlor. She sat in an armchair and I took the couch. I was nervous. I was thinking about her body and the look she had given me over her shoulder. I thought about Diana. I thought about getting the hell out of there. Instead, I got down to business.

"Mrs. Brey, you're in the Auxiliary Territorial Service, rank of subaltern, correct?" I tried to sound like your typical uninterested cop.

"I'm sure you know that, Lieutenant, don't you?"

"Ah, yes, I do. Just checking."

"Tell me how I can help you . . . did you

say your name was Billy?"

"Yes, ma'am."

"Well, if I'm going to call you Billy, you must call me Victoria. But not Vicky. Only Richard calls me that." I looked up on the wall behind her at the framed photo of a young man in an RAF uniform. He stood next to a bomber, a wide smile on his face, the RAF roundel showing in back of him. Both man and machine long gone.

"Victoria, I don't mean to pry into your private life, and I want you to know that I'm not compiling a written report or anything. . . ."

"My goodness, Billy, whatever are you going to ask me about?"

"I understand that you were in Jens Iversen's room early, very early in the morning on the day Knut Birkeland died."

She nodded. "Yes, I was." Calm and cool. No embarrassment, no anger at the question.

"And he escorted you from his room back to your room?"

"Part of the way. He didn't want to be seen, so he took me down his hallway, down the staircase, and then turned back."

"I should tell you, Victoria, that Jens didn't tell me your name. I wouldn't want you to think he betrayed your confidence."

"Why would I care what that little worm thinks?"

Whoa. That took me by surprise. I had thought they had a hot romance going. How did Jens get to be "that little worm"?

"Weren't you and he . . . close?" I asked.

"All he wanted was sex," she said disgustedly. "He pretended to be my friend and to comfort me, but all he wanted was to get his hands all over my body."

I had noticed that whenever women talked about some guy getting fresh with them, they would unconsciously put their hands over their breasts in a protective gesture, checking buttons or pulling at something. But Victoria sat there, one leg crossed over the other, with her hands resting flat on the chair arms. Something was really wrong here.

"I got the feeling he was devoted to you."

"I thought so, too. But evidently not. Did you come here to ask me about Jens?"

"No, no. I'd like to know who or what you might have seen on the way to your room that morning. Anybody or anything out of the ordinary."

"Am I a suspect, Billy?"

"Did you kill Knut Birkeland?" I asked.

"No."

"Then you're in the clear. Did you see

anything?"

"I don't remember. It was very early and I was tired. Do you like music?"

"Yeah, sure, but think back. . . ." She got up with a bored look on her face and walked to a record player.

"Can you stay for dinner, Billy?" I hadn't yet thought about dinner, but I got the feeling she wanted me for dessert.

"No, I need to get back."

"Back where?" She flipped through a stack of records but settled on the one already on the turntable.

"To Beardsley Hall."

"That dreadful place? It'll be after dark before you get back. Stay here tonight. It'll be good to have a man around the house. I'll cook us a nice dinner."

That gave me the shivers. There was no *us,* and I didn't intend on being part of her fantasy. But I also had the feeling she knew something, and wasn't going to give it up easily.

"Maybe. But we need to finish this first. Think about what you saw that morning."

"Do you like Irving Berlin?"

"Sure, who doesn't?" She put the needle down on the record. Hissing and scratching came out of the record player. This platter had been played a lot.

"Let's dance. Then I'll tell you everything, and you can decide if you want to stay." She held her arms outstretched in front of her, a slight innocent smile on her face. One little dance, I thought, in pursuit of the truth. Can't hurt.

"OK." I got up and held her as the music started. She folded my hand holding hers into my chest and rested her cheek on my shoulder. We danced slowly. Her body felt warm, and I could feel her breasts press against me as she breathed. Her hips moved against mine. The words from "I'm Getting Tired So I Can Sleep" drifted out over us. She sang the words in a sad, quiet, high voice. A wish to see her man again, even in a dream. She looked up into my eyes, her eyes only inches from my face. Her cheeks were wet with tears, but she wasn't crying right now. I could feel the heat from her whole body rising up, or maybe it was the heat of the room. Or maybe it was me. My heart was pounding and I felt her chest rise and fall with each breath, a thin layer of sweat glistening against her white skin.

She canted her head and pushed her lips against mine, her mouth open and the dampness from her tears and sweat combining in an unholy alliance against the little willpower I had. My mind said no, my heart said no, but my body was saying, Go right ahead, boy, this dame's delicious.

"Victoria, I can't. . . ."

"Call me Vicky," she said in a small, breathless voice. She took my hand and pressed it against her breast. It was full and her nipple was at attention. So was I and it was getting really tough to stay in control. I felt like she would break into a million pieces if I let go. If I didn't, I'd break a promise I hadn't even made yet. I had to buy some time, and I still had to get some answers. I tried to be a cop and think of her as just another civilian I needed something from.

"Vicky."

"Oh yes, darling!" She smiled, her eyes still closed and her hips thrust against mine.

"Vicky, tell me about the morning you left Jens's room."

"I don't want to talk about him."

"I don't either. But we have to. Who else did you see, on the way back to your room?"

"Another man."

"Who, Vicky?"

"If I tell you, will you stop asking questions? So we can sleep?"

"Sure."

"He was always very nice to me. Kind. He didn't take advantage, like the others."

"Who was he, Vicky?"

"Anders. Major Arnesen. I saw him on the main floor."

"In the corridor near the map room?"

"Yes, I think so. We smiled at each other, but didn't say anything. He must have a girlfriend. I'm glad."

"Did you see anyone else?" The music ended and she stopped dancing. The needle made a quiet hissing sound as the record went round and round and we both stood there, frozen. Her dreamy smile faded into nothing as she came back from that place she had retreated to. Then awareness crept into her face. It was like someone waking up and remembering what they had gone to sleep to escape.

"That's all you want, isn't it?" There was a fury in her eyes that denied any lie I could tell. Her carefully constructed fantasy had just fallen apart. Without wanting to, I had just thoroughly humiliated her. There was only one answer I could give.

"Yes."

I let go of her hand. I was smart enough to not say anything else. She walked over to the record player and raised the needle from the turn table.

"Get out."

"Please, Mrs. Brey, just tell me if you saw

anyone else. Lives may depend on it."

"Lives? How dare you lecture me about lives! I've already given one life to this damned war! The people you're talking about are still alive! They can walk in the sunshine, eat dinner, make love, hold hands . . . what do I care about them?"

Her face crumpled as she tried to hold back a torrent of tears. She raised her hand to her mouth as she made an anguished noise, tears running over her hand and onto the wooden floor, clean little splashes on a thin layer of dust. She fell to her knees and I thought she might actually be sick. I knelt down beside her and put my hand on her shoulder. She trembled as she covered her face with her hands.

"I'm not really a bad person," she said between sobs. Her nose was running, too.

"Me either."

"Don't look at me, please. You must think I'm a hussy."

"Mrs. Brey, you just want to be with your husband, that's all."

She nodded, but she wouldn't look at me. We just sat there for a while. She shuddered a few times as the tears came and went. Finally she took a deep breath and rubbed the back of her hand across her nose.

"Anders was the only one I saw."

"Thanks."

"Is it important?"

"It might be. It just might be." She still didn't move and leaving my hand on her shoulder was beginning to feel awkward. I moved it and she clutched at it, as if she was afraid I'd get away. I tried to think of something to say.

"You shouldn't blame Jens for the transfer, you know. I think he was trying to help."

"Jens?" She sniffled. "What did he have to do with my transfer?"

"Huh? Didn't he. . . ."

"No. Anders issued the order. He said he needed me at the Norwegian Brigade base in Scotland. I was glad to go. I just wasn't prepared to come back here, to all this." She gestured at the room, the house, the memories, everything.

Anders. Anders had been up early in the morning and transferred the only person who had seen him far away from Beardsley Hall. Anders. That made me rethink things. He had been a distant third until now, but this put him tops in my hit parade. Leaving the key in his own room was a nice touch, I had to admit. I hoped Daphne had been able to get his orders to Norway cancelled. That made me think of getting back to the hall. I looked at my watch.

"Billy, please don't go."

"I have to."

"I can't stay here alone another night. I'm leaving for Scotland tomorrow; I don't care about the rest of my leave." She finally looked at me. There was nothing sexy or even pretty left in her face. There was anguish, and shame. Her hand trembled in mine. With the other she grasped the collar of her sundress and pulled it closed.

"OK."

I couldn't leave her alone. I had pushed her, used her, shamed her. I couldn't turn around and leave her, like a piece of rubbish on the floor, now that I had what I wanted. We got up, stood there a second, brushing off our knees and smoothing clothes that weren't all that wrinkled.

"Thank you," she said, barely able to make eye contact. But she did. "Thank you."

She went into the kitchen and started puttering around. I had to admire her for pulling herself together, and I was more than a little relieved that she'd managed to. I got my stuff from the BMW and brought it inside. We ended up cooking together, talking about Boston seafood and English dishes. She opened a bottle of wine and we ate at the kitchen table. We didn't talk about

Beardsley Hall or Richard. I told her all about Diana, except for the secret mission part, and she told me it sounded very romantic. It was nice. I slept on the couch. She took the record upstairs with her, and I fell asleep to the faint sound of "I want to dream so I can be with you," glad that my willpower had lasted as long as it did. As willing as she might have been at one moment, it wouldn't have been worth it the next.

I got up early, but Victoria was already awake and packed. She had tea and toast ready and we ate in silence as we waited for a car to pick her up and drive her to the train station.

I put my gear on the bike and carried her bags outside. I wished her good luck and she said the same to me. Then she gave me a shy peck on the cheek and turned away and sat on the bench in the garden to wait for her ride. Her eyes drifted over the flowers and weeds, surveying her memories and storing them away. The sun came out from behind a cloud, and a bright shaft of light fell between the branches of the trees above her. Patches of sunlight covered her face and heart, like luminous wounds that might fade from sight but never disappear. I got on the BMW and started her up. I didn't bother waving as I drove off. She was already in another world — a world of quiet, carefully tended gardens with an adored husband by her side. I looked back as I turned a corner and saw her sitting just as I had seen her yesterday, as certain a victim of this war as Richard and all the other boys who had come crashing down out of the sky.

CHAPTER TWENTY

The sky was clouding over. I could feel a chill creeping into the breeze that swept by me as I sped down the nearly deserted country roads. I had hooked up with the main road going south from Norwich, which would take me directly to Wickham Market and then on to Beardsley Hall. Every time I saw a house I'd wonder if there was a grieving wife or mother inside, and if she was as devastated as Victoria Brey. I began to think that the cost of this war was going to be far higher than anyone had expected, or at least higher than I had anticipated. I tried not to think about a certain house in Boston and my mom getting that telegram: "The secretary of war desires me to express his deep regret . . ."

My kid brother had just turned twenty and would be facing the draft soon. He'd started college, the first person in our family to go. Dad was real proud of that, proud of his good grades, and so proud of his college acceptance letter that he'd had it framed. I thought that was carrying things a bit too far, but I had to admit, I was proud, too. And protective — not that Danny thought he needed it. He was fast with his fists and got into his fair share of fights with the Italian kids from the North End. He usually won, but he was reckless. The Italian gangs carried shivs and weren't afraid to use them. For a smart kid, he could be pretty dumb when he got his dander up. He'd probably volunteer before he got drafted, which would be in a year, right when he turned twenty-one. Didn't look like the war was going to be over by then, but he still had boot camp and field training to go through, so maybe he'd be OK, if we wrapped this thing up and got home by Christmas of '43.

I didn't want to think about Danny anymore, so I tried to focus on the case. Anders was the key as far as I was concerned. He had something to hide, which made him stand out. So far, his lie about not being up early was the most suspicious thing I had found out about anyone. I had nothing on Jens, and my theory about Rolf was just that, a theory with no proof or motive attached to it. I decided to wait and see if

Kaz had discovered anything and if Daphne had been able to put the kibosh on Anders's orders, before planning my next move, which was a way I had of not admitting to myself that I really had no idea what to do.

The miles flew by, and fast-moving clouds started to roll in from the east. They grew thick and dark as I rode through Wickham Market. I passed the pub and saw Mildred out back, digging potatoes in her Victory Garden. Maybe we'd come back here tonight for dinner again. Glancing up at the sky, I hoped the rain would hold off until I got to Beardsley Hall. As I cleared the village, I noticed a thin line of dark smoke up ahead. It drifted off to the left as the wind caught it, smudging the horizon with a gray stain. I didn't pay it any mind until I took the last turn toward the estate and saw that it was coming dead-on from the direction of the hall. I got that same sinking, fearful feeling that I used to get as a kid when I was walking home from school and a fire engine would roll by, lights and sirens blazing. I always thought it was going to my house, and I'd always breathe a sigh of relief when I got in sight of home and it was still standing. It was silly, just a kid's bad daydream, but I accelerated anyway. Beardsley Hall was hardly home, but it would be nice to confirm that everything was all right and that today was just brush-burning day.

I turned a corner and across the heath I could just make out the hall with that plume of smoke right next to it. Fog was starting to rise, and it was hard to see clearly at that distance. The smoke sort of hung in the air, like a question mark, reanimating my childhood fears. My heart raced and my palms felt clammy. I shuddered, not wanting to believe what my body was trying to tell me. A British military truck with the big red cross on the sides sped down the road toward me. As it neared, the driver put on his siren, the wailing sound echoing in my ears as it went by.

The parking lot was full of people, grouped around the source of the smoke. Scattered debris and small sputtering ground fires marred its usually neat surface. Harding and Jens stood watching me pull in, or the ambulance pull out, or both. As soon as I could make out the expressions on their faces, I knew something terrible had happened. I skidded to a halt in front of them and switched off the motorcycle.

"What happened?" I asked. "Who's in the ambulance?"

"Boyle, I. . . ." Harding looked surprised to see me, and seemed to have trouble getting his words out. "I thought you were in London."

I didn't know what that meant, and I didn't care.

"Jens," I asked, "Who got hurt?"

"Kaz. They are taking him to hospital. He's badly injured."

"What the hell happened here?" I yelled as I got off the bike.

The two men looked at each other and I realized they were in a state of shock. They weren't going to tell me anything. I went over to the crowd, where several men were using fire extinguishers to douse the fire that was producing the smoke. It smelled like burning rubber. I pushed through the bystanders. Harding followed me and gripped my shoulder.

"No, Boyle, wait —"

It was too late. Too late to stop me from seeing the smoldering wreck of the Riley Imp, with its burning tires still giving off choking black acrid smoke. Too late to see that someone had been at the wheel when something had gone very wrong. Too late to stop me from seeing the charred, unrecognizable corpse that had been caught up in a furious fire from the fuel tank.

The only person who ever drove her beloved red Imp was Daphne.

I felt dizzy as a swirl of smoke blew itself around me, hitting me like a hammer blow with the smell of burnt flesh. The world started to spin. Harding tried to hold me up, but my knees turned to jelly and I went down on all fours, and retched.

The next thing I knew we were in the kitchen. Someone handed me a wet towel and I lowered my head into it. That awful smell of soot was still in my nostrils. I tried to get a grip on things. Daphne was dead. Kaz almost. This was bad, real bad. I had to pull my head out of the wet towel, but I couldn't. I couldn't face it. What the hell was happening? Why?

"Billy."

It was Jens. I tried to straighten up, and managed to wipe my face and look at him. He didn't say anything. We were at one end of a long wooden table, and there were people milling all around us, buzzing, talking, whispering. Harding was seated next to me, a medical orderly wrapping his hands in bandages. I tried to ask about that, but no words came out.

"Major Harding tried to get into the car to pull Daphne out," Jens explained, "but it was impossible. The flames were everywhere, all of a sudden, as if there had been an explosion."

"What happened?" I managed to croak. I held up my hand before either one could answer. "Tell me everything, exactly, from start to finish." Something in the back of my mind was trying to get through to me, but I didn't know what. I needed to know everything.

"Take it easy, Boyle," Harding said with real concern. "It must've been a loose fuel line or something."

"It was an accident, Billy," Jens said, "a terrible accident. What else could it have been?"

I couldn't accept their assurances. It didn't matter. It didn't matter that they both outranked me and that Harding could ship me off to the Aleutians.

Daphne. I couldn't believe it. I told myself to hold on, to think, to figure this out before I fell apart. I had to pull myself together and get the story from them, just like a cop interviewing witnesses. That's it, just be a cop. I took a breath, trying to ignore the taste of black soot at the back of my mouth, and fell back into that role. My screaming brain slowed down. I could do this.

"Tell me everything, and don't stop before you get to the end!" I said.

I felt Harding's eyes on me as the orderly finished his bandages. He looked at Jens, nodded slightly, then winced as he tried to flex his hands.

"I should start with yesterday then," Jens said. "Daphne drove in at midmorning in that red sports car. She asked for Major Harding, who was in conference with the king. She told me it had to do with Major Arnesen, that you wanted his orders canceled, that he was not to leave England." He looked at me for confirmation.

"Right," I said. "Go on."

"She had to wait for Major Harding. I told her Anders was under orders from the king, but that the British government, as our host, could certainly request a change of plan. Then things got busy. Rolf returned unexpectedly. He asked if I had heard from you. I said I had not. He didn't explain himself further."

"When did Kaz get here?"

"Late afternoon. By that time Daphne had spoken with Major Harding and Major Cosgrove. Kaz came bursting in, looking for you and Daphne. He wouldn't speak to anyone else. He and Daphne went into the library and stayed there for quite a while."

"OK, stop for a second," I said, trying to keep everything straight. "So Daphne got through to both you and Major Cosgrove about Anders?" I asked, looking at Harding.

"Yes, she did."

"Where is Major Arnesen now?"

"On board the Norwegian naval submarine *Utsira,* somewhere in the North Sea, approaching the Norwegian coast."

"Damn! Couldn't you or Cosgrove get his orders changed, sir?"

"The decision was made not to alter his orders." Now Harding sounded more like himself. Unfortunately, that was a know-it-all hard-ass. I couldn't believe what I was hearing.

"You let him go?"

Harding gave me a cold stare. "Major Arnesen is on a dangerous mission for our valued ally, the Norwegian government in exile. It is hardly a matter of 'letting' him go. He is the king's representative to the Underground army, not an escaped convict."

I tried to take it in. I didn't like it, but I needed to focus on Daphne and Kaz. I nodded to Jens to continue. I thought it best not to say anything right now to Harding, to let my anger settle. I urged myself to make believe I was wearing a blue coat, sitting in someone's Boston kitchen. I'd feel bad that their life had been shattered, but then I'd leave, file a report, head home, and have a beer at Kirby's.

Then it hit me. Diana! Oh my God. Had she left yet? Would she know her sister was dead? Who was going to tell her? And the captain, who had been worried about the wrong daughter! I guess some of what I was feeling showed despite my resolve.

"Billy? Are you all right?" Jens asked.

"Yeah, go on."

"Well, it was obvious that Kaz had some important information, and that he wanted to get it to you. Daphne wasn't sure when you'd return, so they decided to wait here. This morning, I saw Daphne and Rolf standing by her automobile. He was carrying her bag."

"Where was she going?" I asked.

"To meet you in London," Harding answered, as if it were obvious. "You called here and left a message for Daphne and Kaz to meet you at headquarters."

"Who took the message?"

"Rolf," Jens spoke up. "He gave them the message himself."

"And you saw him help Daphne put her things into the car?" I asked.

"Yes. I stopped to chat with them. He was interested in her vehicle. . . ."

"A 1934 Riley Imp. Red," I filled in.

"Yes. She told us it was a gift from her father, and that Kaz was always wanting to drive it, but she saved that pleasure for herself." Jens's face clouded over.

"Soon after, Rolf left in his jeep for Southwold while Daphne waited for Kaz. I said good-bye and went inside to my office. Several minutes later, there was an explosion."

"Did you see it?"

"No," Jens answered.

"I did," Harding said. "I was having a smoke and walked over to a window for some fresh air. I opened it and looked at the countryside for a minute. The car park was to my left. I was on the third floor."

"Tell me exactly what you saw. Sir." Harding half closed his eyes, recreating the scene in his mind.

"Daphne was standing next to the Imp. Kaz came out with his bag and stowed it. I couldn't hear them, but I could tell they were excited. Just as Kaz was about to get in on the passenger side, he stopped. He made a gesture to Daphne like, Wait a minute, and ran back inside, as if he'd forgotten something. Daphne got in the car and started it. She sat there for a minute, idling."

"Did she move the car at all?" I asked.

"Not right away. I saw Kaz come out the door, carrying a briefcase, which is prob-

413

ably what he'd forgotten. He walked toward the car. Daphne must've seen him, and decided to back out, so he could just hop in and they could drive off."

I held my hand up for him to stop. I tried to relax and just let the thought surface. It was right on the edge of getting through. Then, suddenly, I knew.

"As soon as she started to back out, there was an explosion. It was on the passenger side of the car and caught Kaz as he walked toward the car door," I said calmly, seeing it all in my mind. "Then a second or two later, the gas tank went up."

"You're right, Boyle," Harding said in surprise. "I remember hearing a loud noise before the car burst into flames. It happened so fast . . . how did you know?"

"Let's go outside and check the car. I'd like to be certain."

"Are you sure you're all right, Billy?" Jens asked.

"Yeah, I'm fine. I'm a cop, remember? I see this stuff all the time." I stood up and held on to the table for support, trying to convince myself. We went outside.

Men were cleaning up. Daphne's body hadn't been moved, but someone had placed a sheet over her. The wreckage of the Imp was still smoldering and the place stank. Two staff cars that had been parked on either side of the Imp had also been badly damaged. Glass, metal, and charred leather debris littered the area. The Imp was at a slight angle from the others, evidence that Daphne was pulling out of the space when it blew up. I walked toward the passenger side and studied it. It was ripped open. If Kaz had been in the car, he would've been in a dozen pieces even before the gas tank went. A blackened hole in the crushed gravel driveway had been blasted down to the hard-packed dirt. It was right under the passenger seat.

"Tire bomb," I said.

"What?" asked Harding and Jens together.

"Tire bomb. It's a tube filled with plastic explosive and a detonator. One end is flat, and you jam it under a tire. That depresses a switch. The bomb goes off when the tire moves off it and frees the switch. Daphne had the car parked facing in. The device was placed under the left rear tire. When she pulled out, it went off under the passenger's seat and lit up the fuel tank."

"Sabotage?" Jens asked.

"Murder," I answered. "To cover up the murder of Knut Birkeland."

"Where would you get this tire bomb?" Harding asked.

"It's standard equipment for SOE commandos."

"Why would someone want to kill Daphne?" asked Harding.

"The criminal knew Kaz had been snooping around in London. He hotfooted it back here to see if Kaz had found out anything. I bet he had, and he'd confided in Daphne. Then he concocted that phony message from me to get them right where he wanted them. In the car, together."

"Who did?" asked Jens.

"A guy who had access to commando equipment. The guy who gave them the message and helped Daphne out to the car. Rolf Kayser."

Jens opened his mouth, as if to deny it, but the logic of was undeniable.

"But why commit murder?" Harding asked. "Why kill Birkeland?"

"I don't know, sir. But I'll bet Daphne did. And now she's dead. Kaz is our only hope."

I turned and walked inside. I had to wash and change my clothes. The smell of death was everywhere. I scrubbed my face, hands, and hair. I threw everything I was wearing into a pile on the floor and changed into fresh khakis. I still smelled the smoke on my skin.

Twenty minutes later Harding and I were in a jeep heading to the British military hospital in Ipswich. We had left Jens on the phone with the Southwold base, issuing orders in the king's name for Lieutenant Rolf Kayser to be held for questioning as soon as he showed up. For the moment, all I had to do was drive and worry about Kaz. There wasn't time to mourn Daphne yet. I wanted Kaz to be all right, and part of me felt guilty that I might care more about finding out what he'd discovered than about him. I wondered if he knew about Daphne, and hoped I wouldn't have to be the one to tell him. Things just seemed to get worse and worse. How would Kaz take it? He and Daphne were so different, yet so alike. They had been perfect for each other. How could you live, knowing the perfect thing you once had was gone?

"You know what, Boyle?" Harding said. I was grateful to him for breaking into my thoughts. "This means that going after Anders Arnesen would have been a wild goose chase. Now that this has happened, it's obvious he isn't involved."

I hadn't even thought about Anders. I was so pissed at Harding for not stopping him that it hadn't even occurred to me that he couldn't be the killer.

"That's right, sir. But we still need to talk to him. I want to know why he lied about being up and around early that morning."

Harding shrugged, as if what I wanted didn't count for much.

"That reminds me of another thing, Boyle," he said. "I thought you had ruled out Rolf as a suspect because he was with the king when Birkeland was killed?" He finished his question as he pulled up to the gate at the hospital. The sentry asked for our IDs and we went through the drill with him.

"It's a long story, sir. Can it wait until later when I can lay it all out for you?"

"OK." Harding pulled into a parking place. "Let's see how Kaz is doing."

He wasn't doing well. A doctor took us into his room and read from his chart. Broken leg, a large gash on the left side of his face, multiple lacerations, probable concussion, a collapsed lung, and second-degree burns where his clothing had caught fire. Plus they were concerned about the effect on his heart, which wasn't very strong to start with.

I stopped listening and pulled up a chair next to the head of his bed. His face was wrapped in bandages. All I could see was one eye between the layers of gauze. I gently put my hand on his arm, afraid the slightest touch would hurt him.

"Kaz? Kaz, can you hear me?"

"He can't hear you, Lieutenant. The pain medication has put him out," the doctor said.

"When will he wake up?"

"We hope tomorrow. But in his condition, it may be hard to predict."

I didn't ask any more questions. I wasn't crazy about the answers I was getting. Harding went out in the corridor with the doc. I didn't know what to do. Hospitals always made me nervous. But Kaz was my partner, or at least as close as a Boston cop could get to one over here. So I stayed. I looked around to make sure the door was shut, and then I started talking to Kaz. I filled him in on everything that had happened since we left him at Daphne's father's place. Until this morning, anyway. I told him about Southwold, Anders, Victoria Brey, everything I had seen and done.

"That's it, Kaz," I finished up. "Now I just need to hear from you. What did you find out in London? It must've been good."

The slightest of little sounds escaped his lips, just a puff of air. One finger moved.

"Kaz, it's me, Billy."

I could see him try to move his head, but

419

it was too much. He winced. He lifted his hand, holding it as if he wanted to shake hands.

"What do you want, Kaz?" I heard another little sound. I leaned closer to his mouth.

"Bbb . . ."

"Yeah, it's Billy. I'm here."

"Bb . . . Bbbb . . ."

It was like he was trying to say my name but couldn't get it all out. I tried to take his hand, thinking that's what he wanted. He shook me off with an effort that must have been painful. He gasped, then didn't say anything for a long time.

"I'll stay right here, Kaz. When you feel strong enough, try again."

His eyelid fluttered and I could see he was trying to open it. A thin slit appeared and he tried to focus on me. He must have been really doped up, because he faded pretty quick. I waited. Minutes passed. Long minutes.

"Bb . . . bbb." Again, the hand. He tried to open his eye again. This time, he got the lid halfway up. I was sure he saw me.

"Bbb . . . re . . ."

"What?"

He worked his hand again, holding it like he was gripping something. His eye was fully open now, and he held me in his gaze, willing me to understand. I got it.

"Briefcase!" I shouted. "Your briefcase! I understand, Kaz. I'll find it. That's where the evidence is, right?" This time when I took his hand he squeezed it. Yes.

"I'll get it, Kaz, I promise. Then I'll come back to see you."

I wondered if he knew about Daphne, and if I should tell him. But I wanted to get out of there, away from the antiseptic hospital smell and Kaz's suffering. Then I saw the tears leaking from his one good eye. He knew. He had delivered his message and now he was done. All that was left was grief. I squeezed his hand.

"I know, buddy, I know. I know."

I stood up and let his hand slip from mine. I leaned over and kissed him on the forehead, just above his eye, about the only patch of skin that wasn't wrapped in bandages. I sniffed and guiltily wiped my own tears away, glancing around to make sure no one had seen. Boston cops don't cry, much less kiss Polacks.

I stood back from the bed and let out a sigh that came from way down in my gut. Kaz was out, his strength used up by uttering half a word and squeezing my hand. I felt the hardness of the linoleum floor through my feet. The close, warm air of the room brought beads of sweat out on my forehead that dripped down my temples.

It had been a long time since I'd been in a hospital room. I wasn't counting Doc O'Brien's office, where I had taken Danny to get his leg stitched up last summer, or even the emergency room, where I'd escorted my fair share of bums, drunks, and Brunos who thought they could take on a guy who knew how to use a billy club with their fists. No, a hospital room was different; it was a place where they stashed you until they killed you or you happened to get well enough to walk out. At least, that's what most everyone in my family said, ever since somebody's great-aunt got taken down to Cork and put in a hospital she never came home from. I wasn't sure about it myself, but the tightening in my stomach now was the same as it was the last time I'd stood at the foot of a bed like this, hat in hand, trying not to cry and feeling the room close in on me. The uniforms had been blue then, and it had been Dad on the bed.

Uncle Dan had picked me up on my beat, siren blasting away, and brought me straight to the hospital. We didn't know what had happened, just that Dad had been shot and was alive last anyone heard. The place was crawling with cops — out front, in the main lobby, all of them parting like the Red Sea as Uncle Dan looked at everyone and no one, demanding to know where his brother was. Somebody led us up a flight of stairs and down a hall to a room. A room like this: too warm; hard floor; smells of chalky gauze, antiseptic cleaners, and open wounds mingling.

The difference was, Dad could talk. "Bastard couldn't shoot straight" was the first thing he'd said, wincing with the pain the words brought him. He lay on his side, his right shoulder packed with thick gauze front and back, bandages around his chest and neck holding everything in place. Dried blood the color of rust showed through the gauze, and the sheets were pink where blood had dripped and spread. Dad's skin was so pale it was almost as if I could see through it to the flesh and muscle beneath. He looked old, weak, and hurt. That scared me more than the bandages.

"A through and through," Uncle Dan said, his hands clenching and unclenching as his fear turned to anger. "Who did it?"

"Don't know," Dad said. "I heard somebody come up behind me from an alleyway, then a click, like a hammer pulled back." He stopped, closed his eyes for a second, took a deep breath, and then flinched, the act of filling his chest with air causing shred-ded muscle to shriek in protest.

"I started to turn," he said, "and then he fired. I went down, heard another shot, but he missed. Must've been nervous, there were cops close by." He closed his eyes again.

"Where?" I asked. "Where were you?"

"A block from the district courthouse, not ten minutes after I left the D Street Sta-tion."

"Did you see the guy?" I asked. I looked at Uncle Dan and saw him exchange glances with Dad, then look at me.

"Naw," Dad said. "Didn't see a thing."

"Who would shoot you two blocks from the courthouse, in broad daylight? And why?" Dad didn't answer; he just looked at Uncle Dan.

"Well, Billy, I'd say someone who didn't want your da to get to the courthouse," Uncle Dan said with slow certainty.

I had a million questions, about open cases and guys getting out of the slammer, but neither of them wanted to talk. Uncle Dan had given me the keys to the squad car and told me to go home and get Mom, tell her everything was OK. I wasn't so sure it was, but I did as I was told. I took my dad's hand, something I hadn't done since I was a little kid, and held it tight. He squeezed it and smiled, a brave smile, and I gave him one back. As I walked out of the room, I turned to pull the door shut behind me. Uncle Dan was already leaning over Dad, nodding his head as Dad whispered to him. I shut the door and walked down the hallway lined with cops — plainclothes and bluecoats — all thankful Dad was all right, patting me on the back and telling me all I had to do was ask if we needed anything. I remember nodding and saying thanks, all the while wondering what had led to an ambush just steps from the South Boston District Court.

Dad was home in a week and we had constant visitors and meals brought in by neighbors and the wives of cops. Everything from corned beef to platters of cold cuts, pickles, and cheese to lasagna and meatloaf. We needed it all, too, with cops visiting Dad at the end of every shift, sometimes just sitting outside on the front stoop, watching the traffic go by, waiting. Uncle Dan brought some of his IRA pals around, too, quiet men in black suits and cloth caps who spoke Gaelic to each other whenever someone they didn't know came into the room.

The case was never solved. Dad went back to work, desk duty at first, after three weeks at home. Every day after work one of the IRA boys would pick Dad up at the station and drive him home. That went on for a week, then Basher McGee was found floating in Quincy Bay, hands tied behind his back and two slugs in the back of the head. Just like an IRA execution, although no one commented on that. There was a big police funeral, with black armbands, brass, and bands. After that, Dad took the trolley home.

Someone dropped a tray outside the room, the loud metal-against-linoleum sound echoing in the hallway. I took another look at Kaz, then walked out of the room. The door closed behind me.

It was as if I had walked out into another world, where all the rules were different; everything had changed as sure as the door shutting behind me. Daphne Seaton, a kind, sweet person, was dead. Kaz was shattered and would never be the same again without her. My first two friends in England. Destroyed. I didn't really care about the war any more than I had before. But I did know one thing. The man who had killed them was going to die soon, at my hands. *My* world had been attacked this time and I was going to hit back. *This* was my war.

As I went to look for Harding, it occurred

to me that I didn't give a damn about what happened after that. Maybe I'd get killed, maybe thrown in prison, it didn't make a bit of difference. It was kind of restful not to have to think about the future.

CHAPTER
TWENTY-ONE

Thunder rumbled in from the north as low dark clouds let loose. Hard rain pelted the courtyard of the hall with thick drops, splattering dirt and ash into a gooey ooze beneath my feet. Daphne was gone, the white sheet that had covered her lying in the sooty mud next to the twisted frame of the Imp. I tried not to think of the image of her in the car as I went through the wreckage, trying to find any piece of evidence. Nothing had survived the fire. Cold rain soaked through my Parsons coat; I was glad I was wearing thick-soled combat boots as I struggled through the muck.

I turned my attention to the debris piled up in a corner of the lot. Bits of metal and glass, pieces of the staff cars that had been damaged, and what looked like the charred remains of luggage were heaped together. There were a couple of bicycles that had also been caught in the explosion, and other unidentifiable pieces of who knows what. Shovels and rakes were stacked up against the side of the building, left by the crew that had started the cleanup before the rains came. I grabbed a rake and started to pull the pile apart. The rain couldn't keep the stink of wet ash and burned rubber down. I tried not to breathe too deeply as I looked through the soggy mess I raked out from the pile.

I pawed through the stuff, trying to ignore how raw and cold my hands were, and found some bits of clothing and a pile of burned papers that turned out to be a manual for a Ford sedan. I tossed the bike frames aside and dug deeper. I was soaked to the skin now, and the rain was getting worse, starting to come down sideways. There was a helluva storm brewing up. I was just about to give up the search when I saw a leather grip sticking out from under a partially charred seat cushion. I thought of Kaz's hand holding the handle of a briefcase, and pulled it out from under the cushion. It was a cheap government issue briefcase, more of an attaché case, with hard sides and two spring locks. It hadn't stood up well to the blast. It hung open on a busted hinge. One side was ripped and blistered, as if it had caught fire and smoldered for a bit. There was nothing inside. I looked at the warped case and wondered out loud. "Geez, Kaz, how did you manage to live through that?"

I went back to methodically pulling the pile apart again, looking for the papers or whatever else might have been inside the briefcase. It kept raining. Now lightning was striking the heath all around me. I wasn't having fun. The only good thing was that the rain was washing the mud and ash off me as fast as I became covered in it. After half an hour all I had to show for my efforts was a disintegrating pile of charred papers that could have been the London Times for all I knew. It just didn't figure. Could whatever was in the case have been totally destroyed? It must've fallen out of the broken briefcase when the tire bomb went off. Could it have been burned to ashes?

OK, I thought to myself, time to make like a cop and recreate the crime scene. I walked over to the door enterance to the parking lot. Four stone steps led up to large wooden double doors beneath a small arch. I stood there for a minute, looking at the position of the cars and trying to put myself in Kaz's place.

If I'm Kaz just coming through the doors, the Imp would still be in its original parked position. I went down the steps. Kaz was excited, and would've been hurrying. I took quick steps. Daphne's seen me by now, and she's in a hurry, too. She puts the Imp in reverse, lets up on the clutch, and backs up, probably looking at Kaz. Was there a smile on her face? Boom! I stopped in my tracks. I looked all around. So many people had tramped through here and then cleaned up that nothing remained to show where Kaz had hit the ground. OK, the explosion would've knocked him back, and he would have dropped the briefcase. The briefcase. I should be carrying the briefcase. I marked the spot where I was standing and got the briefcase out of the pile. I tried to force it shut, but it wouldn't close properly. I held it closed and then returned to my spot. The briefcase was slightly blistered on one side. How would Kaz have been carrying it? If he'd held it by the handle, how did one side get burned? I tried to picture Kaz in a hurry.

Two-handed. He would have been running and carrying it in front of him in both hands. He wasn't the most athletic guy, and that would have been easier than having it bang against his leg. I held the briefcase up in front of me, the damaged side toward the car.

Boom, again. I slammed the briefcase into

my chest and sprawled backward, let go of it, and hit the gravel with a thud. The briefcase bounced to my left and fell open. I got up, wondering if the briefcase had saved his life. Not really, I guess. And the contents, whatever they had been, had led to Daphne's death.

I looked at the briefcase now on the ground. OK, it's open. Kaz is probably nearly unconscious. But he sees the car and knows Daphne is dead. What happens next?

Another boom. This time it's the fuel tank. What would that have been like? I shut my eyes and imagined being this close. Close enough for Kaz's clothing to catch fire. Whoosh. A fireball. A fireball pushes out the air around it. Wind. Anything loose in its path would be scattered. The fire reaches out to Kaz, lying there, and just licks him. Heat rises. I imagined a whirlwind lifting papers out of the briefcase, setting them on fire at the edge of the fireball. Where would they go?

I did a 180 standing over the briefcase. If they had gone toward the fire, they would have been consumed. Anywhere else near it, they would have been cleaned up and I would've found them in that pile. Well, maybe I did, and that charred mess of paper was it. Or . . .

I looked toward the hall. The parking lot was on the side of the near wing, the corner of the lot adjacent to the end of the wing. A line of neatly trimmed hedges, about five feet high, ran along the edge of the lawn. They turned the corner and continued along the front of the building. I walked to the edge of the hedge that screened off the parking lot. Nothing. There was a space of about two feet between the hedges and the building itself, probably kept clear so the gardener could get in there and trim. It was starting to get dark, and it was hard to see inside the dank space. I forced my way in, the rain pelting me and the snipped ends of branches tearing at me. I saw some gray-and white shapes ahead and plunged in farther. I bent down and felt glossy paper.

Photographs. They were photographs, some of them charred at the corners, all of them wet and muddy. The blast and the wind must have scattered them, and these had been caught up within the hedge. Maybe there were more out on the lawn. It was too dark to make out what the photos showed. I gathered them up, stuck them under my coat, and backed out of the small space. I went right into the kitchen, leaving a trail of black mud and dripping rainwater behind me. The kitchen staff was preparing dinner. I pushed aside a pile of turnips and laid the photographs out on the wooden table.

"Hva helvetet er De som gjøre?" demanded a cook, a mean look on his face as he advanced toward me with a meat cleaver.

"Excuse me, sir," another guy said in pretty good English. "What are you doing?"

He had a dish towel draped over his shoulder and I grabbed it and wiped away the water that was dripping in my eyes.

"Hold on," I said, using the towel to wipe off the worst of the mud on the photos. They were all black and whites, printed on eight-by-ten glossy sheets. On the back of each was stamped "Ministry of Defence — cleared by censor." At first glance, they were pictures of British soldiers. As I laid them out, I realized they were all commandos. There were a few grinning thumbs-up photos that clearly showed the commando shoulder patch. There were commandos running, firing weapons, but it all looked . . . staged. Publicity photos. That's what they were cleared for. Photos for the papers about the brilliant exploits of the commando chaps. What was the big deal?

As I went through them, I noticed several showed commandos on small boats along a rocky coast. In one, there were several boats

at a dock, burning, with a group of commandos smiling at the camera. This one had
a caption on the back:

The Nazis won't be making nitroglycerin
from fish caught by these boats, thanks
to a recent raid on the Norwegian coast
by a joint British and Norwegian commando unit!

I went back and looked through the photos
again. I realized these were all probably
taken on raids into Norway. In a few, there
were signs in Norwegian. I didn't know
what they meant, but I had seen enough
Norwegian to recognize it.

By now, the kitchen crew was all gathered
around and looking at the photos with me.
They saw the Norwegian, too, and started
chattering. The cook with the meat cleaver
put it down and joined the crowd. I tried to
tune them out and see if I could find what
was special about these pictures. What had
been worth two lives? What would incriminate Rolf Kayser? I flipped through them
again. Then I saw it, as clear as day. A photo
of a commando standing back from a burning wooden building, a can of gasoline in
his hand. It was a two-story structure on a
dock; a small town was visible in the back-

ground. Flames were licking the side of the building, just below the name of the business painted up on the second story, between two windows. Kayser Fiskeri.

I didn't need to ask, but I did anyway.

"What's *fiskeri?*" I asked the group.

"Fishery," said the English-speaking guy. "A fish-processing plant."

Money. It had just been about money all along. Goddamn! Had Birkeland and Daphne died because of Rolf Kayser's family *business?* I wanted to cry, but like I said, a Boston cop doesn't cry. I gathered up the photos slowly and wiped my face one more time. Seemed like there was still rainwater in my eyes.

I decided Harding could damn well wait and went up to my room to clean up. I ran a hot bath, dumped my muddy clothes, and soaked for a while. I was trying to figure out a way to get close to Rolf before they took him into custody. I didn't have any bright ideas, but I knew I didn't want him sitting out the war safely in a cell as the Allied wheels of justice slowly turned and better men and women than he died by the score. I put on fresh fatigues and boots, strapped on my .45, looked at the pictures again, and thought it all through.

Twenty minutes later I was in the map

room, where I found Harding and Jens, sitting across from each other at the long table, drinking coffee. They weren't working, or talking. I tossed the incriminating photograph down between them.

"I learned a new Norwegian word today," I said. *"Fiskeri."*

"What's this?" Harding asked, picking up the photo with his good hand.

"A picture taken less than two months ago on a commando raid on the Norwegian coast. There are other pictures of them burning fishing boats, part of the campaign to cut off the German supply of fish oil, for making nitroglycerin. In this one they're burning a fish-processing facility, evidently owned by the Kayser family. Kayser Fiskeri."

"But Rolf himself went on some of these raids," protested Jens.

"What else could he do? If he refused, somebody else would do the honors. He's not stupid. He probably knew that the issue would be decided when the king appointed the senior adviser and tried to move things in his favor by getting rid of Birkeland."

"Didn't anyone here know about his family's business?" asked Harding with a hard glance at Jens.

"Only what he told us, that his family was

well off, and wanted him to go to law school. It would be difficult to check, and we had no reason to do so. Rolf was with us from the beginning. Kayser is not an uncommon name in Norway, you know." Jens shrugged.

"I'll bet his family owns a whole string of these plants," I said, "maybe fishing boats, too, and he was determined to protect their investments. Kaz may have found some other proof, but this photo clinches it for me. It's the missing motive."

"I follow what you're saying, Boyle," Harding said. "But what about the note that Daphne and Kaz received? And how could Kayser have killed Birkeland when he had gone hunting with the king?"

"No one ever saw the note; Rolf delivered the message personally. As for the time of death, I have a few questions to ask Rolf before I can explain that. I think I have it straight, but I want to talk to him first." Talk to him alone, I thought. "Do we have him in custody yet?"

"There's a little problem, Boyle. He's already left."

"What? Where the hell did he go?"

"Norway," answered Jens. "On a mission to the Nordland province."

"What's going on here? How could you

let him go?"

"Simmer down, Boyle," Harding said. "By the time Jens got through to Southwold, Kayser was long gone. He must have driven straight there this morning. Then he hopped a Sunderland flying boat that dropped him at a base up north in the Shetland Islands. The SOE runs a sort of ferry service between there and Norway."

"How did he just happen to hop on this aircraft and then conveniently catch a boat to Norway?" I asked.

Jens answered, "We wanted to dispatch a team to train Underground Army units in the use of explosives, so they could go into action in coordination with the invasion. Rolf organized the transport, landing areas, contacts, everything. We have been waiting for the right weather for them to take the Shetland Bus."

"The what?" This was getting stranger all the time. I sat down hard, the energy I had received from finding the photographs and learning Rolf Kayser's motive, drained by the distance Rolf had put between us.

"That's what we call the boats that go back and forth to Norway. Most are Norwegian fishing boats that have fled to England. They carry agents and supplies over, mingle with the regular fishing fleet, make their drops, and then bring back recruits. It works quite well."

"Kayser wasn't scheduled to go over," Harding explained. "He added his name to the list at the last minute. Since he had been in on the plan from the beginning, no one questioned it."

"Seems like a pretty loose operation," I said.

"No, not at all," Jens protested. "As a member of the planning staff, it was appropriate for Rolf to fly up to Shetland to check on weather conditions. And once the boat was ready to leave, he could easily join the others. No one else involved in the planning of the mission was there to contradict him."

"This Shetland operation," Harding explained, "the Shetland Bus, is a bit unorthodox in its methods. It's nominally run by the Royal Navy, but the sailors are all volunteer Norwegian fishermen. Very effective, but Kayser could easily take advantage of their informality."

"Can't you radio them? They can't leave until this storm clears, can they?"

"Sorry, Billy, but this is perfect weather," Jens said. "We usually don't make runs in the summer, because of the long daylight. Too much chance of being spotted by German air or naval patrols. But in this weather, they don't go out. There's rain and fog up north. Fishermen are used to it, but the Luftwaffe won't fly and even if they send out patrol boats they won't be able to see two meters in front of them."

"In any case," Harding added, "this is a top-secret mission. Complete radio silence. There's no way to get in touch with them."

There was a note of finality in Harding's voice that depressed me. He looked down at the table, then at his injured hand. What had he seen in those last seconds when he tried to get to Daphne? Had she screamed, and did he still hear her?

"You must know where they're going in Nordland," I said, trying to stay focused. I wasn't ready to give up. "Send someone in after them."

"We don't know exactly," said Jens. "We gave them a list of contacts to make. It was up to the commando team to work out the timing. For security reasons, only one other person, in addition to those on the mission, knew when and where they were to meet those contacts."

"And, of course, that person was Rolf Kayser," I guessed.

Jens nodded.

"He must've had this planned as an escape

option," I thought out loud. "After he drove away, he must've stopped to watch the explosion. He saw that Kaz wasn't dead, or at least he couldn't be certain of it. So he went to Plan B. He got himself to safety behind enemy lines, into his own country, where he can melt into the mountains anytime. He knows we can't track him down."

"Damn!" cursed Harding. We all just sat there for a minute.

"There might be one way to find him," Jens said finally.

"How?"

"I do not know Rolf's schedule, but I do know Major Arnesen's. I planned it out with him."

"What's that got to do with it?" I asked.

"Anders is on a mission to assess the readiness of the Underground Army. Rolf's group was to link up with him and pass on information about the underground groups they'd trained and their ability to conduct sabotage operations with a very large shipment of plastic explosive we will be bringing into Nordland. Remember, part of the invasion plan is to seal off Nordland at its narrowest point."

"When and where is the meet?" I asked.

"At a hut in the mountains above Leirfjord. I will have to check the exact date," Jens answered.

"Major Harding," I said, trying to summon up every bit of military bearing I possessed, "I request permission to apprehend Rolf Kayser at this meeting place and bring him back for trial." Harding looked like the pope had just asked him for a kiss. He sucked in some air, then quickly composed himself. Jens looked surprised, and then smiled.

"Denied," Harding said firmly. "You wouldn't last ten minutes."

"Sir, there are underground units throughout Nordland. Jens could put me in touch with one and they could guide me to this Leirfjord place —"

"I said no, Boyle. You'd either be killed or captured, preferably the former, because if you were captured, the Gestapo would get all of this out of you in nothing flat. I'll not have you endangering the invasion plan. Period. End of discussion." He got up and walked out of the room.

"I think he needs some time to think it over," I said to Jens, after the door slammed.

"We don't have that much time," he answered. He sounded serious.

"We?"

"We. As a Norwegian, I feel responsible

for my countryman's conduct. As one who once counted Rolf Kayser as a friend, I feel betrayed. If we do nothing, as Major Harding suggests, he will certainly get away. Sweden is less than one hundred kilometers from almost anywhere in Nordland."

"Aren't you worried about the Gestapo getting hold of me?"

"I think you are a man of many surprises, Lieutenant Boyle. I think others should worry about you. Rolf Kayser, especially."

Jens called for sandwiches and whiskey and we got down to some serious study. He rolled out a huge map and showed me the route Anders would follow by submarine from Scapa Flow and the shorter route Rolf was taking from the Shetland Islands. They both ended up off a little island, Tomma, on the coast of Nordland province.

"Tomma is about thirty kilometers south of the Arctic Circle. A small local boat can ferry you from it to the mainland here," Jens pointed, "at Nesna. You take the main road from there to Leirfjord. I'll draw a map of the path to the hut for you to memorize."

"When would I need to be there?"

"By the 22nd of July. You have just under two weeks."

"And how do we accomplish that, against

the wishes of my commanding officer?"

Jens drummed his fingers on the table, looking at the map and then me. The drumming stopped.

"Let me see the orders Daphne typed up for you."

I gave him the envelope. I realized that in all the excitement I hadn't thought about Daphne's death for several minutes. And suddenly, it was as if I had just found out again. I stared at the map while Jens read through the orders, and managed to regroup. Norway sure was a long way away. There was one advantage, though. Rolf Kayser would never expect me to come after him. What would be the German reaction to me if I was captured? I wasn't so sure.

"Look, Billy," Jens said excitedly, jabbing his finger at the papers. "Your orders are still valid. The cover sheet says thirty days, AAA priority, and identifies the issuing office. U.S. Army ETO headquarters, in this case."

"Yeah, great," I said. "But that and a nickel will get you a phone call."

Jens looked up quizzically, but then went on. "The second page is the actual listing of orders, see? Then the third page contains the last order, an instruction to all Allied personnel to assist you in your duties. That is followed by the signature of Major Harding for General Eisenhower and Major Cosgrove for the Imperial Staff. Very impressive."

"It only goes so far, Jens. At Southwold I couldn't even get four wheels. . . ."

While I was talking, Jens had laid out the three sheets next to each other. He then removed the middle sheet containing the actual orders and substituted a blank sheet of paper.

"Holy shit, Jens. You're a genius. We can add whatever we want."

He smiled triumphantly, but the smile faded quickly. "No, Billy. You should rather say we can add whatever you are willing to add. It may cost you your life."

It was nice that Jens was thinking about my life expectancy, but something else was stirring in my mind. The last piece of the puzzle. I took away the first and second sheets and just stared at the third sheet, all by itself.

It was so simple. So damn simple that a real clever guy like me had never even had a chance.

CHAPTER
TWENTY-TWO

Everything had been so easy, I knew there had to be a catch. Jens had doctored the orders, and late that night I was back at Southwold, returning the BMW no worse for wear and grabbing some of the winter gear the GIs had been issued. I jumped an air transport to Scotland the next morning. I had a Thompson submachine gun, my own .45, a couple of grenades, and I felt ready to take on the whole German army. Then I realized that was exactly what I was about to do.

The orders got me into Scapa Flow, the huge Royal Navy base in the north of Scotland, no problem. I found the Fifteenth Motor Gunboat Flotilla and presented my paperwork. Jens had selected this unit because he had worked with them before and knew they were used to operatives showing up at all hours with top priority orders. The Fifteenth specialized in clandestine operations and was involved in ferrying agents in and out of Norway. This was right up their alley; a strange officer showing up unannounced with secret orders was routine. Even though my orders instructed the Fifteenth Motor Gunboat Flotilla to provide me with "immediate" transport to the island of Tomma off the coast of Norway, the commanding officer told me I'd have to wait two days for a moonless period. Motor Torpedo Boat 718 was due to leave then to pick up some downed British airmen and could be rerouted to drop me off at Tomma first. Not wanting to kick up a fuss and have my phony orders looked at any more closely, I graciously agreed. It didn't bother me since I still had plenty of time to make the rendezvous. I was more worried about Harding. Jens was going to tell him I'd gone to Southwold to try and get firm evidence that Rolf Kayser had stolen a tire bomb. It wasn't much of a story, but it would do to buy me a day or two.

Standing on the dock the morning of our departure, my gear slung over my shoulder, I looked out to sea at the rough water and low clouds, and then back at MTB 718. There was a catch all right. She looked big enough for a fishing trip off Cape Cod, not a rough North Sea crossing. She was about a hundred feet long and very low in the water. A voice hailed me from the boat.

"You there, Yank! Are you our Joey?"

"My name's Billy," I said. Laughter rolled through the crew until an officer showed up at the gangplank.

"Welcome aboard, Lieutenant Boyle. I'm Lieutenant Harold Dickinson, Royal Navy Reserve." He was tall, thin, graceful, and hatless. His head of thick blond hair blew in every direction in the freshening wind. He wore a soiled fisherman's thick white turtleneck sweater, and could've been a Harvard kid getting ready for a sail, except for the twin-mounted .50 caliber machine guns he was leaning against.

"Don't mind the lads. We call all our passengers 'Joeys.' That's what Aussies call a baby kangaroo, carried safely in its mum's pouch. Don't know if that's where it got started, but there it is."

I climbed aboard and saluted. I had seen guys salute when they boarded ships in the movies and thought I'd try to look like I knew what I was doing.

"I thought you Yanks were supposed to be rather informal," said Dickinson, returning the salute nonchalantly and glancing around at his men. "We don't bother with a lot of that here, do we boys?"

"Too busy keeping old 718 afloat for that," one of crew said with a grin as he descended belowdecks with a toolbox. I suddenly became nervous.

"Everything belowdecks working OK, Lieutenant?" I asked.

"First, call me Harry. And second, don't worry about a thing. The lads keep her in tip-top shape. They're just having their fun with you. We're on our own a lot and don't have time for rubbish about spit and polish. Engines and weapons, that's what we spend our time on. Plenty of opportunity between wars to polish the brass."

"I like the way you think, Harry. How many of these trips have you made?"

"To France and Norway, or just Norway?" A crew member walked by, a bearded fellow clenching a pipe in his mouth, trailing smoke, who laughed as he looked at me.

"OK, forget it. I'm sure you know your job. I'm a little nervous."

"Nervous? Why, Lieutenant Boyle, whatever for? We're just about to leave on a six-hundred-mile trip through enemy-infested waters, with a big, fat low-pressure system just sitting over us, dumping buckets of rain and churning up waves taller than houses, in order to land you alone in Nazi-occupied Norway, just south of the Arctic Circle, and leave you there. Why should you be nervous?"

"Houses? Waves taller than *houses?*"

"Rather large houses."

I huddled in the galley as we got under way, sitting on a bench and sipping a cup of hot, sweet tea. Or trying to. The boat was rocking and I was trying to match the rolling motion while bringing the cup to my lips.

"Ever do any sailing back in the States?" Harry asked as he came in. I could see by the half smile on his lips that he doubted it.

"I once rode the ferry across Boston Harbor."

"Boston! Where you colonials wasted all that perfectly good tea?"

"The same."

"Serves you right, then."

"What does?"

"This crossing. This mission."

"Well, I asked for it. Is this tub going to make it?"

"We've been through worse weather," Harry said, a serious look passing briefly over his face, "but I'd hate to make a practice of it. Old 718 will do just fine. She's got four Packard engines driving four shafts and can do a top speed of thirty-five knots."

"Does that count going up the side of a wave?"

"No," he laughed, "it does not. Calm sea, thirty-five knots. This mess, we'll make fifteen or twenty, tops. It's going to be rough."

"The weather or the Germans?"

"Both, although for now we've only the weather to worry about."

He took a rolled-up map from a shelf above me, opened it, and laid it out on the table, using an empty teacup to hold one side down.

"Here's our position now, northeast of the Orkney Islands. We'll pass the Shetlands and then head due north. Then we leave the North Sea and enter the Norwegian Sea. Here," he marked a spot of open water, "we turn east-northeast and head into Tomma. Then we start worrying about Germans."

"What about the Luftwaffe?"

"They don't fly in this weather. Neither do our chaps, for that matter. This low-pressure system is stalled right now. I doubt it'll move for a day or so. That will give us time to land you and get away offshore before the clouds and fog lift."

"What about German patrol boats?"

"Plenty of those, and they will be out. Luckily, visibility is so limited that they shouldn't be a problem. We can outrun most of them and outgun the smaller craft. It's the Vorpostenboot ships I don't want to bump into in the fog."

"Vorpostenboot?"

"Flak ships, like picketboats. They patrol at a distance from shore, trying to catch incoming aircraft and alerting the coastal defenses. They're slow, but armed to the teeth with AA guns. Machine guns; 20mm, 37mm, and 40mm cannon. Nasty, if they spot you."

"If they're so slow, can't you sink them with your torpedoes?"

"We used to have four eighteen-inch torpedo tubes, but had them removed to make room for more fuel and supplies, and assorted Joeys like you. We've got machine guns and 20mm Oerlikons that can give smaller boats or aircraft a good fight, but the Vorpostenboots would turn this ma-hogany into kindling." He knocked on the polished wooden hull.

"Let's stay away from them then."

"Capital idea, Lieutenant! Trust a Yank to see straight to the heart of the matter."

"Call me Billy, and stop putting me on, Harry."

"Now what fun would that be, Billy?" Harry laughed and clapped me on the shoulder. He stood and bounded upstairs, into the wind and salt spray. I tried to drink my tea without spilling it all over myself. We all prefer to do what we do best.

I was getting beat up pretty badly below deck as the boat rolled, smashed headlong into waves, and dropped ten feet all at the same time. I grabbed some rain gear and headed up, trying to stay upright but not doing too well. I slammed against the ceiling, the wall, and then the deck, all within five seconds. I figured at least up top there'd be no ceiling to hit my head on, so I grabbed the handrail and pulled myself up the stairs as fast as I could. The topdeck was open unprotected from the wind, rain, and waves. Harry was at the wheel, soaked and grinning insanely.

"Welcome to the North Sea, Billy. How do you like it so far?"

He had to yell above the noise of the sea and our motors. He never moved his eyes, which were watching each wave as it broke across the bow. The boat crested a wave and slammed down as if it had been hit with a sledgehammer. The piece of deck I was standing on came up and struck me in the face. I fell back, sliding on the wet planks and spitting blood from a cut lip. It took my mind off being seasick, for a minute.

"Are we almost there yet?" I asked as a crewman helped me up.

"Still a bit of a way to go. Keep your knees flexed and try to roll with the boat."

I made my way to the railing and flexed my knees, which was an excellent position in which to throw up breakfast. I let the water whip my face for a while and then staggered back to Harry.

"Feel better?" he asked.

"Actually, yes. This is almost fun."

Harry risked a quick glance at me, and then laughed.

An hour or so later things started to settle down. The waves were still high, but they weren't as rough as they had been and the wind was definitely lessening. Harry began to glance up at the sky. There were some patches of faint light showing where before there had been only continuous dark clouds.

"Lookouts to your posts!" he shouted. Men with binoculars scrambled to the gun mounts.

"What's the matter?" I asked.

"Can you feel that?"

"What?"

"The wind direction changed. It's coming from the west. Pushing the low-pressure system east. It could clear up faster than we planned."

"That's not good, right?"

"Well," Harry said with a grimace as he turned the wheel sharply and advanced the throttle, "the good news is that we can increase our speed now that things have calmed down a bit. We'll try to stay with the system as it moves east."

"You left out the bad news."

"In order to stay with the front, we have to turn east now, instead of tomorrow. It means we'll cut north tomorrow right through the most heavily patrolled coastal areas."

"Those V-boats you mentioned?"

"Yes. Vorpostenboots. Lucky chap, you might get a chance to see one up close!"

I was about to tell Harry it wasn't funny when a shaft of sunlight broke out from between two gray clouds like a bright wound opening in the heavens and lit his face. He didn't look like he was joking.

CHAPTER
TWENTY-THREE

I didn't think I had slept at all until I awoke from a dream. It was about Daphne. She was sitting at a table quietly, while Kaz and I talked. She watched us serenely, as if she knew some sweet secret that was beyond us. Kaz and I fell silent. Then I asked her, "Aren't you supposed to be dead?" Her face lost all expression. I felt a deep pit of sadness open up in my stomach and the dream ended abruptly.

I woke up with a start in my small, damp bunk and looked around for some clue as to where the hell I was. My heart was beating like a bass drum in a Saint Paddy's Day parade. I took some deep breaths to calm down. Oh yeah, I'm on this boat in the middle of the ocean. Great. I dropped my head back on the pillow and tried to sleep. Something kept me from nodding off. I tried to think, but I was still half asleep, or half awake, I couldn't tell. The boat had kept me up, with its rocking, all night long. . . .

I realized everything was still. I could feel the boat moving and the deep *thrumming* of the engines, but the up and down wave-smashing motion was gone. The smell of diesel fuel and sweat was heavy in the cramped quarters. I stumbled out of the bunk and moved through the narrow passageway, instinctively but unnecessarily clutching the walls for support. I stopped myself and stood unaided for a second. I was still dizzy, but the boat was on the level, except for a slight slant to the deck, as the four Packard engines at the stern lifted the bow out of the water. I trudged forward, tired, wet, and worried.

A cold blast of air hit me as I emerged from below deck. Harry was still at the wheel, where I had left him when I hit the sack last night. His blond hair was blown back and his face was red from the wind. He looked straight ahead, only glancing down at the compass in front of him. The ocean was calm, completely flat as far as I could see. Which wasn't far at all, since we were enveloped in fog. There was no horizon, just a white wall of mist that rose up all around us and seemed to curve just above the boat, like the white satin lining inside the lid of an expensive coffin. It seemed as if that I could reach up and touch it. The top of the radio mast vanished just a few feet above my head. We seemed to be moving fast, but nothing was changing — not the water, our direction, or the fog. Men were at their stations, their binoculars useless. They strained forward, trying to peer through the fog or perhaps to hear the muffled sound of a distant engine. Besides our engine noise and that of the hull cutting through the water, the only sound was the occasional hydraulic whine of a twin .50 caliber machine gun mount being traversed, searching sky and sea for a threat that might be lurking just beyond the thin veil of fog. No one spoke a word.

I stood next to Harry. He acknowledged my presence with a quiet nod. I didn't say anything. I had the odd feeling that I was in a church. This silence in the midst of roaring engines, our small, isolated cocoon moving across the wide, flat sea, seemed otherworldly.

"Tea, Captain. And you, too, sir." A young crewman wearing a stained white apron offered up a tray with two thick white porcelain mugs of steaming tea.

"Thank you, Higgins," Harry said, taking the tea without looking away from the few yards of water visible beyond the bow. I took mine and nodded thanks.

"Never seen you run her wide open in thick soup before, sir." Higgins's unspoken question to Harry hung in the air as he looked at me.

"Not to worry, Higgins. Jerry is probably sticking close to the shore. I'm more worried about hitting a bloody big log. Now finish up in the mess and get up here. We could use an extra set of eyes."

"Aye, sir!" Higgins said, untying his apron as he turned to go below. He sounded excited.

"So this isn't SOP?" I asked Harry in a low voice.

"There's no such thing as standard operating procedure out here, Billy. This would be a damn silly thing to do anywhere else, but we've got to get to Tomma before the weather clears. And it will soon."

"And when it does . . . ?"

"Then we better be well out to sea, and you safely on dry ground, or else we'll be trapped close to shore, sighted by patrol craft or Germans on land, and they'll send out the Luftwaffe. Not a good thing, I assure you."

"Should we wait for nightfall?"

Harry shook his head.

"Nowhere to wait. When the fog clears, the Germans will send out everything they have. They'll want to make up for lost time. We could go a hundred miles and chances are they'd spot us. We've got to get you ashore now."

"But what happens to you after you drop me off? When the weather clears?"

"We take our chances, old boy. Just like you."

For the first time it occurred to me that my little unauthorized jaunt could cost others their lives. I didn't want that and hadn't planned on it. Everything was supposed to work out as Jens and I thought it would. The weather was supposed to cooperate, damn it! This was supposed to be a milk run, just another day on the job for these guys.

I thought about Uncle Ike. How many guys would he send to die, thinking he had everything figured out, only to have something uncontrollable go wrong at the last minute? I guess I wasn't so different from the big brass. I hadn't even considered the risk to Harry and his crew, just what *I* needed to get done. It didn't feel good. The only difference was I was here, and about to go ashore in enemy territory just under the Arctic Circle. When the brass felt bad they sat back in their big leather chairs, lit up a cigar, and cursed at junior officers. It was like my dad always said: a rich guy can have the same problem we do, but he can smoke a dollar cigar in a nice big house while he worries about it.

"Just like me," I replied. I started looking for floating logs, but gave up when I realized there wouldn't be time to say anything before we hit. Higgins scrambled up to the bow and strained his neck forward, keeping watch as Harry had instructed.

"Good lad, Higgins," he said, nodding toward the young crewman. "Worked on river barges on the Thames before he came to us. He's been through the worst of the Blitz, but this is just his third mission with us. He's a little nervous. I thought giving him something to do would help."

"We don't really need to worry about big logs?"

"Only if worrying would help. Otherwise it's best not to think about it."

Harry gave me a grin and a quick wink. The more I tried not to think about logs in the water, the more I imagined them bobbing along in front of us. I looked up instead. I could see the top of the mast.

"Harry . . ."

"I know, Billy." It was getting even lighter

and warmer as the sun gained on the fog and started to burn it away. I could feel the humidity in the air now; the breeze wasn't as cold.

"Action stations!" yelled Harry. Men donned helmets and those without life jackets put them on. Someone handed me a life jacket and one of those flat British helmets. I thought of a picture of my dad and uncles from the First World War. I tried not to think about their brother wearing one of these helmets, who hadn't made it back, or about those boys who'd been on the destroyer with Diana.

Several crewmen came up bringing two Bren guns and a box of ammo. They made their way to the stern, past the 20mm Oerlikons mounted amidships, and settled into each corner above the engines with their machine guns.

"We like to discourage pursuit as much as possible," said Harry. "You'd better get ready, Billy. There may not be much time if things heat up."

He didn't need to tell me twice. I went below and put on the winter parka I'd been issued at Southwold. I got my gear and the Thompson and then headed back above deck. With the life jacket on over the parka, I could barely move through the narrow passageway. But I was relying on the life jacket to keep me afloat if it came to that.

Back on deck, it was a lot brighter still. I put a clip into the Thompson and worked the bolt. I didn't know if the Jerries would get close enough for me to use it. It was probably useless, but I didn't have much else to offer.

"If I'm right," said Harry, "we've about fifteen minutes more cruising time. Then we turn due east and head in for Tomma. That will keep the island between the mainland and us. We'll have to slow down to muffle the motors. When we get close enough, we'll launch one of the surfboats, and two of the lads will paddle you in. You may have to get your feet wet. I've told them to toss you over as soon as they see bottom." He was smiling, but he wasn't kidding. I looked up and didn't blame him. The sky was blue.

"OK."

Fog was still rising off the water. Maybe we wouldn't be visible from the air, maybe we would. Anyway, we wouldn't have the fog much longer. By the time Harry turned east, visibility was about fifty yards. He slowed and the engines went from a roar to a low throaty growl. We churned up less of a wake as we cut across the water, and I guessed not announcing ourselves so clearly was worth the reduction in speed.

"Almost there, Billy. Enjoy the ride so far?"

"It's been more than I bargained for," I said, which certainly was true in more ways than one. "I'm going out by sub and —"

"Shut up, Billy! Don't tell me how you're getting back, you damned fool! What if we're captured? Haven't you heard that line 'Ve half vays of making you talk?' It's true, you know. Drugs, torture, whatever it takes. Don't the Yanks teach their agents how to keep their bloody mouths shut?"

"Sorry, it slipped out," I said. "It was just a cover story anyway. Santa Claus is really coming down from the North Pole to airlift me out."

"Saint Nick himself, eh? Not bad."

Harry smiled readily, but I thought I detected a worried look on his face as he studied me. I could tell he was comparing me to previous British agents he had brought in. Experienced agents who knew how to keep their stiff upper lips firmly pressed against their lower ones. I knew the comparison wasn't favorable.

"Ship! Two o'clock!" Higgins yelled as he pointed to the right. Moving away from us was the gray form of a small ship, maybe a trawler. As we drew closer and the fog thinned, several men at once spotted two more small craft, a larger one in front and another smaller one, behind. For a second all guns swiveled toward the three ships.

"Keep a good lookout there!" Harry yelled angrily. "This isn't a sightseeing cruise!" The gun crews and lookouts returned to scanning the horizon in all directions.

"Think they'll spot us?" I asked.

"Too soon to tell. We're very low in the water and they are moving away from us. Maybe not."

"Is that a V-boat?"

"Yes. Being escorted by two E-boats. German patrol craft, much like ours."

"Not as good as ours though?" I asked hopefully.

"Goes without saying, old boy!"

Harry was doing his best to keep everyone's morale up. It worked until the line of three German vessels abruptly turned simultaneously, at about a forty-five-degree angle.

"Jesus! Did they spot us?" I really needed another morale boost.

"Damn!" Harry muttered. "No, but they soon might. It looks like they're on maneuvers. Simultaneous changes of course under low-visibility conditions. Good practice for not bumping into each other. Very practical, those sodding Teutons!"

"What's the problem with that?"

"They won't keep moving away from us. If their next movement is an about angle to starboard, they'll be heading straight toward us and we'll be spotted for sure."

It was cold and windy, but I started to sweat. Harry kept on the same course and speed.

"Should we make a run for it?" I asked, trying to keep the desperation out of my voice.

"Worst thing we could do," he answered. "We'd kick up a bigger wake, and the movement might catch their eye. We've got to count on steady movement, distance, and a low profile. Plus the fact that they shouldn't be expecting anyone to appear out of this fog."

"Meaning no one in their right mind would have come through that storm?"

"Exactly, Billy! See, there's nothing —"

Harry snapped his head toward the enemy ships. He'd seen something. By the time I saw the tracers, they were halfway to our boat, and I heard the sound of firing catching up across the distance. Sparkles of brightness appeared on the bigger ship, and now all three were turning, heading straight for us. Harry jammed the throttle forward and I grabbed onto the rail as all guns aimed at the Germans.

"Hang on!" Harry yelled as he turned the boat to port and geysers of foam exploded in front of us, whole rows of them.

"Why aren't we shooting back?" I yelled, gesturing with my Thompson.

"Don't worry, Billy, they'll be close enough very quickly. That's the heavy 40mm stuff from the V-boat. Pretty inaccurate at this range. The E-boats can close on us, though. We'll have to deal with them before we put you ashore."

As Harry hollered back at me he was zigging and zagging, still keeping on the same general course.

"Won't they trap you inshore? Shouldn't you abort the landing?"

"Billy, this is what they pay us for. Not much, but it is our job. We'll land you and then dart in and out of these little islands. They'll either think we were just trying to throw them off the scent, or that we landed a dozen agents. They won't know where to look for you. If I were you, though, I'd get off Tomma before they close in and search it."

I didn't answer him. I was thinking about the Norwegian Underground Army contacts waiting on Tomma to pick me up. I added them to my list of possible lives lost in my pursuit of Rolf Kayser. Then I added myself.

I watched as the bright tracer rounds arced lazily through the sky toward us, looking more like fireworks than cannon fire. Then I remembered that usually for every one tracer round there were ten regular rounds, and realized that the sky was actually full of more lead than I could see. Again the geysers sprouted around us.

"Ready!" yelled Harry and slewed the boat to starboard, running at the lead E-boat. Machine guns and the forward 20mm started firing, seeking out the E-boat as it closed on us and we on it. Cannon fire from the V-boat was flying over our heads and hitting the water where we had just been. Harry was talking at me, but I couldn't hear a thing. I watched his face, still focused on the water ahead of us, as he opened his mouth and yelled. No words could be heard, only the chatter of machine guns, the roar of wide-open engines, and the splashes of near misses all around us. The twin .50 caliber machine guns on either side of us were firing rapidly, shell casings spewing out, clinking and smoking on the deck around us. The 20mm gun was firing at a slower rate, a steady *pow, pow, pow* as the gunner scored several direct hits on the E-boat. Suddenly he was cut down as a line of machine-gun fire hit the bow of our boat and chewed up the deck, hurling him back against the wheelhouse. Higgins ran to the 20mm and braced himself against the shoulder harness. He fired, wildly at first, but then found his target. The other gunners did, too, and one E-boat was soon blazing, dead in the water.

Harry leaned over to me and said something. All I heard was "mix it up." He pointed to my Thompson. I got it. He was deliberately getting in close to the E-boats so the slower Vorpostenboot couldn't fire without risking hitting the E-boats. The shooting had slackened off, and now the remaining E-boat was running a loop around Harry, firing and then circling to get back to the safety of the bigger boat, where we couldn't follow.

"Make smoke!" Harry bellowed into the intercom, as he turned hard to port and tried to cut off the E-boat. Plumes of thick smoke began to appear out of a rear-facing funnel, and the E-boat turned to starboard, trying to bring all guns to bear at once. Harry had anticipated this and was turning toward port again, doing to the Germans exactly what they were trying to do to us.

The E-boat was raked by our fire, but one of its forward machine guns found us as well. I ducked as shells splintered the wood all around the wheelhouse. Harry yelled again and turned the 718 away from the E-boat, seeking the safety of the smoke screen he had just laid. I ran back to the stern and fired my Thompson at our pursuer. I was putting in a fresh clip when a blast hit just below me, churning up water at the stern and sending chunks of the hull flying. There was a muffled explosion belowdecks and suddenly we were making black smoke. Not artificial smoke, but the real thing, from an engine fire. The E-boat finally turned away, our return fire scoring direct hits all over it. Our bow became heavy as if we were was taking on water. Then we entered into the smoke screen and everything went gray.

I made my way forward. Men were being carried up from belowdecks, coughing and hacking as thick black smoke curled up out of the passageway.

"Report!" demanded Harry. His left arm dangled uselessly at his side, a stream of blood collecting in a pool at his feet. With the other arm he gripped the wheel, keeping the boat on course and probably holding himself up.

"Can't see much yet, Cap'n," said a short, barrel-chested seaman, grease and soot darkening his features. "Looks like number one and two have had it. Three's damaged but working, number four is fine. And you're wounded, sir, left arm."

"Casualties below?" Harry ignored his last comment.

"Two men dead, Cap'n. One other, burned pretty bad."

"Very well, Chief. Shut down one through three and make repairs as you can."

"Aye, sir. Better get that arm bandaged now, sir." The chief waited until Harry nodded, then went back down into the smoke. A crewman with a medical kit came into the wheelhouse from the bow and ripped away the sleeves from Harry's sweater and shirt.

"How's Higgins?" Harry asked.

"Dead, sir."

Harry winced as antiseptic was poured over his wound. "A good lad . . ." Harry looked faint and I grabbed him before he fell over.

"Hang on, captain. There's a splinter. . . ." Before he could finish, the crewman pulled a long, sharp piece of wood out of Harry's upper arm. Blood gushed. More antiseptic was poured and the shock of it probably kept Harry conscious.

"Not as bad as it looks, sir," said the crewman as he applied a gauze pad and wrapped the wound tight.

"Oh, I'd say it's as bad as it looks, wouldn't you, Billy?"

Harry glanced around at the boat, bullet holes everywhere, two men dead above deck, two men dead below, and three engines out of commission. His face was pale and beaded with sweat.

"Yeah, Harry, it's bad. Now how do we get to Tomma?" I asked.

"That bit's easy."

He checked his compass as the crewman rigged up a sling and gently placed his arm in it. He winced, and then adjusted course slightly. "We're headed there now, with the smoke between us and the Germans. That E-boat won't follow, and the V-boat will stay offshore, looking to hit us when we come out. We'll circle a few islands and drop you at Tomma, then . . . well, then you'll have other worries."

"How can you make it on one engine?"

"Slowly. But we can make it. If the Vorpostenboot and the Luftwaffe cooperate."

I couldn't look at him. The truth of the situation was written all over his face, and I felt sure guilt was etched on mine. Buried deep within the smoke screen, there was nowhere else to turn my eyes and escape the reality of what I had created. I looked forward and saw the bodies of young Higgins and the other gunner. I turned away and looked to my rear. The black smoke was thinning out and I could see lines of bullet holes where they had struck the engine compartment. Empty shell casings rolled back and forth on the deck, and worried men gripped their guns in white-knuckled embraces. They were wide-eyed and jumpy. I didn't like looking at them either. I felt that they would be able to see right through me, to see that I had brought them to this place, perhaps to die here. I closed my eyes.

"First time in action, Billy?" Harry misread me, and his question caught me by surprise. It had been, and I hadn't been scared. Not what I had expected. I did feel awful now, but I realized it actually had been exciting.

"Yes."

"Well, you didn't try to hide or jump overboard, so you'll probably be all right."

"I feel sort of strange now."

"Yes," Harry nodded. "It happens to me all the time. It's almost magical, the feeling of being alive, isn't it?"

"I don't really feel very magical, Harry.

Just scared."

I didn't want to go into my real reasons for feeling bad. There were four dead men on my conscience and I didn't want any more.

"That's good, Billy. Means you still have your senses about you. And you're going to need them."

"What do you mean?"

He took his eyes off the water long enough to look me in the eyes. Right now he wasn't the happy-go-lucky pirate captain he played for his crew. Right now he was dead serious, delivering news he knew wasn't good.

"Billy, I can't stop to row you ashore. With only one engine, we can't slow down and allow ourselves to be cornered. We'd never get out and your mission would be compromised."

"I don't like the way this sounds, Harry, but go ahead."

"We'll continue making smoke as we head around Tomma. When we get behind it, I'll double back and go out through our smoke screen. I'll bring her in as close as possible, but you'll have to jump ship and swim to shore. We can't let you take a boat, because the Germans would find it and then there'd be hell to pay."

"How far?"

"I can probably get you close to some rocks you can climb ashore from. Perhaps a hundred-yard swim. You can swim, can't you?"

"Sure. But not weighed down with all this gear."

"Right. It would take you to the bottom. Get rid of the parka. You won't need it anyway. No matter how cold it is out here, it's still summer, even at the Arctic Circle."

I took off the parka and helmet. I left the Thompson and most everything else, except for my .45 and one grenade that I stuffed into a cargo pocket in my utility pants, along with an extra pair of wool socks. Harry gave me a lightweight blue seaman's coat with the English markings removed.

"You might not be noticed so easily if you wear this. Most of the locals are fishermen and wear similar gear. Get ready now, we're almost there. We've just passed Lovund and Sleneset."

Those were two outlying islands. Tomma was next. I put on the lifejacket over the coat and stood near the railing. Tomma was coming up on the horizon. It was about six miles wide and it would be less than that to the mainland. It was a good choice for a landing. Not obvious, with the mainland so close. Big enough to hide out in. Unless we were being observed, the Germans wouldn't search it first thing. So my little swim made sense. I guess. I watched the island draw closer.

Harry's first mate took over at the wheel as he came down to stand by me.

"It's time. Sorry to dump you off like this, Billy, but things often don't go as planned."

"True," I said sadly. "No, they don't. I'm sorry about all this."

"What do you have to be sorry about, Billy? This isn't on your head. Someone in a cozy office in London thought this up, and now we're here to pick up the pieces as best we can. That's the nature of war."

"Or is it the nature of man?"

Or my nature, I wondered. To pursue Rolf Kayser no matter what the cost to others, because he had offended me by killing my friend?

"If I had time for philosophy, Billy, I'd give that some thought. But right now I just drive the boat." He grinned, wearily this time.

"Yeah, and I just jump off the boat." I shook hands with Harry and then did that very thing.

CHAPTER
TWENTY-FOUR

It was like jumping into a barrel of ice. I went in deeper than I thought I would, then struggled to the surface, my arms flailing, panic just about to take over. The freezing water shocked me and I gasped for air. The Atlantic was cold along the North Shore back home, even in July, but it wasn't anywhere near the Arctic Circle, like this water.

I kicked my feet as hard as I could, surfaced, and began to swim toward a line of rocks that jutted out from the shore. I heard the single working engine of MTB 718 resonate through the water and glanced back to see it disappear into its own smoke screen. I felt alone, abandoned. I knew that was irrational, as this was my own plan, but now that it was happening I would've given anything to be back on that boat.

The cold went right to my bones. My teeth were chattering and I had to work to keep my limbs moving, to remember to make each stroke. It was easy enough to float, but it was hard work kicking with those heavy combat boots. I wasn't making much progress, and I started to worry, thinking I was about to go under and stay under. I felt my heart rate go up and knew I was afraid, and that fear could take over and kill me. I had to get up onto the rocks. I forced my legs to kick for all I was worth. I was breathing pretty hard and swallowed a bunch of water. Gagging, teeth chattering, I kept kicking. If I stopped I knew that I would die here.

Finally, my arms hit an underwater rock a few yards out from the first outcropping of rocks. I let my feet down to see if I could touch bottom. I could stand, but the water was up to my nose. I bobbed along, trying to walk, bounce, and climb the slippery underwater slope. Grabbing onto a jagged piece of rock, I pulled myself up. Cold water ran off me as I stumbled and tripped along the line of rocks that led toward shore. I made it to a gravel-strewn beach and fell to my knees, taking in big gasps of air as I pulled off the life jacket. I felt dizzy. A shudder ran through my chilled body and I doubled over and threw up seawater, the salty taste mixing with bile, the foulness staying in my mouth. After a few minutes' rest, I found a large flat rock that I could move. When I lifted it a few inches above the wet gravel, small crabs darted out. Just like playing at the beach back home. I stuffed the life jacket underneath it and let it down with a wet *thump* before sitting on it, my clothes soaked and cold against my skin, shivering, but alive.

Then I heard the crunch of boots on the shingle. I tried to open my coat to get at my .45 but my fingers were too numb to work the buttons. I was still fumbling with them when four men came around a large boulder. They were dressed like fishermen, except for the British Sten guns they carried. The first one said something to me in Norwegian. He sounded angry.

"I don't speak Norwegian."

"Napoleon," another of them said slowly. That was the password. They were waiting for my response.

"Waterloo," I said. Some of the tension left their faces. I stood.

"Why have you come now?" the English speaker demanded. "In daylight, with much shooting?"

"We had to —" I tried to explain.

They cut me off, speaking to each other in Norwegian. Their spokesman turned to me and said, "Is not good. We must go. Quickly." They turned and walked off at a fast pace. I followed. Welcome to Norway. *Is not good.*

They took me to a rowboat, stowed their guns in a burlap sack, and rowed me to another island, Hugla, about one mile south of Tomma. I blew on my hands to warm them, but it didn't help. They were red and raw from my cold scramble over sharp rocks. The icy water dripped from my clothes, making a dirty gray pool beneath my seat. As we beached the rowboat, I heard the drone of engines. From the south, coming from the mainland, a flight of three Bf 110 twin-engine fighter-bombers flew over us toward the ocean.

"Is not good," my new best friend in Norway repeated. "Is not good for boat. Not good." He shook his head. I didn't want to think about that boat right now.

"Cold," I said. "I am cold. Not good. Understand?"

"Yes. Come."

We walked across the pebble beach to a path that led through scrub brush, up over boulders and into a forest of small firs. A half hour later we were at a log cabin, at what was probably the highest point on the small island. The roof was covered with dirt, and moss, grass, and even some small fir trees grew from it. The cabin had a very narrow first floor, which was entered through a doorway above three granite steps in the middle of a rough-hewn pine-log wall facing a small clearing. The second floor was wider and jutted out over the bottom floor. The entrance led into a single room with a stairway and benches along the wall. I followed my rescuers upstairs and one of them got a fire going in the large stone fireplace. There were chairs and a table near the hearth. It was rustic but very comfortable, the kind of place that would have been great for a fishing vacation, if you weren't being hunted by the Germans. From the single window I could see across to the mainland. The town of Nesna hugged the opposite shore, with steep mountains rising above it on two sides. There was an inlet — a fjord, I guess — that went past the town and vanished around a curve in the mountains. Fishing boats and other small craft went back and forth. It looked very peaceful. I knew looks could be deceiving.

Once the fire got going I undressed. They wrapped me in a blanket and sat me in front of the hearth. My clothes were hung to dry on wooden chairs they pushed close to the warmth.

"We sleep here, this night," my talkative friend said. "Ferry to Nesna in the morning, yes? Is best."

"Ferry is good?" I asked.

"No, ferry is not good," he answered with what might have been a smile. Then he shrugged. "Is best." He didn't know many words of English, but the ones he knew, he seemed to know precisely.

They brought out bread, cheese, and dried fish. We ate in silence. We heard more planes overhead. They pointed out German patrol boats passing the island. I nodded. *Is not good,* I knew. It was nine o'clock at night and still bright outside. They kept the fire stoked to dry my clothes, and I stared into the flames, wondering. About Kaz, about Rolf, about Diana, her father, and Harry. About Uncle Ike and how I'd let him down, not even able to complete my first assignment without screwing up and disobeying orders. Hell, forging orders.

Finally the heat made me sleepy. There were wooden bed frames along the walls with feather mattresses on them. I flopped down on one and let my weariness take over. My last thought before I drifted off was that I didn't want to dream. But I did.

There was smoke and fog, and Daphne was back. I couldn't see her clearly and it was like slogging through molasses to get to her. We were on a boat and then we weren't. It was all jumbled up. We were in a log cabin, then in my house back in Boston, in the kitchen. Daphne was sitting at the table, talking with Higgins. She looked up at me, placed a hand on Higgins's arm, and said, "I didn't ask for this, Billy. Why are you doing it?" Higgins looked up at me, too, a question forming on his lips. Thankfully, I woke up before he asked it. Or before I had to answer Daphne.

Two of the Norwegians were gone. The English speaker was still there. I tried to make conversation. "No names. No talk." That was all I got. Well, I thought, they're used to Englishmen, I can't really blame them. He made some awful coffee and we ate bread and cheese. When I made a face after trying the coffee, they both laughed. "Ersatz." The German word for a manufactured substitute for any item unavailable due to wartime shortages had become slang for anything fake. I didn't ask what was in the brew.

There was a single knock at the door. They both grabbed their Sten guns and stood at the head of the stairs. A voice spoke to them in Norwegian. They answered and returned to the table frowning.

"No ferry today. Germans stop all boats. Search Nesna. Is not good."

"Is not good for us?" I asked, wanting to know how serious this was.

"No. Good for us. Search Nesna for British fliers. Boat. . . ." He tried to think of the right words in English.

"The fliers the boat was to pick up?" I asked slowly.

"Yes. Boat not pick up."

"How do the Germans know about the fliers?"

He shrugged. "Someone talk too much. Maybe they have boat crew. They talk too much. Maybe."

"Why is it good for us?"

"Germans will find British fliers. Eight men too many to hide. Then they stop search. Then we go. Easy."

"Easy is good," I said.

"Yes! Easy is good!" He smiled as if pleased with a new way to say "is good." I didn't. I thought about eight bomber crewmen who were going to spend the rest of the war in a POW camp, in the service of justice. My justice.

We sat around after breakfast. I cleaned my .45 and dressed in dry clothes. That was the highlight of my day, until someone brought some more food, bottles of beer, and the news that the British fliers had been captured. The search was off. We drank a toast to our good fortune. For them, the war was over. *Is good for us.*

We took the ferry the next morning. There were German sentries at the ferry landing, but they were inattentive. Probably all searched out. There were other fishermen and locals on the ferry and we didn't attract any attention. We walked through town and up a steep road to a farmhouse. They stashed me in a hayloft, inside a long stone barn, above the cows. As hiding places go, I'd smelled better, but it was warm. My escorts brought me more bread and cheese from the house, and a bottle of apple juice.

"I must go fish," my friend told me. "We go. Good luck." We shook hands and he left me alone in the barn.

For the next four days, I was moved in small leaps westward, toward Leirfjord. Always by somebody different, sometimes through the woods, other times on the road, via horse cart or on foot. I didn't see a single German. I didn't make any more friends either, although one farmer lent me a razor and his wife heated water for a bath. That might have been in their own self-interest, though. Either way, it felt good. There was always enough to eat — plain food, usually dried fish, cheese, bread, a few eggs, and even butter. I walked so much that I sacked out easily enough each night, usually in a barn or a small cabin in the woods. Never in anybody's home. They could always claim they didn't know about the American gangster hiding in their barn, but if the Germans found me in a house, it meant a bullet in the head for the owners.

On the day before the planned meeting between Anders and Rolf, I found myself on a country road with an old Norwegian farm woman. Her horse cart was filled with milk cans, and we slowly clip-clopped through the town of Leirfjord before dawn, heading east. Without speaking a word, she pulled up on the reins and stopped her horse. She pointed in the direction of a well-worn dirt path that disappeared into a stand of pine trees. I got down, smiled, and waved. She shook her head and must've said "giddyup" in Norwegian, since the horse quickly started down the road. The creak of the wooden wheels, the sound of the empty metal milk cans clunking against each other, and the rhythmic sounds of the horses' hooves faded as the road curved to the left, off into a deep pine forest. In a minute I was alone. It was quiet. I looked around. Green fields and meadows of wildflowers stretched out on either side of the road. Steep mountains rose up around the little valley. Pine forests climbed halfway up the mountains, then pale gray rock took over, jutting up into a beautiful clear blue sky with lazy white clouds drifting across it. The air smelled clean and fresh, the smell of the outdoors. A bird sang. I took a deep breath, turned, and began my hike up to the hut. To kill a man.

CHAPTER
TWENTY-FIVE

Jens had said it would take an hour to reach the hut. Well, maybe for him, but we didn't have mountains in Boston and I wasn't used to this. I had to stop a few times and catch my breath. It was pretty steep, with lots of switchbacks and boulders to scramble over. After about two hours I spotted the hut up ahead. By my count it was July 21st and Rolf wasn't due to show up until the next day. I decided to play it safe, in case Rolf was early or Anders was trigger-happy. I watched the place for a while. Finally I saw Anders emerge and go around to the side of the hut. He was dressed in civilian clothes, dark green pants with suspenders over a heavy gray shirt. A woodman's work outfit. I began to hear the sound of an ax hitting hard wood; he was splitting firewood.

I walked up to the hut, watching each step, trying not to make a sound. I reached the door, still hearing the sound of the ax, and of pieces of wood falling into a pile of kindling. Another swing of the ax, and I stepped around the side of the hut, my arms outstretched to show I wasn't a threat.

"Anders —"

I stopped. A revolver pointed square at my chest. The ax was sunk into a stump that had a pile of wood next to it. Anders stood behind the stump, facing me, with two hands gripping the gun, knees slightly bent, in a classic shooter's pose. I had as much chance as a paper target at ten paces, if he fired.

"Anders, don't shoot. It's me, Billy." He didn't speak or relax. But he didn't shoot either, so I figured I was ahead of the game. A quizzical expression replaced the grim look on his face, as he tried to take in what he was seeing and hearing.

"Why are you here?"

"It's a long story, Anders —"

"Who is with you?"

"I'm alone."

He looked skeptical. He also looked all around, resting his darting eyes on me every couple of seconds. I didn't move a muscle.

"All right, you're alone. Are you armed?"

Funny question, I thought.

"Not enough to suit me. Just my .45." I opened my jacket to show him. The gun stayed aimed at my chest.

"Let's go inside." He casually pointed at the hut with the revolver. It wasn't aimed at me anymore, but it wasn't back in his holster either. He let me precede him, opened the door and motioned for me to enter first. I didn't think he was being polite. The hut was one open room, with a table and chairs, a bench in front of the hearth on the left where a woodstove served for cooking and heating, and a couple of beds along the other wall. There were windows on either side of the door and one at the back. It was a nice place in the mountains, except for the gun in my back.

"Have a seat, Billy." I sat at one end of the table and he poured a glass of water from a wooden jug and placed it in front of me. One-handed, since the revolver dangled from his right hand. He walked to the other end of the table and sat down, placing the gun on the table. Within easy reach. I took a drink and put my glass down, within easy reach. It wasn't as comforting as a gun. The cabin smelled of pine and ashes.

"Don't get much company up here, Anders?"

He smiled. "I'm very careful about who gets invited here. And you are not on the guest list, Billy. Tell me why you are here, and how you know about this place." Anders leaned forward, locking his gaze on to me. His arms were folded, his right hand just inches from the revolver.

I didn't like the way this was going. I knew it would be tricky, coming up on Anders unexpectedly, but I thought that after he saw it was me, there'd be slaps on the back and old home week. Not the third degree, with a gun on the table.

"You could've killed me out there, you know."

"Or you me. In my business, a man sneaking up on a secret location usually means trouble. For me, unless I make it trouble for him."

"I can explain that. Rolf Kayser is due here tomorrow, right?"

"Yes," Anders answered. "Why, and how do you know that?"

I relaxed a bit. He was curious — that was better than suspicious. "Jens told me. He told me about this place and how to get to it, and that Rolf Kayser was due to meet you here tomorrow."

"Yes. The underground brought the message several days ago. I was surprised to learn Rolf himself was meeting me. I didn't know he was in on this mission. What are you doing here, Billy?" His hand went up to rub his chin. Away from the revolver, a good sign.

"I've come because of the murder of Knut Birkeland. And the murder of Daphne Seaton."

"What! Daphne? Who killed them? Was it Rolf?" Shock and surprise showed on his face, his mouth hanging half open as he tried to take in what I'd told him. Now he was hooked.

"Yes. He also tried to kill Kaz."

"My God! But Kaz is alive?"

"Barely. Do you know much about the Kayser family?"

"No. What do they have to do with this? Slow down, please, and explain."

I told him. About the pictures, the explosion, the family fish-oil business. I left out the part about Victoria Brey and how she had seen Anders early on the morning Birkeland had been killed. It didn't seem necessary, especially with a loaded gun on the table.

"So you must have suspected me also?" Anders asked.

"I did, but I couldn't see a motive for you. But Kaz found out about Kayser's property from those propaganda photos."

"Billy, propaganda is what the other side does. We do public relations. But what about the timing of the murder? Didn't you say that it took place while Rolf was out shooting with the king?"

I told him my theory. He sat back and thought a while.

"Yes, it all fits, except for the note. How could Rolf have gotten Knut to write such a note? He was hardly the type of man to give in to intimidation."

"I don't know for sure, but I got an idea when Jens doctored my orders."

I told him about how we had concocted a new set of orders authorizing this trip.

"So you are not here officially? Only Jens knows you are here, and he could be court-martialed if his collusion became known?"

I hadn't looked at it that way before. I didn't like the direction the conversation had taken.

"I'm sure he's told Harding by now. Both he and Major Cosgrove must be aware of it."

Anders spread his fingers on the rough wood table. It was marked with cigarette burns around the edges; a thin layer of varnish had long ago faded into the grain. He looked at the tabletop, as if it held an answer to a question. Then he looked up at me.

"Billy, you are playing a dangerous game.

You are on a secret mission within a secret mission. You could be betrayed and no one would ever know."

"Except my betrayer."

"Yes. For some, that would be a burden. For others, a relief. Tell me, why have you come?"

"For Rolf Kayser."

"I didn't ask for whom. Why?"

"He's a killer. A murderer. He killed for his own gain first, and then to cover it up, he killed Daphne. He'll probably escape into a new identity and never be brought to justice if I don't stop him."

"Billy, people are being killed every day. Innocent or not. By accident or design. Bombs fall from the sky on cities all across Europe. Ships sink. Soldiers are shot, blown apart, maimed. Think how meaningless those two deaths are in the midst of all this killing."

"They're not meaningless to me. I knew Daphne. I know what she wanted out of life. What she'll never have. What Kaz has lost. I don't know all those other people. There's nothing I can do about that. That's war."

"But justice for one person, that you can do something about?"

"Yes, I can. I have to."

"Why? Why you?"

Fair question. One night, long enough after his shooting that we didn't think about it all the time, I was having a beer with Dad down at Kirby's. We were finishing up, about to head home for supper, when I blurted it out. I asked him what Basher had given him that day when they argued and he had thrown the package away. He knew I was asking a bigger question, but those were the only words I could get my mouth to utter.

"Too much," Dad had said, as he started to slide out of the booth. Then he stopped and moved back.

"There's a balance in life, Billy. There's the law, and then there's what people do every day, the rules that they live by. The two aren't always the same, but they can't run head-on into each other, or else everything falls apart. We enforce the law, and do a good job at it. We also do what we have to do to take care of our families and each other. In this world, son, no one else will. Basher didn't understand that. He wanted everything, more than he needed. But he couldn't do it alone. He needed others, and he was working his way through the force, looking for the right kind of partners. It was too much, Billy, it was pulling everything out of balance."

"What was it in that package?" I'd asked. Dad had looked down at the table, drawing the flat of his hand across it, clearing something off that I couldn't see.

"The truth is, Billy boy, I don't know. He told me it was worth a fortune. I'm no angel, I know that. But I also know I wasn't about to sell my soul for a fortune or for a plugged nickel. The package went out in the trash. Now let's go home."

We did. We had pot roast and never spoke about it again.

Anders's hand was flat on the table, too.

"So everything won't fall apart," I said in answer to Anders's question, feeling myself my father's son.

Anders reached for his revolver. I held my breath for a second, the muscles in my legs and arms bunched, ready to upend the table and run for the door. He put it in his holster. I breathed out, relaxed, and felt as if I had just passed a test.

"It will be difficult to take Rolf out of here as your prisoner."

"I imagine it will be."

Anders looked at me for a minute. I could see he was making up his mind about something.

"We need a plan," he finally said.

■ ■ ■ ■

The evening mountain air was cool. Anders and I sat on a rough wooden bench in front of the hut. He was reading a worn paperback book with a picture of three Viking warriors on the cover. I was smoking a Norwegian cigarette and thinking what a demand there would be for Lucky Strikes after the invasion.

"What's that?" I asked.

"The *Edda.* An ancient Norse poem. I studied it at university, and we had to read it in English as part of language class. I always enjoyed it, and picked up this copy in London. It seems to me to see into the future."

"How so?"

He flipped through the dog-eared pages and began to read.

The one who squats at the end of the sky
is known as Engulfer of Corpses
a giant in eagle form;
they say from his wings comes the wind of
     the world.
Brothers will fight and kill each other,
siblings do incest;
men will know misery,

adulteries be multiplied,
an axe-age, a sword-age,
shields will be cloven,
a wind-age, a wolf-age,
before the world's ruin.

"Cheery," I said.

He laughed. "It's also a story about the theft of gold. Sound familiar? There are many parallels to Europe today. We have our own Engulfer of Corpses, and this is certainly an axe-age and a wolf-age."

"And men certainly do know misery, some more than others."

"Some deservedly so, some not." He gazed out over the fjord with a distant look in his eyes.

"Well," I said into the silence, "let's hope tomorrow is Rolf Kayser's ruin, not the world's. Or ours."

Anders put down the book and looked at me. "Remember, Billy, I need Rolf alive. He has information to give me about the Underground Army in Nordland. It is very important. Once I have that, he's yours."

"I understand. It should be easy if he doesn't suspect anything."

"He may be very careful. He knows that at this rendezvous is the only location anyone in England knows he will be at."

"Right. But I can't think of any better way to take him alive."

Our plan was simple. I would sit right out front tomorrow, dressed in Anders's British battle dress. I would watch for Rolf coming up the trail. There were several places where it was visible, and with binoculars you could even make out the road below in the valley. As soon as I saw him, I'd wave him up and walk inside the hut before he got too close. Anders would be hidden in the woods, about twenty yards from the hut. He'd have a clear view of Rolf all the way and would follow him inside, once Rolf had gone through the door. Easy.

"Yes," agreed Anders. "Alive, there is no better way."

He closed his book.

CHAPTER
TWENTY-SIX

It was another beautiful day. I was surprised at how nice it was this far north, especially after all those rainy and chilly summer days in England. What I did on my summer vacation, I thought idly, remembering childhood September essays. Never anything like this. I leaned back on the bench, so that its front legs came off the ground and my back rested against the hut. I felt the sun warm my face and would've taken off the wool jacket I wore if it hadn't been a disguise. A black bird cawed above me, drifting on the wind with its wings outstretched. I put the binoculars up to my eyes and scanned the road down in the valley for the hundredth time.

There it was. The milk wagon on its morning run. It stopped at the path and a figure got off, dressed in the same British browns I wore. He didn't stop to wave good-bye to the old lady. I could almost make out the rhythmic metal clanking sounds of the milk cans echoing up the hillsides as the cart wobbled on down the dirt road. I signaled to Anders, who was hiding at the tree line. We were on.

I caught sight of Rolf several times as he hustled up the trail. He was faster than I had been. I made a show of walking back and forth in front of the hut, so he would see me. I guessed he'd signal me as soon as we sighted each other. That was my cue to go into the hut.

Finally, I saw him stop. He put his hand across his brow, to block out the sun. It felt like he was looking straight into my eyes. I waved one arm back and forth in a slow, deliberate motion. He waved back. I changed to a "come on up" motion, and stood watching him for a few minutes. He disappeared and reappeared as the trail dipped and turned. His head bobbed up once and I could almost make out his features. Time to go. I made sure he could see as I opened the door to the hut. I stepped inside and pulled out my automatic, flipped off the safety, and chambered a round. The sharp *snick* of the slide snapping back was reassuring, comforting in a lethal sort of way. I took a deep breath and tried to calm myself. I felt my heart thumping against my chest and breathed deep again, willing myself to slow down, to listen to every sound outside, and not to my own blood pumping through my veins. I waited.

I stood away from the windows so he couldn't see me as he approached. I tried to watch the path from the back of the room, but the window was too small. I sat down on the edge of one of the beds, pistol ready. I figured he'd come in tired, expecting to find his friend, and his guard would be down. It should be easy. I told myself that three times. Piece of cake. I waited.

Ten minutes passed. What the hell was he doing? Maybe he was winded and had taken a break. I got up, sneaking a peek out one of the windows. Nothing. I opened the door just a bit and listened. Nothing. A slight breeze blew through the fir trees and made a gentle *swishing* sound. I stepped outside, onto the stone step below the door, and craned my neck to either side. Nothing. I stepped to the side and looked over to where Anders was hiding. I heard a bird singing, then the flutter of wings as it flew away. The sound of glass breaking was louder than the wind.

I barely had time to realize that sound was completely out of place when a tremendous blast came out of nowhere. My eardrums felt as if they had split. A flash of bright light, then a vortex of glass and wood came flying out of the hut, slamming the partially open door flat against the wall. It knocked me to the ground. Everything was spinning, the hut and the pine trees all revolving as if I were tumbling through space. My gun wasn't in my hand anymore. I tried to get up. It didn't work out too well. Dust and debris from the explosion settled over me. Blood from my hands and face made red rivulets in the gray dust. I tried to shake off my confusion; a little voice from the back of my head was telling me to find my gun.

I heard somebody yelling. I looked up and saw Rolf Kayser standing six feet away, Sten gun gripped tightly in his hands, the murderous snub-nosed barrel pointed at my chest. The only thing I had going for me was the look of utter surprise on his face. His dark eyes were wide, and his whole body seemed to be shaking, as if not killing me then and there was causing him to short-circuit.

"Boyle! *Gud forbanner De!* What are you doing here? Where is Anders?"

I could barely understand him over the ringing in my ears, but I could hear and see his confusion, which at least bought me time.

"Maybe we should start off with why did you try to kill me with that grenade?" I asked as I started to get up. I noticed my .45 lying a few feet to my right. I took an unsteady step toward it and fell back to my knees as if I was weak, which wasn't hard to do. This maneuver brought me closer to my piece.

"I didn't try to kill you, you fool! I came here to kill a traitor. I didn't expect to find you here. Now, where is Anders?"

Good question, I thought. Rolf advanced until he stood next to me. He kicked at my shoulder with his boot until I was flat on the ground, looking up at him. I could see how tightly his left hand was gripping the magazine of the Sten gun and the little black hairs on his trigger finger. He was unshaven and there were bags under his eyes, so that they looked bruised. I wondered if he had sleepless nights.

"Where is Anders?" he demanded again, through gritted teeth.

"Right here." The calm voice came from behind me. I could see Rolf's eyes look up. He didn't move the Sten gun.

"Well, hello, old friend," Rolf said, a maniacal smile creeping onto his lips. "I'm sorry this didn't end quickly, as I had planned."

"Let him go, Rolf," Anders said evenly. "There's been enough killing."

"Not enough! Not while you live, traitor!"

"Rolf," I said, "what are you talking about?"

"You don't know?" Rolf demanded, keeping his eyes firmly on Anders and the barrel of the machine gun about twelve inches from my nose. It didn't inspire me with confidence in our plan.

"Anders, I assume you've got him covered, right?"

"Yes, Billy, just as he has you covered."

"Put the gun down, Anders, or I'll kill him," Rolf growled.

"And then me," Anders answered. "If I am a traitor, why would I care about an American's life? It's just one life among many."

"Boyle," Rolf said, jabbing the gun at me, "what are you doing here with this turncoat?"

"You came here to kill him?"

"Of course. I am many things, Boyle. You know that much by now. But I'm not a traitor. I know something about my friend Anders, something I couldn't tell you back in England."

"Because it would have incriminated you."

"Yes. I couldn't tell you that the night

Birkeland died I saw something. I was someplace I wouldn't have been if what I had told you was true."

Two and two were adding up pretty fast.

"You saw Anders go into the map room. When you came down from Knut Birkeland's bedroom. After you killed him."

For the smallest part of a second his eyes flicked downward toward mine. In a flash they were locked on to Anders again.

"There was no reason for me to have been in that part of the building. I couldn't risk explaining myself."

"So you did the next best thing and hid Birkeland's key in Anders's room for us to find."

"I had planned on throwing it into the woods, but then I realized that it might incriminate Anders. If he couldn't be hung as a traitor, then convicting him of murder would do."

"Anders," I asked. "What do you have to say?"

"We all have a part to play here, Billy," he answered. "Some parts are just more complicated than others."

I wished I could see Anders's face, but I could only listen and think fast how to get the muzzle of Rolf's gun out of mine!

"I am sorry about your friends, Boyle, but

I had to get away," Rolf said. "I know what they found out, and it would have meant my life if I was still in England."

"So it was their lives instead?"

"This is war, Boyle. I'm trained to kill or be killed. If Anders reached the Germans with the invasion plans, it would mean death for thousands and the end of our hopes of liberation. I have to stop him and I couldn't do that facing a hangman in England."

"Just explain one thing to me," I said. I wanted to keep Rolf talking. If I could get him to take his eyes off Anders long enough, well, I wasn't sure what would happen. Anders might kill us both. Or not.

"How did you get Birkeland to write that note?"

"That's all you want to know? You know everything else?"

"I know you never really lost the gold coin. You made up that story so you could leave it next to Birkeland's body to suggest he was feeling remorse about stealing the gold. I know when you really killed him and how you tried to deceive us about the time of death. I know about Kayser Fisheries and what you hoped to gain. I know about the Tire Bomb. I can guess that you broke Birkeland's neck with some fancy commando move. I just can't figure how you got him to write that note."

"It was simple. He had already written it. I destroyed the first page and left the last."

That's it, I thought. Keep talking. Keep telling us how smart you are.

"It was perfect!" He was gloating now. I had seen this before. No matter how smart a criminal, no matter how long he kept his mouth shut, once he started talking, it was hard for him to quit. He had been so clever and had no one to share it with. Once he started, it was too difficult to stop.

"Birkeland was writing his resignation from the government. Remember the page I left you?

I know this is a great disappointment. I have always tried to serve Norway and my king as best as I could. This final step is unfortunately necessary given the current situation.

He was handing in his resignation; that was the final step. I knew the king would never accept it, that he would be forced to give Birkeland the senior adviser post instead. I had gone that night to try one last time to convince Birkeland that his policy was ruinous for all of us, for Norway itself. It would have utterly destroyed my family's business. When he told me about the letter, even showed it to me, I knew what I had to do. It was his death sentence. Now, Lieutenant Boyle, have you come here to arrest me or to let a German spy get away? Make up your mind!" Rolf was sweating now, drops from his brow splashing my face.

"Rolf, put your weapon down!" Anders yelled. "I'll shoot. Pull that trigger and I'll shoot. No matter who or what each of us is, we've been through too much together for that."

"Damn you, Anders, or whatever your name is! I wish we'd left you to those ski troops. It would have served you right for your own kind to have killed you!"

"I know I owe you my life, Rolf. That's why I don't want to kill you now. Let us each go our own ways."

"Rolf, listen," I said, trying to turn down the heat a bit. "I'm a cop but I also know what side I'm on. We can't let this guy go. He knows too much."

"True, but so do you. About me."

"Yeah, but so do Jens and Major Harding and a bunch of others in England by now. If you vanish into the countryside, they'll never find you. I won't go after you. That was your plan, right? After you took care of

Anders?"

I could see Rolf was confused. His only leverage over Anders was that Anders owed him and didn't seem to want to kill him. Somehow he had to break the stalemate. I decided it was time to do it for him. I started to crawl toward my gun.

"Rolf, listen. We can't let this guy go. Let me take him in. The lives of thousands of men depend on it!" I said.

"Stop! I'm warning you," Rolf shouted. He was straddling me, the gun barrel shaking in his hands. I stopped inches away from my .45.

"Rolf," Anders yelled, "we can still work this out!"

"Rolf, let me help you!" I yelled at the same time.

"Stop! Stop it!" He was yelling, trying to drown out the voices that were confusing him. His hands were shaking. I watched his face. Involuntarily, his eyes squeezed shut for a second as he screamed.

I extended my arm and grabbed the automatic, in one motion bringing it up and firing into Rolf's chest. I fired again as his mouth opened in shock. His eyes flickered back and forth between Anders and me. He staggered and tried to shift the barrel of the Sten back to me. I fired again and didn't stop until he fell over on top of me, the Sten gun going off as he fell, kicking up dirt and rocks into my face, his ruined bloody chest hitting me like a side of slaughtered beef.

The next thing I remember, Rolf had been rolled off me and Anders was washing my face with a wet rag. I was covered in blood. It hurt.

"Can you get up, Billy?"

I tried to focus on him. It was hard to see.

"I think so." I rolled over, got to my knees, and let Anders help me the rest of the way. He sat me on the bench.

"I'll get you some water to wash your eyes out with. You've got powder burns on your face and dirt in your eyes, as well as cuts and bruises."

"How long have I been out?" I asked as he brought back a pitcher of water.

"About twenty minutes."

"You could have been long gone by now. What if some of Rolf's men came along?"

"Waiting here is not as dangerous as what you did, Billy."

"Something had to give. I could see he was getting shaky. We were about to lose control."

I looked over to Rolf's body. Things were clearing but still a little out of focus. He was a blurry mass of red. It was almost funny. He had come here to do the right thing, to be a good Norwegian soldier and save his country. Instead he'd gotten killed for doing the wrong thing, to the wrong person. I might have been tempted to let him get away with killing Birkeland, but I had to avenge Daphne.

The weapons had all vanished except for a Sten gun slung over Anders's shoulder. As he set down the pitcher of water on the bench, he let it hang there, like an afterthought.

"I'd say we're even. You're a German spy yet you didn't gun both of us down. That would have been a simple solution for you."

"Simple, yes. Right, no."

"Whose side are you on anyway?" I asked, feeling a pang of guilt at talking so matter-of-factly with the enemy.

"I think, Billy, that is a very difficult question for you and me at the moment."

We sat there a while. There wasn't much more to say. He got up. "I have to go, Billy. With all this shooting, someone may come up here."

"Your side or mine?"

"Perhaps we both need to leave. In opposite directions." Anders went inside the ruined hut. He came out with a blanket and laid it over Rolf.

"Whatever he was, and whatever I am, we were once comrades."

After a minute he went inside and returned with Rolf's Sten gun and my pistol. He laid them on a rock, removed the clips, and tossed them down the trail. Far enough that by the time I found them, he'd be long gone in the opposite direction. He walked over to me. He had on an old green wool sweater and was wearing a small pack.

"I'm going over the mountain, Billy. Can you make it down the trail?"

"Yeah, I can make it."

"You have a plan to get back home?"

"Home? No. England? Maybe. I probably shouldn't say too much about that."

He laughed. "We both should probably not say too much about this entire affair."

"I can't promise what I'll say," I said, thinking about how I'd explain all this if I ever got back to England.

"I understand, Billy." He smiled weakly and reached into his pocket.

"Please accept this gift from Captain Karl Fredriksen." He handed me the book of poetry. *The Edda,* it said on the cover, which displayed three Viking warriors holding their shields proudly.

"Karl. OK, Karl. Take care of yourself." He walked away, then stopped and turned.

"There's one thing I'd like you to know, Billy. This whole operation was my own idea, to get my father out of Dachau. He's an opponent of the regime. Not anybody important, just an old man who complained too often and too loudly to the wrong people. He fought in the last war, and did not wish to see his son fight in another."

"Yeah, same with my father."

"The difference, Billy, is that in my country opposition meant imprisonment. The Nazis do not like anyone to speak as their conscience dictates."

"How are you going to get him out?"

"I have a deal with the Gestapo. If I bring them military secrets, he will be freed. When I saw how fast things were falling apart in Norway, I knew I could blend in and end up in England. My mother was Norwegian, and we had spent summers there. No one ever doubted me."

"You think the Gestapo will uphold their end of the bargain and let your father go?"

"If he is still alive, perhaps. I have no idea if he has survived, but it is the best chance I have. So you see, Billy, I do understand justice for one person."

Then he was gone.

CHAPTER
TWENTY-SEVEN

It was a long journey back to England and to ETO headquarters at Grosvenor Square. I'd walked down the mountain and made my underground contact for the trip back home, just as Jens had planned. This time there was a fishing boat right in the fjord, to take me out to a rendezvous with a Free French submarine. They had two other agents with them and picked up a navigator from a Lancaster bomber, the only survivor from his crew. The return trip was slow, lots of it underwater, which was just fine with me. My eyesight cleared up and most everything healed. All the wounds that had bled, anyway. I spent a lot of time reading that volume of poetry, the only book in English on board.

When I got off the sub at Portsmouth, there was a detachment of American MPs waiting for me. Not an honor guard. They hustled me back to London, escorted me to my room at the Dorchester, and ordered me to dress in my Class A uniform. It was very politely done, they called me "sir" at all the right times, but they made it clear I wasn't the one giving the orders. A new set of clothes had been laid out on the bed and I dressed, wondering if a court-martial had been organized already. Welcome back, you're guilty, proceed directly to Leavenworth.

The MPs deposited me at headquarters and I was signed over to the sergeant of the guard like a delivery of Spam. A clipboard with orders changed hands and I tried to sneak a peek, but the MPs were too fast for me. They left, and two sentries with Thompsons slung over their shoulders, leather straps gleaming with polish, escorted me down a hall and up two flights of stairs. One in front, one behind.

Minutes later I was sitting on a hardback chair in a hallway, the two GIs guarding me as if I were Hermann Göring. A door opened and Major Harding stepped out. He snapped his fingers at me like I was a tardy waiter and crooked his finger.

"Boyle, in here."

"Good to see you, too, Major," I said.

"At ease, boys," I said to my guards as I stood. No reason for me to start acting polite now.

"Shut up, Boyle, and get inside." Harding sounded tired and disappointed. He shut the door behind me as I walked into the room. Curtained windows provided the long, narrow room with an atmosphere of gloom, and a cloud of cigarette smoke hung in the light of a lamp over the table. Along the wall on my right was a large map of Norway, covering it from floor to ceiling, marked with red arrows launched from Scotland and points south. The invasion. I imagined right now "Anders," or whatever his real name was, might be standing in front of a map just like this, briefing some Kraut generals. They probably looked happier than the trio who confronted me. A large rectangular table dominated the center of the room, with Uncle Ike seated opposite the door. The dark wood, probably walnut, shone; it must have been waxed and polished for a hundred years. I could see Uncle Ike's reflection in it and he didn't look any happier there than right side up. He held a cigarette in his hand and tapped it on the rim of a glass ashtray full of butts and ashes. Major Cosgrove sat on one side of him. Harding gestured for me to take the seat opposite the general. He sat on the other side. Uncle Ike studied me as I sat down. I felt the color drain from my face and my heart race. I didn't want to hear what was coming next. I looked down to avoid their eyes and found my own staring back up at me. I put my hand flat on the table, covering my reflection, and, for the first time, realized what my father had tried to brush away from that tabletop at Kirby's.

"William, first let me say that I'm glad you're not hurt, and that you are back with us," Uncle Ike began. I nodded, too nervous to get a word out. It was swell that my own relative was glad I wasn't dead. I couldn't really expect more than that. I put both hands on the table to keep them from shaking.

"Having said that, there are some very serious charges leveled at you, and we need to get to the bottom of them. These issues go beyond your personal desire for revenge, or justice, or whatever misguided emotion led you to take these steps in the first place."

He ground out his cigarette and didn't say anything: my invitation to explain myself.

"I . . . I'm sorry, General." I managed to sputter out the words. "I didn't think this would involve you. I know I'm going to be punished, sir, but I don't want any blame to fall on you."

"That's very considerate, William, but everything here involves me. Especially when one of my officers, privy to invasion plans, goes off on his own behind enemy lines."

Uncle Ike sat back, lit another cigarette, and nodded to Major Harding. Harding opened a folder with a red tab and consulted it.

"Lieutenant Boyle, we understand that with the help of Captain Jens Iversen, you doctored legitimate orders signed by me and Major Cosgrove, to provide yourself with transportation to Norway for the purpose of pursuing Rolf Kayser. Correct?"

"Essentially, sir, except that Jens had nothing to do with it. I retyped the orders myself."

"Don't bother, young man," Cosgrove said huffily. "We have a signed statement from that officer." He pushed a sheet of paper over to me. He was right.

"As you say, sir."

"And you tracked down Rolf Kayser at a rendezvous he had planned with Major Anders Arnesen?"

"Sort of, sir. I got there first and waited for him at a hut. With Anders." They looked at each other. Uncle Ike raised an eyebrow, Cosgrove harrumphed, and Harding nodded slowly. What the hell did all that mean?

"Tell us what happened there," said Harding, as he scribbled a note in the folder. Evidence for the prosecution.

"I told Anders that Rolf was Birkeland's murderer and Daphne's, too, and described the photographic evidence Kaz had found. We came up with a plan to capture him. Anders wanted me to take him alive so Rolf could give him some information he needed about the Underground Army. We planned a trap. We switched uniforms so I could get Rolf to follow me into the hut, where we could nab him."

"So what happened?" Uncle Ike asked.

"First I have to tell you about Anders —" I started.

"Yes, we know he was the spy," Harding said. "Please continue."

"You knew? But —"

"Just continue, William," Uncle Ike said gently, drawing on his cigarette and blowing smoke over the papers in front of him. I was confused. How could they know about Anders? But I had to keep going.

"OK. Sir. Anyway, it turned out Rolf had seen Anders go into the map room the night Knut Birkeland was murdered. He couldn't say anything at the time because the reason he was in that part of the building was that he was coming downstairs after killing Birkeland. He had no excuse for being there. He had actually tried to pin the murder rap on Anders by planting that key in his room."

"What does this have to do with what happened in Norway?" asked Cosgrove.

"Well, Rolf admitted to the murder, but said he wasn't a traitor, and he didn't want to let Anders escape. The last thing he intended to do before disappearing was kill Anders. He very nearly did, and me, too."

"Tell us exactly what happened, Billy," said Harding. "Exactly."

Harding stared at me and I saw they were all looking at me, waiting for something. Tension seemed to buzz in the air, as if they could barely contain themselves while they waited for me to tell my story.

"I went into the hut to wait for Rolf, disguised as Anders, in his uniform. Instead of coming inside where we could take him, Rolf threw a grenade through a rear window. If I hadn't stepped outside at that moment. . . ."

"Was Anders killed then?" Harding asked.

"No. Nor me either, Major." Thanks for the concern, buddy.

"What happened next?" said Harding, as if I didn't matter.

"A lot, sir. But basically I shot him. Dead."

"Anders, the spy?" Cosgrove asked, grasping the arms of his chair and moving his bulk forward, agitation showing in his raised voice.

"No! Rolf, the murderer. Of Knut Birkeland and Daphne, remember?"

"We remember, William," Uncle Ike said. "It's just important that we get this straight. What happened to Anders?"

"Nothing. He helped me after Rolf almost blew my head off, and then he left."

"You let him go?" asked Cosgrove.

"Yeah. I was unconscious for a while," I said. "Anders could've killed both Rolf and me while we were struggling. He tried to get Rolf to give up, and he didn't gun me down when he could have."

I shrugged. There was just no way to explain it that made sense. I'd let an enemy agent with the secret invasion plans go free. Period. Lock me up. I watched three sets of eyes flick back and forth, until Harding and Cosgrove settled on Uncle Ike and each gave him a slight nod of the head.

"Excellent!" said Uncle Ike, slamming his fist on the table. "Excellent, William!"

"Well done, old chap," Cosgrove said, falling back into his chair, and pounding the arm with his hand. "Well done!"

Harding actually smiled as he closed the folder.

"What the hell is going on . . . sir?"

I looked to Harding, then Uncle Ike. This didn't make any sense. I had forged orders, caused four undeserved deaths that I knew of, and let an enemy spy go. I expected to be clapped in irons, not clapped on the shoulder.

"Major Harding, please explain to William. He deserves the truth now."

Harding raised an eyebrow and paused for a second, his hand on the red-tabbed folder. "The whole truth, General?"

"The whole truth. It's good to keep in practice. We'll need to remember what it's like when the war's over," Uncle Ike said, his easy grin lighting up his face.

"We knew all along that Anders Arnesen was an enemy agent," Harding began. "Major Cosgrove had captured and turned Anders's contact early in the war. We knew he was coming, his code name, the works. We steered him to the Norwegian Brigade and allowed him to gain influence with the king's government to provide him with the opportunity to learn about the invasion."

"So it was all a fake?" I asked, the entirety of their deception slowly dawning on me. The sloppy security at Southwold, the winter gear being distributed so openly, the map case that anyone with a jackknife could jimmy open. . . .

"Yes, a rather elaborate ruse actually," Cosgrove said. "But we were worried that Arnesen would find it all too easy and convenient. So we decided to conduct an investigation, but one that would have little chance of succeeding. We wanted him to feel the heat and leave the country as soon as possible. That's why King Haakon gave his permission for him to go back to Norway."

All of a sudden the lightbulb went off, the final piece that I hadn't understood.

"That's how you knew in advance about me, being from Boston and all. I was the investigation that couldn't succeed! You were counting on me to screw up!" Now I started to get steamed.

"Calm down, Boyle," Harding interjected. "Yes, Major Cosgrove was not fully briefed and made some untimely remarks." I could see looks passing between them and knew Harding was finessing some sore points.

"With the murder of Birkeland," he continued, "things became complicated. I had to keep your search for the killer from uncovering our spy before he got out of the country. You were pretty hard to keep on a short leash."

"Can you just explain a few things about the murder of Knut Birkeland?" Cosgrove asked. "We understand the motive now, and we've surmised that the note Birkeland left was really part of another note."

"Yes. He was offering his resignation. That was the final act he referred to."

"To force the king's hand," Harding suggested. "To induce the king to appoint him rather than Skak as senior adviser." I nodded.

"But what about the timing of the murder?" asked Cosgrove, a confused look still on his face. "Wasn't Rolf Kayser off hunting with the king when the murder took place?"

"Based on the condition of the body, I thought so at first. But there were several small clues that finally came together. I found out that Rolf was big on medical training for himself and for his men, so they could treat their wounded in the field. He knew enough basic first aid to be pretty familiar with how the body works. I also remembered that when I examined Birkeland's body he was very clean, as if he had just bathed. But there was stubble on his face. I wondered then why a guy would bother to clean himself up and not shave."

"What does that mean, the stubble?" Uncle Ike asked.

"A lot of people don't know it, but hair continues to grow after death. Remember, Birkeland had a heavy, thick beard. I realized he hadn't been killed when we'd thought, but several hours earlier. Unfortunately, I didn't think of that until I went for a swim in the cold waters off the coast of Norway." I decided not to tell them how or when it had really come to me.

"Cold water?" Cosgrove was really confused now.

"Yes. Cold water and old plumbing. The night of the murder, I had a little too much to drink. I wanted a nice big glass of cold water and some aspirin. Well after midnight there was hardly any cold water in the pipes. That was because Rolf had Knut Birkeland's body in the bathtub, running cold water over it continuously, and turning it regularly for hours. Slowing down the onset of rigor mortis. And overtaxing the ancient plumbing. Turning the body kept the blood from pooling and delayed lividity. The cold water slowed down the natural process of decay. Kayser probably shaved Birkeland in the bathtub, not knowing his whiskers would begin to grow back, enough to be noticeable to the touch in the morning."

"Then he dressed him, tossed him out the window, left the last page of the note with his gold coin, and went off to meet the king, certain that the condition of the body would suggest a time of death that would clear him as a suspect," said Harding, ticking the points off on his fingers.

"Yes. And then coming down from Birkeland's room, he saw Anders breaking into the map room. He hotfooted it back upstairs to stash the key in Anders's room, where he hoped we'd find it. And here we are."

"William," Uncle Ike said, "your investigation was remarkable. We sorely underestimated you. You were resourceful and courageous in finding the perpetrator of these crimes. Not only did you apprehend a murderer; you saved the life of Anders Arnesen. If Rolf Kayser had killed him, he never would have made it back to Germany with the invasion plans. In no small part we owe the success of this operation to you."

"So there is no invasion? All those troops and commandos, the underground, was that all a fraud?" I was still having a hard time taking it all in.

"No, William," Uncle Ike said. "Not a fraud. A plan to save Allied lives. A deception. We're going to turn Norway into the biggest German POW camp you ever saw, for the rest of the war. Right now, the Germans are transferring more infantry units to Norway. Infantry that we, or the Russians, won't have to face elsewhere. Good job, son!"

They each shook my hand. I was stunned. Now I was a hero. Now that I wasn't the total fuckup they thought I was, it was time for congratulations and pats on the back. It was a dirty, rotten low down trick. It made me feel like a little cog in a big machine, two-timed by people I had trusted, including my own uncle.

"Wait a minute, sir," I said. "Was there anybody else in on this deception?"

Uncle Ike seemed to understand. He nodded to Harding and Cosgrove to leave us alone. They filed out and Uncle Ike waited, standing by the window and looking out at the quiet park in the middle of Grosvenor Square.

"No, William. Daphne didn't know. She didn't deceive you, we did. Lieutenant Kazimierz doesn't know, and won't. And no one else will either. This has been your initiation, William, and you've passed with flying colors. But with that comes responsibility. You've saved countless lives by your actions. Now you simply need to keep quiet about it. Do you understand, William, I mean, really understand what I'm telling you?"

"Men died, General. Others were captured. . . ." I shrugged, unable to finish, feeling confused and betrayed. I stood by Uncle Ike and looked out the window as he lit another cigarette. Late afternoon shadows reached like fingers across the small green park below.

"This is war, William. Nearly everything I do is a calculation balancing lives against victory. Men did die on your mission, and it was totally your responsibility. There's no way around that, is there?"

"No, sir. No way."

"But you also saved many, many more. You're ahead on this one, William, if you can stand to do the calculation at all."

"I understand."

He gripped my shoulder. "I wish you didn't have to, with all my heart."

The famous Ike grin vanished. All that was left was a weary sadness. He gave my shoulder a tight squeeze, turned, and walked out of the room. He had left a cigarette half stubbed out in the ashtray, and the blue smoke rose lazily up, a thin strand pooling under the lamp, dulling the light in the room. I did understand, God help me, I did. I was glad their plan had worked, understanding the lives it had saved.

But I had been out on that boat and seen Higgins and the other crewmen, alive one minute, cut down the next. I had killed them, just as much as any German sailor. I could do the calculation all right, but those few numbers on one side of the equation had faces that I would always remember. Daphne had a face.

I put my palm on the window, feeling the coolness of the glass. I watched a GI and a young girl stroll arm in arm through the park. Was he headed for the real invasion? Maybe I'd saved his life. A group of sailors rounded the corner, laughing, pushing each other playfully. Maybe them, too. I looked down the street to the crosswalk. A stream of uniforms hustled across the street, American, British, who knows what else. All of them, too? I wanted to run out, look each of them in the face, ask their names, look at pictures of their girlfriends.

I didn't. I stood there, counting. I could have stayed there all night. But Harding collected me and walked me down to his office.

"Just one more thing, Billy," he said as he paused in front of his door. "I want you to know that I admire what you did. It took guts. And if you ever do it again I'll string you up by your balls. Got it?"

"I get it, sir. This is my initiation, remember? I get to play the numbers game now."

"Shut up, Boyle. Now that we're not going to shoot you, there are people waiting to see you."

He opened his door and shoved me in. The first person I saw was Diana. There were others behind her but they were just a blur.

"Billy!" She flew across the room and flung her arms around me.

"Thank God you're safe," we both said at exactly the same time. She looked deep into my eyes. We just stood there for an eternity, until we heard a polite cough.

"Diana, move aside, will you, there's a line forming, dear." That was Kaz, in a wheelchair, pushed by Captain Richard Seaton, guiding it with his one arm.

"Kaz!" I bent down and gave the little guy a bear hug as best I could. "Kaz, how are you? God, it's good to see you!"

"I'll be fine, Billy, if you don't squeeze the life out of me," he said, looking up at me with a sad smile. A red, raised scar split the side of his face. It wasn't pretty, but at least he was alive. His leg was wrapped in a plaster cast but otherwise he looked to be in one piece.

"Lieutenant Boyle," Captain Seaton said, "I'd like to personally thank you for what you've done. It showed great loyalty and determination. Traits I admire."

He extended his hand and I knew that buried within what he had said was an apology. A proud guy like he was would never say it straight out, but there it was anyway. I held on to to his hand for a few seconds.

"Thank you, sir. I'm . . . I'm so sorry, about Daphne."

"As are we all," said Diana.

Kaz looked down at the floor. Moisture softened the captain's eyes, but after a pause, all he said was, "Yes, well, we're here for a more pleasant duty. Kaz has arranged for a quiet meal back at the Dorchester. We want to hear all about your exploits, how you pulled it off!"

"Great, I'll tell you everything," I lied.

We piled into a cab for the short ride to the Dorchester. The wheelchair folded inside the capacious front seat of the taxi next to Diana, and Kaz hobbled into the back, holding on to my arm for support. It winded him, and we had to work at swinging his leg with the heavy plaster cast safely into the car. The captain and I sat on the jump seats. Kaz grimaced as the cab pulled away from the curb and kept his eyes shut during the ride. He was paying a price for meeting me today, and I wondered at the price he'd pay every day for the rest of his life.

We pulled up to the Dorchester and there were more hands to assist, doormen springing up to unfold the wheelchair to bring it to the door and help Kaz out. He gave them all a smile and called them by name. There was tenderness in how they treated him, and I was glad that at least he had a home here.

"By the way," said Kaz as I wheeled him through the door to his rooms, "I've had your few pitiful belongings brought down from that tiny garret. You'll have the sitting room. I have too much space here as it is."

"Kaz, I can't . . ." I caught a glance from Diana that said, No, don't dare refuse, he needs you here.

"Hell, it'd be great. Thanks."

Kaz didn't reply. He wheeled himself over to the table and changed the subject.

"I should be rid of this cast and up and about in two weeks. Not soon enough, if you ask me."

"How are you otherwise?" I asked.

"They say I'll have a permanent scar," he said, fingering the healing rip on the side of his face. I could see that the stitches had just recently come out. His eyes wandered around the room. There are scars and then there are scars. There was a silence for a while. Then Kaz came back, and brightened up.

"Billy, do you know I've been assigned to you? As soon as I'm back on active duty."

"Assigned to me? What for?"

"Don't be so modest, Lieutenant," Captain Seaton said. "You're among friends here. You and the baron are now Eisenhower's Office of Special Investigations. A name like that covers a multitude of sins, don't you think?"

I couldn't agree more. If they only knew how many. The captain poured champagne and we drank a toast to great multitudes of sin. He poured again, and offered another toast.

"To Daphne."

We clinked our glasses and said her name, and I half expected her to walk through the bedroom door in a gown, apologizing for being late as she fiddled with an earring. The door never opened. We sat, gleaming silver and shining china before us on the table illuminated by candles.

Here in this room, haunted by memories, surrounded by friends and the promise of a future, a little of the past seemed to drop away. I didn't feel as terrible as I had before about my part in causing those deaths. Maybe it really was for the best. Maybe I had been used, but in a good cause. Daphne's killer wasn't out there still enjoying life. He had paid for his crime. And some other guys might not get knocked off in the real invasion when it came. The guilt was still there, however, whenever I thought of Higgins and Harry and all the others the course of whose lives I'd had a part in altering. It would always be there with me, I knew, like a tune that I couldn't stop humming even as I grew to hate it. But the people in this room had faces, too, and we were alive and together for now. That, too, went into the equation.

Most of all, Diana was safe and here, with me. I looked over at her and felt a shiver go through my body. It was part joy at being with her and part fear at the thought of losing her. But there was guilt, too, a wrenching guilt that made me ashamed of feeling happy whenever I looked at Kaz and saw the scar that marked his loss. Now that I really had joined in this war, much of the time joy and fear, life and death, decision and responsibility were jumbled together. Things were intense, awful, terrible, and then sort of majestic when it was all over and you forgot the dirt, smoke, and stink, and were grateful you were alive. I had never thought about being grateful for life before: it was just there, like air and water. Now, it felt like I owed it to the dead, even to those who had yet to die in this war, to be grateful for the simple grace of drawing breath.

Captain Seaton poured again, filling our glasses. I watched him and saw lines in his face that hadn't been there a few weeks ago. Maybe it was better for him now, knowing Daphne's killer was dead. Maybe not. Maybe it was just better for me, I don't really know, and I wasn't going to ask.

"I have a toast," I said, pulling out a tattered paperback from my pocket. "It's from an old Viking poem, from a place like Nordland. I think it's about the promise of justice."

I cleared my throat and read from the page words that had haunted me since I first saw them.

I know a hall whose doors face North
on the Strand of Corpses far from the sun.
Poison drips from lights in the roof;
that building is woven of backs of snakes.
There heavy streams must be waded
    through
by breakers of pledges and murderers.

I set down the book, the three Vikings with swords drawn still marching in the same direction, toward battle.

"Let them beware," said Kaz, with a dark look as he raised his glass.

We drank.

AUTHOR'S NOTE

Billy Boyle and his immediate circle of friends and suspects are, of course, fictional. The historical settings and circumstances of *Billy Boyle: A World War II Mystery* are not.

In 1940, with invading German forces just hours away, the Norwegian government began the daunting task of removing over eight tons of gold bullion from the Bank of Norway. With the assistance of soldiers, police, and civilians, a caravan of over thirty-five vehicles began the journey from Oslo to the west coast, hoping to meet up with an Allied ship before the German forces found them and confiscated the gold. They were successful. With the widespread cooperation of the people of Norway, the incredible smuggling operation brought more than a hundred million dollars (in 1940 dollars) out of Norway safely to banks in the United States and Canada, where these gold reserves helped support the

Norwegian government in exile during the war. In actuality, not a single gold coin was lost.

Operation Jupiter was, in fact, an Allied deception campaign aimed at convincing the Germans that Norway was a likely invasion target. Eisenhower exploited Operation Jupiter fully, even to the extent of issuing winter-weather gear to troops in England who were actually about to depart for the invasion of North Africa. His desire to make Norway into one big prisoner-of-war camp was fulfilled. When the Germans invaded Norway in 1940, they did so with five divisions. In 1941, they had a total of thirteen divisions on occupation duty in Norway. That increased to sixteen and a half in 1943, including armored forces. Over 375,000 German soldiers, sailors, and airmen sat idle in Norway by the end of World War II.

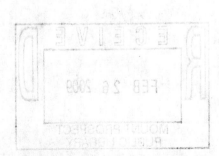